W9-ABT-783

BEYOND THE BLUE MOON

Simon R. Green

A ROC BOOK

ROC
Published by New American Library, a division of
Penguin Putnam Inc., 375 Hudson Street,
New York, New York 10014, U.S.A.
Penguin Books Ltd, 27 Wrights Lane,
London W8 5TZ, England
Penguin Books Australia Ltd, Ringwood,
Victoria, Australia
Penguin Books Canada Ltd, 10 Alcorn Avenue,
Toronto, Ontario, Canada M4V 3B2
Penguin Books (N.Z.) Ltd, 182–190 Wairau Road,
Auckland 10, New Zealand

Penguin Books Ltd, Registered Offices:
Harmondsworth, Middlesex, England

First published by Roc, an imprint of New American Library,
a division of Penguin Putnam Inc.

First Printing, November 2000
10 9 8 7 6 5 4 3 2

ℝ₀ℂ REGISTERED TRADEMARK—MARCA REGISTRADA

Printed in the United States of America

CHAPTER ONE

Haunted by the Past

It was spring in Haven, and no one gave a damn. Everywhere else in the world, it was a time for life and love and a joyful new start to all living things; but this was Haven, the infamous rotten apple of the Low Kingdoms. An independent city-state at the arse end of the Southern lands, where swords and sorcery, religion and politics, life and death, were just familiar coins in the everyday trade of a dark and twisted city. Set at the intersection of a dozen thriving trade routes, Haven had blossomed over the years, like the great gaudy bloom of a poisonous flower, and people and creatures of all kinds came in search of the city's many secrets and mysteries. You could find anything at all in Haven, if you were willing to pay the price, which was sometimes gold and sometimes lives, but nearly always, eventually, your soul. Haven; the city of your dreams, including all the bad ones. A place of wonders and horrors and everything in between. Hungry eyes watched from shadowed side streets, not all of them human, not all of them even alive.

In Haven there were glories and mysteries, messiahs and abominations, pleasures and depravities in all their forms. Heroes and villains and a whole lot of people just trying to get through the day. And—just sometimes—a few good men and women, honorable and true, doing their best to hold it all together, punish the guilty and protect the innocent; or at least try to keep the lid on.

Two such were Hawk and Fisher, husband and wife and Captains in the city Guard, possibly the only honest cops left in Haven. They'd never taken a bribe, never looked the other way, and never once given a villain an even break. Unless it was to his arm or leg. They lost as many battles as they won, but they'd won a few big ones in their time, and even saved the whole damned city more than once. It didn't win them promotions, or even much in the way of raises or commendations, because of the many influential enemies they'd made along the way, through their uncomfortable regard for truth and justice. But still they fought the good fight. Because that was who and what they were.

And if sometimes their methods were excessive, and overly violent, and if occasionally it seemed you could always tell where they'd been because they left a trail of bloody corpses behind them . . . well, this was Haven, after all.

Their beat was the North Side, the poorest, most desperate, and most dangerous part of the city; and the most dangerous things in that infamous quarter were quite definitely Hawk and Fisher. People tended not to bother them. In fact, people tended to cross to the other side of the street when they saw them coming. Hawk and Fisher had built quite a reputation during their years in Haven, all of it earned the hard way.

Hawk was tall, dark, and no longer handsome. He wore a black silk patch over the empty socket where his right eye had once been, and a series of old scars ran raggedly down the right side of his face, giving him a cold, sinister look. He wore a simple white tunic and trousers under a thick black cloak, his only touch of color a blue silk cravat at his throat.

But still, at first glance he didn't look like much; lean and wiry rather than muscular, and building a stomach. He wore his dark hair at shoulder length, swept back from his forehead and tied at the back with a silver clasp. Thirty-five years old, he already had thick streaks of gray in his hair. It would have been easy to dismiss him as just another bravo, a sword for hire perhaps a little past his prime, but there was a dangerous alertness in the way he carried himself, and the cold gaze of his single dark eye was disturbingly direct and unwavering. On his right hip Hawk carried a short-handled axe instead of a sword. He was very good with that axe. He'd had a lot of practice.

Fisher walked at his side as though she belonged there, and always had. Thirty-two years old, easily six feet in height, her long blond hair fell to her waist in a single thick plait, weighted at the tip with a polished steel ball. She was handsome rather than beautiful, with a raw-boned harshness to her face that contrasted strongly with her deep blue eyes and generous mouth. She dressed in pure white and black, just like Hawk, without even the softening touch of a cravat. She left her shirt half unbuttoned to show a generous amount of bosom, mostly to distract her opponents. She wore her shirt sleeves rolled up above the elbow, revealing arms corded with muscle and lined with old scars. She wore a sword on her hip, as simple and unadorned as a butcher's tool, and her hand rarely strayed far from it.

Some time ago something had scoured all the human weaknesses out of her, and it showed.

Hawk and Fisher; partners, warriors, reluctant heroes. Because somebody had to be. They tended not to get the ordinary, run-of-the-mill assignments. They got the hardest, weirdest, most dangerous cases, because Hawk and Fisher were who you turned to when you'd tried everything else, including closing your eyes and hoping it would just go away. Even so, the early hours of this particular morning promised an unusual case, even for them.

"I can't believe they're sending us to sort out a haunted house," said Fisher, kicking moodily at some garbage in the street that didn't get out of her way fast enough. "Do I look like an exorcist?"

"It would seem more a job for a priest," said Hawk, just to keep the peace. "But if it means spending the coldest hours of the morning inside a nice warm mansion, with perhaps a nice cup of mulled wine and some civilized finger food close at hand, well, a man must go where duty calls. I can knock on walls and wave crucifixes around with the best of them. Ghosts always pick the biggest and most expensive houses to manifest in—have you noticed that?"

Fisher sniffed, staring straight ahead. "You're the one who reads those stories. I'm not sure I even believe in ghosts. We've run up against more than our fair share of weird shit in our time, from vampires and werewolves to Beings of Power from the Street of Gods, but we've never come across a single haunting. Hell, considering the number of people we've had cause to kill over the years, if there were such things as ghosts, we'd be hip deep in them by now."

"Well, whatever it is that's upsetting the Hartley family, they're apparently sufficiently well connected to put pressure on our superiors, so we get the job of sorting it out. Probably turn out to be nothing more than a few squeaky floorboards and a case of bad conscience, and we'll just get to sit around in comfort waiting for something spooky to show up. Preferably while picking through a nice selection of cold cuts, and perhaps a little garlic sausage. In chunks. On sticks. I could really go for some garlic sausage right now."

Fisher looked at him for the first time, and sighed heavily. "I don't know why I bother putting you on diets. You never stick to them. You've no self-control at all, have you? I've seen hibernating bears with less of a paunch on them."

Hawk glared at her. "It's all right for you. You can eat anything you like, and never put on a pound. I only have to look at a chocolate cookie and my waistline goes out another inch. It was turning thirty that did it. I should have never agreed to it. It's all been downhill ever since. I'll be wearing slippers next."

"And you wouldn't even touch those nice nut cutlets I made specially for you."

"Let us talk about the haunting," said Hawk determinedly. "Suddenly it seems a far more profitable subject for conversation. The Hartley house is right on the edge of the North Side, where things become almost civilized. Proper street lighting and everything. Family made its money in ornamental boot-scrapers, and other similar useful items. If you've ever scraped shit off your boot in this city, you've put money in a Hartley's pocket. The trouble started when the head of the family, one Appleton Hartley, finally and very reluctantly died of old age, and his heirs took over the family house and business. The ghost started acting up the moment they moved in. Spectral apparitions, unearthly noises—(though how those differ from earthly noises has never been clear to me)—and foul and appalling odors. If it was me, I'd just check the drains, but . . . Anyway, the disturbances have been going on nonstop ever since, and none of the Hartley family have been able to get any sleep for four nights running. This has apparently made them somewhat cranky, and very determined to find an answer for the haunting, which is where we come in. So, as well as everything else, we are now officially ghostbusters, licensed to kick ectoplasmic arse. Acting unpaid, of course."

"Oh, of course." Fisher sniffed again. She could put a lot of emotion into a good sniff when she had a mind to. "All right, lead me to the ghost. I'll tie its sheet in knots, and then maybe we can get back to some real work."

The Hartley house turned out to be a quiet, unremarkable, three-story house in good repair, not obviously different from any of its neighbors, and set halfway down Hedgesparrow Lane. The house was still in the North Side, and miles from anything even remotely like the countryside, but that was creeping gentrification for you. The street as a whole seemed calm and civilized, even modestly salubrious. Hawk and Fisher strolled down the well-lit street as though they owned it, and the few private guards in their special and highly colorful uniforms found pressing reasons to look the other way. They weren't being paid enough to mess with Hawk and Fisher. In fact, there wasn't that much money in Haven.

The current owners and reluctant occupiers of the Hartley house were standing outside the closed front door, waiting for them. Hawk and Fisher had been briefed on the current crop of Hartleys. Leonard and Mavis Hartley were both in their early forties, plumply prosperous and dressed to within an inch of what was currently fashionable. It didn't suit them. Leonard was the taller, with a shiny bald head and a rather unfortunate attempt at a mustache. His hands jumped nervously up and down the buttons on his vest, unable to settle. His wife, Mavis, was shorter and stouter, with a fixed glare and a jutting chin that gave new meaning to the word *determined*. Hawk had an uneasy suspicion that she might just dart forward and bite him somewhere painful if he was insufficiently courteous.

Their son, Francis, stood behind his parents as though embarrassed to be there. Tall and thin and more than fashionably pale, he wore his long stringy hair in curled ringlets, and was tightly buttoned inside an old-fashioned black outfit, trimmed here and there with black lace. There was just a hint of mascara around his eyes. Hawk knew his sort immediately. One of those decadent Romantics who wrote bad poetry about death and decay, and held private absinthe parties for his equally gloomy friends. Considered vampires the epitome of Romance (because he'd never met one), held secret seances, and thought himself frightfully daring and rebellious for dipping a toe into such dark waters.

An idiot, basically.

Hawk and Fisher strode up the path to the house, kicking gravel out of their way, and crashed to a halt in front of the Hartleys, who immediately fell back a pace and started looking around for their private guards. Hawk introduced himself and his partner, and the Hartleys' faces became an interesting study in contradictions, as relief and alarm fought it out in plain view. Relief that the Guard had finally sent someone to help them with their problem, and alarm because . . . well, because it was Hawk and Fisher.

"You won't break anything valuable, will you?" asked Leonard Hartley. "Only there's a lot of really expensive items in this house. Irreplaceable items. Apart from the sentimental value, of course."

"Expensive items!" snapped Mavis Hartley. "Tell him about the porcelain figures, Leonard!"

"Yes, the porcelain figures—"

"Are very fragile!" said Mavis. "And don't even go near the glass cabinets. Those collections took years to put together. Any breakages will come out of your salaries."

"Any breakages—" began Leonard.

"Tell them about the ghost!"

"I was just going to tell them about the ghost, Mavis!"

"Don't raise your voice to me, Leonard Hartley! I remember you when you were just a milliner's assistant! Mother always said I married beneath me."

"I was a very *high-class* milliner's assistant . . ."

This argument seemed quite capable of maintaining itself without any intervention from Hawk and Fisher, so they turned to the son, Francis. He goggled at them with his slightly protuberant eyes, folded his long slender fingers together across his sunken chest, and smiled dolefully.

"What can you tell us about the haunting?" asked Hawk, raising his voice to be heard above the ongoing fight between Leonard and Mavis.

"Oh, I think it's all frightfully fascinating. Gosh! An actual intrusion from the worlds beyond. I'm one of the children of the night, you know. A lost soul, dedicated to act on all the darker muses. A seeker on the shores of Oblivion. I've published verses in some almost very well-known journals. You won't hurt the ghost, will you? I've tried talking to it, but I don't seem to be getting through. I've tried reading it my poetry, but it just vanishes. I think it's shy. I wouldn't mind being haunted myself, I mean, it's just so empowering to be able to just casually drop into the conversation with the other children of the night that I have personally encountered a lost spirit of the night. . . . All my friends are *so* jealous. If only the ghost would just let me get some sleep. . . . I mean, I may be a night person, but there are limits."

"Never mind him, Captain!" said Leonard Hartley, trying hard to sound authoritative, and not even coming close.

"Oh, Daddy, really!"

"That's right, Leonard," said Mavis. "You talk to them. Take control of the situation."

"I am telling them, Mavis—"

"Well, get on with it! Be a man! You pay taxes . . ."

Hawk and Fisher looked at each other, and then strode past the Hartleys. Anything useful they got from these people would in all probability turn out to be not worth the trouble and time it took to extract it, so they might just as well get on with the job. The front door looked perfectly ordinary. Hawk turned the heavy silver door handle, and pushed the door open. It receded smoothly before him, without even a hint of a creaking hinge. So much for tradition. Hawk and Fisher strode forward into the main hall. Gas lights flickered high up on the walls. All seemed calm and still. There were wood-paneled walls, thick carpeting on the floor, delicate antique furniture waxed and polished to within an inch of its life, and a few noncontroversial scenes of country life hanging on the walls directly below the lights. Hawk shut the door behind him. The continuing raised voices of the Hartleys were cut off immediately, and it was suddenly, blessedly, quiet.

"At least it's warm in here," said Fisher. "Where do we start?"

"Good question. Apparently there's no obvious focus for the hauntings. The ghost comes and goes as it pleases." Hawk looked about him. "I suppose . . . we check the rooms one by one until either we find something, or something finds us. Then we . . . do something about it."

"Such as?"

"I'm considering the matter."

"Oh, good. I feel so much more secure now."

And then they both spun around, weapons drawn in an instant, as the sound of approaching footsteps suddenly broke the quiet. It only took them a moment to realize that something was descending the main stairs at the end of the hall. Hawk and Fisher started slowly forward, their faces grim and focused on the situation at hand. They stopped at the bottom of the stairs, took one look at the garish vision bearing implacably down on them, and decided they'd gone quite far enough. A tall, heavyset woman wrapped in gaudy if somewhat threadbare robes crashed to a halt in front of them. She had a wild friz of dark curly hair above a face covered in so much makeup, it was almost impossible to discern her true features. Her mouth was a wide scarlet gash, and her eyes were bright and piercing. She had shoulders as wide as a docker's, and hands to match. She looked large and solid and all too horribly real. She fixed Hawk with a terrible stare, held out a shaking scarlet-nailed hand, and spoke in deep sepulchral tones.

"Be still, my friends. You have entered an unholy place, and we are not alone here. The spirits are restless tonight."

"Oh, bloody hell," said Hawk. "It's Madame Zara."

"You know this . . . person?" asked Fisher, not lowering her sword.

"You know me, Captain?" asked Madame Zara, taken aback for a moment. She withdrew her hand and struck a dramatic pose. "I cannot say I recall the occasion. Though, of course, my fame has spread . . ."

"It was a while back, during the Fenris case," said Hawk grimly. "I chased that spy right through her parlor. Madame Zara is a spiritualist. A medium. Or whatever makes the most money this week. A second-rate con woman and a first-rate fake."

"Sir!" said Madame Zara, drawing herself up. This took a moment, as there was quite a lot of her to draw up. "I resent the implication!"

"I notice you're not denying it," said Hawk. "Last time we met, you were using ventriloquism and funny voices to fake messages from the dear departed. Including, if memory serves, entirely unconvincing yowls from a departed pet cat."

Madame Zara thought about taking offense, considered that this was Captain Hawk, after all, and decided it wasn't worth the trouble. She shrugged, crossed her large arms over her even larger bosom, and fixed Hawk and Fisher with her best intimidating scowl.

"I have every right to be here, Captain. The Hartleys came to me, as one of Haven's most prestigious mediums, wishing to establish contact with their dear departed uncle, Appleton Hartley. There were things they desperately needed to say to him, questions they needed to ask. Most definitely including, What happened to all the money he made? The will left Leonard and Mavis everything, but it seems that a few months before Appleton died, he liquidated his entire business, cleared out all his bank accounts, and took the lot in hard cash. According to the firm's books, there should have been a great deal of money for the descendants to inherit, but there's no trace of any of it anywhere. The family have been tearing this house apart, but the ghost won't leave them alone long enough for them to get anywhere."

By now Hawk and Fisher were nodding in unison. The case was suddenly starting to make a great deal more sense.

"So, the Hartleys came to me, the great Madame Zara. I was unable to contact the actual spirit of their dear departed uncle, due to . . . conturbations in the spirit world. They asked me to investigate and cleanse this house, and lay its uneasy spirit to rest." Madame Zara gave Hawk and Fisher her best other-worldly look. It looked a lot more like indigestion. "I have made some headway. I am almost sure the revenant here is in fact that of a little girl. A child, lost and alone, reaching out to make contact." She paused sharply, and jerked her head oddly. "Aah! She is here, now, with us! Don't pull at my hair, dear . . ."

Hawk looked at Fisher. "I don't know whether to kick her arse or applaud. Any minute now she'll be asking if there's anyone here called John."

"I am a mistress of the mysteries! A conversant with powers and with dominations!" Madame Zara's eyes bulged furiously as she leaned forward, reminding Fisher irresistibly of a bulldog with a wasp up its backside. "I am not to be trifled with!"

"I didn't bring a trifle," Hawk said to Fisher. "Did you think to bring a trifle?"

"Knew I forgot something," said Fisher.

Madame Zara was about to say something really cutting when she caught a glimpse of something in the handsomely mounted mirror on the wall beside her. She looked at it sharply, and then relaxed a little on seeing only her own familiar reflection. Hawk admired her courage. If he'd seen anything like that looking back at him out of a mirror, he'd have fled the house and called in a really hard-core exorcist. And then, as they all watched in stupefied silence, the face in the mirror grew suddenly even uglier. Warts and boils and lesions broke out all over the face, pushing aside the heavy makeup, and blood and fouler liquids ran down the face to drip sluggishly off the chin. The eyes became bloodshot and bulged unnaturally from the widening sockets. The mouth stretched impossibly, blackening lips revealing sharp and pointed teeth. Curled horns burst up out of the bulging temples.

By now the real and unchanged Madame Zara was whimpering loudly, her entire bulk shaking and shuddering. All the natural color had dropped out of her face, leaving it as pale as a sheet behind the gaudy dabs of makeup. And then the demonic face burst out of the mirror, the fanged mouth reaching hungrily for the medium's throat. Madame Zara let out a pitiful howl, gathered up her billowing robes, and crashed down the stairs like a runaway avalanche. Hawk and Fisher moved hurriedly out of her way, and Madame Zara hurtled down the hallway, running for her life. Hawk and Fisher watched her go, and then moved cautiously up the stairs toward the mirror, weapons at the ready. By the time they got there, it was just a mirror again, showing nothing but their own familiar faces. Fisher prodded the surface of the glass with a cautious finger, but it was stubbornly solid and normal. Hawk smashed the mirror with the butt of his axe anyway, on general principles.

"Seven more years bad luck," said Fisher, kicking shards of glass off the stairs.

"Mirrors should know their place," said Hawk firmly. "At least now we can be sure there really is something unnatural going on here."

And then they both fell silent as the quiet house suddenly erupted with a cacophony of spectral sound. The wall beside the stairs boomed loudly, like a great drum, as though struck repeatedly by some huge immaterial force. The knocking traveled up the wall and along the next landing, where all the doors suddenly began slamming, over and over again. The noise was deafening, but Hawk and Fisher didn't flinch. They held their ground and waited for something threatening to come their way. The pounding stopped abruptly, and all the doors fell silent. A low moaning began, distinct but eerily faint, as though its terrible pain and despair had traveled unknowable distances to reach them. The moan rose to become a howl, and then a scream, and finally maniacal laughter, full of dread and horror. Hawk and Fisher held their ground. The laughter broke off abruptly, and silence returned. Hawk cradled his axe in his arms, and applauded politely.

"Very impressive. Derivative, but nicely varied. What time is the next performance?"

Animal roars and screeches filled the air now, wild and ferocious, along with the thunderous growls of something very large and extremely hungry. Hawk and Fisher watched patiently until that, too, finally died away into silence again. Hawk looked at Fisher.

"I am not impressed. Are you impressed?"

"Even less than you," said Fisher. "After surviving the Demon War, this is strictly amateur hour."

The roaring started up again. Hawk roared right back at it, and the original sound broke off abruptly, as though shocked into silence.

"Nice one, Hawk," said Fisher.

And then they both looked around sharply as heavy footsteps sounded from the other end of the hall. Starting at the closed front door, they advanced slowly toward the stairs, and there was something of eternity in the pause between each increasingly loud impact. The floor and the walls and the stairs shook with each step, and the sound seemed to shudder in Hawk's and Fisher's bones. It was like listening to God walking across the sky with Judgment Day on his mind. Hawk and Fisher looked at each other, and then started back down the stairs to face the advancing footsteps, axe and sword at the ready. The thunderous footsteps moved slowly, inexorably, toward them.

Hawk and Fisher reached the foot of the stairs, and kept right on going. The sound of approaching footsteps hesitated, and then stopped. Hawk and Fisher stopped. It was now very quiet, as if the whole house were listening. There was a single heavy footstep in the hall. Hawk stepped forward to meet it. After a pause he took another step forward, and another. And the heavy footsteps retreated before him. Hawk kept going, Fisher now at his side, and the footsteps retreated rapidly toward an open door on the left. They no longer sounded loud or threatening, or in the least Godlike. Hawk and Fisher followed the footsteps through the door and into the main parlor, where they suddenly ceased.

Hawk and Fisher looked about them. The parlor was large, comfortable, and almost cozy in the dim amber light from the turned-down gas jets in the ornamental lamps. The heavy furniture had been pushed out of position into the middle of the room, and the edges of the carpet were no longer nailed down. Someone had been searching for something; apparently with no success. The room was silent. The disembodied footsteps were gone, at an end, with no trace anywhere as to what might have made them.

"Well," said Hawk. "That was interesting."

"Right," said Fisher. "Whatever it was, I think we frightened it. I know we've always had a dangerous reputation, but spooking a spirit has to be a new high, even for us."

"This may be just the overture," said Hawk. "Feeling us out. Seeing what our weaknesses are. Everyone's afraid of something. You wait till the headless body appears, with a great headsman's axe in its hands."

Fisher sniffed. "I've faced liches before. Zombies are easy to take out, as long as you keep a clear head. And make sure you've got some salt and fire handy."

"Still," said Hawk. "Dead men walking can be pretty upsetting. Salt and fire don't always work. And then . . . how do you kill something that's already dead?"

"We'd find a way," said Fisher.

Hawk had to smile. "We probably would at that."

"You know," said Fisher, "you don't have to hold my hand quite so hard, Hawk. I hadn't realized you were so nervous."

Hawk looked at her. "Isobel, I'm not holding your hand."

Fisher's face went blank for a moment as she took in just how far away from her Hawk was. And then they both looked down, to see the large disembodied hand firmly holding on to Fisher's left hand. It looked very real and very solid, but the end of the wrist faded away to nothing at all. Fisher's lips drew back in a disgusted snarl, and she clamped her fingers around the disembodied hand, crushing it with all her considerable strength. There was a sudden sound of bones crunching and breaking. The hand fought desperately to get loose, but Fisher just piled on the pressure, and more bones splintered and snapped inside her implacable grip. The hand suddenly melted away into unraveling mists, accompanied by a pained howling from somewhere far away. Fisher flapped her hand a few times, to disperse the last traces of mist, and then brought her fingers up to her face to sniff them.

"Sulphur. Brimstone. How very unoriginal."

The howling died away. Hawk looked reproachfully at Fisher. "I think you've upset it."

"Good. Teach it to sneak up on me like that. . . . Hawk?"

"Yes?"

"The eyes from that portrait on the wall behind you are following us around the room."

"Just a trick of the light. All portraits are like that."

"No, I mean *really* following us."

Hawk turned slowly, following Fisher's gaze, and there behind him, floating unsupported on the still air, were two disembodied eyeballs. They were bloodred, with huge dark pupils, and threads of something drippy hanging off the back, as though they'd just been wrenched out of the eye sockets. The eyeballs glared at Hawk, full of mute menace.

"You have got to be kidding," said Hawk, and slapped both the eyeballs away with the flat of his hand. There was another agonized howl somewhere far off as the eyeballs banged together, compressing somewhat under the impact, and then caromed across the room to bounce off the far wall like two miscued Ping-Pong balls. Hawk started after them, struck by a sudden desire to see if he could get them going in different directions, but they both quickly vanished as he bore down on them.

"That must've hurt," said Fisher.

"Well, at least now we can be sure someone here is keeping an eye on us," said Hawk.

The door behind them swung open, slamming back against the wall with a deafening crash. Hawk and Fisher spun around, weapons at the ready. Facing them in the doorway was a tall, imposing figure, wrapped in an autopsy sheet that covered it from head to toe. Blood had thickly stained the gray cloth in a long line, where the body had been cut open from throat to crotch, and smaller stains marked the eyes and mouth, giving the figure a rudimentary face. A hand as gray as the sheet emerged slowly from under the wrappings, holding out a length of steel chain, from which blood dripped steadily onto the expensive carpet. Hawk and Fisher looked at each other.

"Traditional, but effective," said Hawk. "Nice use of bloodstains, too."

"And using the actual autopsy sheet was a good touch," said Fisher. "Can't say I see the point of the chain, though."

"All ghosts rattle chains," said Hawk. "It's expected. It's—"

"Traditional, yes, I know."

They advanced unhurriedly on the sheeted figure. It made a low moaning noise that would have raised the hackles on anyone else's neck, and rattled the length of chain noisily.

"Nice try," said Hawk. "Are you frightened yet, Fisher?"

"Not in the least. You?"

"Not even close."

"Good," said Fisher. "Let's see if it's got anything else under that sheet that I can crush in my hand."

The sheeted figure started to back away. Hawk and Fisher increased their pace. The sheeted figure turned to run, dropping its steel chain, which vanished before it hit the carpet. Hawk grabbed one edge of the bloodstained sheet and whipped it away, revealing a skeleton, which spun round unsteadily before coming to a halt. The skull chattered its teeth menacingly at Hawk and Fisher, then reached out with its bony hands. Hawk and Fisher hit the skeleton simultaneously with axe and sword, and after a few hurried and very violent moments, nothing remained of the skeleton but a pile of broken and splintered bones on the carpet. Hawk kicked at a few with his boot. Far away, something was swearing loudly. Hawk sniggered. Fisher looked around hopefully for something else to hit. The bones disappeared, along with the autopsy sheet Hawk had pulled off.

"You know, this is getting to be fun," said Hawk. "I wonder what he'll come up with next?"

"Something quaint and archaic, no doubt," said Fisher. "This Appleton Hartley must have read the same Gothic romances as you. Maybe he'll come in as a nun next. Nuns are big in haunted palaces and the like."

"A cross-dressing ghost? I think he's got enough problems as it is."

One by one the lights began to go out. The blue flames of the gas jets died away to nothing, and the few lit candles sputtered out. A heavy gloom filled the parlor like a dark tide. The only illumination now came from the streetlights outside the sole window, and even that was slowly fading, as though something were blocking it out. Hawk and Fisher moved close together.

"Everyone's afraid of something," said Fisher. "And you and I have good reason to be scared of the dark."

"That was the Darkwood," said Hawk. "This is nothing compared to the long night." But his voice didn't sound as sure as his words. Some things could never be entirely forgotten.

"It's getting really dark, Hawk. No light anywhere."

"Put the lights back on, or I'm going to set fire to something," said Hawk loudly. "I mean it."

"He really does," warned Fisher. "And some of that furniture looks quite expensive, and very easy to set fire to."

"I'll burn your whole damned house down, if I have to," said Hawk, his voice calm and certain again.

There was a pause, and then the gas lights flared up again, and the light in the parlor returned to normal. Hawk and Fisher breathed a little more easily.

"I thought so," said Hawk. "This house was Appleton Hartley's pride and joy; you only have to look at it to see that. He filled it with every expensive piece of bric-a-brac that took his fancy. He's been defending his home against the dreaded Leonard and Mavis, and their attempts to tear it apart in search of the missing money. He couldn't risk us damaging it."

"Fine," said Fisher. "Nicely reasoned, as always. What do we do now?"

"I think it's time we all sat down and had a little chat," said Hawk. "Appleton Hartley! Come out, come out, wherever you are! Or we'll think of some really destructive things to do to your furnishings and fittings."

The ghost of Appleton Hartley walked in through the open door, his head tucked under his arm. It would have looked quite impressive, if the head hadn't had to squint its eyes to see where it was going. Apparently the viewpoint from hip level was disconcerting him. The late Appleton Hartley was wearing the best Sunday suit he'd been buried in, and it didn't fit him any better now that he was dead than it had while he was alive. The headless body lurched to a halt before the somewhat bemused Hawk and Fisher, and the head's face looked briefly seasick.

"This is my house," said the head in a high and somewhat reedy voice. "And you are both trespassing! Leave my property immediately or face my terrible wrath. My righteous anger shall be unconstrained, so flee now while you still can. Or face my fury from beyond the grave!"

"How the hell is he talking like that?" said Hawk. "I mean, his voice box is still in his throat, isn't it? And even if it isn't, how are the lungs getting any air to it?"

"Maybe there's some kind of ectoplasmic connection that we can't see," said Fisher. "That would account for the hand and the eyeballs. Then again, his chest isn't moving, which would suggest he isn't using his lungs—"

"What's that?" said the head sharply. "Speak up! Don't mumble, dammit!"

"We are not mumbling," said Hawk. "It's just that you have an arm covering one ear and the other is pressed against your chest. I'm surprised you can hear anything."

"Oh. Yes. Right." The head frowned as Appleton considered the matter. "I'm rather new at all this, actually."

"Get away," said Fisher.

Hartley's body juggled his head out from under his armpit, and held it forward with both hands, like an offering. Unfortunately, the splayed fingers of the supporting hands now covered the eyes. The mouth swore indistinctly, the fingers fumbled for a better hold, and the head slipped through both hands and crashed to the floor. There was a solid-sounding thud as the head bounced, and all three of them winced. The body stumbled forward, reaching down blindly with its hands, and one foot caught the head and kicked it across the floor.

"Oh, go and help him, Hawk," said Fisher. "We'll be here all bloody night otherwise."

Hawk sighed, pushed past the headless body, and strode over to the detached head. It looked up at him imploringly, and tried an ingratiating smile. Hawk sighed and picked up the head by one ear. He gave the grimacing head back to its body, which grabbed it firmly with both hands, and immediately poked itself in one eye. Hawk and Fisher looked at each other and got the giggles. Hartley's head glared at them and stuck out its lower lip sulkily. Hawk had to bite his own lip to keep from laughing. Fisher turned away, her shoulders heaving.

"Put your head back on your neck, Hartley," said Hawk. "Please."

The ghost did so, head and neck rejoining with no trace of a seam. Hawk indicated to Fisher that it was safe for her to turn back, and they studied the reassembled Appleton Hartley standing somewhat uncertainly before them. He appeared to be solid enough, if you overlooked that somehow he'd managed to get his left ear on back to front. Hawk decided he wouldn't point it out.

"Go ahead," said the ghost. "Laugh it up. You think it's easy being a ghost? The condition doesn't exactly come with an instructional pamphlet, you know. I haven't even figured out how to walk through walls yet. And you have to concentrate on your shape every minute, or you start losing track of the details. So embarrassing. It's not easy being dead, you know. Who are you anyway, and what are you doing in my house?"

"First, we are Captains Hawk and Fisher of the city Guard," said Hawk. "And second, this house now belongs to Leonard and Mavis Hartley. You left it to them, remember?"

"They don't deserve my house," said Appleton Hartley. "My lovely house. They don't appreciate it. Have you seen what they've been doing? Vandals! And what do you plan to do, Captains? Arrest me? The law only applies to the living. And you can't exorcise me, because I'm not at all religious."

Fisher frowned. "Hold everything. You mean you don't believe in life after death?"

The ghost hesitated. "All right, I'll admit I'm still a little shaky on that bit—"

"What are you doing here?" asked Hawk, pulling the

conversation back onto safer ground. "This *was* your house, but you willed it to Leonard and Mavis."

"Only because there was no one else. Bunch of freeloaders. Never wanted to know me when I was alive. Didn't even wait till I was cold in my coffin before they were in here tearing up the floorboards and turning the place upside down. This is my house, my home, and I'm not leaving. Don't I have any rights?"

"Well, no, not really," said Hawk. "You're dead. You're supposed to . . . move on, leave material things behind."

"And leave my lovely house in the hands of these philistines? Never! If I can't take it with me, I'm not going. Here I am and here I stay. We'll see who weakens first."

"Get his family in here," said Hawk to Fisher. "Maybe we can bash out some kind of compromise."

"I wouldn't put money on it," said Fisher, heading for the door. She walked right through the ghost, just to remind him who was in charge, and Appleton shuddered violently.

"You have no idea how repulsive that is," said Appleton Hartley.

It took a lot of persuading to get Leonard and Mavis and Francis Hartley to reenter the house, but Fisher could be very persuasive with a sword in her hand, and surprisingly soon, the whole Hartley family, living and deceased, were standing in the main parlor, glaring at each other. Hawk was hard put to decide which side of the family looked more disgusted with the other.

"*Some* people have no sense of propriety," said Mavis loudly. "Hanging around when it's clear they're no longer welcome, *haunting* . . . I don't know what the neighbors must be thinking. We've never had a . . . revenant in the family before. And after we paid all that money for the funeral, too! Professional mourners, tears on demand, and a real oak coffin. With a velvet lining and real brass handles. Tell him, Leonard!"

"Real brass handles—"

"And the flowers! Do you realize how much wreaths cost

these days? I don't know how they can stand to ask for
the money."

"The professional mourners were good," said Francis.
"Did some lovely keening."

"You call that racket mourning?" said Appleton heat-
edly. "You knew very well I wanted to be cremated, with
a purely secular ceremony! You didn't even have them sing
my favorite song at the funeral."

"Certainly not," said Mavis primly. "It was quite unsuit-
able for a public ceremony. Nothing more than a drinking
song, full of vulgar references to women and . . . body
parts."

"What's it like being dead?" Francis asked the ghost
wistfully. "I think a lot about being dead."

"If I had your parents, so would I," said Appleton. "And
if you keep annoying me, boy, I'll arrange a firsthand experience for you."

"You see! You see!" Mavis went purple in the face. It
suited her. "He's threatening us now! Do something,
Leonard!"

"What the hell am I supposed to do against a ghost?"
said Leonard, feeling very definitely put upon.

"Don't you dare take that tone of voice with me, Leonard Hartley!"

Leonard gave Hawk a long-suffering look, full of plead-
ing, as one married man to another. Hawk sighed and
stepped forward.

"Can we at least decide exactly what this argument is
about? Why are you so determined to remain in your old
house, Appleton, instead of . . . moving on?"

"Because I spent years getting this place just right, and
they're destroying it!"

"In search of the money you've selfishly hidden here!"
countered Mavis. "Money that is ours by right!"

"Ah," said Fisher, finally on familiar ground. "Every
time there's a family argument, you can bet money's at the
bottom of it."

"When Appleton liquidated his business and took all his
money out of the bank, it took two coaches to transfer all

the cash here!" said Mavis. "That money is ours, and I want it!"

"You can want all you like," said Appleton, grinning nastily. "But you won't get it. Oh, I took hundreds of thousands of ducats out of the bank. A lifetime's savings. But it's all gone now. When I found out I was dying, and there was nothing magic or doctors could do to save me, I cashed in everything and spent the lot on wine, women, and song." The ghost paused to consider. "Well, wine and women, mostly. Had a hell of good time, while it lasted. . . ."

Mavis was finally struck silent. Leonard looked like he might faint. Francis smiled for the first time.

"You crafty bastard," he said appreciatively. "If only I'd known, I'd have joined you."

"Francis!" said his mother.

"Should have done it years earlier," said Appleton. "But I was always too busy running my business. Never married. Never had any fun. But when I knew I was dying, everything was suddenly very clear to me. Why spend your life making money just for some ungrateful relatives to inherit? So I spent all my money on a pre-wake and had the best time I could stand. Toward the end it was a rush as to what would kill me first, the disease or the wine and women." Appleton sighed happily. "I had more fun dying than I ever did living my old life."

"There's no money?" asked Mavis in a broken whisper. "None at all?"

"Well, you might find the odd coin lost down the back of the sofa, but that's about it. And you needn't think about selling my house, either. Rather than see you make a penny profit out of dismantling my home, I'll haunt it till you're all dead and gone. Think of me as a sitting tenant with a really long lease."

"You people don't need an exorcist," said Fisher. "You need family counseling. And possibly a good slap on the side of all your heads."

"Right," said Hawk. "This could drag on for years, except I haven't got the patience. So this is what we're going to do. You, Leonard and Mavis, will agree to sell this house to someone who will appreciate and look after it. And you,

Appleton, will agree to this, or Fisher and I will burn the
whole place down."

"You wouldn't!" said Leonard, Mavis, and Appleton
together.

"Oh, yes, we would," said Fisher, and everyone there
believed her.

"We are now leaving," said Hawk. "Sort out the details
among yourselves. Only keep the noise down, or we'll be
back."

"Right," said Fisher. "And next time we'll bring a social
worker with us."

"No need to be nasty," said Hawk.

Sometime later, though not soon enough for either of
them, Hawk and Fisher were back on their beat in the
North Side. It was still the early hours of the morning, but
the streets weren't really any less crowded now than during
the day. In many ways, the North Side really came alive
only after all the honest, hardworking souls had turned in
and gone to bed, leaving the streets to those who made the
real money. You could buy anything in the North Side, if
you weren't too fussy about its provenance. Or the kind of
people you had to deal with. Hawk and Fisher strolled casually along, and everyone took pains to avoid their eyes.
Businessmen hustled customers into shadowy back alleys,
and everyone else suddenly remembered somewhere else
they had to get to in a hurry. For their own peace of mind,
Hawk and Fisher tended to work on the principle that if
they couldn't see it, it wasn't happening. Otherwise, they'd
never get anything done.

The sun was just starting to rise above the horizon,
splashing thick swathes of blood across the reluctantly lightening sky. The first birds were coughing on the sooty air,
sewer rats were ganging up on the cats, and the latest
plague was bubbling wetly in the open sewers. Just another
day in Haven. Hawk and Fisher had seen entirely too many
sunrises just recently. They'd been working a double shift
for three weeks now, replacing a pair of Guard Captains
they'd been forced to arrest. Captains Karl and Jacie Gav-

riel, another husband and wife team with a hard reputation, had been running their own private protection racket on their beat. Nothing new or particularly unusual about that, but these Guards became greedy, raising their price so high that even the hardened denizens of the North Side were moved to make an official complaint.

Hawk and Fisher were sent to investigate, and they wasted no time in establishing the truth and then lowering the boom on the Gavriels. However, the Gavriels refused point-blank to come quietly, and there then followed a certain amount of unpleasantness, not to mention blood loss and property damage, before Hawk and Fisher were able to subdue them. Karl and Jacie Gavriel were currently chained to their hospital beds, awaiting trial, while the same people who'd made the original complaint were now threatening to sue Hawk and Fisher over the property damage. As a reward for bringing in their crooked compatriots, Hawk and Fisher were required to cover the Gavriels' shift in the North Side as well as their own, until replacements could be arranged.

No good deed goes unpunished in Haven.

"The Gavriels," said Hawk, brooding. "They're part of what I'm talking about. About what living in Haven does to you. They were clean once. Good thief-takers. Are they our future? Are they what we could become?"

"We're nothing like the Gavriels," said Fisher firmly. "You worry too much, Hawk."

"One of us has to. You know, more and more it seems to me like we haven't really accomplished anything, for all our time in Haven. Name one thing we've really changed for the better. Oh, we've caught a lot of bad guys, and killed even more. But Haven's still Haven. The North Side's still a cesspit of poverty and despair. The same old evils are still going on, the same poor bastards are still suffering every day. We've changed nothing."

Fisher adjusted the knuckle-duster under her glove, and tried to see where Hawk was going with all this. "We're doing well just to keep the lid on things. You can't hope to put right centuries of ingrained evil and corruption in just a few years. We've made an impression. Stopped a lot

of bad things, and bad people. Even saved the whole
damned city more than once. We've done our best."

"But who have we become in the process? Sometimes I
look in the mirror and I don't recognize the man looking
back at me. This isn't who I wanted to be. Who I meant
to make of myself."

Fisher stopped walking, and Hawk stopped with her. She
looked at him directly, face to face, deep blue eyes meeting
his unflinchingly. "So what do you want to do, Hawk? Just
turn our backs and walk away, leaving the good people
undefended? There are good people here. If we don't protect them from scumbags like the Gavriels or villains like
St. Christophe, who will? You can't walk the straight line
in Haven and expect to get anything done. We are what
we have to be, to get results."

"I used to know who I was," said Hawk quietly. "I was
an honorable man, and I led and inspired other men,
through my own good example. But that was a long time
ago."

"No," said Fisher. "That was yesterday."

They looked at each other for a while, remembering.
Finally Fisher sighed and looked away. "We were younger
then. Idealistic. Maybe . . . we just grew up."

At that point someone was dumb enough to try and steal
Fisher's purse. Had to be someone new to the city. He'd
barely gotten his hand around her purse before Fisher
punched him out without even looking around. This would-
be cutpurse hit the ground hard, his eyes unfocused. Somehow he got his feet under him, and staggered away. Fisher
was so surprised, she let him go.

"Damn. I must be getting old. They never used to get
up after I hit them." She shook her head then turned back
to Hawk. "Look, Hawk, we do what we can. You can't
clean up the North Side with just brute force. Even I know
that. The sorcerer Gaunt tried that approach with the Devil's Hook, using his magic and the threat of his reputation,
but it didn't last. Things slipped right back to their bad old
ways the moment Gaunt left the city. The nature of the
North Side is mostly determined by its absentee owners, be

they landlords or drug lords, and all of them are out of our reach. The law is nothing in the face of political connections. We could fight them, but we'd be on our own. No other Guard would join us. Hell, they'd probably be ordered to stop us. It would be just you and me, against impossible odds."

Hawk smiled slightly. "That never stopped us before. When we knew we were right."

"Perhaps not," Fisher conceded. "But if we were going to take on established villains like St. Christophe and his army of bodyguards, I'd need a hell of a good motivation. I don't think I believe in miracles anymore. This is Haven. It doesn't want to change."

Hawk shrugged and looked away. "Maybe I'm just feeling my age. Turning thirty-five shook me. That's maybe half my life gone. I don't feel old, but I don't feel *young* anymore. Some days its feels like I'm on the downhill slope now, and I'm running out of time to do all the things I meant to . . ."

"And you've got a bald patch."

"I know! Trust me, I know! I'm beginning to wonder if I should get a hat to cover it."

"You hate hats."

"I know!"

They continued on their way again, walking side by side in thoughtful silence. People came and went around them, saw their frowning faces, and gave them even more room than usual. Quite a few decided to call it an early night, and went home to hide until Hawk and Fisher had calmed down again.

"I find it harder to care about things these days," Fisher said finally. "When you see the petty evils of Haven repeated over and over in front of you every day . . . it wears you down. Even the sharpest blade will dull if you slam it against an unyielding surface often enough."

"There was a time when what we did mattered," Hawk said stubbornly. "And so, we mattered. We had purpose, and ideals. And what we did changed the world for the better."

"That was long ago," said Fisher. "In another land. We were different people then."

"No," said Hawk. "That was yesterday."

And then they both stopped in their tracks, as a call from the Guard communication sorcerer filled their ears. First a burst of pleasant flute music, to get their attention. It used to be a gong, but that rattled Hawk's back teeth so much that he went and had a private but very forceful word with the communications sorcerer, and after that it was flute music. Hawk was very popular with the other Guards for a while.

"All Guards, hold for an important message," said a calm voice in the back of their heads. It used to sound just behind their eyes, but too many people found that unnerving. "All Guards, hold for an urgent message."

"Damn," said Fisher as a simplistic syrupy guitar melody filled their heads. "Why do they always have to play such crappy music?"

"I think it's a franchise," said Hawk. "Lowest bidder and all that. Don't worry until you start enjoying the music."

"All Guards report to the main docks, in the North Side," said the sorcerer's voice, cutting abruptly across the guitar music. "Striking dock workers are gathering in large numbers. Probability of riots. All Guards to the docks, and prepare for action. No exceptions."

The communication broke off and Hawk and Fisher looked at each other. "I thought things would get out of hand in the docks eventually," said Fisher. "Lot of angry people there."

"I hate riots," said Hawk. "You never can tell what a mob will do when it gets the bit between its teeth. People in a mob will do things they'd never dream of on their own. They might even forget to be afraid of us."

"No one's *that* stupid," said Fisher.

They changed their direction and strolled unhurriedly toward the Devil's Hook and the adjoining docks.

"Strange they didn't call us in before," said Hawk. "I mean, we are the closest Guards to the scene."

"But the docks aren't our beat," said Fisher. "Presumably the Guards on the spot thought they could manage, and then had their minds changed in a hurry when the crowd started turning into a mob."

"Always good food to be had down by the docks," Hawk said thoughtfully. "Maybe we could pick up something tasty for dinner while we're there. But no more crab meat; that last batch gave me a really nasty rash."

"I remember," said Fisher. "Two degrees of temperature, and you thought you were dying."

"And no lobsters, either. They always want you to choose a live one, and then I feel too guilty to enjoy it. Besides, all those long wavy legs and antennae make me queasy. Far too much like some of the demons we fought in the long night."

"There's always the sea slugs," said Fisher, just a little maliciously. "You know, those long white things. Always lots of meat on them."

"I am not eating something that looks like it's just dropped out of a whale's bottom," said Hawk firmly.

"You never want to try anything new. Though admittedly, it must have been a brave or bloody hungry man who ate the first sea slug."

They crossed over into the Devil's Hook, the dark and seedy heart of the North Side, where crime and general wickedness were condensed through grinding poverty and desperate need into conscienceless violence and pure evil. The dilapidated buildings in that square mile of slums were crammed close together on either side of dark narrow streets, each filthy room packed with as many people as the floor could bear. There were few street lamps, mostly just flaring torches, and the streets were thick with refuse. Beggars huddled under threadbare cloaks, one hand held mutely out for whatever fortune might provide. People hidden behind hoods strode purposefully down the dark streets, looking neither to the left nor the right, ignoring each other as they went about their private business. They still managed to give Hawk and Fisher a wide berth, though.

The two Guards strolled through the deadly street, apparently entirely unconcerned, and calmly discussed the current situation in Haven's main docks. The dockworkers' guild was mad as hell, not for the first time, because the dock owners, Marcus and David DeWitt, had brought in zombie scab labor to break the ongoing strike by all dockworkers. They were striking because three men had been killed, and five crippled, by a collapsing dock structure. Everyone knew the docks were in a terrible state, but repairing and making them safe would cost a lot of money, which the DeWitt brothers didn't feel like spending until they absolutely had to. They also professed no interest at all in paying compensation to the aggrieved families of the dead and injured workers. The guild threatened a strike on the families' behalf. The DeWitts told them all to go to hell, the dockworkers went on strike, and the DeWitts brought in zombies. Lots of them.

The DeWitts had also been using their private guards to crack down on the workers smuggling goods out of the docks, thus cutting into the dockworkers' long-established money-raising ventures. Half the drugs in Haven came in through the docks, and the dockers always made sure they got their cut. It was one of the few good reasons for being a docker. Nothing was ever simple in Haven.

Hawk and Fisher knew all this. The Devil's Hook and the docks might not be their beat, but it was their nearest neighbor. So they made it their business to keep an eye on things. Because you never knew when neighbors might come visiting. If the dockworkers' troubles spilled over into the North Side, Hawk and Fisher wanted to be prepared.

There had been a bill before the city council to force the dock owners to provide safe working conditions, but the bill's proposer, Councilor William Blackstone, had been murdered, and his bill died with him. So far, no one else had proved brave or ambitious enough to challenge the very wealthy and very well-connected DeWitt brothers. Hawk and Fisher had been Councilor Blackstone's bodyguards. They'd failed to keep him alive.

They passed deeper into the Devil's Hook. People were crowding the gloomy streets now, despite the early hour. The kind of businesses that operated in the worst slums of Haven never closed. You could find or buy anything, including the pleasures that might not have a polite name, but certainly had a price. On the slightly more respectable front, there were sweatshops everywhere; whole families crowded into a single room, working twelve- or fourteen-hour days, every day, creating goods for a few pence that would sell for a few ducats in the finer parts of the city. Everyone in the family worked, from the grandparents down to the smallest children. Some were born, lived their short lives, and died in those grimy single rooms, never leaving the only world they knew. Company representatives took care of their few needs, at fixed prices, and discouraged anything that might interrupt the family's work. Everyday business in the Devil's Hook.

There were hotels that rented rooms by the half hour, and simple doss houses, ranging from flea-infested mattresses laid side by side on a communal floor, to the darkened rooms where a penny brought you the right to sleep standing up in a queue, with ropes under your arms to support you. They really crammed them in such establishments, and no one objected, because at least the warmth of crammed-together bodies was better than the cold of the streets. And everywhere, the beggars; lining the streets like so much discarded furniture, or so many broken and thrown-aside toys. They held out bowls if they had them, or hands if they didn't, showing off their various deformities to their best advantage. Some were birth defects, or the result of disease or war, but others had deliberately disfigured themselves, or their children, through cunning artifices or cheap back-street surgery, to tug more efficiently at the heartstrings of those who passed, on their way to the docks. Like everything else in the Devil's Hook, begging was a harshly competitive business.

Every beggar had to have a license. As always, the city took its cut.

There were no animals in the Devil's Hook. If it moved, and was smaller than them, the occupants ate it. Sometimes they even cooked it first. When times got really bad, in the depths of the harshest winters, when the bitter cold kept paying customers off the narrow streets, the occupants had been known to eat each other. People with any sense avoided the Hook in winter, and sometimes barricades were erected across the entranceways to keep the occupants in.

It was rumored that the Devil's Hook was where plague rats went to die, because they felt at home there.

The general smell was appalling, but Hawk and Fisher didn't flinch. They were used to it. But when they'd finished their shift, they knew they'd have to fumigate their clothes and beat them with a stick to get rid of the smell, and whatever tiny wildlife they'd picked up along the way. They stuck to the middle of the street, and were careful where they put their feet. Hawk looked around him with more than usual attention.

"In a city full of disgusting spectacles, this has to be the most appalling. Every time I come in here, I think it can't get any worse, and every time it is. When people die here and go to hell, they must feel right at home. Is this what we're fighting to protect, Fisher? Is that what we put our lives on the lines to support?"

"We support the law," said Fisher.

"What about justice?"

The Hook fell away suddenly, like a vampire presented with raw garlic, as the slums gave way to the docks, and the foul stench of too many people packed into one place was pushed back by the sharp, clean smells of the docks, and the open sea. Gulls keened overhead, getting an early start on the day. The dock buildings formed a wide semicircle surrounding the bay, which was currently crammed full of ships from a dozen countries and city-states further up the coast. Flags of all colors and designs flapped proudly in the gusting breeze, and the tall soaring masts made a kind of forest against the slowly lightening sky. Hawk was briefly struck by a kind of homesickness, though it had been many years since he had last walked in the Forest Kingdom. He brushed his feeling firmly aside and studied the situation with a soldier's eye.

A vast crowd of protesting dockers had formed at one end of the dock, facing off against a thin line of gaudily clad private guards bolstered by the handful of city Guards who normally patrolled the area. The crowd of striking dockers numbered in the hundreds, backed up by their wives and families, and the prevailing mood was not good. Tempers had been pushed to breaking point by the introduction of mass zombie scab labor, and the strikers were spoiling for a confrontation. A few placards were being waved here and there, for the few who could read their simple messages, but mostly the dockers and their families put their feelings across by mass chanting. Simple slogans, crude insults against the DeWitts, declarations of defiance, all of them in voices ugly with rage and resentment and growing desperation. Savings were fast running out, bellies were empty, and the strikers were determined that if they had to back down and return to work, someone was going to pay first. There was also the unspoken fear that the zombies might replace them entirely. The thunderous roar of the massed chanting drowned out all the other sounds in the docks. Hawk couldn't help noticing that every man and woman in the crowd was armed with something, from the steel hooks and claws and hammers of their trade, to clubs and lengths of chain and broken glass, and every man and woman looked more than ready to use them.

Hawk counted twenty private guards, each with a drawn sword, but there was no telling if they'd have the guts to hold their ground and use those swords if the crowd tipped over into a mob and surged forward. They were more used to bullying individual workers, or ganging up on the occasional smuggling ring. Hawk had already decided that if there was going to be a fight, he was going to make damn sure the private guards were between him and the dockers. That way they wouldn't be able to turn and run.

All along the harborside, zombies were hard at work, moving slowly and silently back and forth from the ships, unloading their cargo and transferring it to the waiting transports. They carried heavy weights seemingly with ease, and they never stopped to rest. There were hundreds of them, going about their business with no sense of confusion, and Hawk had to admit he was impressed. He'd never seen so many corpses in one place before. Creating a zombie from a dead body was a simple if unpleasant business, but very expensive. Not many sorcerers specialized in necromancy, given the kind of deals they had to make for power and knowledge in that field, and they charged accordingly. Certainly, controlling so many dead bodies simultaneously had to involve a lot of power. In fact, if he hadn't seen it with his own eyes, Hawk would have said it was impossible. The DeWitts must have imported a new necromancer, and a real heavy hitter at that. Hawk frowned. If someone that powerful had come to town, he should have known about it before now.

Zombie scab labor wasn't a new idea. Various businesses in Haven had tried replacing recalcitrant living workers with more compliant dead men in the past, but the expense and difficulty in controlling the corpses had always made the idea impractical. Besides no one liked having zombies around. They were just too upsetting.

The DeWitts had used smaller zombie forces in the past, to force striking dockers back to work, but the strikers usually took them out fairly quickly, by guerrilla tactics involving stealth and salt and a lot of running. This was the first time an entire work force had been replaced by zombies, so the strikers and their families were out in force. They knew they were fighting for their livelihoods, with nothing but the workhouses and the cold streets in their future if they failed. Desperate times breed desperate people, and Hawk knew no one fights more fiercely than a man who believes he has nothing left to lose.

Hawk and Fisher hung back in the shadows for a while, studying the situation. The mood was ugly, and just their appearance might be enough to spark something. Everyone knew that Hawk and Fisher were only called in after all thoughts of diplomacy had been abandoned. The dockers' chanting was now degenerating into name-calling as the strikers goaded the outnumbered private guards. The crowd wasn't quite ready to commit itself to action yet, but the threat of sudden violence hung heavily on the air like a brewing storm, dark and ugly and unpredictable.

"I really don't like these odds," Fisher said quietly. "Even if every Guard in the city turns up, right down to the lowliest probationary Constable, we're still going to be outnumbered."

"The strikers haven't actually broken any laws yet," said

Hawk. "A lot of this is just letting off steam. Gives them the feeling they're doing something. They must know that the Guard is on its way, and that if they start something, a lot of them are going to get hurt, maybe even killed. They're not trained fighters, like us. It could be that a large enough Guard presence will take some of the wind out of their sails, calm them down."

Fisher snorted. "You don't believe that any more than I do. These people are spoiling for a fight. It's all they've got left."

Hawk made a disgusted noise. "If we were really interested in justice, we'd be down there fighting beside them."

"Don't get soft on me, Hawk. If that crowd becomes a mob, they won't care who they hurt. They certainly won't think twice about trying to kill you or me."

"I know," said Hawk. "Let's report in to the DeWitts. See what they want us to do. Maybe we can persuade them to be reasonable."

Fisher raised an eyebrow. "Bets?"

One by one the city Guard assembled in the great cobblestoned yard outside the DeWitt brothers' business headquarters; an impressive three-story building in dark stone that overlooked the docks like a feudal lord's castle. Inside, the hundreds of clerks and customs officers and other paper-shufflers were keeping their heads well down, and trying to persuade themselves that nothing of what was going on outside was any of their business. They didn't even have the gumption to look out the windows at the gathering army of Guards.

Looking around, it seemed to Hawk that more than half of the entire city Guard was there, from Captains to Constables, but even so, they didn't come close to filling the yard. Lamps in elegant frames added to the dim morning light, but still there were shadows everywhere, and a cold wind was blowing in from the sea. They would all have been a lot more comfortable inside the DeWitts' building, but of course there was no way such very important people as Marcus and David DeWitt would ever allow mere

Guards inside their premises. They might need the Guard, but they sure weren't going to socialize with them.

Hawk sighed, and pulled his cloak tightly about him. Orders had come down from above that the DeWitts were to have full cooperation from every Guard, no excuses and no exceptions, and the Guards should follow the DeWitts' instructions in all things. The DeWitts were connected. So crime was allowed to run rampant in the rest of Haven while the dock owners used the Guard as their own private bully boys. Hawk growled something under his breath, and Fisher looked at him uneasily. She just knew he was going to say something impolite and entirely regrettable to the DeWitts, when they finally deigned to put in an appearance, and she and Hawk were in enough trouble already with the powers that be. She seriously considered knocking Hawk down and sitting on him, while there was still time, but he'd only sulk later. Fisher settled for locating the nearest exit, just in case they had to leave in a hurry.

There was a self-important banging noise from above, as the doors on the balcony overlooking the yard finally flew open, and Marcus and David DeWitt strode imperiously out to stare down their noses at the assembled Guard. They were both in their early fifties, well-fleshed, with the easy elegance and arrogance that comes from being born into lots and lots of money. Their carefully backbrushed and pommaded black hair made their fat, pale faces appear washed-out, cold, and impassive as masks. There was a quiet, understated sense of menace in their unwavering self-possession, as though no one and nothing in the world could ever disturb their privileged world.

David was the elder by a year, but otherwise there wasn't much difference between them. They dressed well but soberly, their only jewelry a collection of thick golden rings on their fleshy fingers. David had a cigar, Marcus a glass of champagne. The DeWitt brothers looked down on the Guards in their yard, assembled at their command, and they couldn't even be bothered to look disdainful. They looked more bored than anything, as though forced by duty to carry out some petty but necessary protocol.

"You are here to protect the docks against any threat,"

said David flatly. "Most definitely including the strikers. You are hereby authorized to use any means necessary to ensure the safety of the ships, their cargoes, and the harborside buildings. You first task is to disperse the mob at our doors, and send them packing."

"You shouldn't have too much trouble," said Marcus in a voice eerily like his brother's. "Just be firm, and they'll back down."

"And if they don't?" said an anonymous voice from among the Guards.

"Then you do what you have to," said David. "They're troublemakers. Scum. We want them off our property. Hurt them. Kill them, if necessary. But get that rabble out of our docks."

"If we kill them all," said Hawk in a remarkably restrained voice, "you won't have a workforce anymore."

"We have the zombies," said Marcus. "Now that we have the means to control such a number, they will be our workforce. The living are now redundant. The dead should prove much more reliable. They don't need paying, or cosseting, and you don't get any back talk from them."

"Right," said David. "Should have done this years ago."

"And what about the people who worked for you all these years?" asked Hawk, still dangerously calm. "What right do you have to take away their livelihoods, destroy their lives, throw their families out onto the streets? Aren't there enough beggars in the Hook already?"

"Life, and its riches, belong to the strong," said Marcus DeWitt, entirely unmoved. "To those who have the strength to take what they want, and hold it."

"And you're the strongest ones here?" asked Hawk.

"Of course," said David.

Hawk smiled nastily. "Want to come down here and arm wrestle?"

Several Guards laughed, and then quickly turned their laughter into coughs as it became clear the DeWitts had no sense of humor. Those Guards nearest Hawk and Fisher began to edge carefully away from them, not wishing to be associated with such dangerous people. The DeWitts moved forward to the edge of their balcony, to get a better look at Hawk.

"You are hired help," David said flatly. "You'll do as you're told. Is that clear?"

Hawk's hand dropped to the axe at his side. He was smiling, and a wild light burned in his eye. Fisher grabbed his arm and held it firmly in place. "Hawk, no! Not here. Not in front of witnesses."

Hawk's arm muscles bulged dangerously under her hand, and then slowly relaxed again. Fisher let out a breath she hadn't realized she was holding. The DeWitts glared down at Hawk until it was clear he had nothing more to say, and then they turned their backs on him and left the balcony. Members of their private guard moved slowly among the city Guard, assigning them positions on the harborside and giving them more specific orders where necessary. Hawk was surprised to see a familiar face approaching him. Mistique was a charming sorceress of no uncommon ability, and had impressed him greatly the last time they'd worked together. A tall, slender, constantly fluttering figure in her mid-thirties, Mistique was dressed in traditional sorceress' black, but the outfit was carefully cut in the very latest fashion to show plenty of bare flesh. She had a long, horsey face, and a friendly, toothy grin that made her look easily ten years younger. It also made her look like she was about to take a bite out of you, but then, you couldn't have everything. She had a thick mane of jet black curly hair that fell well past her shoulders, which she was constantly having to sweep back out of her eyes. She had a husky upper-class accent, a disturbingly direct gaze, and wore dozens of bangles and bracelets that clattered loudly with her every movement.

"Darlings!" she said loudly, advancing on Hawk and Fisher with determined cheeriness. "How absolutely super to see you both again!"

"Hello, Mistique," said Fisher, glad of anything that might distract Hawk. "What the hell are you doing here? You're not in charge of all those bloody zombies, are you?"

"Certainly not," said Mistique, pulling a face. "Nasty things. Not my kind of territory at all. No, the city Council appointed me as official bodyguard to the DeWitts, for the duration of their troubles. Just in case the dockers have clubbed together to buy some magical threat. If it was anyone but the DeWitts, I'd have told the Council to go take a long walk off a short pier, but one doesn't turn down the DeWitts. So here I am, darlings, a sorceress of my magnitude reduced to a mere bodyguard. The shame of it. Far too much like real work for my taste. But, needs must when the devil vomits in your shoes. And the job does pay very well. Both Mummy and Daddy are getting on a bit now, and need a lot of looking after, which means I've been raiding the family coffers just a little more than I feel comfortable with, so . . ."

"So we do what the DeWitts tell us, and tug our forelocks respectfully, if we know what's good for us," said Hawk.

"Well, yes, darling. That's life. In Haven, anyway. Though it has to be said that Marcus and David don't have a single social grace between them. I mean, honestly, they've been ordering me about like a bloody servant. I'd widdle in their wine, but with the vintages they prefer, they'd probably never notice."

"Maybe you can tell us why the DeWitts have such a hold over the Council just now," said Fisher. "They don't normally have this much influence."

"Ah, yes. It seems there's a great deal of perishable goods currently waiting to be unloaded from the boats in the harbor. Tons and tons of it. And an awful lot of it could go off, really soon, if it isn't unloaded in a hurry. The DeWitts are currently paying for widespread preservation spells, but if they have to keep that up much longer, the cost will eat up all their profits. So dear David and Marcus are caught between a rock and a descending boot. If they let up on the spells, they'll be left with nothing but tons of rotting food. And if they don't supply that food, in good condition, they stand to lose not only oodles and oodles of money, but also a whole bunch of very important contracts throughout the city. So they really can't afford to allow anything to interfere with unloading the ships."

"And of course the dockers know all about this," said Hawk.

"Oh, of course, darling. Anyway, since the Council doesn't want to face a whole city full of hungry people, with the prospect of civil unrest and even riots, for now what the DeWitts want, the DeWitts get. Bend over and smile, darlings. It'll all be over before you know it."

"How are the DeWitts controlling so many zombies at once?" asked Fisher, on the grounds that changing the subject had to be a good idea.

"They've come into possession of some remarkable magical artifact," said Mistique, tossing her long hair thoughtfully. "Paid a hell of a lot for it, too. Apparently it makes controlling any number of zombies a piece of cake. I don't know what it is. They won't let me see it. They're also being very cagey about who they got it from. Don't blame them. Nothing good ever came from dealing with necromancers."

"Could they really get away with replacing the workforce with zombies?" asked Hawk.

"I don't see why not," said Fisher. "Zombies wear out the longer and harder you work them, but there's never any shortage of corpses in Haven to replace them. In fact, the Council would probably approve. All the main cemeteries have been full for years, and the incinerators are working twenty-four-hour shifts."

"But what about the dockworkers and their families?" asked Hawk. "Does no one care what happens to them?"

"This is Haven, darling," said Mistique, not unkindly.

"And the DeWitts are running a business, not a charity," said a cold voice bearing down on them. The three of them looked around to see the commander of the DeWitts' private guards. He crashed to a halt before them, and took it in turns to favor each of them with his glare. Big, broad, and muscular, he would have looked really impressive and menacing if he hadn't been wearing the DeWitt official private guard uniform. Banana yellow with bloodred piping, topped with a rich purple cloak. He looked very much like a bruise on legs. Hawk and Fisher had to bite their lips.

"Hello, Commander Foy," said Mistique. "Love the outfit."

"Trust me," said Fisher. "You are entirely alone in that."

"I think my retinas are burning out," said Hawk.

"Hush," said Fisher. "What do you want with us, Foy?"

"*Commander* Foy! I run things here, and don't you forget it!" He glared at Hawk and Fisher, who still couldn't meet his eyes. The commander sniffed loudly. "The De-Witts understand that this is not the kind of work the city Guard are used to undertaking. So, to . . . sweeten the medicine, the DeWitts have most kindly authorized me to assure all of you that there will be a substantial bonus, to be paid at the end of the day. A very substantial bonus."

"Bribe money," said Fisher. "Why am I not surprised?"

"We're not taking it," said Hawk.

"Hold everything," said Fisher immediately. "We haven't heard how much it is yet."

"We don't need their blood money," said Hawk.

"Hey, we're going to be doing the work anyway, and you can bet no one else will turn it down."

"We're not taking it!" Hawk yelled.

Fisher looked at Foy. "We're not taking it. But I'll bet we're the only ones."

"No bet," said yet another voice, close at hand. This turned out to be Constable Murdoch. He and his younger brother patrolled the docks. Hawk and Fisher knew them vaguely, from cooperating on a few cases together. The older brother was currently standing face-to-face with Commander Foy, glaring right into the man's eyes, while his younger brother stood impassively at his side, as always. "I'm not taking any part in this, and neither is my brother," said Murdoch. "We're local. Grew up in the Devil's Hook. Our dad worked the docks till the strain of it killed him. Some of those strikers are our friends and neighbors and family. We'll not raise a hand against them." He glared at Commander Foy. "We're not the only ones, either. Your bosses don't have enough money to make us fight our own kind. Not over something like this."

"It may not come to fighting," said Hawk. "If we're a strong enough presence . . ."

"They'll fight," said Murdoch. "You know they'll fight. They've nothing else left."

"We're the law," Hawk said slowly. "We're not supposed to choose which laws we'll uphold, and which we won't."

Murdoch snorted. "That's rich, coming from you, Captain. Everyone knows your reputation. You bend and break the law every day."

"In pursuit of justice."

"Where's the justice here?" said Murdoch. He turned to his brother. "Come on. We're leaving."

"And if they fire you?" said Fisher.

Murdoch shrugged calmly. "Then we'll join the striking dockers. And the next time there's trouble here, and you can bet there'll be a next time, the faces you see over raised weapons might just be ours. What will you do then, Captains?"

He didn't wait for an answer. The Murdoch brothers made their way out of the courtyard, and no one tried to stop them. But no one else followed them. Commander Foy started to say something cutting, and then the words died in his mouth as Hawk gave him a hard look. Foy decided he had urgent business elsewhere, and went off to look for it, trying not to hurry too obviously. Fisher sniffed, and took her hand away from her sword. She looked at Hawk.

"Murdoch had a point. Where is the justice in what we're doing here?"

"I don't know," said Hawk, and suddenly he sounded very tired. "Part of me wants to walk right out of here with the Murdochs, but . . . the law here's very clear. Mob violence has no place in business disputes. If we stay . . . maybe we can help keep the violence from getting out of hand. Sometimes you have to settle for the lesser of two evils. But there's nothing says we have to like it."

The general growl of conversation among the Guards died away as the DeWitts came back out onto their balcony, and looked down like generals surveying their troops. As Foy had intimated, the DeWitts began by committing themselves to a massive bonus, to be paid once the Guards' work was done. Most of the Guards nodded acceptance happily enough. A few even cheered.

"The strikers have refused our lawful orders to leave the docks," said Marcus DeWitt. "You will make them leave, by whatever means necessary."

"Be careful once you get onto the harborside," said David. "Some of the structures aren't very safe."

There was a brief murmur of dark amusement among the Guards. The DeWitts seemed entirely unaware of the irony in what had just been said.

"Do your duty, Guardsmen," said Marcus flatly. "Your city has need of you."

There were a few more cheers, but the majority of the Guards just turned and left the cobbled yard, heading to the docks to do their job.

The first light of true morning spread slowly across the docks as the Guards marched down the harborside to face the striking dockers. Most of the red was gone from the skies, and a thin mist had sprung up, a pearl gray cloud that swallowed up the ships in the harbor, and wrapped itself around the two factions as though cutting them off from the rest of the world. As though nothing mattered but what the dockers and the Guard would do next. They were in their own little world now, with no escape from the violent clash that was growing more real and more inevitable with every moment.

The harborside shook under the massed thunder of booted feet as the Guards bore down on the gathered strikers. The dockers fell silent, but made no move to fall back or disperse. They stood close together, bodies tense with anticipation, their faces full of silent hate and determination. The Guards crashed to a halt facing the strikers, and for a long, long moment both sides just stood and looked at each other. Both sides had weapons in their hands.

In the midst of his fellow Guards, Hawk hefted his axe uneasily. Even now a few calm words from either side might have stopped this. A little give and take from both sides, a few gestures of goodwill, and they could all have turned aside from the terrible thing waiting to happen. But no one was interested in compromise. Hawk looked away, his gaze moving almost desperately across the ships' masts rising above the mists like naked trees, and a sudden surge of wanderlust hit him, almost like pain. He felt an almost physical need to board one of those ships and just sail away. Not just from this particularly unpleasant duty, but from Haven, and all its corrupting evils. To start a new life somewhere else, to be someone else, someone cleaner. . . . Or perhaps just keep traveling. Hawk shook his head angrily. He'd never run away from a hard decision before, and he wasn't about to start now.

He looked at the striking dockers, and they looked back, grim and cold, knowing they were damned, whatever happened. The tension on the docks was so real and focused now, it almost had a cutting edge of its own. The violence was very close, a scent of sweat and adrenaline, a taste of blood in the mouth. Of men preparing to fight, to bleed and maybe die, because they had turned away from every other option. Because it was time.

Hawk looked away again, as though by his refusal to take part, he could prevent the gathering anticipation. Like a child who thinks that if he can't see it, it isn't happening. He studied the zombies, still moving slowly but purposefully back and forth, lifting and carrying and even operating the simple cranes with silent, unwavering precision. Once set in motion, they would work day and night, with no need to stop for rest or food or sleep. They felt no pain or weariness, and nothing short of major damage or actual falling apart would stop or even slow them down. Whoever they might have been in life no longer mattered. They were just machines now, unfeeling limbs and muscles moving to another's will.

They still had their drawbacks. They would perform a task unceasingly, but if conditions changed, the dead were incapable of adapting to that change. They couldn't cope with even the simplest forms of the unexpected. They had physical problems, too. They were dead, after all, and while zombification slowed the processes of corruption, it couldn't stop them completely. As a result, all the zombies were in varying stages of decay. Some had no eyes and could not see, and were limited to only the simplest tasks. Sometimes an unexpected weight or strain would tear a rotted arm or hand completely away. The zombie would mindlessly continue in its work, incapable of realizing it no longer had enough limbs to carry the job out. Some bodies were so far gone, they were literally strapped together with cords and leather thongs to keep them from falling apart.

A few still bore recent autopsy scars, or even the wounds that had killed them. And a few had obviously been stitched together from ill-assorted spare parts. The zombie spell could get a lot of work out of a dead body. Hawk looked hard, but didn't recognize any of the dead faces. He wasn't sure what he would or could have done if he had.

Later, no one was sure how it had started. Maybe somebody said or did something, or someone else thought they did. It didn't matter. Suddenly both sides surged forward and slammed together in the middle of the harborside, and everyone was screaming and fighting in one great milling mass, desperate to hurt and punish the enemy that made this fight necessary. Steel hooks and crowbars faced off against swords and axes, blood splashed on the ground among the stamping feet, and no one had any interest in quarter or mercy. Because if one side or the other did back down, everyone knew that side would never be taken seriously again. So they fought with savage fury, spitting their hatred into one another's faces, and within moments, the first dead went crashing to the bloody ground.

Hawk and Fisher fought with axe and sword and practiced skill. They had to. The dockers would have killed them if they'd hesitated. Hawk parried desperate blows and struck back with vicious precision, and howling men and women fell before him. There was no time to tell whether he'd killed them. The Guards and strikers surged back and forth, the two sides being forced apart into small clashes of fighting men and women as the situation grew increasingly confused. There was no room or time for tactics or planning, just the vicious thrust and parry from every side, and the howling voices of the victorious and the wounded. The strikers outnumbered the Guard, but the Guards were better trained and armed. Blood flew in the air, spattering those around. The wounded on the ground tried to drag themselves away between the stamping feet. And still both sides pressed forward, struggling in the milling chaos to reach their hated enemy.

All too soon, slowly but inevitably the strikers began to give ground, the rage and desperation in their hearts no match for an army of well-trained, well-armed fighters. The Guards' swords and axes rose and fell with methodical brutality as they moved slowly forward, foot by foot, hacking and thrusting, shoulder to shoulder now as they imposed shape and meaning on the battle. They beat and drove the strikers back, and Hawk and Fisher were right there with them. Individual strikers fell wounded, or were separated from their fellows, and some Guards took the opportunity to take out their anger on those defenseless unfortunates. Hawk saw a constable cut down a man armed only with the splintered remains of a wooden club, and then all the Guards nearby moved in to kick the man to death.

The strikers broke, and turned and ran, and the Guards ran after them, bloodlust thrumming in their heads. They cut down men and women from behind, and laughed as they did it. The battle was over, but the violence had its own impetus now, and would not be denied. Hawk saw one Guard corner a lone woman striker against a wall. She was visibly pregnant, driven to fight by desperation and need, her swelling belly in contrast to her undernourished frame. She had two knitting needles in her hands, the wood roughly sharpened into points. She quickly realized there was nowhere for her to run, and she dropped the needles and showed the Guard her empty hands, but he didn't care. He was breathing hard, and grinning, and his eyes were very bright. He put away his sword and drew his nightstick from his belt, and struck her across the swollen belly. She cried out, thrown back against the wall behind her, and he hit her across the belly again. His soft laughter was drowned out by her screams as he drew back his arm to hit her again.

Hawk threw himself on the Guard. He grabbed the man, swung him around, and hit him in the face with all his strength. The Guard's mouth and nose exploded in a cloud of blood. He would have fallen, but Hawk grabbed him by the tunic front and held him up. He put away his axe, and coldly and methodically he set about beating the Guard to death with his bare hands. The Guard struggled at first, and then he screamed, but Hawk didn't care. In the end, Fisher had to drag Hawk off the man by brute force. He was breathing hard, and didn't seem to recognize her for a moment. The Guard lay unmoving on the ground, a bloody mess but still alive. The pregnant woman had disappeared. Fisher looked quickly around to see if anyone had noticed, but the other Guards were still pursuing the retreating strikers. Which was just as well. Fisher was sure none of the other Guards would have understood. Hawk looked at the blood on his hands, as though unsure as to how it got there.

"It's over, Hawk," said Fisher. "The others can deal with the mopping up. Let's get out of here."

"This is Haven," said Hawk, too tired even to be bitter. "Everywhere is just like this."

And that was when everything really went to hell.

The zombies suddenly went insane, abandoning their tasks to attack every living thing in sight. They swarmed off the ships and along the harborside, unliving arms wielding steel hooks and crowbars, and threw themselves on Guards and strikers alike. Those without weapons tore at the living with savage teeth and clawed hands. There were hundreds of them, more than a match for the Guards and the strikers put together, and the living were already exhausted from the earlier fighting. The zombies tore a bloody path through them, hitting the living from all sides, and the remaining Guards and strikers quickly forgot their differences in the name of survival. People who'd been trying to kill each other only moments before now stood shoulder to shoulder and back to back in the face of a far more terrible enemy.

The zombies fell on the living with silent fury, tearing warm flesh with cold hands, wielding their improvised weapons with unnatural strength. Men and women fell howling as the dead bludgeoned them to the bloody ground, and tore them to pieces. The Guards and the strikers fought back as best they could, but what would normally have been deadly blows had no effect on zombies. Cutting off or destroying the head effectively blinded them, but the bodies still fought on, clawed hands reaching out for the warmth of living flesh. Complete dismemberment was the only way to really stop a zombie, and in the press of stamping, shrieking bodies, that was hard and dangerous work. Everywhere men and women screamed in horror as the dead dragged them down, cold hands tearing horrid furrows in yielding flesh. But neither the Guards nor the strikers made any attempt to turn and run. They stood their ground and fought back with grim determination. They all knew that only they stood between the suddenly murderous zombies and the defenseless family homes beyond the docks. If the zombies broke through, and on into the Devil's Hook and beyond, the dead would turn the crowded tenements into one great slaughterhouse.

Hawk and Fisher fought side by side, cutting down any zombie that came near them. Hawk's axe was proof against some magics, and he quickly discovered that a blow from his axe could at least briefly interrupt the magic animating the dead. He sent the zombies crashing to the ground again and again, and Fisher would then move in and dismember the zombie with her sword before it could rise again. It was hard, butcher's work, and there seemed no end to it. Hawk and Fisher fought on, fatigue building in their aching arms and backs as they swung their weapons over and over. Undead faces glared at them from every side, teeth snapping like traps in rotting faces. The recently killed rose up again, all along the harborside, and the line between the raging dead and the helpless families of the Hook grew steadily thinner.

And then the mists along the harborside suddenly came alive, twisting and snapping, and became thick purposeful strands that enveloped the zombies and tore them apart. The sorceress Mistique had finally arrived. She stood at the edge of the fighting, and beckoned desperately to Hawk and Fisher. The zombies struggled against the attacking mists, ignoring Hawk and Fisher as they fought their way through the undead ranks to join Mistique. The sorceress's face was pale and strained as she struggled to control so large an area of mists.

"A rogue sorcerer's taken over control of the zombies!" she said breathlessly as Hawk and Fisher joined her. "He's overridden the DeWitts' control. Which means he's got to be somewhere nearby. And bloody powerful. No one I know in the city at present could do anything like this."

"Can you locate him?"

"I'm trying! It's taking practically everything I've got to take on so many zombies with my mist. I can't maintain this for long." She was breathing hard now, sweat beading on her face. Around them, the Guards and the strikers were attacking the beleaguered zombies with renewed strength and purpose, but already some of the dead were breaking free of the mists, as Mistique's concentration wavered. Her hands became white-knuckled fists as she fought for control. "He has to be somewhere near. . . . Someone so powerful should be easy to detect, but . . . I can't see him! He must be hiding behind some kind of shield. . . . Wait a minute. If he's shielded, look for no magic where there should be some. Got him! Shit! He's hidden himself in the DeWitts' business offices! You two go and get him; I'll stay here and hold the zombies with my mists for as long as I can."

"You're the sorceress," said Hawk. "Shouldn't you—"

"I'm needed here! Move, damn you! I can't control so much mist for long!"

Hawk and Fisher ran back down the harborside, heading for the DeWitts' business offices. They were already deadly tired, but they forced themselves on, pushing the pace as much as they could. The sounds of fighting continued behind them.

"Just the two of us, against a powerful sorcerer," said Fisher. "Not good odds."

"They never are," said Hawk. "I wish we still had those magic suppressor stones we were issued a while back."

"You mean the ones with a tendency to blow the hand off your wrist if you held on to them too long?" said Fisher.

Hawk sniffed, and looked back to see how Mistique was doing. Mists boiled around the sorceress, ripping limbs

from any zombie that got too close to her, but just as Hawk
looked, one of the living dead came up on her blind side,
its clawed hand reaching for the back of her head. Hawk
started to cry out a warning, and then the zombie's hand
closed on Mistique's thick black hair, and ripped it away.
The whole great black mane of hair came away in his hand,
revealing a shiny bald head underneath it. The dead man
looked at it, puzzled, as Mistique howled with outrage. Her
mists streamed into the zombie's mouth, shot down into his
body, and then blew him apart from the inside. Hawk and
Fisher looked at each other as they ran.

"I didn't know she wore a wig," said Hawk. "Did you
know she wore a wig?"

"Shut up and keep running," said Fisher.

"Been a real day of surprises today," said Hawk, and
then he shut up and saved what was left of his breath for
running.

They were soon pounding into the cobbled yard before
the DeWitts' place of business. There were lights in all the
windows, but no trace of anyone anywhere. Hawk yelled
for the DeWitts to show themselves, but there was no response. Even the private guards in their stupid uniforms
were conspicuous by their absence. Hawk and Fisher hefted
their weapons and moved cautiously forward. The front
door stood slightly ajar. Hawk pushed it slowly open with
one hand, tense for any response, but all was still and quiet.
Hawk pushed the door all the way open, and he and Fisher
charged forward into the hall beyond.

What remained of the the DeWitts' personal guard lay
scattered the length of the hall. They lay still where they
had fallen, eyes staring unseeingly, their weapons mostly
still undrawn. Whatever had killed them had hit them hard
and suddenly, and now they just cluttered the hall. Fisher
knelt and examined a few, and then shook her head.

"No obvious wounds. No discoloration to the face, so
probably not poison. Something just . . . sucked all the life
right out of them. Our sorcerer's been busy."

"Maybe he's using their life force to maintain his control
over the zombies," said Hawk, looking quickly about him.
"If so, then the odds are that everyone else here is dead,

too. I suppose it's too much to hope that he got the DeWitts."

"Concentrate on the business at hand," Fisher said sharply. "If this sorcerer is as powerful as Mistique thinks, there could be all kinds of defensive spells between us and him."

"Right," said Hawk. "And one'll get you ten he already knows we're here."

They moved cautiously forward down the hall, stepping carefully over the dead bodies, weapons at the ready, but nothing and no one emerged from the shadows to meet them. The silence was absolute, apart from Hawk's and Fisher's strained breathing. They checked each room leading off the hall, but they found no defensive magics, no creatures appearing out of midair, no elementals descending suddenly upon them from the spirit realms. Only more dead, struck down wherever they happened to be when the sorcerer cast his deadly spell.

Hawk and Fisher ascended the great stairway at the end of the hall, the backs of their necks tingling in anticipation of the attack they'd probably never know till it hit them. They stopped at the top of the stairs and looked about them. Closed doors and unmoving shadows looked calmly back at them. Fisher hefted her sword unhappily.

"This is wrong," she said softly. "There should be all kinds of nasty surprises protecting a sorcerer this powerful."

"Unless he isn't really all that powerful," said Hawk, just as quietly. "And it's taking everything he's got just to keep his zombie spell going."

"In which case," said Fisher, "I vote for charging right in and killing the bastard before he realizes what's happening."

Hawk looked at her fondly. "That's what you always suggest."

"Yeah—and most of the time it works."

"Can't argue with that. All right, we listen at each door until we hear something magical, then we burst in and I'll race you to see who gets to him first."

"Go for it," said Fisher.

They padded cautiously down the landing, listening carefully at each closed door. Their soft footsteps sounded dangerously loud in the quiet, but no one came out to investigate. And finally, at the third door, they heard a voice droning quietly. Hawk and Fisher shared a quick look and a nod. Hawk lifted his axe, but Fisher stayed him with a raised hand. She tried the door handle, and it turned easily. Fisher turned the handle as far as it would go, and then eased the door inward an inch. The hinges were mercifully silent. The air was sharp with tension, like the sea just before a storm breaks. Hawk counted down from three with his fingers, and then hit the door with his shoulder. The door flew open, and Hawk and Fisher charged into the room, weapons raised. Only to crash to a sudden halt as they saw who was waiting for them.

The sorcerer was sitting cross-legged in midair, floating unsupported above a wide chalk-drawn pentacle on the bare wooden floor. Dressed in sorcerer's black, he wore robes hung loosely about a lean, almost emaciated frame. His shoulders were still broad, but his large hands were just bone and skin, and they wavered unsteadily as they moved in slow mystical passes. The dark robes were stained and shabby, nowhere near as impressive as they had once been. The same could also be said of the sorcerer. His pale aquiline features were drawn and strained, and the dark, deep-set eyes were almost feverishly bright. He no longer shaved his head, and his hair had grown back in a dirty gray.

He turned his head slowly to look at Hawk and Fisher, his thin mouth moving in something that might have been meant as a smile. Hawk's first thought was that the sorcerer looked like a drug addict too long from his last fix. Squatting on the sorcerer's left shoulder was a small bloodred demon, barely a foot high, with a pinched vicious face and flaring membranous wings. It hissed at Hawk and Fisher, then giggled nastily. A long, slender umbilical cord ran from the demon's swollen belly to the sorcerer's neck, where it plugged seamlessly into the prominent artery.

"Hello, Hawk, Fisher," said the sorcerer in an almost

normal voice. "I knew it would be you who found me, if anyone."

"Hello, Gaunt," said Hawk, not lowering his axe. "Been a while, hasn't it?"

The sorcerer Gaunt had once single-handedly cleaned up the Devil's Hook, killing all the villains, and made the place almost civilized for a while. But it all fell apart again after he was forced to leave Haven. A good man in a bad city, he'd drawn his considerable power from a succubus, a female demon he'd called up out of the Pit, and bound to him, at the cost of his soul. He'd used evil to enable him to do good, and had no right to be surprised when it all went horribly wrong. The succubus was destroyed, and Gaunt lost his power source. Hawk and Fisher saw it happen. Gaunt had been their friend, then.

"Jesus, Gaunt," said Fisher. "What the hell happened to you? And what the hell do you think you're doing now?"

"What I have to," said Gaunt.

"You look half dead," said Hawk. "And what is that ugly thing squatting on your shoulder?"

"My new source of power," said the sorcerer. His voice was calm, almost emotionless. "After I lost my lovely angel, my succubus, most of my magic went with her. I couldn't protect the Hook anymore, and all the scum I'd kept out came rushing back, wolves with endless appetites returned to prey on the innocent. So I left Haven, in search of new magic. But after what happened to the succubus, the only demons that would answer my call were nasty little shits like this one. It's really no more than a parasite, feeding me magic in return for the life force it drains from me. Not the best of bargains to enter into, but I didn't have much of a choice."

"From what I remember of your succubus," said Hawk, "you've just traded one addiction for another."

The demon glared at Hawk, stretching its mouth impossibly wide to show sharp steel teeth. Up close it looked like a living cancer, bulging red and traced with purple veins, and it stank of sulphur and the Pit.

Gaunt smiled sadly at Hawk. "In the end, power is all that matters. It's all I have left. You want to know how I

could do something like this to myself, don't you? Ah,
Hawk, I was already damned long before you met me.
That's the price you pay for bargaining with the Pit, no
matter how noble your intentions. Trafficking with demons
like this was no trouble at all to what's left of my conscience. I needed powerful magic again, to do what had to
be done, to save the Hook. I failed them, you see. I promised them they'd be safe, promised I'd protect them from
the bastards who used and preyed on them, but in the end
I couldn't back it up. Now I can. I have returned, and this
time I will clean up the docks and the Devil's Hook for
good. The dead shall be my soldiers, and no one will be
able to stand against them. I will spread such horror
through the city that no one will ever dare oppose my
will again."

"Your zombies are killing innocent people right now!"
said Fisher. "Guards and striking dockers, men and women
putting their lives on the line to protect their families. Or
are you saying you can prevent the zombies from slaughter-
ing defenseless people in the Hook?"

"No," said Gaunt. "Some of the innocent always have
to die, for the greater good."

"They're killing everything that moves!" said Hawk.
"You don't have any real control over them!"

"You're wrong, Hawk! Wrong! I planned this all very
carefully. I created the zombie control device, with a little
help from my friend, and I sold it to the DeWitts. Suitably
disguised, of course—they didn't know it was me. But I
knew they'd never be able to resist such an opportunity.
And all along, the control device had my spell hidden at
its heart, so I could override the DeWitts' control at any
time. I knew Marcus and David would be too greedy to
look beyond the profits to be made, by replacing living
workers with zombies. And that greed has brought their
doom upon them."

"Are they dead?" said Fisher.

Gaunt frowned. "Unfortunately, no. They ran like rabbits at the first sign of trouble. It doesn't matter. My zombies will track them down later."

"There isn't going to be a later," said Hawk. "Your zombies are killing innocent people. That has to stop. Now."

"I thought you, if anyone, would understand," said the sorcerer. "The DeWitts weren't the only ones considering the introduction of zombie labor. This . . . carnage I've organized will make people too afraid to ever think of using zombies again. I'm saving thousands of jobs here, Hawk; saving lives and livelihoods all over the city. It's regrettable that some will have to die to bring that about, but you should know; there are no real innocents anymore. Not in a world where the good must damn themselves to hell to gain the power to do good. So don't talk to me of death and suffering; I face more pain and horror than you can imagine."

"Stop this now," said Fisher. "And we'll find a way to save your soul. We've done harder things in our time."

"Right," said Hawk. "No one is ever really lost, who truly repents."

"But I don't repent," said Gaunt. "I wanted power, and I willingly paid the price. I've . . . failed so many times, you see. I never did become what I wanted to be, what everyone said I had the potential to be. I never achieved the things I meant to. I couldn't even protect my friend William Blackstone, never mind the people of the Hook. I have to win this time, Hawk. I have to win, just once. Whatever the cost."

"And we have to stop you," said Fisher. "Whatever the cost."

"You can try," said Gaunt. He gestured almost lazily with one hand, and a bolt of lightning shot toward Hawk and Fisher, crackling and spitting on the air. Hawk brought up his axe, and the lightning glanced away from the great steel blade, smashing through the closed glass window and dispersing in the outside air.

"It's not that easy, is it?" asked Hawk, just a little breathlessly. "Most of your power and your concentration is tied up in maintaining control over the zombies, isn't it? That's why there weren't any defensive spells downstairs. You're not nearly as powerful as you used to be, Gaunt."

"I don't need to be," said Gaunt. "I have all the help I need."

Hawk and Fisher looked around sharply at the sound of slow footsteps dragging along the landing toward them. Fisher ran over to the door and looked out. All of the DeWitts' private guards, dead once but raised again by Gaunt's augmented will, came stumbling down the landing toward her, still wearing their stupid canary yellow uniforms. Fisher slammed the door shut, and looked for a lock or a bolt, but there wasn't one. She put her back against the door, and braced herself to hold it shut. Heavy fists slammed against the other side of the door, followed by the thud of dead shoulders, but Fisher held the door shut. She dug in her heels and glared at Hawk.

"Do something, Hawk! We've got company!"

Hawk looked at her, and then back at Gaunt, lost in concentration over his spell. Through the broken window came the sound of fighting still going on further down the docks, interspersed with the screams of the hurt and the dying. Hawk knew his duty, but he didn't want to do it. The sorcerer had been a good man once. He was still trying to be, in his own mad, twisted way. And once he had been Hawk's friend. The zombies were battering against the closed door now, pounding at it with heavy weapons in dead hands, and the thick wood trembled as Fisher fought to keep the door closed. If they got in, Hawk and Fisher wouldn't stand a chance in such a cramped space. Hawk looked back at Gaunt, torn with indecision, searching desperately for a way to avoid having to kill a man who had once been his friend. The sorcerer ignored him. And Hawk sighed once, and started forward. He knew his duty. He'd always known his duty.

He knew better than to try to cross the chalk pentacle surrounding the sorcerer. He'd seen such things before. The power harnessed in those innocuous-looking lines would fry the flesh right off his bones. Hawk hefted his great axe, aimed, and threw it, all in one strong fluid action. The axe crossed the chalk pentacle, the runes etched on the steel blade flaring fiercely for a moment, and then it sailed on to neatly sever the scarlet umbilical cord linking the demon to Gaunt's neck. The cancerous thing toppled backward, screaming shrill obscenities, and the sorcerer gasped in shock and pain as the source of his magic was abruptly cut off. Hawk was already charging forward, crossing the now harmless chalk lines without hesitation, his attention locked not on the moaning sorcerer but on the tiny red demon. It leapt to meet him, moving inhumanly quickly, just a blood-red blur as it shot through the air to slam against Hawk's chest. He staggered to a halt as its clawed hands and feet sank into his chest, the membranous wings flapping madly as it fought for balance. Hawk cursed at the sudden pain and grabbed the demon with both hands, but its claws had sunk deep into his flesh. Blood soaked the front of his tunic as he lurched back and forth, tearing at the demon. And then its severed umbilical cord whipped through the air like a striking snake, and tried to attach itself to Hawk's throat. The parasite needed a new host.

Fisher abandoned her post at the door and ran forward. She heard the door crash open behind her, but didn't dare look back. She crossed the chalk pentacle, grabbed a hand-ful of Gaunt's hair, and pulled his head back so she could set the edge of her sword against his throat. Tears ran down the sorcerer's face, but his eyes were still closed in concen-tration, and outside the sound of fighting still went on. And through the open door came the slow, steady footsteps of the newly raised dead.

"Stop this, Gaunt!" said Fisher. "Or I swear I'll kill you!"

"No, you won't," said Gaunt, not opening his eyes. "Deep down, you know what I'm doing is right. There has to be change in Haven. The guilty must be punished. Or everything we've done here has been for nothing.

"Hawk's going to destroy your demon."

"It has already given me enough magic to see this through. And you won't kill me, Isobel. I was your friend."

Fisher looked across at Hawk, who was still struggling with the demon. It was trying to plunge the end of its sev-ered umbilical cord into Hawk's neck, but he'd given up his hold on the demon's body to grab the unbilical's snap-ping end with both hands. There was an unnatural power in its jerking movements, and it took all his strength to keep the sucking end away from his throat. He could see his axe, but it was well out of reach, and if he took one hand away to grab for the knife in his boot, the demon would win. It was sniggering now, and its breath was unbelievably foul. Hawk braced himself, and used the last of his strength to turn the umbilical away from him, and plunge the sucking end into the demon's own distended belly. The cancerous face looked briefly startled, and then it shrieked with pain and thwarted rage. It released its hold on Hawk's chest, and he threw it away from him. It tumbled in midair, then sucked its whole body inside itself and vanished in a puff of paradox. Hawk, breathing heavily, looked at where it had been and blinked a few times.

"Well," he said finally. "There's something you don't see every day."

There was the sound of dead bodies falling suddenly to the floor, and Hawk spun around to see the DeWitts' private guards lying slumped and lifeless on the bare wood floor. The nearest was an arm's reach away. From outside, the sound of fighting had also come to a halt. Hawk looked at Fisher. She was standing over Gaunt's dead body, and blood was dripping from the edge of her sword. She met Hawk's gaze unflinchingly.

"I had to do it while he was vulnerable. He would never have given up control of his zombies. They were his last chance for power. His last chance to be somebody."

"Isobel . . ."

"He would have let us both die!"

"Yes," said Hawk. "I think he would have." He sighed once, and went over to pick up his axe. He hefted it once, and then put it away. He looked expressionlessly at the sorcerer's dead body. "He was . . . misguided. He meant well. He was my friend."

"That's why I killed him," said Fisher. "So you wouldn't have to."

Afterward it was mostly about clearing up. The striking dockers went home, taking their dead and wounded with them. The Guards called in surgeons to tend their wounded and began the slow process of clearing the various debris off the harborside. The zombies, calm again without Gaunt's influence, went back to work. The dockers' demonstration was over for the moment, but both sides knew it would have to be fought again, and again, until someone surrendered or there was no one left to fight. A few hardcore zealots on both sides wanted to resume the fighting right there and then, but calmer heads dragged them away in different directions. There had been enough death for one day.

Hawk and Fisher walked slowly along the harborside, stepping around the pooled blood, already dark and drying. All of the dead had been removed; both sides had a dark suspicion that DeWitt might see the bodies as raw material for their zombie workforce. Guards stood in small clumps, drinking and smoking, smiling and laughing and celebrating their survival. Hawk remembered some of them showing unforgivable brutality to the fleeing dockers, and his hand moved to the axe at his side. Fisher took him firmly by the arm and guided him away.

"Gaunt was a good man once," said Hawk. "He really did clean up the Hook for a while. But this . . . is what Haven does to good men."

"You always were too sentimental," said Fisher. "Gaunt was a power junkie who sold his soul for magic long before we ever met him. The road to hell has always been paved with the souls of those with good intentions."

They walked on a while in silence, leaving the docks behind them as they made their way back into the Devil's Hook. The grim gray tenements were strangely quiet, subdued for the moment by the news of what had happened in the docks. The few people on the streets gave Hawk's and Fisher's Guard uniforms hard looks.

"So," Fisher said finally. "We saved the city again. Hark how the grateful populace applauds us."

"We saved Haven for the DeWitts and their kind," said Hawk. "The dockers didn't deserve what happened here today."

Fisher shrugged. "It's politics. I've never understood politics."

"All you need to understand is that the situation in the docks is still unresolved. This will happen again. More dead Guards. More dead dockers. Only next time . . . I'm not sure which side I'll be fighting on." He looked straight ahead of him, not even glancing at Fisher. "This isn't what I came to Haven for. It's certainly not why I stayed."

"We stayed because we thought we were needed," said Fisher. "Because we thought we could make a difference."

"How do you feel about working and living in Haven now? How would you feel if I suggested we leave?"

"I go wherever you go, my love," Fisher said carefully. "You know that. But can we really leave, with so much still undecided? Turn our backs on all the evil running loose in the city? Last time I looked, we were still the only honest cops in Haven."

"I'm worried," said Hawk. "About the lack of purpose and direction in my life. I'm thirty-five now. Not old. Definitely not old. But I'm not young anymore, either. When I was younger, I always thought I'd have my life sorted out by now. That I'd have made all the big decisions in my life. I can't help feeling that I'm just . . . drifting. That I've lost my way."

"I've never been ambitious," Fisher told him. "We survived the long night of the Blue Moon, and the Demon War. Anything else was bound to feel anticlimactic after that. Hell, I fully expected to die back then; every day since has been a bonus. We're doing a good job here, mostly—saving people, helping people. Settle for that."

"We used to be heroes," said Hawk. "Everything we did mattered."

"Do you really want to leave Haven?"

Hawk sighed tiredly. "Where could we go that would be any different?"

And that was when the messenger from a far and distant land burst suddenly into their path, swept off his hat, and bowed deeply to them both. Hawk and Fisher came to a halt and looked, startled, at the messenger as he sank to one knee before them and addressed them in tones of ringing sincerity.

"Prince Rupert, Princess Julia—at last I have found you! You must return at once to the Forest Kingdom. King Harald has been assassinated. Only *you* can uncover the truth, bring the killer to justice, and bring peace and hope to the Forest Land again!"

Hawk looked at Fisher. "Well, that's torn it."

CHAPTER TWO

No One's Who They Used to Be

Hawk looked down at the messenger, kneeling patiently before him, and then glared quickly about him. No one seemed to be paying any special attention, but this was Haven after all, and the North Side, too, where absolutely nothing went unnoticed or unremarked by someone, if only because you never knew what might turn out to be valuable information later on. Hawk found his hand had dropped to the axe at his hip, and he moved it determinedly away. No amount of violence was going to get him out of this dilemma. It was the name that had thrown him, the damned name. No one had called him Rupert in a very long time. He'd been a different person then, leading a different life in a very different world, one he thought he'd escaped forever. He should have known better. The past never really lets go of you, and family ties are the strongest of all.

"Who the hell are you?" asked Fisher, scowling down at the kneeling man. Her voice sounded calm enough, but then, it took a lot to shake Fisher, and always had. Even when she'd been Princess Julia of Hillsdown.

"I am Allen Chance, Your Highness," said the messenger. "I believe you knew my late father, the Champion of the Forest Land."

"Never mind who he is!" snapped Hawk. "Details can wait till we get him off the street. You, Chance—get up. I never did like people kneeling to me. And no more of that *Your Highness* stuff, either. Isobel and I are Captains of the city Guard, and we have a reputation to live down to."

The messenger rose gracefully to his feet and smiled charmingly. "As you wish, Sir Rupert."

"Oh hell, we have got to get him off the street," said

Fisher. "God knows I don't want to hear whatever it is he's come all this way to tell us, but we're going to have to talk to him. And the last thing we need is an audience. Did you come alone, Chance?"

"No, he bloody didn't," said a deep growling voice behind them. Hawk and Fisher looked around, and there facing them was the biggest dog they'd ever seen. His great blocky head was on a level with their waists, and his long powerful body swelled with muscles under gleaming dark brown fur. Half of one ear was missing, and his mouth was stretched in a wide, not at all friendly grin. He had large, sharp teeth. Lots of them.

"Stone me, it's a talking wolf," said Fisher.

"I am not a wolf!" The dog sounded very certain, and not a little annoyed at the very suggestion. "Wolves are stupid, irresponsible, and they run in packs because they're afraid of their own shadows. I am a dog, and proud of it. Chance is my companion, and I'll thank you to adopt a much more respectful tone when addressing him. And if you even look like threatening him, I'll bite your arms off up to the elbows, just for starters."

Hawk was pretty sure the dog meant it. He tried a calming smile on the animal, who didn't look at all impressed. Hawk wondered if he should try and pat the dog's head, but one look at the great teeth was enough to make him abandon that idea. He wasn't too sure just what kind of dog it was. The coat varied in color from all shades of brown, to black at the head and white at the large paws. The face suggested half a dozen breeds, all of them unhappy at the mix. If every dog in the world had gotten together for one great canine orgy, a dog like this would probably be the result.

"This is my companion," said Allen Chance, moving forward to stand beside the dog. "His name's Chappie. He was watching my back, or more accurately yours, just in case. We weren't actually all that sure how you were going to take being discovered after all these years."

"But he can talk!" said Fisher.

"And very nicely, too," said Chappie. "I pride myself on my diction. And just so everybody's very clear about this:

I am *not* Chance's dog. He is my companion. I do not wear a collar, fetch sticks, or come when called if I don't bloody feel like it."

"How did you learn to talk?" said Hawk.

The dog shrugged. "I used to live with the High Warlock, in his Dark Tower. You hang around with a crazy magician long enough, you learn to talk. It's no big deal." The dog padded slowly forward, and Hawk and Fisher had to fight down a strong urge to back away. Chappie sat down and scratched briefly at his ragged half ear with a back foot. "We have met before, but you wouldn't remember me. I was just a pup then. Just another of the High Warlock's animal experiments. There were lots of us once. Now hold still so I can sniff your crotch, piss up your leg, and otherwise act objectionable. It's all part of my doggy charm."

"I think we'll pass on that, thanks," said Hawk. He looked at Chance. "That dog has too much personality for his own good."

"I know," said Chance. "Trust me, I know."

"We have got to get this pair off the street and out of the public eye," said Fisher. "They are just too weird, even for Haven."

"Right," said Hawk. "Our lodgings are too far. Where can we take them that's nearby and private? Somewhere we can be reasonably sure of not being overheard."

"The Dead Dog Tavern," Fisher said immediately. "It was pretty decent drinking before that last hygiene scare."

"You want to take us *where*?" said Chappie ominously. "If this is the kind of establishment that has dog on the menu, I will personally demolish it, set fire to the ruins, and piss on the ashes."

"It's just a name," said Hawk. "Now shut up and stop attracting attention, and I'll get you a biscuit or something."

"Well, whoopie," growled the dog, but made no other objection as Hawk and Fisher took Chance by the arms and hurried him off down a side alley. No one around seemed particularly surprised. They were used to seeing Hawk and Fisher hustle people away, whether they wanted to go or not. The dog took one last look around, muttering under his breath, and then followed the others into the alley.

The Dead Dog was a nearby watering hole, seedier than most, which took some doing in the North Side. You could only get in by intimidating the doorman, and the establishment prided itself on its bad reputation. You got no frills, fancies, or comforts at the Dead Dog; just good booze at reasonable prices, guaranteed privacy, and bar snacks if you were feeling adventurous. Two large and burly bouncers with muscles on their muscles kept the peace. There were isolated tables with clusters of chairs, and plenty of shadows for people to disappear into. It was never really full and never really empty, and the constant murmur of conversations rose and fell like the tides of the sea. Someone was planning a revolution, someone was planning a bank job, and someone was getting the shaft, though he didn't know it yet. Just another day in the North Side.

No one looked around when Hawk and Fisher barged in with Chance between them, though Chappie drew a few uncertain glances. The bouncers drew back just a little to give the two Guard Captains plenty of room. Then they looked at Chappie and drew back even more. Hawk and Fisher chose a table in a particularly dark and distant corner, and sat down with Chance between them. Chappie turned around a few times and then lay down at Chance's feet.

The messenger peered about him into the gloom as those people sitting nearest Hawk and Fisher got up and moved away to other tables. The crowded room was a hot and sweaty place, with many kinds of mostly legal smoke drifting on the still air. A row of shrunken heads with sewn-together eyelids hung over the bar by their hair. Rumor had it they were all that remained of those who hadn't paid their bar bills. Chance looked back at Hawk and exhibited polite distress.

"You used to drink here regularly, Your Highness? What happened, did you lose a bet or something? This looks like the kind of place where plagues start. There aren't any rats here, are there? I can't stand rats."

"I like them," said Chappie. "Crunchy."

"No rats," said Fisher. "If any hang out here, they get sick and die." She looked around her. "Mind you, this place has definitely gone downhill since we were last here."

"How can you tell?" asked Chance.

"Right," growled Chappie. "I've been down sewers that had more ambiance, not to mention better company."

Other people sitting nearby got up to move to other tables. Hawk didn't blame them. Part of him wished he could, too. But if Harald was dead . . . Hawk had always understood duty. Especially where his family was concerned. He leaned forward and fixed Chance with his best glare.

"All right, this is as private as we're going to get. Talk to me, Champion's son. But don't take anything for granted. We may be who you think we are, but that doesn't necessarily mean we care to be reminded of it."

"Damn right," said Fisher. "We had good reasons for leaving the Forest Land, and I doubt very much that it's changed. Even if Harald is dead."

"You are sure about that?" asked Hawk. "I'm damned if I'm going to be dragged all the way back home on a rumor."

"The King is dead," said Chance. "I've seen the body."

"Damn," said Hawk softly. "I never cared much for him, but he was still my brother."

"He was murdered four months ago," said Chance. "No one knows how or why or who. That's why I was sent to find you."

"We were close once," said Fisher. "He wasn't all bad."

She broke off as the innkeeper strode over with a bottle of the very best wine and three glasses. He slammed them down on the table one after the other, just to show he wasn't intimidated, then he glared down at Chappie, who glared right back at him.

"No dogs!" said the innkeeper. "I'm allergic."

"Really?" said Chappie. "What a coincidence. I'm allergic to fat, stupid innkeepers with piggy little eyes. Now piss off, or I'll bite off your balls and gargle with them. Better still, piss off and come back with something tasty and meat-based. I'm definitely feeling peckish."

The innkeeper blinked a few times, gave Hawk his best martyred look, and then disappeared quickly back behind his bar. Chappie looked smug as he laid his head on his paws. Chance looked down at him accusingly.

"You can't be hungry already. It's only a few hours since dinner."

"I have a large and fast-moving metabolism, and a very low boredom threshold," said Chappie, not looking up. "Blame the High Warlock; he designed me."

"Well, try and wait till we get back to our lodgings," said Chance. "I don't want you eating the kind of muck they undoubtedly serve here. I've got something special waiting for you back at the lodgings."

"Oh, I've had that," said the dog, licking his chops reflectively. "Ate the lot. All gone."

"That was for this evening!"

"Who's to say this evening would ever come? Live for the moment, that's my motto. We could all die at any minute. Especially now that we're in Haven. I never wanted to come here in the first place. Poxy bloody hole. When are we going hunting rabbits again, Chance? You promised we could go hunting rabbits again."

"All right," said Hawk. "I give up. You have my complete attention, sir dog. Let's start with your history. What did you mean when you said we'd met before?"

The big dog sighed patiently. "Try and keep up with the rest of us, Your Ex-highness. Remember your first visit to the Dark Tower, when you came to enlist the High Warlock's aid against the encroaching darkness of the long night? Well, if you cast your mind back, you might just remember that the Tower was packed to the rafters with animals. The High Warlock always had a whole bunch of animal experiments going on, mostly for the company, I think. He had a great deal of curiosity about the natural world, a whole lot of magic, plus a complete lack of scruples when it came to asking, *What if?* I was born there, the only survivor from my litter, and I was managing my first few words almost before I could walk. Mostly complaints about the quality of the food.

"And then you came along, full of heroics and high ideals

and all those other things that get you humans killed well before your time, and suddenly nothing will do but he's got to go rushing off to fight in the Demon War. He couldn't take his animals with him, so he put us all into hibernation till he returned. Not that any of us were consulted, of course. One minute I'm getting on with some important scratching and wondering what's for dinner, and the next minute it's a whole different season, and he's come back to the Tower to die." Chappie paused, his great dark eyes far away, fixed on yesterday. "I always thought he'd live forever. Powerful bloody magician like that. But no. He used up all his magic fighting your war, and what was left of him didn't last long.

"I saw you again, when you and blondie here came to say good-bye, before leaving the Forest, and he gave you that axe. He was dying even then, but he put on a good show for you, so you wouldn't be upset. Once you were gone, he let all of us loose. Most went charging off into the woods and the wide world, keen to find some trouble to get into, but I stayed. I thought somebody should. The High Warlock ate a good meal, drank most of a bottle of wine, settled himself in his most comfortable chair, then he went to sleep and never woke up. Not a bad way to go, I suppose. I waited till he was cold, just in case anything . . . unusual happened, and then I left the Tower and set off to see the world. Eventually I met Chance, and hooked up with him. It's a dog's life on your own."

"We heard he died," Hawk said quietly. "We never knew how."

"What happened to the other animals?" asked Fisher. "Were they all as smart as you?"

Chappie sniffed loudly. "Of course they weren't as smart as me! I'm a dog. But they were all pretty special, one way or another. They've been loose in the Forest for some time now, spreading their genes and generally improving the local wildlife, and making life hell for the local poachers." The dog sniggered. "If you go down to the woods today, you'd better go in disguise and be bloody well armed. There's toads that can spit lightning, deer that can be in two places at the same time, and one particular bunch of

teleporting squirrels have been driving the trappers into
nervous breakdowns. Sadistic little buggers, squirrels. I've
always said so. Mind you, rabbits are worse. Bastards!"

"So the High Warlock went easily," said Hawk. "I'm
glad. He looked pretty frail the last time we saw him. And
very tired. He'd been through a lot, because I asked him
to. I hope he made it to heaven, for all his faults."

"All dogs go to heaven," said Chappie cheerfully. "It's
in our contract. We agree to be your best friends, and try
to keep you out of trouble, and in return for that arduous
job, we all get a guaranteed place in paradise. Cats go to
the other place, and serves them bloody well right. Probably feel right at home there, tormenting the sinners." He
stopped suddenly, distracted by the one man still sitting at
a nearby table. He'd pushed away his plate with half the
food still on it. The huge dog stared at the meal as though
mesmerized, and then lurched to his feet and advanced on
the table. The customer looked around and found himself
almost face to face with a huge dog. He went pale. The
dog cleared his throat. It sounded a lot like a growl. The
customer went very pale. Chappie looked meaningfully at
the food on the plate. "You're not going to leave all that,
are you? Perfectly good food, going to waste? There are
millions starving in Cathay!"

The customer looked at the dog, almost afraid to move.
"I'm . . . really not very hungry. Couldn't manage another bite."

"Well," said Chappie, "I suppose I could help you out.
Rather than see good food go to waste. If you're sure you
don't mind?"

"Oh, no. Go right ahead. I'm sure there's somewhere
else I have to be. Very urgently. If you'll excuse me . . ."

He made a dash for the door. Chappie wolfed down all
the food on the plate and then licked it clean before padding contentedly back to collapse at Chance's feet. The
messenger looked at him sorrowfully.

"You have no shame, do you, Chappie?"

"Of course not. I'm a dog. You tell these people your
story, while I have a little nap. And don't embellish it. I'll
be listening."

Chance sighed and turned back to Hawk and Fisher. "I am the son of the late Champion of the Forest Kingdom. His only child. I don't think my father liked women much. Or men, come to that. Apparently he encountered my mother while searching the taverns for the High Warlock, when he was off on one of his drinking binges. He wasn't usually that hard to find. Just look for a window with fireworks coming out of it. Anyway, by the time the Champion found him, the Warlock had passed out cold. It had been a long night, so the Champion made arrangements for them both to spend the night at the tavern. I get the impression he'd had to do this before. My mother was working there, as a tavern slut. She got the Champion drunk . . . and nine months later presented him with a rather unexpected son. Me. He wouldn't acknowledge me at first, though he sent my mother money for my upkeep, in return for her silence and keeping her distance.

"When I was ten, he came for me. No warning. Just this huge, terrifying figure in heavy armor whom everyone, including my mother, bowed low to. He took me away with him. We spent the best part of a week traveling, and I don't think he spoke ten words to me. He finally dropped me off at St. Jude's, a very well-regarded and even more expensive private school on the border between the Forest and the kingdom of Redhart. He rode off without saying good-bye. I never saw him again.

"I inherited his broad shoulders and a tendency to rather more muscles than is usual, but not his killer's rage. My red hair and green eyes came from my mother, along with my somewhat calmer disposition. I never saw her again, either. The school wouldn't let her visit, and she died before I was old enough to leave. Tavern sluts don't tend to live long lives. My father died during the Demon War, but of course you know that. You were there.

"I was twelve years old and all alone. King Harald sent me my only inheritance, the Champion's great double-headed axe. I couldn't even lift it then. There was no money; what little my father left went to settle his few debts. Luckily he'd paid my tuition fees in advance, and I was able to stay on at the school. They supplied bed and board at no cost, in return for the privilege of having a legend's son attending their school. I left the moment I'd graduated, because I wanted to be my own man, not just someone's son."

Chance paused for a moment and took a long drink from his wineglass. It was a very poor vintage, all piss and vinegar, but he politely pretended not to notice.

"I wandered here and there, discovering the world and looking for my place in it, and finally ended up where I always knew I would—at the Forest Castle. King Harald was very gracious, but he made it abundantly clear he had no use for a Champion. He'd abolished the post. Instead he offered me a new position, that of King's Questor. Basically, my job is to be the reasonable voice at Court, to see all sides of every argument and provide a disinterested voice where necessary. Answerable only to the Throne, I have the authority to settle all arguments and disputes, by force if necessary. I am an arbiter, a judge, defender of lost causes, and the court of final appeal. I serve no single cause or faction, only justice. This has made me very unpopular in certain quarters, which I take as a sign that I'm doing my job right. I have to say, I much prefer being Questor rather than Champion. I admire my father's legend, but I don't want to become him."

He drank more wine while Hawk considered what Chance had said and what he hadn't. If Chance had been twelve at the time of the Demon War, he had to be twenty-four now. Which made Hawk feel old, but he decided he wasn't going to think about that just now. He'd heard about St. Jude's School. It was famous for being the toughest school in the Forest Kingdom, or out of it. The pupils had to learn to be even tougher, just to survive it. If you failed a course, they sent your remains home in a sealed coffin. The school mascot was a werewolf, and the swimming pool had crocodiles in it. Rupert's father, King John, had often threatened to send him and his brother, Harald, there, when they were getting out of hand or had displeased him greatly, and it was one of the few threats that actually brought them in line.

St. Jude's would make a man out of you, or kill you

trying. The school specialized in turning out legendary heroes, great scholars, and famous leaders of men. And not a few first-class villains. Only the truly exceptional survived to graduate from St. Jude's.

Men like Allen Chance.

"What academic qualifications did you end up with?" Fisher asked, just to show she was keeping up with the conversation.

"I have degrees in law, philosophy, literature, and military strategy," said Chance diffidently.

"And a fat lot of use any of them were when it came to getting you a job," said Chappie from under the table. "I notice you didn't mention you only went to the Forest Castle because you were desperate for any kind of salaried position."

"I would have gotten around to that," said Chance, a little snappily. "There's a lot of unemployment in the Forest Kingdom, struggling as it is to recover from the long night and the Demon War, and I was . . . overqualified for most positions. The point is, I was very happy being King's Questor. I served Harald faithfully, and I hope well, for four years. I always considered myself to be a reasonable man first, and a warrior second, and the position enabled me to be both."

"Tell them how you got the job," said Chappie.

"Look, who's telling this story? Do you want to tell it?"

"Then get on with it," said the dog. "And hurry it up. I'm getting hungry again."

"There were other applicants for the position of Questor," Chance said carefully. "Many of them famous men, already building their own legends. Quite a few were St. Jude's men. But they all had political backing and not-so-secret agendas. All I had was my late father's reputation, which frankly was as much a hindrance as a help. Everyone agreed he'd been one hell of a fighting man, but the Champion had always been famous in his distaste for all kinds of politics. There were even those who murmured that his sanity wasn't all that it might have been, too. It quickly became clear to me that either I found some backing of my own, or I might as well leave before I was asked to go.

"And that was when the Landsgraves of Gold and Silver and Copper came to me. Their position at Court was much reduced from what it had once been, and they saw in me a chance to regain influence and power. They provided me with all kinds of dirt on my rivals, and those we couldn't discredit, I challenged to duels. Most withdrew from the competition rather than face the Champion's son. But I still killed some good men, just because they wouldn't back down. In some ways it seems I am my father's son. So, I became King's Questor as a result of blackmail and spilled blood. Not at all the bright and glorious future I'd envisaged for myself at the Forest Castle.

"But once appointed Questor, the first thing I did was to reveal the Landsgraves' plotting. They were banished from the Court in disgrace, and I was able to establish myself immediately as a truly impartial Questor, and a bit of a bastard to boot. King Harald found the whole business highly amusing. The Landsgraves swore revenge, of course. For a time I had to have my own food taster, but after I killed the first half dozen assassins the Landsgraves sent after me, they pretty much gave up. They had gambled and failed, and no one at Court had much time for a bad loser. I was Questor, and I had proved I was my own man, but my betraying of the Landsgraves isolated me at Court. No one would be my friend, or even my ally. No one but the King."

"Let's cut to the chase," said Hawk. "Tell me how my brother died."

"It's been four months since the murder," said Chance. "And still no one knows how it was done, or why, or by whom. Cause of death was a single blow from a knife or short sword, directly into the heart, in the King's private chambers. No weapon was ever found. There were no signs of any struggle. Some have whispered darkly of suicide, but they can't explain the missing murder weapon. The most thorough investigations have failed to turn up any clue, or any clear motivation that would single out a specific culprit.

"Strictly speaking, the murder should have been impossible. King Harald was guarded on all sides by armed men, all of whom were examined under truthspell, all of whom saw and heard nothing suspicious. The King was also protected by strong magical wards, courtesy of the Magus, through which only the Royal Family could pass; and the queen was very definitely in Court at the time of the murder, in front of hundreds of witnesses. But someone got to the King anyway, silent and unseen as a ghost.

"The longer the investigation went on without any result, the more gathering tensions threatened to tear the Court apart. So I volunteered to go out into the world and bring back the legendary Prince Rupert and Princess Julia, in the hope that once again they would save the Forest Kingdom in its time of greatest need. As the Champion's son, I was indirectly a part of that legend, so my offer was accepted. And here I am, and here you are."

Hawk stirred unhappily. "Trust me, Chance; there's nothing legendary about Isobel or me. We just . . . did what we had to. Over the years we've heard many variations of the story, of the legend, of what we did in the long night. Most of them expanded and distorted by minstrels and saga writers till I hardly recognize us anymore. Minstrels have always preferred a good story to the truth, and romance over reality. *His strength is as the strength of ten, because his heart is pure,* and all that bullshit."

"Traveling players have been presenting the great romantic drama of Prince Rupert and Princess Julia for years," said Fisher, nodding. "And not once did I ever get top billing. Sometimes the names were the only things they did get right. We saw the Great Jordan's version once. Can't say I was impressed."

"The songs and stories always make it sound as though we defeated the Demon Prince all on our own," said Hawk. "Through the goodness of our hearts. That the whole country rose up to follow me, as its natural leader. That I could have been King, but heroically gave up the Throne for my legendary love of Julia. That I tamed the dragon by taking a thorn out of its paw. It was nothing like that.

"It was running and fighting, and stumbling from one desperate crisis to the next, with no guarantee we'd live to see another hour. It was wading through blood and guts, and seeing good men and women die all around you. For us, the long night was very dark; darker than you can imagine. We all came close to breaking, to going mad from the sheer horror of what we faced. You don't know the whole truth of what happened in the long night, Chance. No one does. Only Julia and I remain of those who were there at the end, and even after twelve years, we still don't sleep well at night sometimes."

"Hush," said Fisher. "Hush."

A thought struck Hawk, and he gave Chance a hard look. "What happened to the Rainbow sword I left behind? Is it still in the Old Armory?"

"Oh, yes," said Chance. "And much revered. Though no one seems too sure just what it actually does. According to some versions of the legend, you called down the Rainbow through your own inherent goodness."

"How come it's always his inherent goodness, and never mine?" said Fisher plaintively.

Hawk shook his head slowly. "It's only been twelve years, dammit. How could the truth have been forgotten so quickly?"

"Be fair," said Fisher. "It was a hell of a mess then, especially at the end. We only knew what was going on because we were right there in the thick of it all. Everyone else only saw their own small part of it. And like you said, most of the people who did know the truth are dead and gone. Maybe that's for the best. The legend is probably a lot easier to live with than the truth would ever have been."

"And afterward," said Hawk, "no doubt dear Harald had the story rewritten by his minstrels, to play up his part in it. A King rules as much by his reputation as his armed forces. And people have always needed their heroes. Since we weren't around to tell our side of things, we ended up being tailored for the traditional roles of hero and heroine. I can't help feeling we'd be a terrible disappointment in the flesh."

"You should hear what they say about the High Warlock," said Chappie, scratching briskly at his ribs with a back foot. "They've conveniently forgotten all about his boozing and his wenching. Or the romance he's supposed to have had with your mother."

"Chappie!" chided Chance quickly. "Sorry about that, Your Highness."

"It's all right," said Hawk. "There are always stories. I know about them. How could I not? But whatever happened between them was over a long time ago, and no one knows anything for sure now. The only people who could have told us the truth are all dead. Now it's just another story—of no more importance than the ones they tell about Rupert and Julia. Truth becomes history becomes legend, and the real people at the base of it all are soon forgotten."

"But . . . you did destroy the Demon Prince," said Chance. "That much at least we can be sure is true."

"Actually, no," said Fisher. "The Demon Prince was a Transient Being. All we could do was banish him from the world of men. He'll be back someday. Some evils are eternal."

For the first time Chance seemed taken aback, even shocked. "But . . . all the deaths, all the destruction of the Forest Land . . . and it's not *over*?"

"It's over for now," said Hawk. "Settle for that. That's the trouble with legends; we demand they have a neat, comforting ending. The truth is rarely that obliging."

"What about my father?" asked Chance. "Are any of the legends about him true? Did he fight heroically and die bravely?"

"Oh, yes," said Hawk. "That was true. He was a great warrior, and a true hero, and he gave up his life defending the Castle, and his King. Bravest damned thing I ever saw."

Chance nodded slowly, looking down at the wine glass on the table before him, and then he clearly decided to change the subject. "So; how did the two of you end up here, in Haven? And why are you both masquerading as commoners when you're Royal born? Even here, in the arse end of the world, surely such an inheritance would bring you social and economic advancement."

"It's a long story," said Hawk.

"No surprise there," said Chappie. He was lying on his back now, paws in the air, eyes closed. "Try for the condensed version, or I'll heckle you."

"We left the Forest Kingdom and headed south," Hawk

started. "We wanted to start new lives, as new people. Free ourselves of the baggage of our past. And contrary to what you may have been told, Harald and I did not part amicably. Julia and I were determined to put ourselves well out of his vindictive reach."

"The King has always said you left with his blessing," said Chance.

"Like hell," said Fisher. "He wanted me as his wife, and he wanted Rupert dead so he wouldn't be any challenge to the Throne. We left him lying unconscious in a pile of horseshit in the stables."

"I didn't want the Throne," said Hawk. "But there were any number of people and factions who would have made me King if I'd stuck around. The Forest Castle just wasn't big enough for Harald and me; one of us would have had to kill the other, eventually. And I didn't want that. For all the anger and bitterness between us, he was still my brother, and we had fought side by side in the Demon War. He was a hero, in his way. So we left the Forest Land. After one last stop at the Dark Tower, to say good-bye to the High Warlock."

"I remember that," said Chappie's voice from floor level. "He prophesied that one day you would both return to the Forest Kingdom." The dog snorted loudly. "Hardly a difficult one, that. Unfinished business has a way of creeping up on you, evade it as you may."

"He gave us gifts," said Hawk. "He gave me my axe, to replace the sword I could no longer wield. I was a first-class swordsman in my time, even gave your father a run for his money, Chance, but all that changed when a demon clawed the eye right out of my head. You can't be much of a swordsman with damn-all depth perception. But axes don't depend on subtlety; all you need is a strong right arm and a certain amount of bloody-minded determination. And this axe has other attributes, too; it cuts through magical protections. Mostly."

"He gave me a gift, too," said Fisher. "I could have had a magical weapon as well, if I'd wanted. But I wielded one of the damned swords, the Infernal Devices, in the Demon War, and that was more than enough for me. I still remem-

ber the evil blade called *Wolfsbane*. It nearly ate my soul.
So instead, I asked for a prophecy. I asked the High Warlock whether Rupert and I would always be together. And
he said yes; until the day we died."

"I never knew that," said Hawk. "I never asked what
you asked him; I figured that was your business. I'm
touched. But I could have told you the same thing, if
you'd asked."

Hawk and Fisher held hands across the tabletop, smiling
into each other's eyes, and for a moment Chance caught a
glimpse of Rupert and Julia, and their legendary love.

"The High Warlock told us we'd never see him again,"
said Hawk. "We'd already guessed that. He looked old and
tired, and so frail, a gust of wind could have blown him
away. Magic ate him up and spat him out, destroying him
even as he'd used it to destroy his enemies. He probably
could have saved himself even then, if he'd really wanted
to. He could have regenerated himself one more time. But
I think . . . he was allowing himself to die. Magic, Wild and
High, was going out of the world, and he knew it. There
was no room left for the kind of man he'd been. He'd had
one last great adventure, and I think he wanted to go out
on a high, while he was still remembered as a hero of the
Demon War, rather than the bitter recluse he'd been before
I found him. All his old friends, and all his old enemies,
were dead and gone, and Julia and I were leaving, too. He
was alone."

"He had me," said Chappie. "But he said it was well
past time I struck out on my own. After all his animals had
left, and he was dead, the Dark Tower sealed itself around
him, the many windows disappearing one by one, and the
Tower became his tomb. But then, it always was, wasn't
it?"

"We took the unicorn Breeze back to his own kind,"
said Fisher. "Back to the herd he'd been taken from, so
long ago. Rupert had promised him that. It took a while,
but we found them in their hidden valley; and no, I'm not
going to tell you where. The few people who knew, who
captured Breeze, are all dead, and their knowledge died
with them. Let it stay that way. Breeze is happy now, run-

ning free with the unicorns. That's all anyone needs to know."

Hawk looked down at Chappie, seeing how he stayed close to his companion, Chance, and he remembered how close he and Breeze had been.

"The hero always has a companion in his travels," Hawk said finally, smiling down at the upside down dog. "I had Breeze and you have Chappie."

"I beg your pardon," the dog said immediately. "He doesn't have me; I have him. And a bloody nuisance he is, sometimes. I only stick around because God only knows what trouble he'd get into if I wasn't there." The dog rolled over onto his side, sniffed at the air, and was suddenly back up on his feet again. He padded over to a table and stared accusingly at the occupant. "You're never going to eat all that, are you? It's not good for you. Here, let me help you out." And the dog ate everything on the plate. The table's occupant watched him do it, looking like he might burst into tears at any moment. The dog licked the plate clean, and then swaggered back to sit beside Chance again. "You know, the food's terrible here. And such small portions."

Fisher couldn't keep from grinning as she looked at Chance and the dog. "How the hell did you two get together?"

"I took a thorn out of his paw, gave him a bowl of milk, and he's been with me ever since," said the dog. "Actually, we both got a little too close to the Darkwood, for reasons that seemed good at the time, and ending up fighting a bunch of demons together. We made a good team, so I let him hang out with me. Now tell me what happened to the dragon. He was always my favorite part of your legend. Was he really as big as they say?"

"Bigger," said Hawk. "Thirty feet long if he was an inch, and God alone knows how many tons in weight. He was the last of his kind, the last dragon in the world of men. Wild magic personified. He was already dying when he left the Castle with us. He hung on just long enough to reach his old cave in Dragonslair Mountain, and then he just laid down and waited for Lady Death to find him. He was very old, older than the Forest Kingdom itself, and he had suffered so very much in its defense. He'd flown to the top of the mountain; the rest of us had to get up there the hard way. By the time we arrived, he was fast asleep, surrounded by all his precious things. Watching him die was like watching all the wonder going out of the world. Afterward we set a fire in his cave, as he'd asked. He didn't want his dead body being plundered for the valuable hide and organs."

"I remember the fire," said Chance. "You could see it burning at the top of Dragonslair for days, like a great beacon in the night. What happened to his hoard? Was it tons of gold and silver and precious jewels, as everyone said?"

"It was butterflies," said Fisher. "He collected butterflies. He had dozens of cases of the things, all carefully mounted and labeled. I never did figure out how he caught them. I mean, I can't see a thirty-foot dragon chasing across the fields in hot pursuit, brandishing a bloody big butterfly net. Well, actually I can, but I very much prefer not to."

"He was good at sneaking up on things," said Hawk.

"He'd have to be," said Fisher. "Anyway, his butterflies burned with him."

"Dammit, isn't anybody you knew still alive?" asked the dog.

"Well, the goblins were fine when we left them," said Fisher. "Every bit their usual obnoxious selves. Are they still making a nuisance of themselves in the Forest?"

"Surprisingly enough, no," answered Chance. "The fate of the goblins is something of a mystery. They disappeared into the woods soon after you left, and no one's seen hide nor hair of them since. Their old home, the Tanglewood, never grew back. No one's sighted a goblin anywhere in the Forest Land for years, and mostly everyone's just rather relieved. I mean, they were . . ."

"Yes," said Hawk. "They were. But still they fought beside us in the last great siege of the Forest Castle, and not one of them broke or ran. I was always very proud of the appalling little creatures."

"Move it on," said the dog impatiently, "Or we'll be here all bloody night. Your companions are gone or dead, and you're traveling out of the Forest with a sackful of jewels you liberated from the Castle. What happened next?"

"The jewels didn't last long," said Fisher. "Rupert always did have a soft spot for a hard-luck story. He gave it all away, little by little, for this cause or that, trying to do good or just help people who needed it. A whole lot of it went to hiring an army of mercenaries. Not one of our better decisions. There was this Prince we met, who'd been thrown off his throne, and out of his own country, so that a bunch of bad guys could seize control and run things their way. As you can imagine, this struck something of a chord with us, so we put together an army of mercs for hire, led them into battle, and put the Prince back on his throne. Only to discover that he was an even bigger bastard than the ones we'd overthrown for him."

"Right," said Hawk. "Our first clue came when he had us both arrested, dragged off in chains, and thrown into the dungeons. Where we met a very interesting class of people, most of whom had very interesting stories to tell us about just why the Prince had been chucked out in the first place. We escaped from the dungeons, took to the hills with our own mercenaries snapping at our heels, and used most of what was left of our money to fund a popular uprising that threw the Prince out of power again. He was beheaded this time, and a distant cousin took power, saying all the right things . . . but at the end of the day there were a lot of dead people, a country devastated by civil war, and not a lot of real change to show for it all. We stayed out of politics after that."

"With most of the jewels gone, we didn't have much choice," said Fisher. "I don't think we're meant to have money."

"We used what was left to buy passage on a ship sailing down the coastline to the Southern Kingdoms," said Hawk. "The *Revenge* wasn't exactly a luxury ship, and the crew were one step up from pirates, but we didn't have a lot of choice. There aren't many ships or crews brave or foolhardy enough to risk the long journey down the coastline, past the Deadlands."

"What are they like?" asked Chance, leaning forward

eagerly. "The Deadlands, I mean. There's hardly any real information about them, even in the great libraries at St. Jude's."

"What are they like?" Hawk repeated. "Hell on earth. Centuries ago, or at least so long ago that no one now can say when with any certainty, two wizards fought a duel. The last great clash of Wild Magic in the world of men. The wizards' names and motivations are lost to us, but their battle destroyed thousands of miles of territory, leaving it horribly transfigured. Whole countries and their populations were wiped out, their very names lost to history and legend. To enter the Deadlands even now is to die, slowly and horribly.

"We only ever saw the edges of it, from a distance, but that was more than enough to shake us. The land . . . it's never still, never settled. Mountains rise up and then fall again, great cracks open and close, and tides move slowly across the disturbed earth. Awful things live there, bigger than houses, howling and screaming in voices loud as thunder. Life still somehow survives in the Deadlands, but it is altered and transformed by terrible unseen energies. It's not life as we would recognize it."

"There were things in the sea, too," said Fisher, frowning as she remembered things she'd put a lot of effort into forgetting. "Just swimming in the dark waters by the coastline had been enough to change the life there in harsh, unnatural ways. The crew of the *Revenge* might have been pirates once, but we had good cause to be grateful for their swordsmanship when things came crawling up the sides of the ship at dead of night. They were pale as corpses because their skin never saw the sun, and they had no eyes because they had no need of them in the dark depths of the sea. They had spikes on their spines and mouths stuffed with jagged teeth. They moved as silently as ghosts and fought like demons, but they screamed like men when they died."

"There was a kraken half the size of the ship," said Hawk. "Red as a rose, with long barbed tentacles that wrapped around the bow of the *Revenge* and tried to drag it under. And once we saw a serpent, huge and magnificent, three times the length of the ship. It swam in circles around us for over an hour, raising its great feathered horsehead high into the air to look down on us small things. It was every color of the rainbow, and it looked at us with eyes that knew every secret in the sea . . .''

"Most ships that make the long voyage down the coastline never reach their destination," said Fisher. "The Deadlands have a long reach."

"Anyway," said Hawk, "eventually we ended up here, in Haven, pretty much broke and with nowhere else to go. So we looked around, thought we could do some good here, or at least make a difference, so we settled down as city Guards. We thought we were needed."

Fisher sniffed loudly at that, but had nothing else to add.

"How did you find us?" Hawk asked. "I thought we'd covered our tracks pretty well."

"It wasn't easy," said Chance. "Not least because you don't look at all like your official portraits. When I first saw you, back in the Devil's Hook, I barely recognized you."

"Hold everything," said Fisher. "There are official portraits of us? Where?"

"In the great Hall of the Forest Castle," said Chance. "Huge things, almost nine feet tall, painted by the most fashionable portrait artists in the North. No expense was spared for the two legendary heroes of the long night. There are statues, too. Lots of them, all over the Forest Land. Some of the peasants even leave offerings before them, even though that's officially discouraged."

"Oh, I'll bet," said Hawk.

"But of course, since neither of you were available to sit for your portraits, the artists had to work from people's descriptions, and their memories," said Chance. "So not surprisingly, the end results were rather . . . idealized. To be honest, about the only things they got right were your hair colors. Still, I never expected the likenesses to be that good. I'd seen the official portrait of my father, the Champion, and I knew that couldn't be accurate. No one could have that many muscles on their upper torso and still stand upright.

"You covered your trail pretty thoroughly, but luckily I

didn't have to follow that. I had a magical gem from the Old Armory, the Crimson Pursuant, that was designed specifically to track down and recognize members of the Forest Royalty. It brought me right here, to you. Would you like to see it?"

"Yes, I think I would," said Hawk. "Not least because I never knew such a thing existed."

Chance took a small leather pouch from his belt, pulled it open, and spilled out onto his palm a small polished ruby. It lay on his palm like a drop of blood. It seemed perfectly unremarkable, until Hawk leaned forward for a better look, whereupon the ruby blazed with an inner fire, pulsing like a heartbeat. Chance closed his hand around the ruby and dropped it back into the pouch. Hawk looked quickly around him, but everyone else in the tavern was ostentatiously minding their own business.

"King Harald left instructions in his will," said Chance, putting the leather pouch away, "that in the event of his death, this gem was to be taken from the Armory, and used to track you down, or your heir, so that the Forest line could continue if anything happened to Prince Stephen."

"He could have tracked us down at any time," said Fisher. "He just chose not to."

"He should have sent you sooner," said Hawk, almost glaring at Chance. "When he first realized he was in danger. Then we might have got back in time to save him."

"He would rather have died than beg us for help," said Fisher. "But he knew his duty, to his Kingdom and his son. He knew Rupert would have to return, to avenge his killer's death."

"He would have done the same for me," said Hawk. "How long have you been looking for us, King's Questor?"

"Oh, almost a week now," said Chance.

Hawk and Fisher stared at him incredulously. "A *week*?" said Hawk. "It took us months to get this far south!"

"Well, yes," said Chance. "But you took the long way, down the coastline. I came through the Rift. You have heard of the Rift, haven't you?"

Hawk and Fisher looked at each other. "Just rumors,"

said Hawk slowly. "We're pretty cut off from the mainstream down here. Tell us about the Rift."

"It's the greatest wonder of the modern age!" said Chance. "A sorcerous gateway, an opening in space itself that has linked the north with the south for the first time in centuries. You step through the Rift in the north, and step out of the Rift in the south. Simple as that. And vice versa, of course. The Deadlands are no longer a barrier between north and south. All kinds of trade and other interactions have been going on for years now."

"We never knew," said Hawk. "We could have gone home anytime."

"If we'd had a reason to," said Fisher. "Who created this . . . Rift?"

"The Magus," answered Chance. "The High Warlock's successor at Forest Castle. A sorcerer of great and subtle powers. He came to Harald's Court to announce the High Warlock's death, and proclaim himself the Warlock's chosen successor."

"I could have told them that was a lie," said Chappie from under the table. "And I did, later. But no one ever listens to me."

"Not now, Chappie," said Chance.

"See what I mean?"

"The Magus proved his worth and his power by opening the Rift," said Chance. "Though it took him nearly a year to set the spell up. After that, he was the darling of the Court. Officially, the Magus has sworn fealty to King Harald and his line, but unofficially he's never closed his door to anyone. If you can afford it, or if you've got something or someone he wants, you too can have the Magus perform a wonder on your behalf. He never worked openly against the King, but no one was ever too extreme or too unpopular to be denied the Magus' ear. Still, the Rift was everything he promised it would be, and more. Trade and other influences have transformed the Forest Kingdom almost beyond recognition in the last ten years."

"What's the Magus like?" asked Fisher, frowning.

"Spooky," said Chance.

"Too bloody right," agreed the dog on the floor. "Makes

my fur stand up on end every time he's anywhere near. Do you have any idea how painful that is? And he smells wrong."

"Let's put the Magus to one side, just for the moment," said Hawk. "Tell me about Harald. What happened to him after we left and he became King?"

"King Harald married Princess Felicity of Hillsdown," said Chance. "He was obliged to marry one of Duke Alric's daughters under the terms of a contract signed long ago by your father, King John, and since Princess Julia was . . . no longer available, he married the next in line. Felicity. It was a magnificent wedding. Everyone came. Everyone who was anyone, from the Forest and Hillsdown. Or maybe it just seemed that way; the Castle was packed solid for months on end with friends and relations. The servants ended up sleeping in the stables. King Viktor and Queen Catriona came all the way from Redhart, just to bless the wedding. The new Royal Couple seemed happy enough, and everyone said they looked very well together. Even so, it was still a number of years before Queen Felicity gave birth to their only child, Stephen."

"I can't believe it," said Fisher, shaking her head. "*Felicity* is Queen of the Forest Land? That idiot? There is no God, there is no justice . . ."

"Do I take it you and she never got on?" asked Hawk, amused.

"I have had fungal infections I thought more highly of. Felicity was and no doubt still is a bitch of the first water, with no principles and even fewer scruples. She did everything I ever did and a whole lot more, and never once even looked like getting caught. She always found someone else to carry the blame and take her punishments. Sometimes me. She slept with everything that breathed, plotted treason with anyone stupid enough to trust her, and never did a day's work in her life. She used to have servants following her around all the time, just in case she dropped something."

"Well," said Hawk. "At least she and Harald had a lot in common, then."

"She is vile, evil, and appalling! She is no more fitted to

be Queen of the Forest Kingdom than one of the Four Horsemen of the Apocalypse! In fact, they'd probably do less damage in the long run!"

"I'm assuming this wasn't a love match," said Hawk, ignoring Fisher's raised voice with the ease of long practice. "How did Felicity and Harald get on?"

"They were always polite enough in public," Chance said carefully. "And if there were lovers or dalliances, they were both very discreet. But servants will gossip, and some stories arose often enough to become more than credible. Apparently their rows could go on for hours, and they weren't above throwing things. Sometimes large, heavy things with points on them. And it wasn't unknown for them to go days on end without speaking to each other except in public ceremonies. I'm amazed they cooperated long enough to produce an heir."

"I have a nephew," said Hawk. "How about that."

"He stands to inherit the Forest Throne when he comes of age," said Chance. "If he lives that long. For the moment, his mother rules on his behalf, as Regent. Of course, you also have a claim to the Throne, Prince Rupert. You could replace the Queen as Regent, or even put aside your nephew and take the crown for yourself, for the good of the Kingdom. Have you any children of your own, to continue your line?"

"No," Fisher answered quietly. "It never seemed to be the right time."

"Our lives have always been . . . complicated," said Hawk. "Not to mention constantly bloody dangerous."

"Tell us more about how Harald was murdered," said Fisher. "I still haven't heard anything that explains why Hawk and I have to go back. Don't you have your own investigators? And what about the Magus? If he's such a hot-shit sorcerer, why can't he tell you who the murderer is?"

"That last is a very good question," said Chance. "Especially since the magical wards protecting the King were designed and maintained solely by the Magus, who swore there wasn't another living sorcerer with enough power to break or penetrate them. He's been conspicuously silent about that since the murder, except to say that his wards were still intact after the murder. Which was supposed to be impossible. The whole thing seems impossible. There was a small army of guards watching every entrance to the King's private quarters, but no one saw anything. Harald was on his own for less than an hour. One of the guards heard him fall, looked in, and found the King already dead, with no one else present. And now you know as much about how Harald was murdered as anyone else. And that's after months of investigative work."

Hawk and Fisher were both frowning thoughtfully. "Sounds like a variation on a locked room murder mystery," said Hawk. "They're always bastards. Were you present in the Castle when my brother was killed, Chance? Did you see anything unusual?"

"Unfortunately, the King had already sent me on a mission to the Darkwood, sometime previously," said Chance. "That's when I met Chappie, and we fell in together. I wasn't there when my King needed me."

"Were there any other sorcerers present who could confirm the Magus' wards were unbroken?" asked Fisher.

"Oh, the Castle's crawling with magic-users these days," said Chance. "But they're all pretty low level. Anyone with any real magical abilities was killed off during the Demon War. We don't have anyone powerful enough to challenge the Magus."

"Then the next obvious guess has to be that the Magus was somehow involved in the murder," said Hawk. "He might even be the murderer."

"Then why bother with a knife?" asked Fisher.

"Misdirection?" Hawk suggested.

"A lot of fingers have been pointed at the Magus," said Chance. "Mostly when he's not around. The Magus is a very powerful figure at Court. But he's never shown any direct interest in politics, or in gaining political power for himself. He's currently the main protector of the Queen and her young son. Along with Sir Vivian, High Commander of the Castle Guard. They watch each other pretty closely. Vivian and the Magus have never liked or trusted each other."

"I remember Vivian," said Hawk, just a little coldly. "He was a Lord then. And a traitor. He plotted to murder my father."

For the first time Chance looked openly shocked. "I never heard any of that before! The legend has it that Vivian gave up his Lordship to fight beside and protect the peasants during the long night. King Harald granted him a knighthood on his return to the Castle after the War."

"You don't want to believe everything you hear in legends," said Fisher. "A lot of things happened during the long night that only the inner circle ever knew about. Vivian plotted to kill one King when he thought his duty drove him to it. Who's to say he wouldn't try again, with another King?"

Chance shook his head slowly. "I can't believe I'm hearing this. Sir Vivian is one of the greatest heroes in the Forest Kingdom, looked up to and respected by all. Everyone knows the legend of the Hellstrom brothers, Vivian and Gawaine, defenders of Tower Rouge. King John knighted both of them for that, and later made Vivian a Lord. How could such a man be a traitor?"

Hawk smiled tiredly. "You'd be surprised what duty and necessity can drive a man to. But you're right. The Vivian I remember would have more reasons than most to protect Harald. Tell me about the Queen. Felicity. Isobel doesn't seem to think too highly of her. How do you see her position in all this?"

Chance hesitated, choosing his words carefully. "She was fond of King Harald, in her own way. For all their arguments, they always stood together against any threat from outside. If she'd wanted him dead, she'd had plenty of opportunities before, and knowing Felicity, she would have had no trouble in making it look like an accident, or even a purely natural event."

"But right now she's ruling the Forest as Stephen's Regent," said Fisher. "A monarch in all but name."

"Her powers are severely limited as Regent," said Chance. "If enough factions got together, they could remove and replace her with another Regent. So far, the factions are too busy fighting each other, but . . ."

"Who backs the Queen?" Hawk asked.

"Sir Vivian has sworn himself her protector, on his blood and his name. He's taken his failure to protect the King very hard. And there's the Magus." Chance frowned. "But that's about it. Everyone else has their own agendas, or ambitions. The Queen has an abrasive personality, and is more respected than liked."

Fisher snorted. "I can believe that."

"Most people who currently accept her as Regent, or at least don't openly oppose her, do so out of loyalty to the young King-to-be, Stephen. But the Prince is not immune from danger. There are many factions in the Court, some of them quite extreme, desperately trying to turn the situation to their own advantage. The most obvious being Duke Alric of Hillsdown. He is currently visiting Forest Castle, along with a company of his soldiers. He couldn't bring any more than that for fear of being seen as an invasion, but he could call his army into the Forest at any time, and everyone knows it. Officially, he came to offer comfort and support to his grieving daughter, but she hasn't done a lot of grieving, not in public anyway."

"You can forget the comfort part," Fisher said flatly. "My father never gave a damn for anyone but himself. He's never been anything more than a coldhearted, endlessly scheming politician, whose only use for his children was as pawns in his ambitions. He used up four wives producing his nine daughters, and never missed any of them." Fisher smiled coldly. "But the joke was on him. His daughters were never supposed to be anything more than possessions that he could marry off in return for power and influence outside Hillsdown. Daddy always was ambitious to be more than just a Duke. But with no sons to cramp our style, we daughters blossomed in our own right. And we had all learned from dear Daddy to be just like him. Though, of course, in my case he had the last laugh, when he signed my death warrant."

She was almost spitting out the words at the end, shaking with rage and bitterness. Hawk put a comforting hand on her arm, but she barely noticed, eyes lost in yesterday.

"Anyway," Chance said awkwardly, "he's made it clear

he wishes to see the Forest and Hillsdown become one Kingdom again, as it used to be long ago, before the original Starlight Duke led his rebellion and made Hillsdown into a separate nation. When Stephen becomes King, he will have a legitimate claim to the Thrones of both the Forest and Hillsdown, since the Duke has no son of his own to inherit. Of course, this is just another reason why a great many people would rather see Stephen dead right now. The main political factions—"

"If I were you, I'd send for another round of drinks," interrupted Chappie, lying on his back on the floor again. "This is going to take some time."

"It's not really all that complicated," Chance said quickly. "It's just that the Rift has made it possible for all kinds of new philosophies, political and religious, to reach the Forest Kingdom for the first time. In particular, the doctrine of democracy and constitutional monarchy has seized the imaginations of many. In fact, the democrats would be by far the biggest faction, if they weren't hopelessly split into dozens of quarreling splinter groups, all with their own dogmatic dogmas and agendas. Essentially, you have Sir Vivian preaching slow cautious change and reform; the Landsgrave Sir Robert Hawke, who wants a purely figurehead monarch and an elected Parliament; and the Shaman, who preaches fire and brimstone politics, and the removal of the current powers-that-be by force. The only thing they can all agree on is that they don't want Queen Felicity as Regent."

"I knew there was another reason why we got out of politics," said Fisher. "It makes my head hurt."

"Oh, it gets worse," said Chance. "You have to understand, the population of the Forest Land has changed dramatically in nature since you left. A large proportion of the original population was wiped out during the Demon War. After the long night ended, there was a massive influx of people from Redhart and Hillsdown, to take over the abandoned farms and land, and all the jobs that needed to be filled to keep the Kingdom's business infrastructure going. Even with the new immigrants the Forest Land came perilously close to famine and bankruptcy. The Forest needed help and couldn't afford to be fussy about the forms it came in.

"As a result the Forest population is much more . . . varied than it used to be. The newcomers brought their own ways and traditions with them—political, religious, and social. The ground was ripe for change. This situation was further complicated by the opening of the Rift. A lot of people took one look at the devastated Forest, compared it with the freedoms and luxuries of the southern Kingdoms, and voted with their feet by immigrating south through the Rift. The Forest lost a hell of a lot of people before King Harald put guards on the Rift, to stop the outpouring. He also set up a Customs barrier, laying a heavy duty on all goods coming through from the south. Which was a good and a bad thing. Good because the revenues are helping to repair the damaged Land, and bad because goods are now much more expensive in the north than in the south. Much of the Forest is still dead and blighted by the long night. Its regeneration needs all the help it can get. But as a result, a great deal of the Land's food has to be imported from the south, which makes it expensive. And hungry people tend to think with their bellies.

"King Harald was one of the few surviving heroes of the Demon War. That was about all that kept the Land from open revolution. Now he's gone . . ."

"What about the Darkwood?" asked Hawk. "Is it still limited to its original boundaries?"

"Oh, yes. It's quiet now. There's no Tanglewood to be a barrier anymore, but demons rarely venture outside the darkness these days. When they do, we mostly just shoo them back in."

Fisher raised an eyebrow. "Since when is the Forest soft on demons? Evil bloody things; they killed a lot of good people. Including your father."

"You don't know," said Chance slowly. "I did wonder if the truth about the demons had traveled this far south."

"What truth?" Hawk asked.

"I'm sorry," said Chance. "There's no easy way to tell you this. After the Blue Moon and the long night had

passed, and the Demon Prince had been . . . banished, all
that had been touched by the Wild Magic returned to normal. Including all the dead demons, who changed back into
dead people. Did you never wonder where all the thousands
of new demons were coming from? Every man, woman, and
child who perished in the long night rose again, transformed
into demons, in all their many monstrous forms. That's why
demons always killed their prey. They were making new
demons."

"Oh, God," said Hawk. "I never thought . . . we were
all fighting our own family and friends, and killing them
again." He looked almost angrily at Chance. "Could we
have turned the demons back into people? If we'd known,
back then?"

"You didn't know," said Chance. "You couldn't know.
And no one's come up with a cure in the past twelve years.
Though the Magus insists he's working on it."

"All that time we spent killing demons, always thinking
we were doing the right thing," said Hawk. "If we'd taken
our fight straight to the Demon Prince, defeated him
earlier . . . how many people might we have saved from
being living nightmares?"

"Hush," said Fisher, putting a hand on Hawk's arm.
"Hush. We didn't know. We had no way of knowing then.
Change the subject, Chance. Tell us about the Castle. Any-
thing new happening there?"

"Oh, yes," said Change. "After the Demon Prince disappeared, the last traces of the astrologer's old spell vanished
with him, and the once missing, now returned South Wing
became entirely normal again. However, something else appeared, right in the middle of the Castle. The Inverted Cathedral. This gets kind of complicated, but bear with me.
A lot of this is only recently rediscovered knowledge, dug
out of the oldest sections of the Castle libraries; knowledge
forgotten, and perhaps repressed, for centuries.

"The Cathedral existed before the Castle. It was built
long ago, so far back that history becomes legend becomes
myth. In those far-off days, the building of Cathedrals was
both an art and a science. Cathedrals were constructed for a
specific reason: direct communication with God. The whole

structure, the very shapes, angles, and stresses, all had meaning and purpose. The finished building was designed to resonate, like some gigantic tuning fork. When people worshiped in their Cathedral, the structure took their voices and their faith and sent them flying up to God, in one great more-than-human sound. And God would hear, and send his love and grace back, transmuted down the long tower of the Cathedral into a form the people could accept. Direct communication with God.

"They say in those days the power of Good radiated from the Cathedral, bathing all the Forest land in its sanctity, so that the Forest and its people grew straight and true, strong and sure in the love of God.

"So of course it all went horribly wrong. Somebody with a hell of a lot of magic, and I use the word *hell* advisedly, inverted the Cathedral. Instead of soaring up into the sky, the great structure now plunged down into the earth. And what had once sent prayers up to God, now sent mortal voices down to . . . what? And who was listening? The sanctity was gone from the Forest, and new darker influences spread across the Land. The first Forest King ordered the Forest Castle built *around* the Inverted Cathedral, to contain it and guard it, and then used magic to keep the Cathedral subtly out of phase with the rest of the Castle, sealing it off forever in its own private place. No more worship there, from anyone to anything.

"Even so, just the presence of the spell was enough to account for the Castle's singular physical nature, whereby its interior is far larger than its exterior. But something in the long night, in its coming or its ending, broke the old spell, and the Inverted Cathedral has returned.

"The first investigative team that King Harald sent in didn't come back. Neither did the second, the third, or the fourth, even though each team was increasingly larger and better armed. The Magus wouldn't even go near it for all his vaunted powers. Only one man returned, from team five. He was quite mad. He'd met and spoken with something that destroyed his mind. Since then, he has only ever spoken three words. *The Burning Man.*"

"And the significance of that?" asked Fisher after a moment.

Chance shrugged. "Your guess is as good as anyone's. The Magus tried to interrogate the man and lurched out of his room only a few minutes later, trembling and vomiting. The madman's been kept in strict isolation ever since, for his and our protection. King Harald declared the Inverted Cathedral off limits to absolutely everyone, and had the Magus set up powerful protective wards to keep the damned structure strictly isolated. There are currently teams of scholars reading their way through every old library in the Land, in shifts, searching for more information. Meanwhile, there are strange lights in the sky, strange voices deep in the earth, and livestock have been born with two heads, speaking unknown languages."

"Jesus," said Fisher, shuddering suddenly despite herself. "And people are still living in the Castle, with that thing in their midst? How do you stand it?"

"How did you cope with the missing South Wing?" asked Chance. "Remember, we've had twelve years to get used to it."

"If we'd known, we would have come back," said Hawk. "We thought all the evil was destroyed. We should have known better."

"What about the Infernal Devices?" Fisher asked suddenly. "There was a rumor a few years back that one of those damned swords had returned."

"Yes," said Chance. "*Wolfsbane*. Luckily it wasn't around for long, and did no real damage before it was lost again. There's been no report of *Flarebright* resurfacing since it was lost in the long night, and *Rockbreaker* was destroyed."

"We know that," said Fisher. "We were there. The Demon Prince broke the damned sword across his knee. I heard it scream as it died."

This time it was Chance's turn to shudder. "I've heard all the legends, but every now and again it strikes me hard. You actually met the Demon Prince, the personification of darkness upon the earth. What was he like?"

"I don't remember anymore," said Fisher. "I put a lot

of effort into forgetting. But still, sometimes, I see him in my dreams."

"The past rarely lets go of you," said Hawk. "And the future never stops making demands. Right, Champion's son?"

"There's only a little more to tell," said Chance.

"Good," said a voice from under the table.

"The Landsgraves of Gold and Silver and Copper aren't what they were," said Chance. "With such a reduced population, the Forest was faced with a much smaller tax base, which meant Harald was forced to ask Redhart and Hillsdown for help in rebuilding. He paid for this aid by selling off a large proportion of the Land's mineral rights. I was the Landsgraves' last desperate grasp for power, and with that failure, their day was over. There is only one Landsgrave now; Sir Robert Hawke. One of the many now fighting for democracy and peasants' rights.

"His main opponent is that enigmatic personage, the Shaman. He was a solitary hermit for many years, living deep in the Forest, far from anything even approaching civilization, wanting only to be left alone. But slowly he gained a reputation as a holy man and a spiritual leader, and the peasants went to him for help. He had a strange kind of magic, and a desperate need to be of use. One day last year he just strode right into the Forest Castle and said he'd come to demand fair treatment for the peasants, or else. The guards tried to throw him out, and he turned each and every one of them into small, green, stupid hopping things. The Magus went to meet him, they stared at each other in silence for a while, and then the Magus turned and walked away, saying there was nothing he could do. The King refused to meet with the Shaman, so he set up camp in the great courtyard, preaching peasants' rights to anyone who'd stand still long enough."

"I hate would-be saints," said Hawk. "Every one I ever met was a royal pain in the arse."

"One last piece of dispiriting news, Your Highness," said Chance. "As I'm sure you remember, most of the Forest's fighting men died during the long night. In order to maintain an army strong enough to dissuade Redhart and Hillsdown from invading while the Forest was still vulnerable, Harald called in a large number of mercenaries. The bulk of the Forest army is currently composed of professional fighting men from a dozen countries, with no ties to the Forest Land but their pay packets. They're a continuing drain on the Forest economy, and very unpopular. Harald used them mostly to keep the peasants in line and enforce the new taxes."

"We'll have to do something about that," said Hawk.

"Are you really thinking about taking on a whole army?" said Fisher.

"Why not? We've done it before."

"I know! I still have the scars."

"Are you saying you're willing to return to the Forest Land, Your Highnesses?" said Chance.

"It seems we're needed," said Hawk. "I've always understood my duty. And I have my nephew's safety to think of. But if we are going back to the Forest, it won't be as Prince Rupert and Princess Julia. Those names carry too much baggage. We'll go back as Hawk and Fisher, two investigators authorized by Rupert and Julia to find Harald's murderer and take care of business. I'll write us a letter to that effect. I've still got my Royal seal somewhere."

"Sounds good to me," said Fisher. "I've no wish to go back to being Princess Julia again. Far too limiting. Besides, I'm not who I used to be."

"No one ever is," said Chance.

"Which is sometimes a blessing," said Hawk. "But I'll tell you this: If we really are finally leaving Haven for good, we've got a lot of business to clean up here first."

"Right," said Fisher.

CHAPTER THREE

Taking Care of Business

When Hawk and Fisher announced that they were making a quick stop at their lodgings before they went any further, Chance wasn't at all sure what to expect. So far the legendary figures of Prince Rupert and Princess Julia had been, certainly not a disappointment, but nothing at all like the people he'd imagined finding at the end of his journey south. He wasn't sure exactly who or what he'd expected, but nothing in the legends, official or otherwise, had prepared him for Hawk and Fisher. Or Haven, come to that. And he definitely hadn't expected to find the two greatest heroes of the Demon War living in a one-room apartment over a somewhat shabby family café.

The area was quiet, and people nodded politely if not warmly to Hawk and Fisher as they passed. It was midday now, and pleasant aromas of newly prepared food drifted from the open door of the café. Chance's stomach rumbled loudly, reminding him it had been more than a while since he'd last eaten. But Hawk and Fisher ignored the café's open door, heading instead for a rickety wooden stairway on the side of the building. From the look of the battered wooden steps, the whole structure hadn't been painted or repaired since it was first erected. Chance watched the stairway shake and shudder under Hawk and Fisher's weight, sighed once, loudly, and went after them. It took all his strength to drag Chappie away from the café's enticing aromas, and even more determination to get the reluctant animal to ascend the wooden steps.

"We took this place when we first arrived in Haven," said Fisher over her shoulder. "It was supposed to be just a temporary measure, while we looked around for something better, or at least less appalling, but somehow we never got around to moving. What with one thing and another, we rarely get to spend much time here anyway. It's a good enough place, I suppose. Warm in winter and cool in summer, and nobody bothers us. We get free meals at the café below, because burglars, thieves, and protection thugs have learned to give it a wide berth rather than annoy us."

"Is the food any good?" asked Chance politely.

"It's free," said Hawk shortly.

"Best kind," said Chappie.

The quivering stairway ended at last at a heavy wooden door with three heavy steel locks, and a varied assortment of protective runes and sigils carved deep into the wood. Hawk produced a set of keys on a ring, from which dangled not only a rabbit's foot, but also what looked suspiciously like a human finger bone. He unlocked the three locks, pushed open the door, and Fisher barged right past him, plunging into the room beyond with sword in hand. She looked quickly about her, and only then put her sword away and gestured for the others to come in.

"You can't be too careful, not in Haven," she said offhandedly. "We've made a lot of enemies here over the years. Came home one time and found an iron golem waiting for us. Luckily its weight was too much for the floorboards, and the damned thing crashed right through into the café below. Last I heard, they were still using its belly as an oven. Make yourselves comfortable while Hawk and I grab a few things."

Chance looked interestedly about him as Hawk locked the door and slammed home two heavy bolts at top and bottom. The apartment was one long room, taking up the whole upper floor of the building. The three narrow windows were barred, and what little light crept in only served to show up how gloomy the rest of the place was, even at midday. Fisher lit a lantern, and a warm golden glow filled her end of the room. There wasn't much furniture, and belongings lay piled in heaps on the floor next to the walls. Rugs and carpets of varying design and quality covered the floor, scuffed and worn smooth in places. Everything in the room looked like it had been bought secondhand, to no

overall plan or design. Periods and styles clashed rebel-
liously, but still the apartment had a warm, cozy feel to it;
of comfort and ease and peace of heart.

Chance wandered slowly round the room, looking at this
and that, trying to get a feel for Hawk's and Fisher's char-
acters from the way they lived, but really the only word
that immediately came to mind was *slobs*. Chance couldn't
help noticing the protective wards carved into the window-
sills, and even on the walls and ceilings. He recognized just
enough of the simpler spells to feel very uneasy about what
had presumably tried to get in sometime in the past.

"There are more defenses you can't see," said Hawk casually, searching through the rumpled sheets on the unmade bed at the far end of the room. "People will always
find the courage to strike from a distance, and Haven is
crawling with magic-users for hire."

Chance nodded, taking in the string of garlic buds hanging on one wall, next to two crossed silver daggers and a
large vial of what he assumed was holy water. "You have
troubles with vampires and werewolves here?" he asked,
trying hard to sound casual.

"Just now and again," said Fisher, pulling off her boots
and wiggling her toes with unrestrained satisfaction. "That
stuff's just tools of the trade in a city like Haven."

On the wall next to the tools of the trade was a plain,
unadorned crucifix, and Chance crossed himself automatically. "I see you still kept your faith, so far from home."

"You need something to believe in in a cesspit like this,"
said Hawk, staring dubiously at a pair of rolled socks.

"A lot's changed in the Forest Church since you've been
gone," said Chance. "It's a lot more organized and influential than it used to be. The long night put the fear of God
into a lot of people."

"We saw heaven once," said Fisher, pulling on a pair of
scruffy boots that looked to Chance entirely identical to
the ones she'd just taken off. "Or at least, something very
like it."

"You mean you *died*?" asked Chance, uncertainly.

"Yes," said Hawk. "But we got over it."

Chance decided he wasn't going to ask. He didn't think

he wanted to know. He looked around to see what mischief Chappie was getting into. The dog was ambling happily around, sniffing at everything and sticking his nose into every dark corner he could find. He found something on the floor, gobbled it up, and then spat it out at speed. He realized Chance was watching him, and grinned widely.

"Interesting place you've brought me to, Chance. I've known stables where all the horses suffered from bloat and wind that smelled more fragrant than this dump. And you've got mice here. I've found some droppings, if anyone's interested. And a whole pile of clothes absolutely begging to be hauled off to the laundry. Don't you people ever clean up in here?"

"We're between maids at the moment," said Hawk. "Ah, I wondered where I'd put this."

He was holding up what appeared to be a small doll made out of twisted raffia, decorated with slender colored ribbons, each studded with tight little knots.

"What is it?" Chance asked politely.

"Well, it started out life as a dream-catcher, but I had a sorcerer acquaintance of ours boost its power. I won't tell you exactly how, but the goat was never the same afterward. Now this little mannikin functions as a general protective ward against all kinds of offensive magic. It won't last long once it's been activated, but while it's awake, nothing short of a major summoning will be able to get to us."

"You think we're going to need that kind of protection?" asked Chance.

"This is Haven," said Fisher. "And we're going to be stirring up one hell of a lot of trouble before we leave." She looked reflectively at the mannikin in Hawk's hand. "I remember when we got that. The case of the Collector of Souls and the Dread Mandalas."

"Yeah," said Hawk. "That was a bad one."

Hawk and Fisher looked at each other for a moment, and then went back to rooting through their piles of possessions. Chance went back to looking about him. Half of one wall was taken up with a bookcase, mostly crammed with cheap Gothic romances. Chance pulled out a couple at random, and nodded to see the familiar garish covers of tousled gypsy lasses half falling out of their blouses, while in the background was the usual brooding mansion with one lighted window. There were times when Chance felt very strongly that the invention of the printing press had a lot to answer for. When he was at school in the north, reading wasn't something just anybody did. He put the books back, and Hawk caught the movement.

"I know," he said unapologetically. "But they're cheap and cheerful, and when you limp home in the early hours at the end of a double shift, you need something not too demanding to unwind to. I like the spooky stuff; Isobel mostly goes for the romantic elements."

"We do have other books," Fisher pointed out huffily, but couldn't seem to come up with any other titles on the spur of the moment.

Chance went back to wandering around the long room, stepping carefully over the empty wine bottles and an occasional discarded sock, to look at a jigsaw of impressive size, almost finished on a wide wooden board. It was a forest scene, with tall trees and bursting green foliage. Chance didn't feel any need to comment. Everyone deals with homesickness in their own way.

"We would have finished that," said Fisher, trying to force something large and woolly and recalcitrant into a backpack. "But Hawk's only good at doing the borders. And he lost the last few pieces."

"I did not lose them!" Hawk said hotly. "I don't think they were in the box in the first place. And I can do more than borders. I just don't have the time, mostly."

"You're still upset because we didn't get the mountain scene you wanted."

"I didn't want it," said Hawk, in that extremely patient tone that drives women mad. "I just said it had more colors, and would have been more challenging."

Hawk and Fisher came together in the middle of the room, and looked quietly about them. They were both carrying bulging backpacks, crammed full of essentials. The mannikin peered out of the top of Hawk's pack like a watchful sentinel. Chappie came and sat beside Chance, chewing happily on something he'd found. Chance knew better than to inquire what.

"We really should get going," said Hawk.

"Yes," agreed Fisher. But neither of them moved.

"Not a lot to show for ten years," said Hawk. "But then, I think I always knew we were just passing through."

"You know we can't take much," said Fisher. "It would only slow us down."

"Yes, I know. But I shall miss this place. Hard to think we'll never see it again, once we close the door behind us."

"Do us good," Fisher said briskly. "We were getting into a rut here anyway."

"Part of me doesn't want to leave," said Hawk. "We were comfortable here. Safe. Safe from having to be heroes and legends."

"We don't *have* to go . . ." Fisher said slowly.

"Yes, we do," said Hawk. "Vacation's over."

They left the apartment securely locked behind them, because to do otherwise would only call attention to their leaving, and tied their packs to the horses Hawk had requisitioned from a nearby stable. Hawk sent Chance and Chappie back to their hostelry to pick up his horse and belongings, while he and Fisher went to make their good-byes at Guard Headquarters. They studied the streets along their way with more than usual interest, the knowledge that they'd never be seeing them again allowing Hawk and Fisher to see them with fresh eyes. After so many years in Haven, they'd become inured to far too many sights and sounds, and all the many familiar evils.

It was time for one last crusade in Haven, one last chance for justice, retribution, and the casting down of the guilty. And to hell with what the law had to say about it.

Guard Headquarters was busy as always, with any number of colorful people bustling in and out. No one paid Hawk and Fisher any unusual attention as they tied up their horses outside, tipped a Constable to keep a watch on them (because otherwise they'd have come out to find nothing left but their horseshoes), and then moved purposefully through Headquarters toward the main Stores.

The Storemaster objected loudly to their unannounced visit, and demanded to see the necessary paperwork. Hawk gave him a hard look, Fisher let her hand rest on her sword's hilt, and the Storemaster decided he was needed urgently elsewhere. He left at not quite a run, and all the clerks at their desks became very interested in their work as Hawk and Fisher strolled casually through the Stores, helping themselves to whatever they liked the look of.

There was a lot to choose from. Guard scientists were always coming up with new ideas, to help the poor souls on the beat survive another day on the mean streets of Haven. Hawk and Fisher loaded up with concussion grenades, incendiary devices, and as many throwing knives as they could carry. Hawk was particularly taken with the chaos bombs. They were new, very much untried and untested in the field, and as expensive as prototypes always are, but they were rumored to be quite amazingly destructive, and that was enough for Hawk. He stuffed all six of them into his belt pouch, and looked hopefully around for more goodies. Fisher had to smile. Hawk always loved the latest toys. Even so, they quickly decided to pass on the other latest development, drug bombs filled with black poppy dust. The one and only time the things had been used in the field, the bomb saturated the whole room with poppy dust, and criminals and Guards alike had just sat around holding hands and giggling a lot until the effects wore off.

"How about the new handcuffs?" asked Hawk. "They're supposed to be guaranteed escape-proof."

"I don't think so," said Fisher. "First, I wasn't planning on arresting anybody, and second, the last time those things were used, they ended up having to cut the poor bugger out of them. I think we've got enough toys, Hawk. Let's go and hit the Files room before word gets out."

Hawk nodded reluctantly, and they strode briskly out of the Stores and down the main corridor. People took one look at their determined faces, and hurried to get out of their way. The Files room was currently enjoying one of its more accessible periods, thanks to a poltergeist that had moved in recently. The unseen ghost had a thing about order, and everything being in its place. It wasn't an especially logical or useful order, but the general feeling was that some was better than none, and everything possible was being done to make the poltergeist feel at home. However, the bureaucrat in charge, one Otto Griffith, a long bony specimen with a face like a slapped behind, still saw the Files as being his personal territory, and defended them with all the spleen at his command.

"You don't have a chit, do you?" he demanded immediately as Hawk and Fisher walked in. "You never bother with the correct procedures and paperwork. Well, this time I've got the Commander on my side. He said I don't have to let you have anything, unless you can show me the correct necessary acquisition forms. In triplicate."

"We don't have time for this," said Hawk. "And I really don't give a chit."

He nodded to Fisher, and they each took hold of the piled-up In and Out trays, and tossed their contents high into the air. Papers flew like escaping birds, flying in all directions, and only reluctantly fluttering back to the floor across the widest possible area. Otto Griffith's face went several interesting colors in turn, and he looked like he was about to burst into tears.

"You're barbarians! Uncivilized Northern barbarians!" He scrambled out from behind his desk and began snatching up the scattered papers, clutching them to his chest like injured loved ones. Hawk and Fisher left him to it, and headed purposefully toward the rows of great oaken filing cabinets. Digging out information on their chosen targets went remarkably quickly, and soon they had all the necessary information on where their targets could currently be found, and details of their defenses. They waved Otto a cheery good-bye as they left the Files room, and he responded with a detailed and quite appalling curse that someone of his background and standing shouldn't have known.

Outside the Files room Hawk and Fisher came to a sudden halt. Their way was blocked by a dozen armed Guards, their weapons already in their hands. There was a long tense moment as both sides considered each other carefully, weighing the situation, and then one of the Guard Constables explained, very politely and only a little uneasily, that the Day Commander would very much like a word with Captains Hawk and Fisher. In his office, right now. If it wasn't too much trouble.

"And if it is?" said Fisher.

"He wants to see you anyway," said the Guard Constable. There was a sheen of sweat on his upper lip, but the sword in his hand was steady. "We're to escort you there, and see you don't get lost along the way."

"How considerate of the Commander," murmured Hawk.

He and Fisher glanced at each other. They could probably take a dozen Guards, but they didn't want to. The Constables were just doing their job. So Hawk and Fisher nodded calmly, took their hands away from their weapons, and said they'd be delighted to accompany the Guards to the Day Commander's office. The dozen Constables immediately looked extremely relieved, and escorted their charges down the main corridor. None of them put away their swords, though.

The first real surprise came when Hawk and Fisher were very politely ushered into the Commander's office, and found not only the Day Commander but also the Night Commander as well waiting to see them. Given how much the two men detested each other, and how jealously each man defended his own territory, it was almost unthinkable to find them both in the same office at the same time. They were standing behind the desk, apparently because there was only the one chair, and neither was willing to let the other sit in his presence. Neither of them looked at all pleased to see Hawk and Fisher. They both nodded pretty much in unison to the accompanying Constables, who backed out of the room with almost indecent haste, and shut the door behind them.

Commander Dubois currently ran the night shift. Short and stocky and as bald as an egg, he'd been a Commander for over twenty years, and it hadn't improved his disposition one bit. He'd been quite a thief-taker in his time, but these days he needed a stick just to get around. Some years

back half a dozen thugs had taken it in turns to stamp on
his legs till they broke. He was a harsh, intolerant man
whose only saving grace was that he hated crime and criminals with a fine passion, and so was very good at his job.
He glared at Hawk and Fisher from behind the desk, and
Hawk and Fisher nodded respectfully in return.

Looming over Commander Dubois was the tall blocky
figure of the Day Commander. Glen had just hit fifty, and
resented it fiercely. He had a permanent scowl, a down-
turned mouth, and a military-style haircut that looked like
it had been shaped around a pudding bowl. He'd been an
Army officer before he came to the Guard, and never let
anyone forget it. Hawk and Fisher gave him a sloppy salute,
because they knew how much that irritated him.

Still, seeing Dubois and Glen together made it clear to
Hawk that somehow news of their intentions had already
gone around. Nothing else would get these two men together in one room. Hawk supposed he shouldn't have
been surprised. No one can hope to keep a secret long in
a city like Haven, where information is often a life and
death matter, not to mention money in the pocket. Now it
just remained to see how much the two Commanders knew,
or thought they knew, about Hawk and Fisher's plans for
a final vengeance. And then Dubois spoke, and all Hawk's
planned evasions went out the window.

"So, you're leaving Haven," said the Night Commander
heavily. "It hadn't occurred to you to come and tell us this?
That there might be urgent arrangements we'd have to
make, like finding replacements to cover your beat? Much
as I am loath to admit it, you are two of the most successful
Guards in this city, and your leaving will make one hell of
a difference."

Hawk regrouped quickly. "We thought we'd let our de-
parture come as a nice surprise," he said smoothly. "Just
think of the good it'll do your ulcers, not having us around
to apologize for."

"You can't go," said Commander Glen flatly. "You're
needed here."

"No, we're not," said Fisher, just as flatly. "It's people
like you who've kept us from making any real changes in

this damned city. You've always been more concerned with
the letter of the law than with the spirit of justice."

"It's not your business to decide what is and isn't just!"
snapped Glen. "The whole point of the law is that no one
person gets to decide what's right and wrong. That's why
we have a Council instead of a King."

"The law is supposed to give people a chance for justice," said Hawk. "But when the law is corrupt, drafted by
the rich and influential to protect the interests of the rich
and influential, when it can't or won't protect the people
from those who would prey on them, that's when you need
people like us. We're not infallible, but we're better than
the alternative."

"We know," said Dubois, surprising both Hawk and
Fisher. "That's why you can't leave. We need people who
can be . . . flexible, in the cause of justice. Guards the
people can respect. You've both done a good job, in your
way. Which is why we'll have a hell of a time replacing
you."

"We never quit," said Glen, standing almost rigidly at
attention. "We never turned away from the job, no matter
how hard it got. They crippled Dubois, and he still wouldn't
give in to the bastards who think they run this city."

"But what have you really achieved here?" asked Fisher,
almost tiredly. "You've given your lives trying to get this
city to act civilized, and it's as big a cesspit now as it's
always been."

"If it's a case of more money—" said Dubois.

"It's not," said Hawk shortly.

"Then how about a promotion," said Glen, taking Hawk
and Fisher by surprise again. "We never meant for you two
to be Captains all your lives. Dubois and I always thought
that one day you two would be ready to take over our jobs,
and then we could retire at last. I might have given my life
to the job, but I don't want to die behind this desk. If you
leave, where the hell are we going to find two more honest
Guards in Haven?"

"It has to be you," said Dubois. "There's no one else
we can trust."

Hawk shook his head slowly. "We're needed more, elsewhere. Somewhere we can make a real difference. We can't stay."

"All right," said Glen. "What *could* we offer you to make you stay?"

"Not a damned thing," said Fisher. "We don't intend to die here, either. And like Hawk said, we're needed more somewhere else. So we're leaving."

"And just what were you planning on doing before you left?" asked Dubois. "We've heard about your little visits to Files and Stores. Poor Otto was almost in hysterics. We've had to send for his mother. According to him, you've seized confidential information on practically every main villain in Haven. And you've loaded up with enough weapons to start your own war. If you're intending to take the law into your own hands, and pay off some old grudges before you go, you must know we'll have to stop you, by whatever means necessary."

Hawk smiled. "You can try."

"Right," said Fisher.

The tension in the small room mounted as Hawk and Fisher and the two Commanders glared at each other, equally determined and unflinching, and there was no telling who might have said or done what, when the door suddenly burst open, and the sorceress Mistique came rushing in, more than a little out of breath. Hawk and Fisher both stared immediately at the long thick mane of black hair they now knew to be only a wig, and then they quickly looked away again, not wanting to be caught staring. The sorceress nodded briskly to the two Commanders, either not noticing or politely ignoring the atmosphere in the room.

"All right, I'm here! What is so damned important that the communications sorcerer has to nearly blow my head off with his urgent message? For a moment I thought one of the family gods had finally found out where I lived. So, what is it? Are they rioting in the docks again? I don't know where they get the energy . . ."

"These two Guards are under the misapprehension that they're leaving the city," said Commander Glen tightly. "You are hereby authorized to use all necessary measures to prevent this, until we can beat some sense into their stubborn thick heads."

"You have got to be joking," Mistique said immediately. "I'm not doing one damned thing that might get those two mad at me, and neither will any other sorcerer you've got working for you with two brain cells left to rub together."

"We're leaving Headquarters now," said Hawk. "If anyone gets in our way, we'll mail them back to you. In a whole lot of small packages."

"Never mind the golden handshake or presentation clock," said Fisher. "I always get emotional at those to-dos anyway."

They walked out of the office without waiting for any reply. The Constables who'd escorted them in had long since made themselves scarce. The more sensible ones were hiding until it was clearly all over, and safe for them to come out again. Hawk and Fisher strolled unhurriedly out of Guard Headquarters, and no one tried to stop them.

"So," said Fisher. "After all we've done for them, after all the times we saved this poxy city, we're on our own now. No help, no backup; just you and me against everyone else."

"Best way," said Hawk. "No complications or obligations, no clash of interests or conflicting loyalties. Just us, against everyone else."

"Us against the world," said Fisher. "Just like old times, really."

They joined up with Chance and the dog Chappie at the deserted harborside by the docks, as arranged. It was very calm now, and very quiet; all the Guards and all the strikers were currently licking their wounds at home and plotting new strategies. The only things moving now were the zombies, working endlessly, efficiently, unloading the ships and carting off the goods with calm, eerie precision. Up above, carrion birds filled the sky, soaring silently, drawn to the dead but unable to reach them due to the harbor's protective wards. Hawk and Fisher and Chance had had to tie their horses up well away from the docks before they could enter; just the smell of the working dead had been enough to make their mounts put back their ears and roll their eyes. Chappie's eyes had narrowed into slits, and he stuck close to Chance as he padded along the harborside, muttering dangerously under his breath.

"Tell me again this is a good idea," said Chance, ignoring the dog with the ease of long practice. "Just the four of us, against people as well-connected as the DeWitts seem to be? They're bound to have their own army of private guards."

"Most of those are dead and injured, after what happened here earlier," said Hawk calmly. "The DeWitts have undoubtedly sent their agents out to the local hiring halls to arrange for reinforcements, but they won't have had time to put together a real force yet. And they sure as hell won't be expecting more trouble this soon. They think they're safe from people like us."

"And if you're wrong?" said Chance.

"Then we walk right through them," said Fisher. "David and Marcus have a lot to answer for, and nothing and no one is going to stand in our way."

Chance felt a sudden chill across the back of his neck. The cold determination in Hawk's and Fisher's faces and voices reminded him yet again that he was in the company of legends. At that moment, Chance thought he believed every word he'd ever heard about them.

The cobbled yard before the DeWitts' business building held only a dozen private guards, uncomfortable in their new garishly colored uniforms. They did their best to look menacing, but barely half of them were holding their weapons like they knew how to use them. Hawk and Fisher drew their weapons and broke into a loping run, howling their old Forest war cries as they closed rapidly on their foes. Chance drew his father's great axe and hurried after them, Chappie already bounding happily ahead. The private guards broke and ran. Hawk and Fisher chased them into the building, kicking in the door as the last few guards tried desperately to slam it in their faces. The guards huddled together to make a last stand, basically because there was nowhere left to run, but when Chappie came charging in, the guards threw down their weapons and put their hands in the air. One of them actually burst into tears.

"It's not fair!" he said loudly. "No one told me I'd have to fight Hawk and Fisher and a bloody wolf!"

"Right," said the guard next to him. "They're not paying us enough for this. Hell, there isn't that much money in Haven."

"I am not a wolf!" snapped Chappie, showing all his teeth. The guards gave frightened little cries and huddled closer together. Chappie turned to glare at Chance as he finally caught up with them. "Tell them I am not a wolf, Chance!"

"They'd be better off if you were," said Chance, just a little breathlessly. The late Champion's great double-headed axe had not been designed for running with. "I wasn't expecting prisoners, Hawk. What do you want to do with them?"

"We could feed them to Chappie," said Hawk, and grinned unpleasantly as the guards did everything but try to climb into each other's pockets. "Hell, I haven't got time for this. Shoo, the lot of you. And don't let me see you again, or I'll have Fisher fillet you."

The private guards shuffled hesitantly past him, smiled weakly at Fisher, and then bolted the moment they reached the door. Chance looked around the deserted entrance hall. If reinforcements from inside the building had been coming, they would have been here by now, which suggested there were no more guards.

"Which way now, Hawk?"

"Beats me," said Hawk. "We only ever saw the DeWitts on that bloody balcony. But the word is they're still in here somewhere. So I guess we just kick in doors and generally terrorize people until we find them."

"Amateurs," growled Chappie. "Take hours to search a building this size. Get out of the way and let me do it. Won't take me long to sniff them down." He raised his long head and sniffed ostentatiously at the air, then stopped short and frowned. "That's odd. There's something new in the building. Coming this way. It smells like . . . smoke, with sulphur in it."

And that was when the thick gray mists came rolling down the entrance hall, and enveloped all four of them in a multitude of thick, grasping strands, tenuous as cobwebs but strong as steel. Hawk and Fisher lashed out, but the gray strands evaded their weapons with serpentine ease, and lashed their arms to their sides in a moment. Chance did no better, and the gray strands all but cocooned Chappie rather than take any risks where he was concerned. Hawk and Fisher fought the enveloping strands until they contracted sharply, squeezing all the breath out of their lungs, and after that they just stood there, rocking unsteadily on their feet as they fought for air. Chance didn't waste his strength. He murmured to Chappie to be still, and then stood quietly, waiting for some opportunity to present itself.

The billowing mists parted to reveal a slender dark figure, and Hawk made a disgusted sound. "Mistique! Never trust a sorceress."

"How the hell did you get here ahead of us?" asked Fisher, scowling darkly. "And how did you know we'd strike here first?"

"Well, honestly, darling, I am a sorceress," said Mistique calmly. "I'm supposed to know things like that. Don't bother struggling; the mists are as strong as I think they are, and I think they're unbreakable. I really do apologize for this; it's not as if I want to be here, but the Commanders threatened to fire me, and right now I need this job, so I can look after poor Mumsy and Daddy. So I'm afraid none of you are going anywhere. You're going to stay safely wrapped up in my clever little mists until you come to your senses. Or until the Commanders find some way to pressure you into doing what they want. They're really very good at doing things like that."

All the time the sorceress was talking, Hawk strained surreptitiously against the mists, but there wasn't an inch of give in them. The High Warlock's axe would probably cut right through the mystic strands, if he could just bring the weapon to bear, but his arm was trapped at his side. Hawk stopped struggling and thought about that for a moment. His arm was trapped, but his axe . . . Hawk grinned suddenly, and opened the fingers of his hand. The weight of the axe pulled it free from his grip, and it fell toward the floor, tearing through the gray mists it encountered along the way. Mistique shrieked, threw up her hands, and collapsed in a decorous heap on the floor. Immediately the enveloping mists began to unravel and dissipate, and within seconds the captives were free again, as they swept their arms vigorously about them. Chappie couldn't resist biting at some of them, and grimaced at the taste. Chance looked dubiously at the unconscious sorceress.

"Does she often faint like that?"

"The mists are magical extensions of her own mind," said Hawk. "When my axe cut through them, she felt it personally, and the magical feedback knocked her out. Just as well. She didn't really want to fight us."

They strode past the unconscious sorceress, Chance dragging Chappie along when he wanted to stop and urinate on her, and headed down the hall, following Chappie's keen nose as he sniffed out the DeWitts' trail. Fisher leaned in close to Hawk.

"That was a bit easy, wasn't it?" she asked quietly. "Not to mention convenient?"

"She was faking it," Hawk murmured just as quietly. "Now she can report back to the Commanders that she did her best, but we were just too much for her."

"Why bother with the act?" said Fisher.

"Because you can bet there are any number of unseen eyes watching us," said Hawk. He grinned suddenly. "The next guy who tries my trick on Mistique and expects it to work is in for a very unpleasant surprise."

They followed Chappie's nose along a convoluted trail, passing back and forth through the great building. Clerks at their desks watched with wide eyes as they passed, but made no attempt to raise the alarm. They stuck to their desks and kept their heads well down. Most of the rooms were empty. Chappie followed the trail out onto the balcony and back again, his nose very close to the floor now. He never once hesitated or looked confused, even when the trail finally ended at a broom closet. He snuffled noisily at the door, then stepped back to look meaningfully at Chance. Chance tried the door. It was locked, but one blow of his father's axe took care of that. Chance pulled the door open, and there were Marcus and David DeWitt, huddled together like frightened children.

"Surprise!" said Chappie, and the two brothers cried out in shock and fear.

"Come out of there," growled Hawk. "Don't make me come in there and get you."

And then Marcus DeWitt thrust forward one pudgy hand, holding out the zombie control stone. It flared up brightly as Marcus spoke the activating word, and Chance suddenly fell back a step, clutching at his head. Chappie collapsed on the floor, whining and whimpering. Hawk and Fisher swayed on their feet as something rushed through their thoughts like an icy river, numbing their minds, but then it was gone, and they were themselves again. Hawk glared at Marcus.

"What the hell was that?"

"The control stone," Marcus said breathlessly. "At this range, it can control any mind or body."

"Like hell," said Fisher. "After all the Wild Magic we were exposed to, a simple geas like that is just water off a duck's back to us. Now hand that thing over before I make up my mind which of your orifices I'm going to stuff it into."

David DeWitt laughed suddenly, a soft relieved sound. "You may not be affected, but your companions are. They belong to us now."

Hawk and Fisher looked around sharply. Chance was standing stiffly, his face and eyes dangerously blank. Chappie was back on his feet, and growling menacingly.

"Kill them!" said Marcus DeWitt viciously. "Kill them both! Now!"

Chance stalked forward, raising his axe. Chappie snarled once, and lurched toward Hawk and Fisher. They backed slowly away, not wanting to get too far from the DeWitts in case they tried to make a run for it.

"I thought that stone only worked on zombies!" hissed Fisher.

"Gaunt must have done a better job than he knew," said Hawk.

"So what do we do now? I don't want to have to hurt Chance or the dog."

"I'll hold them off, you get that stone away from Marcus. But make it quick—Chance and Chappie don't look like they're bluffing."

Fisher nodded, and the two of them lunged forward with the precision of long experience. Hawk's axe swept up to parry Chance's descending blade, and the two heavy axe-heads slammed together in a bright flurry of sparks. Chance's eyes were vague as he fought the DeWitts' will, but he swung his axe with practiced skill and commitment. The two axe-blades rang loudly in the still air of the narrow corridor as the two men struck fiercely against each other, neither of them yielding so much as an inch.

Chappie came lurching forward, stiff-leggedly, snarling like a long roll of thunder. Fisher moved quickly to put the two fighting men between her and the dog, and then darted forward to grab at the control stone in Marcus' hand. Her fingers closed around his, but he wouldn't give it up, prying desperately at her fingers with his other hand. Chappie swung around the fighting men and stumbled toward Fisher. David DeWitt tried to hit her. She lashed out with the back of her hand holding her sword, and he cried out as he fell back into the closet, blood gushing down his face from a broken nose. Chappie was very close now, almost within lunging range. So Fisher threw all her strength against Marcus' grip, and bent back his wrist until it broke. He shrieked briefly, and then again as she jerked the control stone out of his hand. Chance stopped fighting immediately, and stepped back, lowering his axe. Hawk watched him carefully.

"Damn," said Chance thickly, shaking his head. "*Damn,* that was unpleasant."

"Got that right," growled Chappie, shaking his head, too. "Like having someone else behind my eyes, making me do things. I'm going to bite someone's arse for this."

"Get in line," said Hawk, finally lowering his axe. He looked at the DeWitt brothers, both of them sniveling together in their hiding place. They shrank back under his gaze. Fisher studied the control stone thoughtfully. Seen up close, it seemed too small and ordinary to have been the cause of so much woe. Hawk reached into the closet, grabbed Marcus by the shirt-front, and dragged him to his feet. He glared right into Marcus' tear-filled eyes, their faces so close, they were almost touching. When Hawk finally spoke, his voice was little more than a whisper.

"How many good men and women died on the harborside today because of you? How many were crippled, or beaten so hard, they're pissing blood? How many families will starve because you took away all the jobs, replacing men with your stinking zombies? You're worse than an assassin, DeWitt. You don't just kill men; you kill lives and families and hope. Why should they die? Why shouldn't you die, instead?"

He raised his axe for a killing blow, and Marcus screamed as he saw no mercy in Hawk's cold eye, no mercy at all.

Fisher moved quickly in beside Hawk, and though she didn't touch him, her voice was right there in his ear. "Don't do it, Hawk. He deserves to die, they both do. But I've been thinking. If the DeWitts die now, the docks will be paralyzed for months while their heirs fight it out over the will. You know how this city loves a good lawsuit. No work for the dockers, no food for the city. If the DeWitts die now, at our hands, innocents will suffer."

"If the DeWitts live, innocents will suffer," said Hawk, not lowering his axe.

"There is another way," Fisher said carefully. "Not as satisfying for us, but then, that's not supposed to be why we're doing this."

Hawk finally lowered his axe and looked at Fisher. "All right. I'm listening."

Chance studied them both as Fisher murmured in Hawk's ear. For the first time he had seen true rage in Hawk's scarred face, and the sheer violence of it had shocked him. He had no doubt at all that Hawk would have killed his helpless victim in cold blood if Fisher hadn't intervened. This wasn't the Prince Rupert of legend. This was someone else, someone far more terrifying, and Chance wasn't at all sure how he felt about this new Hawk. This wasn't the man he'd come south to find, to save the Forest Kingdom. And then he was surprised to see a slow smile spread across Hawk's face as Fisher stopped murmuring and stepped back.

Hawk took the control stone from Fisher and strode over to a nearby window. He gestured for the others to join him, and they did, including the DeWitts after an admonishing glare from Fisher and a scowl from Chappie. They all looked out the window and down below, the harborside and the docks spread out before them under the midday sun. It was getting uncomfortably warm now, but the zombies toiled unceasingly in silence, feeling none of the heat. Hawk held the glowing control stone aloft in his hand, spoke the activating word he'd heard Marcus use, and concentrated, sending out his will to the dead men working below. And as one they stopped what they were doing, abandoned their tasks, and turned away to walk slowly but purposefully into the sea. One by one, they vanished beneath the dark waters, disappearing in their hundreds like so many slow-moving lemmings, until there were no more zombies left anywhere in the docks.

"They'll keep walking across the bottom of the sea forever," said Hawk. "Or at least until something eats them, or they fall apart. And just to make sure you two bastards don't get your hands on any more . . ."

He opened his hand and let the control stone drop onto the floor. And as the DeWitts watched disbelievingly, Hawk smashed the stone with one blow from his axe. The glowing crystal shattered into thousands of delicate slivers with a soft tinkling sound, and that was that. Marcus and David DeWitt moaned quietly. The only sorcerer who could have made them another was dead and gone. They had invested all that wealth and made all those plans for nothing.

"You'll have to deal with the unions now," said Fisher. "And after the way you've treated them, they're going to drive a real hard bargain before they let you woo them back again. Better tighten your belts, boys. Profits are going to be way down this year."

*   *   *

Things got bloody after that. Hawk and Fisher had their list of evil men and women, and more than enough reason to go after all of them. They went where no Guards had ever dared go before, and brought death and terror to the city's predators in one fast rampage through the darkest parts of Haven's underworld. Villains who had long thought themselves above or beyond the law now discovered they were not beyond the reach of Hawk and Fisher, and the long-postponed rage in their hearts. Chance and Chappie knew they were just along for the ride, and mostly settled for watching Hawk's and Fisher's backs as they brought their own savage brand of justice and retribution to those who had so long evaded it.

Not all that long afterward, they were studying a first-class restaurant in the very civilized hub of the city, around which the other Quarters revolved. Here were the very best establishments, for shopping and cuisine and the latest fashions. Only the very richest shopped here, of course, and there were private guards everywhere to keep out the merely curious. The crime rate was astonishingly low for Haven, because anyone who even considered making trouble there very rarely survived to stand trial. This was the playground of the moneyed and the powerful and the fashionable, and they liked their peace and quiet and privacy. They strolled unhurriedly down the pleasant tree-lined streets, arrayed in all their finery like so many preening peacocks. The foursome observed their target restaurant from across the street, in the concealing shadows of an alley mouth. As long as they stayed close to a tradesmen's route, they were, for all practical purposes, invisible, as the higher orders would never stoop to recognize a servant's presence.

The restaurant was currently packed, and there were large armed men guarding the door to ensure that no one else so much as paused to read the handwritten menus in the windows. Surprisingly, no one objected to this. They knew who was dining within, though they pretended not to. Chappie sniffed at the air appreciatively, licking his chops.

"By God, someone in there knows what he's doing. I can smell every kind of meat there ever was, and a whole bunch of sauces so good, they make my teeth ache. Tell me we're going in there, Chance. I promise I won't bite anyone. Unless it's a particularly slow-moving waiter."

"We're going in, but not just yet," said Hawk. "And when we do, feel free to bite anyone you like. Basically, just go for anything dangling."

"You're my kind of guy, Hawk," said Chappie happily.

"Is everyone in there a villain?" Chance asked. "What are they all doing together in one place?"

"This," said Fisher, "is where the heads of Haven's more organized crime get together, once a week, to sort out internal problems and discuss territory violations. All very calm and businesslike, enforced by a small army of bodyguards. You're looking at some of the wickedest men and women in Haven, and the most powerful. At their word or whim, people suffer and die every day. The Guard have strict orders not to go anywhere near this place when these people are in session. They have enormous political influence. Hell, some of them are politicians."

"Which is as good a reason as any for killing as many of the blood-sucking bastards as possible before we leave Haven," said Hawk. "But we can't afford to drag this out. We go in, cause as much murder and mayhem as we can, and then vanish back into the alleys again. There's a lot of private muscle here, all of it well armed, and even we can't fight an army. And, since word of what we're up to has no doubt reached Glen and Dubois by now, you can bet there are a hell of a lot of Guards out in the city looking for us, with orders to bring us in no matter what it takes. Isobel, you still got those concussion grenades?"

"Oh, yeah," said Fisher. She reached into a pouch at her belt and brought out a handful of small silver orbs. She hefted them lightly in her hand and grinned at Chance. "They don't look like much, but these really are something special. We don't often get permission to use them, because they're so expensive and difficult to manufacture. Basically, they're fragments of time and space seized from the heart of a raging hurricane, trapped in a magical shell like insects in amber. A moment out of time, contained indefinitely.

All I have to do is prime and throw one of these little
beauties, and that restaurant is history."

"Better make it two," said Hawk. "Just to be on the
safe side."

"You're spoiling me. Have you got the incendiaries
ready?"

"Of course. And the chaos bombs."

Fisher scowled unhappily. "I'm still not sure about those
things. There's a good reason why they're still on the forbidden list. No one really understands chaos magic yet, and
the one time someone tried to explain it to me, I had a
headache that lasted all day. Those things are just as likely
to take us out as the bloody enemy. Promise me you'll only
use them as a last resort, Hawk, or I'm not going in there
with you."

"Fuss, fuss, fuss," Hawk said calmly. "Whatever happened to your sense of adventure?"

"What happened to your sense of survival?"

"Can we please leave the marital discord for later?" said
Chance. "You did say we were running short on time."

"Spoilsport," said Chappie. "It was just getting interesting. Doggy romance is much more practical. You just—"

"I *know* what you do," snapped Chance. "And it never
fails to disgust me. The High Warlock might have increased
your intelligence, but he did damn all for your instincts."

The dog sniggered. Fisher chose one of her silver orbs,
and wound up for a throw. "Party time. . . ."

The concussion grenade exploded right in the front doorway, in the midst of the bodyguards. They just had time to
see a quick silver glow and reach for their weapons, and
then suddenly a hurricane was raging right there amongst
them. The front of the restaurant disappeared in a moment,
disintegrated by the raging winds, and the bodyguards were
torn apart, blood and mangled flesh flying high up into the
air along with broken bricks and scraps of wood. The winds
died quickly away with no real storm to maintain them,
and a ghastly rain fell upon the pretty streets. The rich and
fashionable cried out in shock and horror as wreckage and
offal fell from the sky. Hawk and Fisher were already

charging across the street, weapons in hands, Chance and Chappie right behind them.

They burst into the restaurant through the shattered front, to find thirty-nine crime bosses and their entourages already on their feet, pushing their chairs back from the tables and demanding to know what was going on. Hawk and Fisher hit them hard, throwing bombs and incendiaries around with wild enthusiasm. Fires broke out all over the restaurant, fanned and encouraged by the savage winds now surging inside the delicately appointed room. People went flying in all directions, some of them on fire. Several more took one look at Chappie, shouted the familiar *Wolf!*, and ran. Then Hawk and Fisher hit the first bodyguards, and it was all flying swords and clashing blades. One by one the bodyguards fell, no match for the fire and fury that drove Hawk and Fisher. Chance did his best to guard their backs, swinging his late father's huge axe with deadly skill. Chappie ran happily back and forth, doing terrible things to the slower moving, and defying anyone to stop him.

The crime bosses quickly realized that their only hope for safety lay in numbers, and they backed away together to form a half circle bristling with weapons at the back of the room, from where they watched numbly as the last of their bodyguards were cut down. Fires raged uncontrolled all over the room, the last of the winds whipping up the flames around the dead and the dying till what remained of the restaurant looked very much like hell. And the scariest things in that hell stepped over the last few fallen bodyguards and advanced on the crime lords: Hawk and Fisher, blood dripping from their weapons and bloodlust in their eyes. All those years of being ordered to turn their heads away from evil, while the guilty went unpunished, were finally over.

Chance hung back. This was their fight, their personal vendetta. He called Chappie to him, and the dog trotted over, grinning with red mouth and teeth.

Hawk and Fisher stopped just out of reach of the crime lords' weapons, and the two sides studied each other silently, the only sounds the low moaning of the dying, and the crackling of burning furniture. The fires were spreading.

Soon the whole restaurant would be a blazing inferno from which no one could hope to escape.

"Why now?" asked Marie ab Hugh, owner of a very profitable gambling house where the odds were squeezed till they screamed, and the only breaks a sucker got were in the arms and legs of his children when he couldn't pay. She knew Hawk and Fisher, and her eyes were hot with vindictive fury. "Why come after us now? You must know you can't take us all, and you can be sure the survivors will retaliate in ways you can't even imagine. You'll die, your families and friends will die, everyone who ever had a civil word for you will die, and you'll all die screaming in agony. Your names will become a curse on the lips of the city."

"We thought you'd say something like that," said Fisher calmly. "And you're right; two against thirty-nine is bad odds, though we've faced worse in our time. But we're in something of a hurry, and more interested in justice than in savoring our revenge. So, for all those who suffered at your hands, or your orders, for all those who bled or grieved or died because of you, we've brought you a little present. Go ahead, Hawk. Bring a little chaos into their lives."

Hawk already had the chaos bomb in his hand. A small golden orb, dully gleaming, and quite possibly the most dangerous weapon he'd ever contemplated using. He'd heard all the horror stories, the terrible things that had happened to the first few Guards entrusted with the prototypes. What was left of them had to be buried in unhallowed ground, and some said you could still hear muffled voices screaming from under the earth mounds.

This new version was supposed to be much safer, but only because no one had gotten around to testing it yet. Truth be told, Hawk didn't really give a damn. He had vowed to punish as many of the guilty as he could before he left Haven, and this was his best chance. He spoke the priming word and threw the chaos bomb at the crime bosses huddled together before him. Several flinched away, clearly expecting another incendiary, or more hurricane winds, but one of the braver souls stepped forward and slapped at the bomb with his hand, trying to send it right back at its thrower. Of course, he was the first to die.

The bomb activated the moment his hand touched it. The golden orb shattered, and something trapped within woke up and came out. No one there could tell what it was, whether it was a living thing or a force of nature or some magical construct. It was just too different, too unnatural, to be easily defined by human senses. It spread out across the smoky air, an awful presence unconfined by reason or logic, and everything it touched screamed. The man who'd activated the chaos bomb with his touch suddenly became a man-shaped mass of butterflies, which flew away in separate directions. It was almost pretty. The two men on either side of him melted and flowed away in thick liquid streams, calling for help in increasingly gurgly voices. The crime bosses started to scatter and run, but it was too late. Several slammed together in the growing panic, and merged into one great fleshy form, with too many arms and eyes, and mouths that howled in unknown languages. The changes spread quickly through those who were left, transforming the crime lords in awful ways, until even Hawk and Fisher had to look away.

The last man standing was a grossly fat protection racketeer, his back pressed against the far wall as he watched the chaos do its awful work on his business associates. It is said that inside every fat man there is a thin man screaming to get out. Hawk and Fisher watched despite themselves as the fat man suddenly split apart from throat to crotch, blood flying thickly on the air as a thin bony hand emerged from inside the great crimson rent. The fat man's screams were choked with blood as first the hand, and then an arm, and finally a shoulder emerged from his dripping guts, the thin man tearing the gross bulk apart in his eagerness to be free. Bones broke and fat tore, until finally a terrible thin man stood in a pile of discarded guts and skin, and laughed and laughed and laughed.

Chance had to fight to keep from vomiting. Chappie pressed close against his legs, tail clamped between his back legs, whining unhappily. Fire roared around them, consuming what was left of the restaurant. Fisher looked at Hawk.

"Did even they deserve that?"

"I don't know," said Hawk. "If you like, we can ask some of their victims before we leave."

Fisher looked uneasily about her. She could feel the unnatural presence still coiling and writhing on the air, unsatisfied and beyond any control they might have had over it.

"Hawk, that shit doesn't look like it's interested in dispersing. If anything, I'd say it's spreading, and heading in our direction. Time we were leaving, I think. In a hurry."

"You're probably right," said Hawk. "Any idea what the range on that thing is?"

"Don't ask me," said Fisher, backing quickly toward the shattered front of the restaurant. "You're the one who reads up on these things."

"Shut up and run," said Hawk, and they did. Chance and Chappie were right there behind them.

Outside the restaurant a crowd had gathered to watch. Hawk and Fisher yelled at them to get back, and the fashionable people took one look at the bloodstained weapons in their hands, then the expression on their faces, and did as they were told. Hawk didn't stop running until he was safely back in the alley mouth on the other side of the street. He looked back, Fisher at his side, both of them panting for breath. Chance and Chappie tucked themselves in behind the two Guards, and peered cautiously past them.

"Tell me," said the dog conversationally. "Have you people ever heard of the word *overkill*? I've seen forest fires that do less damage than you two."

"Right," said Chance. "I'm impressed. Really. Can we go now? If whatever you let loose in that place isn't limited to the restaurant, I for one am heading for the nearest horizon and not looking back till I'm in a different country."

"Race you," challenged Chappie, sniffing at the air unhappily.

Hawk was about to say something cutting when the whole restaurant vanished suddenly and silently, leaving only a great hole in the ground where the foundations had been. The watching crowd made various noises of awe, and called loudly on several gods. A few clapped. Hawk blinked a few times.

"It would appear the chaos force has gone back to wherever the Guard sorcerers got it from," he said finally. "And taken the restaurant with it."

"Good riddance," said Fisher. "Now let's get the hell out of here. One of the people we were looking for wasn't there. And we can't leave Haven without saying good-bye to him first."

"Oh, hell," said Chance. "Haven't you killed enough people for one day? How much will it take to satisfy your need for revenge?"

"You'd be surprised," said Hawk, and something in his voice made Chance decide not to say anything else. Hawk looked broodingly at the great hole in the ground. "One man wasn't there, the greatest villain of them all. He never gets his hands dirty himself, but he takes a cut from everyone else's business in return for financing their various schemes. A great fat leech, feeding on the blood of the city."

"St. Christophe," said Fisher. "He has a personal army of over four hundred men, and a mansion better protected than Guard Headquarters. We were hoping he'd be here with the other scumbags, but apparently he's too important these days to appear in person. So we'll have to go after him the hard way."

"Hold everything," said Chance, trying hard to sound firm and decisive. "There is no way the four of us are going to fight our way through an army of *four hundred men,* dammit. I don't care what the legends said you did. And Hawk, if you even look like you're thinking of unleashing another of those chaos bombs, I am going to knock you unconscious for your and everybody else's good."

Hawk smiled slightly. "Well, you could try. But you're right. No more chaos bombs. Not until I have a much better idea what their limits are. And we'd never fight our way through four hundred men to reach St. Christophe. So we'll just walk up to his front door and demand to see him. He'll let us in because his pride won't let him do anything else. And then we'll have him."

"And just how do we get out afterward, past the four hundred armed men?" said Chance.

"Oh, we'll think of something," said Hawk airily. "In fact, I think we ought to take a little present with us, a little something for St. Christophe's personal bodyguards."

"Of course," agreed Fisher. "I have just the thing in mind. We'll pick it up along the way."

Chance looked at Chappie. "We are dead. Very, very dead."

Chance didn't know where he'd been expecting to stop off to pick up St. Christophe's little present, but a sewer opening sure wasn't it. Hawk levered open the heavy iron grille with the edge of his axe, and shouted down the hole. There was a long pause as several appalling odors wafted up into the street, and then a voice singing something vaguely melancholy could be heard drawing gradually nearer, along with the sounds of boots sucking deep into something Chance preferred not to think about. Finally a gray and grimy head appeared through the sewer hole, and the smell in the street was suddenly worse. Much worse. Chappie retreated, coughing and spluttering, and Chance felt very much like doing the same. But Hawk and Fisher held their ground, so he had to, too. Hawk nodded amiably to the grimy head, which smiled pleasantly in return.

"Greetings, Captains. Isn't it a simply lovely day?"

"So it is," said Fisher. "Chance, this is Gently Northampton; he knows the sewers under Haven better than anyone."

"Sewers are my life," said Gently. He blew his nose on a filthy handkerchief that Hawk wouldn't have touched with two pairs of gloves on, and then smiled again. "You can't beat the sewers for a bit of peace and quiet. No one bothers you. I haven't paid taxes for years. Though you'd be surprised what you can find down here some days. We've had to block off the tunnels under Magus Court. I don't know what those magicians have been up to, but there's something big and white in the passages now, and it's giggling. We've had to call in the SWAT team. Mind you, the sewers under the East Side are lovely this time of year. There's flowers there as beautiful as anything in the gentry's gardens. And, of course, they eat the rats, which helps keep the numbers down."

"Fascinating as always, Gently," said Fisher. "Did you get our message about what we need?"

"Certainly," said Gently. "Anything for you, Captains. One bagful, as requested."

He ducked back in his hole and then handed up a large cloth sack that writhed and bulged ominously. Fisher took the sack, tested its weight with one hand, and grinned unpleasantly. "Thank you, Gently. That will do nicely."

"Time to go see St. Christophe," said Hawk as Gently's head disappeared back into the sewers. He levered the iron grille back into place and stamped it down.

"Then can we please go back to the Forest?" said Chance, just a little plaintively. "I didn't feel this threatened during the Demon War."

"Some people just don't know how to have a good time," said Hawk, and Fisher nodded solemnly. The sack bulged and kicked.

St. Christophe's mansion was reputed to be the single largest personally owned residence in the city, and Chance could quite believe it. Four stories high and what looked like several acres wide, it dominated the quiet residential area. The thick stone exterior walls were topped with iron spikes and broken glass, and the only entrance into the grounds was a great stone archway that featured not only a lowered steel portcullis but also half a dozen heavily armed private guards. They took one look at who was approaching them and immediately sounded a general alarm. Hawk strolled unconcernedly up to the steel bars of the portcullis and smiled charmingly.

"You know who we are. Just once, what say we do this the easy way? We're here to see St. Christophe. You let us in, or else."

"Or else what?" asked the leader of the private guards.

"Or else we'll improvise," said Fisher. "Suddenly and violently and all over the place."

The guard leader thought about it. Technically speaking,

he was perfectly safe behind the thick steel weight of the portcullis . . . but this was Hawk and Fisher. Plus someone with a big axe, and a wolf. He looked unhappily at Chappie for some time, and then decided this was all too much for him. He sent one of his men up to the big house for instructions, and then everyone stood around and smiled patiently for a while. Fisher hefted her sack now and again to keep it quiet. Finally a butler turned up, in full frock coat and powdered wig, and ordered the portcullis raised. He would escort the Captains and company up to the mansion to meet St. Christophe.

The private guards looked at each other, took it in turns to shrug unhappily, and then did as they were told. The wheels of the portcullis turned, the heavy steel bars rose, and Hawk and Fisher sauntered through the archway like they owned the place. The butler bowed briefly, and then led the way up a raked gravel path that meandered through the extensive lawns and gardens. Behind them came the sound of the portcullis crashing back into place. None of them looked back. The butler's pace was nicely judged to suggest his master's impatience, while at the same time slow enough for the company to be impressed by the specially imported trees and flowers and the exquisite landscaping. And then Chappie spoiled it all by chasing a peacock and coming back with a mouthful of feathers.

The butler went berserk. Did they have any idea how rare peacocks were in this part of the world? How expensive they were to acquire and maintain? He wanted the wolf killed, stuffed, and mounted, not necessarily in that order. Chappie invited the butler to step right up and try his luck. A certain amount of unpleasantness followed, until Chance was finally able to coax Chappie back off the butler's chest, and allow the man to get up again. The butler led the party the rest of the way in dignified silence, pretending nothing at all had happened.

At the front door he passed them over to the head butler, resplendent in a uniform finer than most admirals, and he led the party down a great hall lined with ancestral portraits and two silent lines of armed men, and finally into a dining room, where St. Christophe sat at a feast. He was seated at the end of a long table of heavy mahogany, which was all but bowing under the weight of so much food. There was enough provender at that table to feed a dozen families, but St. Christophe was the only one eating. He dominated the room with his malign presence, his huge bulk contained in an exquisitely tailored suit of dazzling white, the only color a single bloodred rose on his lapel.

St. Christophe was over six feet tall, and weighed four hundred and fifty pounds if he was an ounce, but rumor had it that there was a lot of muscle under all that fat. Rather more disturbing rumors had it that he got that big by eating his enemies. His great round face was blank, almost childish, his features stretched smooth by his fat until he had the enigmatic brooding look of an oversized baby.

His gaze was flat and unwavering, and full of calm menace. He wore no weapons. It had been a long time since St. Christophe had fought for anything but his own pleasure. He left the necessary brutalities of his business to the twelve female bodyguards who went everywhere with him, each of them naked but for their swordbelts. They were reputed to be the twelve deadliest fighters in Haven, every one of them undefeated. So Hawk and Fisher made a point of ignoring them, and concentrated instead on the sumptuous furnishings and fittings of the dining hall. Hawk was particularly taken with the massive steel and glass and diamond chandelier hanging overhead. There were no visible supports, which suggested it was held aloft by some hidden magic. An expensive whim for something so monstrously tacky. St. Christophe casually threw a scrap of meat to one of his bodyguards. She caught it neatly on the point of her sword, conveyed it to her mouth, and chewed it calmly, all without once taking her eyes off the new visitors.

"Show-off," said Fisher.

Chappie sneaked up behind one of the bodyguards and stuck his cold nose up her bottom. She squeaked loudly, and then tried very hard to look as though she hadn't. The dog sniggered loudly. Chance didn't know where to look. Spending most of his life in an all-boys private school had done nothing to help him deal with so much female nudity.

He found it all very distracting, but he was still smart enough to realize that that was the point.

"So, Captains," said St. Christophe, in a slow voice as implacable as an avalanche. "What could be so important that you must disturb me at my repast?"

"Oh, nothing much," said Hawk easily. "We're just here to kill you, burn down your house, and cripple your extensive criminal operations. We're leaving Haven, you see, so we won't get another chance. You should be flattered, Christophe; we saved the best for last."

St. Christophe chuckled fatly. "Insubordinate as ever, Captain Hawk. Must I remind you that I am a perfectly respectable businessman, with no criminal record of any kind? The law has no interest in me."

"We're not the law anymore," said Fisher. "We answer to a higher cause. How many lives have you ruined over the years, Christophe? Do you even know?"

"Of course not," said the big man, patting delicately at his rosebud lips with a monogrammed silk napkin. "I have people who keep track of such things for me. I really have no interest in continuing this conversation, Captains. Because of my admiration for your many exploits, I offer you this one chance. Leave my home, and this city, and never look back. While you still can."

"Good thinking, having nude women as your body-guards," said Fisher calmly. "Men are so easily distracted by things like that. I, on the other hand, am not. So I considered the problem dispassionately, and decided to bring your bodyguards a little present. Or two."

She undid her sack, upended it with a flourish, and out of the sack dropped twenty of the foulest, fiercest, hugest, and most vicious sewer rats to be found in all of Haven. They all hit the floor running, mouths snapping, and went straight for the nearest undefended food; in this case, the dozen sets of bare female feet. The bodyguards shrieked, and scattered in disarray and confusion as the rats bit at their feet and tried to run up their legs. One rat made the mistake of going for Fisher, and she casually booted it the length of the room.

St. Christophe surged to his feet, a squat giant in blinding white. He pushed back his chair, and snatched a sword from a bodyguard as she ran past him with a rat rooting in her hair. Hawk and Fisher drew their weapons and advanced on him. Chance slammed the only door shut and wedged it with a sturdy chair. Chappie meanwhile was having a fine time, chasing the darting rats and female bodyguards with equal glee.

Hawk and Fisher closed in on St. Christophe, who wielded his sword with surprising strength and speed, parrying their every blow. He moved impossibly quickly for one of his great bulk, and there was real power in his attacks. Try as they might, Hawk and Fisher couldn't pierce his defense, even when they came at him from two different sides at once. St. Christophe backed slowly away as Hawk and Fisher pursued him, not even breathing hard. Servants and guards were already hammering on the other side of the door Chance was guarding. Hawk and Fisher fought well and hard, but it had been a long day, and they were tiring fast. Steel clashed on steel, and St. Christophe smiled mockingly at his old adversaries. His fat face was slick with sweat. Both sides stopped for a moment, to regain their breath and call up new resources.

"You can't win," said St. Christophe. "The best you can do is arrest me, and my lawyers will have me out in under an hour. There won't be any trial. I am protected on levels you can't even imagine. You're just the city's attack dogs, and I have the means to muzzle you. Leave my home, or die here."

"Somehow I just knew you'd say something like that," said Hawk. "You think we can't touch you, and you're wrong."

He threw his axe at the point where the massive chandelier hung from the ceiling, and the rune-etched blade sheared through the simple magic supporting all that weight. St. Christophe looked up, and just had time to realize where Hawk and Fisher had maneuvered him into standing, and then the whole immense weight of crafted steel and glass and diamonds came crashing down, and smashed him to the floor. The reverberating sound seemed to go on for ages, and everyone turned to look. St. Chris-

tophe lay pinned beneath the chandelier, only his head and
one hand showing. He tried to force himself up, throwing
all the strength of his great bulk against the weight holding
him down, and for a moment the chandelier actually
moved; but it was only shifting its mass, and St. Christophe
groaned loudly as his strength gave out, and the chandelier
pressed him even more firmly to the floor.

Those female bodyguards not immediately concerned
with fighting off sewer rats stood watching numbly, bemused by a sight they'd never thought to see. The pounding
on the closed door grew louder. Chance wedged another
chair against it, and then backed away, sword in hand.
Chappie came to join him.

St. Christophe breathed heavily, and glared up at Hawk
and Fisher. "My people will break through soon. They'll
free me. And then you'll die slowly and horribly for this
indignity. Because I'm St. Christophe, and you're nobody!"

"Shows what you know," said Hawk. He reached out
and retrieved his axe from among the glass and diamonds
of the chandelier, and hefted it thoughtfully. And then he
raised it with both hands and brought it swinging down
with all his strength. The heavy steel blade sheared clean
through St. Christophe's thick neck, and buried itself in the
floor beneath. The head rolled away across the floor, still
wearing its last expression of outrage and surprise. Hawk
watched the head roll until it finally came to a halt, and
then nodded, satisfied.

"I have to say," Chance said slowly, "that wasn't exactly
honorable, was it?"

"Bloody well is in Haven," said Fisher.

Sometime later Hawk and Fisher and Chance sat on their
horses in a high place, and looked out over the city. There
was chaos in the streets, with lots of shouting and screaming, and here and there a thick plume of black smoke from
an out-of-control fire. Most of the Guards were out on the
streets, struggling to maintain order while not looking terribly hard for the people responsible for it all. Chappie sat
beside the horses, chewing happily on the last of something
with a lot of feathers.

"Time to leave," said Hawk.

"Right," agreed Fisher. "I think we've done as much damage as we can for one day."

"Won't you be at all sad to leave this place?" asked Chance. "I mean, it's been your home for ten years now."

Hawk and Fisher looked at each other. "No," they said together, and laughed.

They had one last stop to make before they could leave; the retreat of an ex-con man Hawk and Fisher had known for some time. Zeb Tombs lived in a quiet little house in a quiet little cul de sac in a very respectable area that knew nothing of his checkered past. Hawk knocked on Tombs' door.

"He's not in!" said a voice from behind the door. "He's gone away, and he was never here anyway. Tombs? Never heard of the man. Stay away! This is a plague house!" There was the sound of really repulsive coughing. "And it's haunted!"

"Open the door, Zeb," Hawk said calmly. "You wouldn't want Fisher to have to kick it in, would you?"

There was the sound of opening locks and sliding bolts, and then the door swung open. A distinguished-looking gentleman in his early fifties, resplendent in a fine embroidered smoking jacket, looked quickly up and down the deserted street and then glared at Hawk and Fisher. "You leave my door alone! I just had it painted. What did I do to deserve you back in my life? I haven't shot an albatross in ages. Oh, hell, come in, come in, before the neighbors notice. If they haven't already. Some days you can't walk down this street for twitching curtains. And wipe your feet!"

Hawk led the way in, followed by Fisher, who nodded cheerfully to Tombs as she barged past him. Chance and Chappie brought up the rear. Tombs gave the dog a hard look, but said nothing. He waved his guests into the parlor, a comfortable room furnished with all the ill-gotten gains of a long career of separating the more gullible well-off from as much cash as Tombs could carry away in one journey. He'd done very well for himself in Haven, until he made the mistake of trying to sell shares in a silver mine to Commander Dubois, who didn't know much about mining, but was pretty sure you didn't find much of it going on in land he knew to have been underwater for a hundred years. He set Hawk and Fisher on Tombs' trail, and that was that.

"What do you want with me now?" asked Tombs. "I've been good. It's been ages since I've done anything . . . creative."

"We're leaving Haven," Hawk said briskly.

"Allow me to be the first to wave good-bye."

"But we need disguises first."

"Good idea," said Tombs. "If I were you, I'd want to look like someone else, too. And anything I can do to help you on your way will be a real pleasure." He glanced dubiously at Chappie, and then at Chance. "Your wolf is housebroken, isn't he?"

"If one more person calls me a wolf, I am going to do something really distressing to them!" said Chappie, showing all his teeth.

Tombs backed quickly away and put a heavy chair between him and the dog. "Hey, if it was up to me, you could be anything you want. But trust me, the teeth and claws and fur are a bit of a giveaway."

"Never mind Chappie," said Fisher. "He's just being himself. Concentrate on coming up with disguises for Hawk and me. What have you got?"

"Well," said Tombs reluctantly, "it's not as easy as it might have been, since *certain people* made me dispose of all my old gear, but I do just happen to have a transformation spell I was saving for a rainy day."

"They don't work on us," Hawk said immediately. "We were exposed to a hell of a lot of Wild Magic in the long night, and these days any change spells just slide right off us."

Tombs blinked a few times. "You're full of surprises, aren't you, Captain? But I've nothing else to offer you except the standard makeup and hair dyes."

Hawk and Fisher looked at each other, and then they looked at Chance, who studied them both thoughtfully. "You really don't look much like your official portraits, and it has been a long time. . . . I think the scars and the eye patch are really all you need, Your Highness."

"Highness?" said Tombs quickly.

"Shut up, Tombs."

"Yes, Your Highness, shutting up right now."

"What about me?" said Fisher.

"Dye your hair black and no one will know you," said Chance, just a little hesitantly. "Nearly everyone you knew back then is dead. The few still alive probably only ever saw you briefly, and from a distance. The dye should be enough."

"Is she a highness too?"

"Shut up, Tombs. Or I'll let the wolf have you."

Dying Fisher's long mane of hair jet black was a messy but fairly quick process, and there was no denying that afterward she looked different. She studied herself in Tombs' bathroom mirror, scowling fiercely with her new dark eyebrows, and then looked back at Hawk lounging in the doorway.

"Tell me the truth, or you're dead meat."

"You look very striking," Hawk assured her, careful to keep all traces of a smile off his face. "And most importantly, nothing at all like Julia. Settle for that. Now I really think we should be going. The Guard will probably do everything they can to avoid finding us, but you can bet all the villains we didn't have time to get round to will be lining up for one last chance at us before we leave."

Fisher nodded, and followed Hawk back into the parlor. Chance kept a straight face while Tombs openly boggled. Chappie hid behind Chance's legs and had a prolonged coughing fit.

"So, what now?" asked Chance brightly.

"We ride for the city limits at full speed, and we don't stop for anything," said Fisher. "How far do we have to travel to reach the Rift? More than a day?"

"I have a special charm from the Magus," said Chance. "Once we're outside the city, I can summon the Rift opening right to us. Then all we have to do is ride through, and we'll be back in the Forest again."

"As simple as that," said Hawk. "Assuming we get out of the city alive. We've made a lot of enemies here over the years."

"For all the right reasons," said Fisher.

"Are you people ever going to leave?" asked Tombs. "All this talk of enemies is making me very nervous. I can think of any number of people who'd cheerfully firebomb this whole street just to get at you. I've sometimes felt that way myself."

"Relax," said Hawk. "We're on our way."

"Don't I get any payment for my hard-earned expertise?"

"What do you think?" said Fisher.

"Grrr," added Chappie.

Hawk, Fisher, and Chance rode their horses full tilt through the crowded streets, Chappie loping along beside them, while arrows and knives and blunt objects of all kinds rained down from above, and spells and curses crackled helplessly on the air, repelled by the protective mannikin peering out of the top of Hawk's backpack. People threw themselves out of the horses' way, shouting threats or encouragement, or just the latest official betting odds on their getting out of the city alive. The few Guards they encountered looked the other way, determined not to get involved. Hawk and his companions ran the gauntlet, come and gone so quickly, no one could touch them. But the mannikin was burning out fast, and the horses couldn't maintain such a pace for long. And more and more horsemen were taking up the chase behind them.

Hawk led the way, trusting to his extensive knowledge of the city streets to get him out of Haven by the fastest possible route. The streets flashed by, buildings and crowds nothing more than a blur. He could see the edge of the city from where he was, but he couldn't get at it. There was no direct route, only a maze of narrowing streets and alleyways.

And then he rounded a corner at top speed, and saw that the end of the street ahead was blocked by a massive barricade. Armed men stood waiting before it. They'd clearly dragged all the furniture out of the surrounding tenements and piled it up into one great impassable wall. Hawk kept going. He couldn't even slow down, with the pursuing riders so close behind. The barricade drew closer. No way around, too high to jump. The jagged ends of broken chair legs thrust out of the barricade like so many vicious spikes.

And Hawk remembered another barricade, in the long night of the Demon War, in the last great battle outside the Forest Castle. The Blue Moon burned sickly overhead, blue and diseased, and the only barricade between Prince Rupert and the legion of demons was the increasingly high pile of his own fallen dead comrades.

Fisher pulled alongside him, reining her horse in close as they raced forward. "You see that barricade?"

"Of course I see it!"

"Any ideas?"

"Not yet."

"We'll have to jump it," Fisher told him.

"We can't! It's too high!"

"We don't have any choice!"

And then someone stuck a blazing torch into the mostly wooden barricade, and the whole thing went up in soaring flames. Fisher scowled.

"All right, we won't jump it. We need an idea, Hawk. And you'd better come up with it bloody soon, because that barricade is getting really close now."

Another minute and they'd be on top of it. Hawk's horse was already beginning to slow, despite his urging, as the flames leapt high into the sky. Quick glances around showed that the only side streets were blocked with armed men. Someone had put a lot of thought into this. There was no way out. So if you can't go through, or around . . .

"Follow me!" yelled Hawk, and steered his horse sharply to the left. Right in front of them was a bulky steel fire escape, leading up to the second story and the roof. The horse took one look and tried to balk, but Hawk drove him on with spurs and oaths and a merciless grip on the reins. The horse plunged forward, its steel-clad hooves striking sparks as it clattered up the fire escape. The whole structure shook under the sudden weight, but held. Fisher and Chance urged their mounts after Hawk's, and Chappie brought up the rear. Two armed men darted out of the shadows at the base of the fire escape.

"They're getting away!" yelled one. "At least kill the bloody wolf!"

Chappie gave them his best snarl and a really hard look, and both men stopped sharply in their tracks. "*You* kill the bloody wolf!" said the second man. Chappie grinned as he followed the horses up the steps and onto the sloping tiled roof.

The whole stairway tried to tear itself away from the supporting wall, but somehow it held long enough for all of them to reach the roof. Hawk's horse was growing increasingly upset, but he drove the animal on, whooping wildly with the thrill of it all. Slates and tiles shattered under the horses' hooves as they plowed on, leaping recklessly from one roof to another. The shock and startled cries from down below seemed very far away. This high up, Hawk could see the city boundary clearly, agonizingly close. He spotted another fire escape plunging steeply down to the ground, and headed his horse toward it. He could hear Fisher and Chance following close behind. Fisher was laughing. Chance sounded as though he was praying.

They thundered down the fire escape and slammed back into the street again, the blazing barricade safely behind them. There was hardly anyone left now between the riders and the edge of the city. No one had really thought they'd get this far. One last heavy-duty curse crackled on the air around them, and all of Hawk's hair stood on end. He could feel the magic struggling to find a hold on him, slow and vile and malevolent, but the charm in his backpack still protected him. And then the mannikin screamed shrilly, waving its raffia arms, and burst into flames. The curse had been deflected, but their protection was gone.

Hawk and Fisher and Chance left the city port of Haven at a gallop, and never once looked back. Chappie was still right there with them, tongue lolling out the side of his mouth as he panted for breath. He was built more for stamina than speed. Before them lay the ragged coastline and the sea, and a whole lot of open ground. If horsemen came out of the city after them, there was nowhere they could hide, or defend, and their horses were too exhausted to run much further away. Hawk looked across at Chance.

"We need the Rift. Now!"

"We're too close to the city! I need a few more minutes!"

Fisher pulled in close beside Hawk on his other side. "So. We're really going back. Back to the Castle, and the Court, and all its intrigues and formalities. At least Haven was open and honest in its evils."

"The Forest Castle was my home," said Hawk.

"We're not going back to stay, are we? Tell me we're just going back to solve Harald's murder."

"If my duty calls. . . ." said Hawk.

"What about your duty to me?"

Before Hawk could answer, Chance seized their attention by drawing from his pack a Hand of Glory. A severed and preserved human hand, cut from a hanged man right after his execution, the fingers turned into candles. Old magic. Bad magic. The kind that damns your soul. A Hand of Glory could open any lock, find hidden treasures, reveal concealed doors. Hawk and Fisher watched intently as the five candle fingers lit themselves, burning with a warm yellow flame. From behind them came the sound of hot pursuit, but none of them looked back. Just being this close to a Hand of Glory was like having someone drag their fingernails across your soul. And then Chance said a Word of Power, activating the Hand, and everything changed.

Day became night. The sights and sounds around them seemed suddenly far away. Sunlight vanished and darkness slammed down. They were riding through the gloom now, and the stars were out. The horses fought their reins, tossing their heads and rolling their eyes. Night became day, became sunlight, blindingly bright. Day became night again, and the moon above was tinged with blue, like the first signs of decay. Night became day, and the world split open before them, space itself cracking apart to reveal an endless tunnel lit with its own eerie silver light. Hawk had seen this before, when the High Warlock used his teleport spell. He forced his almost hysterical horse on, into the tunnel, and the others were right behind. They all felt as much as heard the tunnel entrance slam shut behind them.

They slowed their horses to a walk in the tunnel. Time and space meant different things here, and with the tunnel closed, they were safe from pursuit. Being in the silver tunnel was like being back in the place where you were before you were conceived and earthed in flesh, so it should have come as no surprise when the dead came to talk with Hawk and Fisher. Ghosts from the past they had turned their backs on.

To Prince Rupert came his dead father, King John. He seemed old and tired and defeated, and when he looked at his son, his gaze was full of sadness. His voice was a whisper, and his words cut like a knife. *My sons have always been a disappointment to me.* And then he was gone, replaced by the awful pale face of the Demon Prince, who smiled his terrible smile and said, *I have always been well served by traitors.* The Champion came and walked beside Rupert, still bloody with his death wounds, and wouldn't look around as he said, *Courage can only take you so far.* And finally there was Harald, dead Harald, who looked at him accusingly. *You always said I'd make a better King than you.*

To Princess Julia, dead King John said kindly, *Never trust anyone. Especially those you love.* Her dead friend Bodeen, his chest still pierced with the death wound she gave him, gave her a friendly nod and said, *Everyone's a traitor to someone.* And then there came the dragon, dead and gone and consumed by fire, who studied her with the empty eye sockets of his charred skull as he said, *Magic is going out of the world. But that doesn't mean it's lost.* And finally to her came Harald, who was once her lover, if not her love, and he held her hand in his cold dead fingers and said, *I did love you, Julia. In my way.*

The ghosts spoke in calm, distant voices, suffused with the knowledge that only comes to the dead, and Rupert's and Julia's hearts hammered painfully in their still-living breasts as they remembered things and feelings they thought long lost. Somehow they knew they were being told things they needed to know, but the presence of so much death diminished them, with their memories of loss and failure and things left unsaid but never really forgotten. The living were not meant to hear the dead, because the human heart cannot bear too much truth.

And then the silver tunnel opened up with a roar and threw them back into the real world, and the Forest slammed into being before and around them. Bright green with the lush foliage of summer, the great trees stood tall and proud. The air was full of the song of birds and the drone of insects, and the rich scents of grass and earth and mulch. It smelled like home. Hawk reined his horse to a halt as the silver tunnel disappeared behind him, and the others stopped with him. He sat there for a moment, breathing heavily with the strain of long-suppressed emotions, and then glared at Chance.

"Why didn't you warn us?"

Chance looked back at him uncertainly. "I'm sorry. I was given to understand you'd traveled through the silver tunnel before."

"Not that," said Fisher heavily. "You should have told us. You should have told us about the dead."

"What dead?" asked Chappie, looking quickly about him.

"They came and talked to me," said Hawk. "Ghosts of the past, long since buried."

"The dead," said Fisher. "Trying desperately to warn me about . . . something."

Chance shook his head slowly. "No one has ever reported such side effects before. The Rift is just . . . a means of transport. Hundreds of thousands of people have gone back and forth through the Rift, and no one ever reported hearing voices. Perhaps it's your exposure to the Wild Magic again."

"And perhaps it's just us," said Hawk. "Still haunted by our past, and the things we had to do in it."

"Who spoke to you?" Chance asked curiously. "What did they say?"

Hawk and Fisher looked at each other. "Maybe we'll tell you. Someday," said Fisher.

"That's far enough!" said a new voice, arrogant with the

privilege of command. "You will have to declare everything you've brought with you from the south before you can be allowed to proceed any further."

They all looked around, and there were half a dozen tents and twenty or so heavily armed men. Hawk and Fisher looked at Chance.

"Customs and Immigration," he said apologetically.

"Welcome home," said Hawk. "Nothing ever changes."

CHAPTER FOUR

Not Really Like Coming Home at All

Hawk looked at the Customs and Immigration people, and just knew he wouldn't get along with them. The owner of the officious voice, a broad, portly specimen dressed in a bright and gaudy uniform of gold and russet, had the upturned nose and supercilious scowl of every civil servant who knows he's been promoted well past his point of competence, but is damned if he'll admit it. The kind of official who knows every rule in the rulebook that will stop you getting what you both know you're really entitled to, all the while saying he's only doing his job. And that it's more than his job's worth to make an exception in your case; unless, of course, you might be willing to grease the wheel a little. The armed men backing him up were wearing traditional Forest trappings and colors, but their voices as they murmured together had distinct Redhart accents. Mercenaries. Certainly they were experienced enough to recognize a possible threat in Hawk and Fisher, and they all had their hands somewhere near their swords as they watched the Customs Officer advance importantly on the new arrivals. Chance dismounted and stood patiently beside his horse, and after a moment Hawk and Fisher joined him, just to show willingness. Chappie scratched vigorously at a flea until Chance nudged him hard with a foot.

The Customs Official stopped just in front of Hawk and tried to stare him down, which was his first mistake. When Hawk calmly refused to be stared down, the official turned his stare on Fisher, which was his second mistake. Fisher glared back at him so venomously that the official actually fell back a step. Somewhat desperately, he turned to the third new arrival, and immediately his manner changed. A wide ingratiating smile took over his face, and he bowed low to Chance.

"Sir Questor, forgive me for not recognizing you immediately! Customs Inspector Ponsonby Stout, at your every service! The whole Kingdom has been anxiously awaiting your return, but no one expected you back so quickly. Did you find them? Have you brought back our beloved Prince and Princess?"

He looked eagerly past Chance, ignoring Hawk and Fisher, as though Rupert and Julia might be hiding behind them somewhere. He'd clearly already dismissed the scruffy figures of Hawk and Fisher as being unworthy of his expectations. Hawk didn't know whether to feel relieved or insulted. The mercenary soldiers took a new interest in what was going on, and strolled forward. Some bowed politely to Chance; some didn't.

"The Prince and Princess will not be returning to the Forest land," Chance said carefully. "They have instead sent these two . . . personages in their place, to investigate King Harald's murder. They are Hawk and Fisher, Guard Captains from the Southern city-state of Haven."

"Haven? Never heard of it!" snapped Stout. He looked reluctantly back at Hawk and Fisher, and tried out his best sneer on them. "But if they are from the south, they'll have to be inspected for forbidden contraband, and pay all relevant taxes and duties on whatever they've brought with them. You, Hawk! Show me your travel documents."

"They don't have any," Chance said quickly. "I brought them through the Rift myself, bypassing Southern Customs by use of the Magus' charm. As Questor, I vouch for them both."

"This is all very irregular," said Stout, quite pleased at having found something he could exercise his authority over. He sneered condescendingly at Hawk's and Fisher's admittedly somewhat grubby outfits, and then his gaze fell on their bulging backpacks. "I want both of those opened! Now! I have to be sure they don't contain any of the proscribed items of contraband."

"What counts as contraband?" Hawk asked Chance, ignoring the Customs Officer.

"Practically everything these days," said Chance. "Let me handle this, Hawk."

But by now Stout had spotted the burned-out mannikin protruding from the top of Hawk's backpack, and his eyes bulged excitedly. "Sorcery! Magical paraphernalia! You must know trafficking such items across the Rift is forbidden, Sir Questor. This is very serious, very serious indeed. Who knows what else such people might have about their persons." He gestured importantly for the armed men to come even closer, and they did so, clearly pleased at the prospect of a little excitement. Stout smiled unpleasantly at Hawk and Fisher while addressing his mercenaries. "I want both their bags searched, and I want these two strip-searched! Be very thorough, gentlemen. I don't like the look of these two at all."

Chance covered his face with his hand. "Oh, no."

Fisher looked at Hawk. "Just how messy do you think we should make this?"

"Minimum necessary," said Hawk. "There's still time for everyone to be reasonable."

"Strip them!" shouted Stout, infuriated by their casual manner and refusal to be at all intimidated by him. "I want a full body cavity search, followed by a strong purge, just in case they've swallowed anything!"

One of the mercenaries reached out an eager hand toward Fisher's bosom, and she punched him right between the eyes. His head snapped back, and he hit the ground like a falling tree. Two more mercenaries reached for her, and Hawk flattened them both before they even knew he was there.

"So much for reason," Fisher said calmly.

"Ah, what the hell," said Hawk easily. "There's only twenty of them."

The other mercenaries were already surging forward, swords in hand, and Hawk and Fisher went to meet them, weapons at the ready. It was a short and not especially bloody battle, as Hawk and Fisher were still on what passed for their best behavior. Chance kept dancing around the mayhem, shouting to Hawk and Fisher, *"Don't kill them! Please don't kill them! They're only doing their job! Oh,*

God, the Queen will have my balls for this." Hawk and
Fisher could have inquired whether the mercenaries would
also be observing such guidelines, but didn't have time or
the breath. It's actually quite difficult to stop a man just by
wounding or disarming him, especially when he's doing his
very best to kill you, but Hawk and Fisher had years of
experience of bringing in suspects more or less alive. Not
too much later, twenty semiconscious or heavily bleeding
mercenaries were sitting together, mumbling, moaning, and
holding their heads while they tried to remember what day
it was, while the Customs Officer looked on with bulging
eyes. Hawk and Fisher examined their work with quiet
satisfaction.

"Start as you mean to go on," said Hawk.

"You have to be firm," said Fisher.

They turned to look at Stout, and all the color drained
from his face. He would clearly have liked to fall back
several steps, but his legs were shaking too much. Hawk
smiled at him, and Stout actually whimpered. "We don't
do Customs," Hawk said firmly. "We also don't do taxes
or duties or any kind of strip search that isn't entirely con-
sensual. Now go and sit down with your little soldier friends
and don't bother us again, or Fisher and I will validate your
credentials with something large and heavy and pointed.
Go."

The Customs Official went. Chance shook his head
slowly, and gestured urgently for Hawk and Fisher to join
him a little distance away. Hawk and Fisher did so, cleaning
the blood from their weapons with dirty pieces of rag.
Chappie lay down by the subdued mercenaries and kept a
hopeful eye on them, just in case. Chance kept his voice
low, but his voice was sharp and severe.

"That was really not a good idea. Those soldiers were
operating on the Queen's authority, and so was Stout. He
may be a prick, but he's the Queen's prick. . . . I can't
believe I just said that. Look, the point is, you have very
little authority here in the Forest. You're not Guard Captains anymore, and you've refused to claim your Royal pre-
rogatives, so all you have left to back you up is your letter
of intent, purportedly from Prince Rupert. That, and my

support as King's Questor, will buy you some leeway, but you can't go on acting like this! You don't have the justification, and there's a limit to how much I can protect you. You're on your own here."

"Best way," said Fisher calmly.

"If I learned anything from my time in the Forest Kingdom," said Hawk, "it's that you have to come on strong, or they'll walk right over you. If Isobel and I act as though we have the authority to take names and kick arses, everyone else will let us. We *are* Rupert and Julia by proxy, and people will respect that as long as we act the part."

"And if they don't?" asked Chance.

"Then we start throwing people off the Castle battlements until they do," said Fisher.

"I wish I thought you were joking," said Chance. "I can't promise to protect you. I'm only the Questor."

"That's all right," said Hawk. "We've had lots of experience protecting ourselves. You worry about who's going to protect the Court from us."

"Oh, I am," said Chance. "Trust me, I am."

Leaving burning Customs tents behind them, they journeyed on through the Forest. The Forest Castle was still several days' hard riding away, but Hawk and Fisher were in no great hurry to get there. It had been a long time since they'd seen the rich colors and splendor of the Forest, and they were enjoying the slow return of old memories. Their horses easily followed the open path, and they were free to just sit back and look around them, drinking in the sights and sounds. It was summer, and the great tree branches were heavy with greenery. The trees soared up into the sky, their highest reaches bending over to form an interlocked canopy through which golden sunlight fell in thick shafts, full of swirling dust motes. The air was comfortably warm, almost drowsy, and full of the clean, fresh smells of living things. Birds sang, insects buzzed, and from all around came the slow cautious sounds of game on the move.

"God, this is a change after Haven," Hawk said finally.

"No more soot and sewers and sorcery; just the woods. It smells like home."

"You're right," said Fisher, almost dreamily. "I'd forgotten how . . . alive and uncomplicated the Forest is. It's a hell of an improvement over Haven, with all its stinks—"

"Trust us, we noticed," said Chappie, padding along beside the horses. "Place smelled so bad, I was beginning to wish my nostrils would heal over. I mean, I like a good roll in some muck as much as anyone, but there are limits."

"It's good to be back," said Hawk, not really listening. "Despite everything that happened here, this is still my home."

"I never really thought of it that way," said Fisher. "The Forest is only special to me because that's where I met you. I'm from Hillsdown, remember?"

Hawk turned in the saddle and looked at her uncertainly. "We could go visit Hillsdown afterward, if you want."

"No," said Fisher. "There's nothing for me there. What memories I have aren't happy ones. You're my home, Hawk—wherever you are."

They smiled at each other, then rode on for a while, enjoying the sharp staccato singing of the birds, and the endless low drone of insects. The horses meandered along, happy to be taking their time, while Chappie made brief darting journeys off the trail into the trees in search of food or amusement. Chance was quiet, watching in what he hoped was an unobtrusive way as Hawk and Fisher remembered who they had once been. For the first time he really began to see them as the legendary Prince Rupert and Princess Julia, who had saved the whole Forest from almost unimaginable horrors and evils. They seemed almost to grow in stature as their memories came back to them.

"I know this place," Hawk said suddenly. "I've been here before, on my way to Dragonslair Mountain. I was so determined to prove myself by finding and slaying a dragon. I thought that if I could do that, all the problems of my life would be solved. I'd be appreciated, respected, and all the rest of my life would be . . . sorted out. I was so young then."

"We both were," said Fisher. "And I was so frightened

of my father. Duke Alric of Hillsdown, undisputed monarch of all he surveyed. Except maybe his own family. I had seven sisters, all of us searching for our own identity by challenging our father in different ways. When he sent me off to die in the dragon's cave, I was almost relieved. It meant the worst was over, and I'd never have to be scared of him again. He could be terrible when he chose to be. At least there was a chance the dragon might be kind, and kill me quickly instead of by inches, like my father was doing. I wonder if I'll still be scared, when I meet him again at Forest Castle. It's been twelve years, and I'm so much more than I was then, but still . . . do we ever really see our fathers differently than when we were children?"

"Oh, I think so," said Hawk. "My father and I never really got to know each other till we were both adults, and better able to appreciate and understand each other. I suppose that's true for lots of people. You never talked much about your father before. It's hard to believe you were ever afraid of anyone."

"You never knew Duke Alric," said Fisher. "And I wish I never had, either."

Hawk smiled at her. "Don't you worry about your father, lass; if he even looks at you funny, I'll kick him up one side of the Court and down the other."

Fisher looked at him fondly. "You would, too, wouldn't you?"

"Damn right," growled Hawk.

"You worry me," said Chance. "Please remember that Duke Alric is an honored guest of the Forest Court, and as such has been promised all diplomatic courtesies and full protection from all forms of harm and harassment."

"That's all right," said Hawk. "I didn't promise him anything. And as Hawk, I'm not a citizen of the Forest Land, so the Court can't be blamed for whatever terrible thing I might do to him. Don't look so gloomy, Chance; we know how to behave diplomatically, if we have to."

"Right," said Fisher. "We didn't kill any of those Customs soldiers, did we?"

"And that's your idea of being diplomatic, is it?" asked Chance heavily. "Not actually killing anyone?"

"Well, mostly, yes," said Hawk.

Chance looked at the trail ahead of him. "If I had any sense at all, I'd turn around and ride away right now."

They rode on through the Forest. Days and nights passed, and all was quiet and peaceful. They met no one, but Chappie always found fresh game from somewhere, and they ate and slept well under the Forest canopy and the starry night sky. Bubbling streams ran fresh and clear, and long summer days were calm and pleasant, and Hawk and Fisher began to relax, almost against their will. They'd never been able to let their guard down in Haven, even when barricaded inside their own quarters. Chance saw the slow change in them, like soldiers home from the war at last, and approved. It was all going well, until they came to the borders of the Darkwood.

The Darkwood, the one place in the Forest where it was always night and the sun never rose. Where the trees were always dead and rotting, and nothing lived but demons. The Darkwood had returned to its original boundaries after the Blue Moon passed and the long night collapsed, but it was an ancient place, and could never be entirely destroyed. Hawk reined in his horse and sat there for a long time, staring into the darkness that fell like a curtain before him. The day ended abruptly in a straight line, the impenetrable dark turning aside the daylight with contemptuous ease. A cold breeze gusted eternally out of the blackness, carrying with it the stench of corruption and death. Hawk's horse wanted to back away from the dark and the smell, but Hawk wouldn't let it. Twelve years had passed since he'd last looked upon the Darkwood, but now he was back, and the horror in his heart was as fresh as yesterday. Fisher moved her horse in close beside him, knowing what he was feeling. They had both journeyed through that long night, and they still carried the scars on their souls.

"Why did you bring us here, Chance?" Fisher asked angrily. "We didn't need to see this."

There was a sudden harshness in her voice, a cold and dangerous edge that Chance had never heard directed at him before, and he paused a moment to be sure his voice would be calm and measured when he answered.

"We had to pass this way to reach the Forest Castle. And I thought we might perhaps use it as a short cut. Just passing through the edge would save us two days' journey."

"You've never been through the Darkwood, have you?" asked Hawk, not looking away from the darkness before him.

"Well, no—it's forbidden. But you'd been through it so many times, I thought you might want to—".

"No," said Hawk. "Been there, done that. I have nothing to prove to myself anymore. We go around."

"We go around," said Fisher.

And so they turned their horses aside, and rode around the boundary of the Darkwood. The cold and silent blackness frightened the horses, and they kept their heads turned away from it. Hawk kept his head turned away too. In his day, there had been a barrier between the Forest and the Darkwood; the Tanglewood. But that was long gone now, destroyed in the Demon War. There was no warning now, to give you a chance to prepare yourself; just a sudden transition from light and life and living things to the soul-destroying horror of the endless dark. Hawk could still remember his first journey through the Darkwood, along with his then companion, the unicorn called Breeze, and how close it had come to overturning his reason. In the cold and rotten heart of the Darkwood he had encountered a spiritual darkness, a stain on his mind and on his soul, and he carried the mark of it with him still.

Even after the driving back of the long night, it had been many years before Hawk and Fisher could bear to sleep without a nightlight.

"I'm sorry," Chance said finally, disturbed by the brooding silence Hawk and Fisher had fallen into. "I should have realized how much this place would affect you. Of course you must have terrible memories, terrible . . . I should have understood."

"You still don't," said Fisher. "It's partly because we don't want to have to kill any more demons, now that we know what they are. Or were. But it's more than that. Asking us to go back into the dark is like asking us to re-experience our own deaths. Haven't you ever talked to anyone who went through the Darkwood?"

"Very few people will speak of it," said Chance. "The only real hero left from that time is the Landsgrave, Sir Robert Hawke, and he can get quite violent if anyone's dumb enough to raise the question with him. He's always happy to talk about his heroics during the Demon War, and his close personal friendship with the legendary Prince Rupert, but . . ."

Hawk snorted, amused. "We were never really friends. We went through a lot together, fought side by side against appalling odds, but I can't say I ever really knew the man. There wasn't time. I respected him, certainly; he was a brave man and a fine warrior. I even took his name for my own when I went south. But we were never friends."

"Be that as it may," Chase said diplomatically, "he parlayed that famous friendship with a legend into a strong political career. Everyone loves a hero." He paused, and then risked another question. "Can you tell me what it was like, in the Darkwood?"

"Dark," answered Hawk. "Dark enough to break anyone."

"I was here once before," Chance said. "This is where I met Chappie. The Shaman had a vision; said he saw demons spilling out of the Darkwood. He made a hell of a fuss about it, so to shut him up, the King sent me to take a look. Just me, mind you; no soldiers or Rangers for backup. Luckily, it turned out the Shaman was only partly right. There was just the one demon, who'd sneaked out of the long night and was now lurking on the outskirts of a small town not far from here. The townspeople were terrified, naturally, but as far as I could tell, the demon hadn't caused any real damage yet. So I went to sort things out."

Chance paused for a moment, looking straight ahead, remembering. "I didn't want to kill it, not knowing what it had once been, but I was prepared to, if I had to. If I couldn't persuade or scare it back into the Darkwood, where it belonged. I wasn't really sure what to expect. I'd never actually encountered a demon before, close up. But

I figured, one demon out of the long night, how much trouble could it be?"

Fisher snorted, amused. "Hell, some of the things we faced in the long night were bigger than houses."

"And even the ones most like humans could still be real trouble," said Hawk. "Where do you think I got these scars on my face from?"

"I was just saying how I felt then," Chance said quietly. "I soon learned better. I found the demon easily enough. Once darkness fell, there it was, sitting in the town cemetery, squatting before the tombstones and reading the names aloud. It was white as a shroud, pale as a corpse, naked as a grub, with a twisted form and a face that was as much human as not. It had long curving claws on its hands and feet. It had trouble speaking because of all the fangs filling its mouth, but I could understand it. The demon made no move to attack as I approached; instead it just sat and studied me, as though trying to remember what I was. We talked for a while. The poor bastard had started to remember that it had once been human, and lived in this town. It had come out of the long night in search of its memories, its past life. It just wanted to go home, basically.

"Of course, it couldn't be allowed to. It was still a demon, with all its drives and appetites. Several pet cats and dogs had already disappeared. So far, it hadn't been able to remember exactly who it used to be, which was just as well. You can imagine the horror of its old family, if this misshapen thing had come hammering on their door, demanding to be let in.

"So I told the demon it had to go back where it belonged now, back into the Darkwood. It pointed out several of the headstones, and read the names aloud in its thick, guttural voice. They were all members of the same family. Maybe the demon's family, back when it had been human, maybe not. It was still very confused. And then it turned and looked out over the sleeping town, and it started crying.

"I patted it on the shoulder, reassuringly, and suddenly it turned on me, all teeth and claws and vicious strength. I should have drawn my axe the moment I saw the damned thing, but it had looked so pathetic. I hit the ground hard,

with the demon on top of me, and it didn't take me long
to realize the demon was much stronger than I was. Its
clawed hands fastened round my throat, and I couldn't
breathe. I pulled at its wrists with all my strength, and
couldn't budge them. And then this huge snarling fury
came flying out of nowhere and slammed into the demon,
knocking it off me. And that's how I met Chappie."

"What happened then?" Fisher asked after Chance had
paused for a long time. "What happened with the demon?"

"I killed it," said Chance. "What else could I do? I
couldn't let it stay anywhere near the town, and it would
have been cruel to make it go back into the Darkwood,
remembering what it had once been. So Chappie pinned it
down, and I cut its head off. Afterward, it turned back into
a human form, so I buried it in the cemetery, next to what
might have been its family. No marker, of course. I never
knew its name, and I couldn't ask in the town. It would
only have upset people."

"You did what you had to," said Chappie. "You had no
choice. You didn't tell them the worst part. The demon
had already dug up several graves in the cemetery, and
feasted on what it found there."

"It just wanted to go home," said Chance.

"Don't we all," said the dog.

"When we got back to the Forest Castle, they told me
King Harald had been murdered in my absence," said
Chance. "His enemies had come for him, and I wasn't there
to protect him. If I hadn't gone off after that demon—"

"The King would have died anyway," snapped Chappie.
"The King was protected by Sir Vivian and his guards, and
the bloody Magus' magical wards, and the killer still got to
him. What could you have done to protect him, that all
those people couldn't?"

"I don't know," said Chance. "And because I wasn't
there, I'll never know."

Not long after leaving the Darkwood behind, they came
to a clearing Hawk recognized. He shouldn't have been
able to; it looked like just another clearing, like so many
they'd already passed through, but somehow he knew. He

could feel the difference in his bones, and in his soul. He stopped his horse abruptly, and looked about him. Fisher had to rein in her horse and come back to join him. Being in the lead, Chance didn't notice for a while, and Chappie had to yell to him to come back. He quickly turned his horse around, one hand near his great axe, but there was no sign of any threat. The birds were singing, the grass was thick and luxurious, the trees stood tall and proud. Just one more Forest clearing.

"You know what this place is, too, don't you?" Hawk asked Fisher.

"Of course. How could I not know?"

"Well, how about letting us in on the secret?" said Chappie as he and Chance came back to join them.

"This is where we met the Demon Prince," said Hawk. "In what was then the sick heart of the Darkwood. This is where I called down the Rainbow to banish the darkness. This is where we emerged from the long night, when the Darkwood was thrust back to its original limits. And this is where the High Warlock told me my father, King John, was dead."

"Damn," Chance said softly. "*This* is the place? All the songs and legends tell of it, but no one ever seemed to know exactly where it was." He looked eagerly about him, trying to see what Hawk and Fisher saw, but all he saw was a Forest clearing. "This is history! There should be . . . I don't know, a plaque or a shrine or something. So people could come here, on pilgrimages—"

"No," said Hawk. "Let it stay a legend. The reality would only disappoint them, just as it's disappointing you. You built this place up in your imagination till no reality could match what you saw in your mind's eye. This place isn't important. It's what we did here that matters."

"And some of what we saw and did here are best kept to ourselves," said Fisher. "We still have nightmares, sometimes."

"I would have given everything I had, to have been a part of such an undertaking!" said Chance.

"That's the legend talking," said Hawk. His hand rose slowly to his face, as though the old scars were bothering him. "The reality was somewhat different. You look at this clearing and see only awe and wonder and the triumph of the light. We look at it and remember horror and pain and how close we came to losing everything. I saw my father betrayed by his oldest friend. I saw my Julia crippled, by a living horror older than humanity. I saw Death stare me in the face and grin. I called down the Rainbow, and it was bright and glorious and wonderful beyond belief, but in the end that's not what I remember."

"We remember the dark," said Fisher. "We always will."

Chance could hear the revulsion in their voices, and looked around the clearing again, straining to see something of what they saw, but he couldn't. For him, it was just a clearing. He decided to change the subject.

"You said this is the last place you saw your father, Your Highness?"

"Hawk. I'm just Hawk now. But yes. He was alive when we banished the Demon Prince, and he lived to see the Darkwood thrown back, but the strain was too much for him. He died here, and the High Warlock magicked the body away. He never would say why; only that he had done what was necessary. And knowing what I know about my father, and his part in the coming of the long night, I never questioned the High Warlock. I didn't think I wanted to know."

"What you're hearing now isn't part of the legend," Fisher said to Chance. "And if you're smart, you won't repeat any of it."

"Of course not," Chance agreed quickly, though there were many questions he wanted to ask.

"For a long time, I wasn't sure whether I really believed my father was dead," said Hawk. "I never saw his body. And part of me didn't want to believe it . . . because I never got to say good-bye. But the more I hear about what's happened to the Forest Land, the clearer it is that King John has to be dead. There's no way he could stay hidden with so much going on. And he would have come back from the shores of Death itself to avenge his murdered son, if he could. So he's dead. Just like Harald. Which only leaves . . . me. The last of my line. There's

Harald's son, Stephen, of course, but he's half Hillsdown. I could be King, if I chose. I have that right. It could be said to be my duty."

"But you don't want to be King," said Fisher.

"No," said Hawk. "I don't."

Time to change the subject again, thought Chance. "There's no doubt about the High Warlock being dead, I'm afraid. The Magus told us when he came to Court to announce himself the Warlock's chosen successor. King Harald needed to be sure the High Warlock was dead, so he sent some admittedly rather reluctant emissaries to the Dark Tower, to check out the situation. They found the High Warlock dead in his chair, and the Tower deserted, so they collapsed the whole damned Tower on top of him, to be his cairn. And perhaps also in the hope that all that weight of stone would be enough to hold his spirit down, and keep it from wandering."

"I'm still pissed off about that," said Chappie. "Barbarians! It was my home, too."

"So much death," Hawk said tiredly. "No wonder we stayed away so long."

They rode on through the Forest. More days passed. There were many areas of dead trees and dead land, places blighted by the fall of the long night that had still not recovered, and perhaps never would. There were trees with no leaves, whose dark trunks crumbled at the touch, rotted away from within, and whole clearings where nothing grew, and the bare ground was cracked and dry. Silent, because no living creature would enter these places, and even the birds and the insects avoided them. Old wounds that would never heal. The horses didn't want to enter these places, either, and on the few occasions when there was no other choice, the riders had to keep a hard rein to prevent the horses from bolting. They tossed their heads, eyes rolling, and their hooves threw up dust and ashes where they walked.

Some parts of the Forest would take generations to recover. And some never would.

Dotted here and there in the woods, in quiet clearings

and open glades, they came across many small churches and shrines. Most were Christian, simple places for worship and celebration, but there were other shrines, too, for older gods and more ambivalent forces. The long night had put the fear of God into the Forest population, and they took their comfort where they could find it. There were standing stones and crude altars, marking old places of power and the occasional genius loci; old battlefields in the never-ending struggle between good and evil, or light and dark. Fresh garlands of flowers lay curled around ancient stones with fresh markings, along with simple prayers written on scraps of paper and weighted down with smooth stones on which open eyes had been painted. Prayers for good weather and better harvests, or just to keep the dark times at bay. There were even occasional small shrines for Prince Rupert and Princess Julia, and old King John, too, with flowers and simple offerings, and pleas for their return someday. Hawk found them touching, but Fisher just turned up her nose. Fisher had always believed that God helps those who help themselves.

They were heading into the more populated areas now, passing through the many new small towns and villages built to replace those lost or destroyed during the Demon War. Bright and shining with freshly quarried stone and new timber, the paint and plaster were still wet on the most recent additions. In the larger towns, new buildings sprouted up amongst the old like new flowers in an old garden. They were all lively, busy places, thronging with people, many of whom still had strong Redhart or Hillsdown accents. The new arrivals had made their mark in other ways, too, showing clearly in unfamiliar architectural styles, and their own transplanted ways and traditions. Hawk found some of these alien ways upsetting, in what should have been the heartland of his old home, but he did his best to hide it. Wherever they had come from, they were Forest people now. His people if he decided to be King. So he smiled and nodded at the friendly faces, and felt more of a stranger in this new Forest Land than they did.

It was early evening when the rain came down, sudden and hard. Thunder rumbled directly overhead, and lightning flared blue-white in the darkening sky. They had come to a place where the trees were widely spaced, and there was no obvious shelter. The horses tossed their heads unhappily, and Chappie slunk in close beside Chance, his tail between his legs and his ears flattened, flinching with each new crash of thunder. Hawk spotted the ancient signpost, half hidden in tall grass, that pointed the way to the small town of Breckon Batch, and they hurried down a narrow trail already fast turning to mud under the driving rain. Chance was the only one with any rain gear, and he didn't have time to stop and put it on, so they were all pretty soaked when the flaring lightning showed them a squat stone tavern on the edge of town, the Starlight Inn. They stabled their horses in the modest lean-to beside the tavern, and hurried inside, though Hawk paused to give the swinging sign a dubious look. The Starlight was a clear reference to the original Starlight Duke, who'd rebelled against a Forest King long ago, and split off his own territory to form what was now Hillsdown. In Forest history, the Starlight Duke was an infamous traitor, and in Rupert's day naming a Forest inn after him would have been an open treason.

Not surprisingly, the Starlight Inn turned out to cater mostly to Hillsdown immigrants. The patrons fell silent as the newcomers came crashing into the dim smoky room, stamping their boots on the stoop and shaking the rain from their cloaks, but they warmed up quickly once Chance introduced himself. It seemed the Questor's good reputation was known throughout the Kingdom. Hawk and Fisher looked on just a little jealously as the inn's patrons made a fuss over Chance and gave him the best seat by the fire. The tavern owner produced jugs of hot mulled ale, and wouldn't hear of them going any further that night, not in such terrible weather. He had rooms available, at very competitive prices, and he wouldn't take no for an answer. He called for the serving wench to bring dry clothes, and room was made for Hawk and Fisher at the fire. Chappie lay as close to the flames as he could get, steaming happily.

Soon they were all dry and comfortable, and more able to take an interest in their surroundings. The crowd seemed pleasant enough, though their thick Hillsdown accents sometimes made their speech impenetrable to Hawk. Chance and Fisher were more used to it, so Hawk just sat back and let them do most of the talking. He was more interested in studying the changes the immigrants had brought with them, even to something as simple and basic as a tavern. Most obviously, there was the sign of the fish everywhere, instead of the cross; reminders that these people had their own separate Church. Many of the drinks on offer behind the wooden bar were unfamiliar, and when hot food finally arrived, it consisted of traditional Hillsdown delicacies, most of which Hawk just looked at dubiously. The main offering was a deer's entrails steamed in a sheep's stomach. Fisher attacked it ravenously, saying loudly that it had been a long time since she'd had a chance at such good food.

"It's the spices that make all the difference," she said to Hawk, somewhat indistinctly. "Eat up; this'll put hairs on your chest."

"Then why are you eating it?" muttered Hawk, prodding the steaming mound before him with a fork.

"If you don't want it, I'll have it," said Chappie.

"Now there's a surprise," said Chance. He was eating his portion with no apparent problems, so Hawk reluctantly tried a small mouthful. He then decided he was rather hungry after all, and did his best to eat without thinking too much about what he was actually chewing. The spices did make a difference.

The innkeeper bustled over, a broad-shoulder and barrel-chested man who had clearly been a soldier at some time in his life. "Is all to your liking, Sir Questor? Here, let me stick the hot poker in your ale again, warm it up some. And is there anything else your servants would be needing?"

"We are not his servants!" said Hawk, looking up sharply.

"My apologies, sir. And what might you be, then?"

"His companions," said Fisher as Hawk struggled for an answer. "We're on our way to the Castle."

"Good luck to you all then, sir and madam; 'tis a very unhappy place at present, so I've heard. What with the King so sudden dead, God bless him, and no one any clearer as to the who or why."

"How did you feel about the King?" asked Hawk. "I mean, he wasn't your King for long."

"He was our King," said the innkeeper firmly. "We all swore allegiance to him when we first became Forest citizens. And proud we were to do so. The old Duke, he ruled well enough in Hillsdown, I suppose, but he never really cared for his people, or for what they thought of him. Wasn't a bad sort, really. As long as you paid your taxes on time and kept your mouth shut about things that didn't concern you, he mostly left you alone. But King Harald, he was a hero; saved us all from the long night. A good man, so I've heard tell."

"Do you find things better then, here in the Forest?" said Hawk.

"Well, yes and no, Your Honor. There's more land for every man, but that means more work in the tending of it. More freedom, I suppose, but the price of everything in the markets is a damn sight higher. And it doesn't *feel* like home here yet, if Your Honor understands me."

"Yes," said Hawk. "I think I do. This was my home, but I've been away a long time. And much has changed in my absence."

"Change is in the air," said the innkeeper, moving among them to top off their jugs with fresh ale. "With the King gone, God bless him, there's talk of politics everywhere. I mean, the Queen does her best as Regent, God bless and save her, but her son, Stephen, is many years off being a man's age. There are those saying we should seize the opportunity, and make changes now, while we can."

"What sort of changes?" said Fisher.

"Any and all sorts, ma'am," said the innkeeper cheerfully. "News from the south tells of all kinds of political systems, and the idea of democracy is on every man's lips. Though every man seems to have his own idea of what that should mean. There's speeches and gatherings all over the place, and representatives from the rich and the powerful promising a lot in return for support. With the King gone and the Queen so weakened, God bless them both, it seems like everyone's getting ready to toss their hats into the ring. And then there's Duke Alric, of course." The innkeeper frowned for the first time. "Supposedly he's here to comfort the Queen in her time of loss, but more likely he's here to tell the Queen what to do, and none of us like the sound of that. We came here to get away from the Duke."

The conversation went on for a while, as tavern conversations have a way of doing, going around and around with everyone chipping in, but never actually getting anywhere. Eventually the talk wound down, and the tavern patrons left to go to their homes, lurching and bumping into each other. The innkeeper showed a by now very sleepy Chance and Hawk and Fisher to their rooms. The Questor got the best room in the tavern, of course, as befitting his stature and good reputation. But he did have to share it with Chappie, who still smelled distinctly damp. Hawk and Fisher got a small, pokey room that was little more than an attic. They wouldn't give the innkeeper the satisfaction of an objection, so they just smiled and nodded till he left, and only then looked unhappily about them.

There was a very uncomfortable-looking bed, under a blanket that looked like it was more used to covering a horse; an inch of candle in a pewter holder; a bucket in the corner whose smell told them exactly what it was for; and one tightly shuttered window. Outside, the storm was still going strong, with the rain hammering on the roof overhead. Hawk and Fisher stripped off their borrowed clothing in weary silence, and finally cuddled together under the rough sheets. With the candle blown out, the room was pitch dark, save for the occasional flash of lightning that showed eerily around the edges of the shuttered window.

"Does the dark bother you?" Fisher quietly asked Hawk.

"No. Not as long as you're here."

"Me neither. We'll be at the Castle in a few days."

"Yes."

"Then what do we do?"

"Play it by ear. This isn't the Forest we remember. Things are different now. Odds are the Castle will be different, too. But it doesn't matter. We'll find Harald's murderer and see the guilty punished. Because we're Hawk and Fisher, and that's what we do."

"Damn right," said Fisher.

They laughed quietly together, lay awhile listening to the storm, unable to reach them for all its fury, and then they both slept soundly until morning.

And just a few days later they at last came in sight of Forest Castle. They stopped awhile where the tightly packed trees fell away suddenly to form the edge of a huge clearing, so Hawk and Fisher could savor the moment. Or perhaps just so they could put off the moment when they'd have to go home. Beyond the wide clearing was the dark-watered moat, and beyond that, Forest Castle. Truth be told, it didn't look like much from the outside. To the untutored eye, it looked like just another time-battered Castle, and a good sight smaller than most. The great stone walls were cracked and pitted from long exposure to the elements, and here and there could clearly be seen patches of white against the gray, where new stone had been brought in to make repairs after the demons' final assault in the last hours of the long night. The tall, crenelated towers had a battered, lopsided look, and the flags on the battlements hung limply in the hot, breezeless day.

But within the walls that had served fifteen generations of Forest Kings was contained a much larger Castle, with a thousand rooms to every wing, banquet halls and ballrooms, servants' and guards' quarters, stables and kitchens and courtyards. And more than a few wonders and mysteries. Of which the most recent, or the oldest, depending on how you looked at it, was the Inverted Cathedral.

Hawk looked at what had once been his home, and actually felt vaguely nostalgic for a while, until he remembered how they'd treated him the last time he'd come home, bringing with him Princess Julia, and a dragon he'd been supposed to kill.

"You're scowling again," Chance said wearily. "All right, what is it this time? Don't you have *any* good memories of your past life here?"

"Not many," said Hawk. "I don't know what the legends say about my early days, but the truth is, I was despised, discounted, and unnoticed by just about everyone. I was the second son, never to be King. That was always Harald's destiny. He always looked the hero's part. I never did. So my father sent me out on a quest, ostensibly to prove my worth, to find and slay a dragon. In reality, I was supposed to take the hint and just keep on going, into exile, and thus remove a potential threat to Harald's succession. Only I was too honorable, or too dumb, to see that. So I made my way through the Tanglewood and the Darkwood, climbed Dragonslair Mountain, and found my dragon. And Princess Julia. I befriended them both, and brought them back home with me.

"I think it fair to say absolutely no one was pleased about that. Harald actually challenged me to a supposedly friendly duel, so he could knock me about in front of an audience, and put me firmly back in my place. As he'd done so many times before. But I'd learned a lot in my time away, and I cut him to ribbons, right there in front of everyone. That felt so good until the Champion did the same thing to me. He did everything but carve his initials on me, to remind me of my proper place. He did so enjoy proving he was still the best. You look shocked, Chance."

"I can't believe they never respected you, your . . . Hawk. Were you always treated like that?"

"Pretty much," answered Hawk.

"They behaved vilely toward him," said Fisher. "They never appreciated him, even though he was always the best of his family."

"Well, you'll find much has changed here since then," said Chance. "Your memory is revered now. And yours, Fisher."

"Some things never change," said Hawk. "I'll probably still have to kick arse and generally act up to get anything done. I'm quite looking forward to it."

"Me, too," said Fisher.

They grinned at each other, remembering happy times, and Chance stirred uncomfortably in his saddle. Every now and again he wondered if he was doing the right thing in bringing back Hawk and Fisher to a Court that already had more than its fair share of troubles. He decided it was time for another change of subject.

"The Castle interior is probably much as you remember

it. Rooms and locations still change back and forth, according to their own impenetrable logic, and directions still vary according to which day it is when you ask. Though it must be said those rooms nearest the Inverted Cathedral tend to change places more rapidly than most. Perhaps because they're afraid to stay close to it for any length of time. The Seneschal is still the only one who knows where everything is at any given time. He and his staff are still on top of things. Mostly."

"How is the old stick?" said Fisher warmly. "He was always a game old bird. He never approved of me, but no one did back then. Is he still a major pain in the arse?"

"He's mellowed somewhat. Marriage and children, coming late in life, seem to have settled him down. As long as you catch him on a good day."

"How does he feel about the Inverted Cathedral?" Hawk asked.

"Officially, he's still studying it. Unofficially, it scares the crap out of him, just like everyone else. It's the one place in the Castle he's never been, and he has stated loudly, for the record, several times, that wild horses couldn't drag him inside the unnatural construction. But he's still the first one to listen whenever the scholars in the libraries turn up some new fact or story or rumor about the Inverted Cathedral's history."

"That doesn't sound like the Seneschal I remember," said Fisher, frowning. "I was there when he led an expedition to rediscover the missing South Wing. I never saw him frightened of anything, even when we ran into a bunch of demons. The Seneschal I knew never backed down from anything."

"The Inverted Cathedral is different," said Chance. "Where once it rose up into the heavens, now it plunges down into the depths."

"I know, you told us," said Fisher. "So what? I was there when the Seneschal came across an upside down Tower, during our search for the South Wing. It was weird as hell, but he was the first one through the door."

"You don't understand," said Chance. "No one knows

how deep the Cathedral goes now. Some say it goes all the way down to Hell."

There was a pause as Hawk and Fisher considered this. "We saw the Demon Prince sitting on a rotten throne in the heart of the Darkwood," Hawk said finally. "I think we've already seen everything Hell has to offer."

"Sure," agreed Fisher. "And we lived in Haven for ten years. There's not much that throws us anymore."

They rode back into the clearing, and no one challenged them. The quiet of the great man-made clearing, after so long among the living noise of the woods, was almost threatening. The Castle grew steadily larger and more imposing as they approached it. Hawk found his right hand had dropped to his axe without him even noticing. Fisher was scowling so hard, it must have hurt her forehead. Even Chance looked troubled, though Hawk couldn't help thinking that was probably more due to him and Fisher than to the Castle.

They crossed the clearing without incident and came to the moat. It looked pretty much as disgusting as Hawk remembered it. Dark shapes swam slowly through the murky waters, half hidden by the layers of shifting scum on the surface. Hawk stopped his horse just before the lowered drawbridge, and stared down into the moat. Fisher stopped beside him.

"Chance," Hawk said slowly, "is the moat monster still in there, guarding the Castle?"

"Oh, yes," said Chance, reining in his horse. "Him and his offspring."

Hawk and Fisher looked at him sharply. "Offspring?" asked Fisher. "What the hell did he mate with?"

"No one's ever really liked to ask," said Chance.

They rode on across the drawbridge, the heavy wood hardly shaking under the weight of the horses and riders and Chappie. Dark things with improbable shapes popped their heads up through the scum of the water to take a look at the new arrivals, but were always gone again before Hawk and Fisher could get a good look at them. They seemed mostly interested in Chappie, who ignored them all with cutting indifference.

They rode on through the towering stone Keep and the open gatehouse, and on into the Castle's main courtyard. The waiting crowd assembled there could no longer contain themselves. They burst out into cheers and shouting and wild cries of welcome, all but drowning out the brass band's official welcoming fanfare. Hawk's horse immediately tried to turn and bolt, and for a while he was too busy struggling to control his horse to understand what was happening. He actually had his axe half drawn before he realized the huge crowd was actually pleased to see him. Though to be honest, they seemed to be mostly cheering the return of the King's Questor, Allen Chance. He smiled and waved graciously about him, as though perfectly used to such treatment, and Hawk supposed he was. The Questor was a real hero.

The courtyard was packed wall to wall with people jumping up and down and craning their necks for a better view of the new arrivals. A large professionally painted banner high up on the far wall blazed the words "Welcome home! Prince Rupert and Princess Julia! Saviors of the Forest Land!!!" The brass band was oom-pahing through the national anthem with more enthusiasm than skill, but no one was paying any attention. Apparently, garbled word of the Questor's return had preceded him, and the crowd had gathered to celebrate the successful completion of his mission. Two young pages in full ceremonial uniforms stood proudly at attention on a raised dais below the welcome banner, holding the two Royal crowns of the Forest Kingdom on purple velvet cushions.

But already the roar of the crowd was beginning to die away as the people looked eagerly for the legendary figures of Prince Rupert and Princess Julia, and didn't see them. The Questor they knew, and his dog, but the two shabby figures with him looked nothing like the official portraits of Rupert and Julia. So the crowd looked beyond Hawk and Fisher, hoping to see someone else, someone more impressive, behind them, and when it became clear that there was no one else, the crowd's noise died quickly away in confusion. The brass band was the last to get the message, and carried on playing as Chance and Hawk and

Fisher rode their horses slowly through the middle of the crowd. One by one the instruments fell silent as the musicians realized something was wrong, and the three riders and Chappie crossed the last of the distance in stony silence.

Chance reined in his horse at the foot of the great stone stairway leading up to the main door, and dismounted. Hawk and Fisher swung down to join him, in a silence so complete, their every movement could be heard. They kept their hands near their weapons. They knew how quickly the crowd's mood could change, especially if it's just been denied something it really wants. Chance was doing his best to look undisturbed, but Chappie was sticking close to him, glaring at the crowd as though daring them to start something. Hawk caught a movement out of the corner of his eye, and spun around sharply as the main door swung open, and a familiar face appeared, followed by a lot of guards. Hawk and Fisher moved to stand close together as Sir Vivian Hellstrom, High Commander of the Castle Guard, strode down the steps to face them.

Sir Vivian's gaunt, raw-boned face was so pale as to be almost colorless, topped with a thick mane of silver-gray hair. There was a calm and studied stillness to his face that suggested strength and determination, but his eyes gave him away. They were hard and unyielding; fanatic's eyes. He was lean and wiry rather than muscular, but there was a deadly grace to his few economical movements. Once he'd been Lord Vivian, and a major player in Castle society, but Harald, then Prince Harald, had revealed Vivian's plot in a conspiracy against King John, and so Vivian lost his lordship, and his freedom. But because Vivian was who he was, King John gave him a second chance. He sent Vivian out to defend the most exposed peasants in the long night during the Demon War, with the promise of a pardon if he returned alive after the war. Vivian had always been a survivor. So he came back victorious, and a hero to the peasants. King Harald knighted him for his services, and put him in charge of Castle Security.

Vivian Hellstrom, hero of Tower Rouge and a legend in his own right. And a pardoned traitor.

Hawk only knew what Fisher had told him of Vivian's treachery, but he could see the naked suspicion in Fisher's cold gaze as she looked on the High Commander. He stayed close to her, though whether to protect her from Vivian or Vivian from her, he wasn't sure. Fisher had never been one to forgive and forget. A full company of armed and armored guards filed out of the main door behind Vivian, spreading out to take up what could have been either a ceremonial or a defensive formation. Hawk remembered earlier times when he had returned from fighting the Kingdom's battles only to be faced with cold ingratitude from the very people he was protecting. Maybe nothing had changed after all.

Chance cleared his throat loudly, and all eyes turned to him. "Greetings, Sir Vivian," he said easily. "It's good to be home again. Thanks for the welcome. Nice turnout."

"It is good to see you again, Sir Questor," said Sir Vivian in his cold, even voice. "Where are Prince Rupert and Princess Julia?"

"Ah," said Chance. "That's something of a long story, I'm afraid."

As he launched into it, smiling bravely all the while, Hawk took the opportunity to distract Fisher by quietly filling her in on the background of Vivian Hellstrom's legend. He should have done it earlier, when he knew they were going to have to deal with Sir Vivian, but somehow he had never gotten around to it.

In the beginning there had been the two Hellstrom brothers, Vivian and Gawaine, more famous for their parentage than anything else. Their father was the High Warlock, their mother that most notorious and evil sorceress, the Night Witch, who lived alone deep in the Darkwood. The first anyone knew of the twins' existence was when the Night Witch sent them as babies to the Forest Castle, carried tenderly by demons right up to the front door of the Castle. A short note gave their names and their parentage, and a prophecy that one day they would save the Forest Land.

The High Warlock was summoned from a nearby tavern. He stayed just long enough to acknowledge them as his, then turned them over to foster parents and went straight back to his tavern. When the Hellstrom brothers came of age, they enlisted in the Forest army, and saw much action in the vicious border disputes of the time between the Forest and Hillsdown. Most notably, they defended Tower Rouge at Hob's Gateway, standing alone after all their comrades were killed, facing down a whole battalion of Hillsdown troops until reinforcements could arrive. Their brave stand saved the Kingdom from imminent invasion, and made them legends.

King John knighted them both. Songs were still sung about that brave stand at Tower Rouge, and the two noble warriors who would not be beaten, despite all the odds against them.

"You can't trust songs," Fisher said finally. "Hell, you've heard some of the songs they sing about us. I only ever knew Vivian as a conspirator and a traitor. Anything else I ought to know about the Hellstrom brothers?"

"Gawaine's settled in Redhart these days. Left the Forest under something of a cloud, I gather. He has one child, the Seneschal here at Forest Castle. Prince Rupert met their mother, the Night Witch, once—"

"What was that?" Sir Vivian interrupted sharply, looming suddenly over them. "How do you know that? That's never been part of Rupert's legend!"

Hawk decided he was going to have to be very careful in the future what he said about his previous life. "That's the legend as we heard it in the south, Sir Vivian, but I'm sure you know how much a story can change on its travels. Has Chance explained things to you?"

"He has, and I don't believe a word of it. I'm supposed to believe you're here out of the goodness of your hearts? To help a King and a country you know nothing of? Why should you do such a thing?"

"Why did you stand your ground at Tower Rouge against impossible odds?" asked Hawk.

Sir Vivian just grunted, then looked hard at Hawk and Fisher. They did their best to stand easy, entirely calm and unruffled, but this was the first real test of their new identities. Sir Vivian had good reason to remember Princess Julia. But in the end he just grunted again, unimpressed.

"So the Prince and Princess won't be coming back, despite our most desperate need. Perhaps you would care to explain why."

"They're needed elsewhere," said Hawk smoothly. "A matter of conscience and duty. I'm sure you can understand that." He looked about him. The great crowd in the courtyard was still silent, hanging on his every word. Hawk decided to concentrate on Sir Vivian, who was marginally less disconcerting. "We are Hawk and Fisher, Guard Captains. We have a lot of experience in investigating and solving murders. Rupert and Julia authorized us to act on their behalf here; to speak with their voices and exercise their authority."

"And why would they choose you?" Sir Vivian asked coldly.

"Because we're very close," said Fisher.

"You have some proof of your office here, of course," said Sir Vivian in a voice that suggested he very much doubted it.

"Of course," said Fisher. She handed over the letter of introduction Hawk had prepared earlier. "It's in Rupert's own hand, signed by both Rupert and Julia, and bears Rupert's seal at the bottom. You do recognize the Royal seal of the Forest Kings, don't you?"

Sir Vivian scowled, but nodded reluctantly. There had only ever been three Royal seals, one each for John, Harald, and Rupert. Handed down through generations of the Forest line, they were magical constructs and could not be duplicated. The letter might have been forged, the seal, never. He handed the letter back to Hawk, and then glowered at Hawk and Fisher equally.

"What precisely was so important that the Prince and Princess could turn their backs on the Forest Land?"

"That's their business," said Hawk politely.

"I have a right to know!"

"No, you don't," said Fisher. "If they'd wanted you to know, they'd have put it in the letter. All you need to know is they're not coming, but we are here to do everything they would."

"Wonderful," said Sir Vivian, almost viciously. "This will

change everything. The King's death left the Court and the country divided into factions almost beyond counting. Prince Rupert and Princess Julia are legends. Real heroes. All sides had agreed to an uneasy peace, awaiting their return. The Prince and Princess were the only people everyone would have trusted, or at least listened to. Once the news gets out that all we've got is you, the peace will collapse in a second. The last thing the Court or this country needs is two outsiders upsetting the political process and walking all over our customs and beliefs."

"Don't worry," said Hawk. "We know how to be diplomatic."

"Sure," said Fisher. "We just don't bother, usually."

Sir Vivian looked deeply unhappy, and just a little shocked. It had been a long time since anyone had dared talk back to him. As High Commander of the Guard, his position and his legend had always been enough to intimidate anyone not actually of Royal birth. He was about to launch into a ferocious diatribe on correct behavior that would have seared their ears, when his gaze suddenly fell on the axe at Hawk's side. He studied the wide axe head in silence for a long moment, taking in the runes etched into the steel, and then he looked at Hawk with new eyes, and something very like respect.

"My brother, Gawaine, had an axe like that. Our father, the High Warlock, gave it to him after Tower Rouge. Because he wanted to show how proud he was of his bastard sons. I could have had one, too, but I asked for something else, which I later threw away. Where did you get that axe?"

"From the High Warlock," said Hawk. "I did him a service once."

"But how did you get it?"

"Mail order," said Fisher briskly. "Look, are you going to invite us in, or not? We've got a hard job ahead of us, and we'd like to make a start."

"Very well," said Sir Vivian. "Against all my better judgment, I'll take you in and present you to the Court. Though what they'll make of you is not my problem. Follow me.

Stay close and don't wander. And, Sir Questor, we will have words about this later."

"Looking forward to it immensely, Sir Vivian," said Chance, smiling widely and just a little desperately.

"Lies like that will take you straight to hell," said Chappie.

"Shut up," said Chance.

They followed Sir Vivian in through the main door, and the (possibly) ceremonial guards fell in around and behind them. The door slammed loudly on the continuing quiet in the courtyard. Fisher moved in close beside Hawk.

"If Gawaine got an axe from the High Warlock, what did Vivian get that he lost?"

"His lordship," said Hawk.

Sir Vivian gave orders for all further celebrations to be canceled immediately, and led Chance, Hawk, and Fisher to Court by the least traveled route, working on the assumption that the fewer people who knew Rupert and Julia weren't coming back, the better; at least until Hawk and Fisher had been presented and, he hoped, accepted, at Court. He also sent guards off with orders for the rest of his people to prepare for possible civil unrest and even rioting. Many people had invested a lot of faith in Rupert and Julia's return, and there was no telling how they might express their disappointment.

Hawk had to keep from looking happily about him. It was the first time he'd been inside his old home for twelve long years, and everywhere familiar sights and objects leaped out at him, bringing back memories; from old family portraits to suits of ancient armor to assorted bric-a-brac that apparently no one had gotten around to throwing out. Even the most worthless junk can acquire a patina of worth and history if people hold on to it long enough. Especially if there's a story attached to it. Or people think there is, or used to be. The old familiarity of home came flooding back, and it was only with an effort that Hawk remembered how glad he'd always been to get away from the Castle. Prince Rupert had rarely been happy here, and with good reason. Most of the people who persecuted him and made his life miserable were dead and gone now, lost in the

Demon War, but their ghosts still haunted his memory. He glanced across at Fisher to see how the Castle was affecting her, but she seemed to be taking it all in her stride, as she did most things.

From Sir Vivian's reluctant answers, Hawk discovered that the Court was still in session, despite the late hour of the evening, under the Regent, Queen Felicity. The day's business should have been concluded long ago, but apparently with so many factions, political parties, and causes all demanding to be heard, or at least noticed, it was taking longer and longer to reach an agreement on anything. Raised voices and hot tempers were commonplace, and it was a rare session that ended without some level of bloodshed, despite all Sir Vivian's guards did to maintain order. Hawk had to get most of the details from Chance, after Sir Vivian decided he wasn't talking to Hawk anymore. Anyone would think he was upset.

On their way to the Court, they passed through a great hall crammed full of magic-users of every and any persuasions, all of them eagerly demonstrating their powers and abilities to anyone who showed an interest, or would at least stand still long enough. The raised voices, flaring lights, and sudden transformations made for a unique form of bedlam, and Hawk and Fisher stopped to watch, fascinated. Most of the Forest Land's previous magicians had died during the last great battle of the Demon War, poisoned by the treacherous Astrologer. Afterward, rather than be left helpless in the face of possible magical attacks from neighboring Hillsdown and Redhart, King Harald had put out a call for all magic-users in the Land, of whatever cause or quality, to come to the Forest Castle and serve the Land. And so they all came, eager for a chance to be put on the Royal payroll. Since most of them turned out to be meagerly talented, incompetent, or outright frauds, the search went on, even today. The Forest couldn't afford a magic gap.

Everyone in the hall now was waiting to be seen, to be granted an audience at Court to show what they could do. Hedge witches, conjurers, summoners, warlocks, necromancers, and enchanters, and one self-proclaimed messiah. Some had been camped out in the hall for days, and small stall-holders were doing a brisk trade in food, wine, and toilet essentials. The noise was appalling, not least because the Court hadn't actually gotten around to viewing anyone that day. In this, as in so many things, the Court was running well behind schedule.

One magician had apparently duplicated himself several times by accident. He was now standing in a small crowd of himself, arguing loudly over which was the original, or at least the most real. Another magician waved his hands theatrically over an upturned top hat, chanting loudly. The chant was suddenly interrupted when a huge clawed hand shot up out of the hat, grasped the magician by the throat, and then pulled him inside the hat. Those watching studied the rocking top hat for a moment, but there was no sign of the magician reappearing. A few clapped tentatively. One braver soul picked up the hat, turned it over, and shook it, but nothing fell out.

Not far away, a self-proclaimed conjurer of devils and apparitions was loudly offering to teach magic to anyone with the right price. As proof of his abilities he produced several impressive objects apparently out of midair. There was great applause, some cheers, and even a few startled cries. Hawk was not impressed. He'd seen street conjurers in Haven, and knew how most of the tricks were done. Conjurers had to be really impressive in Haven, because if they weren't, the audience would kill them. Of course, if they got too good, there was always the chance someone or *something* would turn up from the Street of Gods, and do something terribly unpleasant to them for trespassing on godly territory. Miracles belonged in churches. Hawk strode over to the conjurer, spun him around twice, and slapped him hard on the back. Several startled doves shot out of the conjurer's sleeves, a firework went off, and an unconscious rabbit dropped out the back of his coat. People began closing in on the conjurer, loudly demanding their money back, and Hawk left them to it. Chappie ate the rabbit.

Sir Vivian invited Hawk, in a somewhat strained voice, to continue on to the Court, and Hawk nodded amiably. Illusions snapped on and off around them as they made their way through the mob of magic-users. Falls of multicolored hail contended with the pale wisps of ghostly butterflies. Here and there clumps of the more intellectual practitioners were having animated discussions over the merits and/or drawbacks of Wild, High, and Chaos magics, and threatening to turn each other into things. One had actually conjured up a blackboard so he could prove his point with angrily chalked mathematics. Somebody else was making women's clothes vanish. Hawk shook his head bemusedly.

"I thought magic was supposed to be going out of the world," he murmured to Fisher.

She shrugged. "If it is, it's not going quietly."

The Academy of the Sisters of the Moon was well-represented, with its own stall, a registration drive, and several graduated witches in their familiar silver gowns, trying hard to look mysterious. According to Chance, the Academy had been turning out witches for some time now, but they had yet to produce anything even approaching a sorceress. But witches had their uses, and their low-level magic made them welcome at hospitals, churches, and in the army. Any witch was potentially capable of becoming a sorceress, but that took time and study and experience, and apparently most witches just didn't survive that long. The world was a dangerous place, and the unseen world even more so.

Chance suddenly broke away from the group and surged forward through the crowd as he recognized a familiar face among the witches. She turned to meet him, smiling sweetly. She was tall and buxom, in a low-cut russet gown, with a magnificent mane of flame-red hair, and huge green eyes full of a happy personal magic. Her name was Tiffany. Hawk and Fisher knew this because Chance had been talking about her all the way through the Forest to the Castle. It seemed he was much taken with Tiffany, though it wasn't clear how she felt about him. Still a teenager, she was the youngest witch ever to graduate from the Academy of the Sisters of the Moon, and great things were expected of her.

Powerful but naïve, she believed in everything, from crystals to tarot to channeling past lives to the healing powers of certain aromas. She was prone to wandering in the woods, picking flowers to give to the poor, whether the poor wanted them or not, and having long conversations with squirrels and birds and butterflies. Chance told Hawk and Fisher all of this at some length, even when they asked him very firmly not to.

By now Chance and Tiffany were clasping hands and smiling into each other's eyes. Hawk and Fisher wandered over to get a good look at this most praised person. Sir Vivian tried to protest, but they just ignored him. Start as you mean to go on. Chance and Tiffany were so wrapped up in each other, they didn't even notice Hawk and Fisher's approach. They tried coughing loudly, but when that didn't work, they just stood there and studied the young witch thoughtfully. Up close, there was no denying Tiffany's beauty, but her gaze and smile were just a little too vague for Hawk's liking.

"It's so good to see you again, Tiffany," said Chance, grinning like an idiot. "You're looking beautiful, as always."

"That's nice," said Tiffany. "So, Allen dear, what have you been doing with yourself?"

"I've traveled through the Rift into the south, in search of Prince Rupert and Princess Julia," said Chance importantly.

"Oh, have you been gone? I hadn't noticed." Tiffany turned her happy smile on Hawk and Fisher, not seeing Chance's crestfallen look. "Are you friends of Allen's?"

"We're Hawk and Fisher," said Hawk. "We're here to investigate King Harald's murder."

"Oh, good," said Tiffany. "Welcome to Forest Castle. I could have told Chance he wouldn't be able to bring back Rupert and Julia. I often channel the Princess, and we have long talks."

"No, you don't," Fisher said firmly. "I know the Princess, and I can tell you right now she's never bloody heard of you."

There was no telling where this conversation might have gone, so it was lucky for all concerned that it was interrupted by the sudden arrival of a large and blocky man in an impressive magician's gown of deepest black. He'd shaped and trimmed his black beard to within an inch of its life, and wore a large golden medallion around his neck. He ignored everyone else to scowl ferociously at Tiffany, who just smiled sweetly back at him. If anything, this seemed to upset the newcomer even more.

"I've told you before, witch, I won't have you spreading your infantile nonsense here! I don't care if you have graduated from the snobby Sisters' Academy, all this new-age waffle is a waste of everybody's time, and threatens to bring us all into disrepute. Crystals! Flower scents! Pyramid power! Nonsense, all of it!"

"Have you had a good bowel movement recently, Mal?" asked Tiffany. "You know missing one always makes you grumpy."

"I am not grumpy!"

"Did you try the enema purge I recommended?"

"Never mind the enema! I want you out of this hall right now!"

"I think we can assume the enema didn't work," said Chance. "Who is this . . . person, Tiffany?"

"I am Malvolio the Magnificent!" roared the magician, pulling himself up to his full height. "Master of the mathematics of the universe! All who live shall bow before my genius!"

"What do you want to bet he's an ex-boyfriend?" Hawk asked Fisher, who nodded solemnly.

"I broke it off," said Malvolio haughtily. "She was too immature for me. Right now, all this flower child frippery is undermining the mystery and awe of magic, and could affect all our chances of making a proper impression before the Court. I want this child out of here, and I want her out now!"

"Have you considered personal counseling?" asked Tiffany. "Just lying down and talking to someone can be very therapeutic."

"You see what I mean!" The Magnificent Malvolio's face took on a dangerous shade of purple, and his eyes bulged half out of their sockets. "Therapy? What kind of talk is that for a real magic-user? Magic is power! And glory! It's all about the domination of the universe and everything in it through the superior will of the adept, and I will not allow this little chit—"

"Tell me something," Chance broke in. "When did you last get your ashes hauled?"

Malvolio glared at Chance. "I take pride in keeping myself pure and inviolate. Power comes from the disciplined mind."

"Thought so," said Chance. "Personally, I've always thought there's more to life than power. I suggest you find yourself a nice healthy girl and settle down together. In the meantime, I think you should leave, right now. Before I decide to show you a trick I know, involving this battle axe and your lower intestines."

"Oh, don't hurt him, Allen!" Tiffany said immediately. "I'm sure he didn't mean to be rude. His aura's obviously out of balance. His spleen must be overproducing."

"If he's still here when I've stopped talking to you, I'm going to get his spleen out so we can all get a good look at it," Chance said firmly.

He looked around slowly and deliberately, just in time to see Malvolio the Magnificent stalking away, his chin held up so high, it must have hurt his neck. Tiffany looked at Chance reproachfully.

"You've upset him now."

"I certainly hope so," said Chance. "Some people should be upset as a matter of principle, on a regular basis. It's good for their souls. You never told me he used to be your boyfriend."

"He was just a friend," Tiffany said guilelessly. "I have lots of friends."

Chance decided to change the subject before it went somewhere he might not like. He reached inside his jerkin. "I brought back a present for you, Tiff. All the way from Haven. That's a powerful city-state in the south."

"Oh, how sweet of you, Allen! I love presents. What have you brought me?"

Chance smiled and brought out from inside his jerkin a flat red box tied with a pink ribbon. Tiffany all but snatched it from him, cooed over the ribbon, and then ripped it away, dropped it to the floor, and pried open the box. She dropped that unceremoniously to the floor, too, as she concentrated on the glowing blue crystal in a delicate silver filigree setting. Tiffany cooed over that as well, turning the crystal back and forth to catch its gleam in the changing light. She leaned forward to peck Chance on the cheek, and he blushed like a child. Tiffany didn't notice. She was already studying the crystal again.

"Oh, Allen, it's lovely! How thoughtful of you. This crystal has very positive vibrations."

And then she peeled away the intricate silver setting with her fingers and let it drop to the floor, so she could hold the unadorned crystal up before her eyes and stare into its depths. Chance looked at the crumpled silver setting on the floor, and then bent down and picked it up.

"We're on our way to Court, Tiffany. I can't stay. See you later?"

"If you like, Allen." Tiffany waggled her fingers at him in a good-bye, nodded briefly to Hawk and Fisher, then stopped and stared at them thoughtfully. Hawk felt an unpleasant prickling at the back of his neck. Witches had the Sight, and were reputed to be able to see the future, as well as other things. Witches often knew things they weren't supposed to. Tiffany looked from Hawk to Fisher and back again. She frowned. It looked out of place on her pleasant, unlined face. "You have both been touched by Wild Magic," she said slowly. "I can see it hanging about you, like chains to a terrible past. You bring blood and change. You have two shadows, behind and before you. I see you going down and down . . . to an awful place . . ." She shuddered suddenly. "You scare me. I can see the Blue Moon in your eyes."

"That's enough, Tiffany," said Chance. He took her by the arm and pulled her firmly away from Hawk and Fisher. "We have to be going now."

He gathered up Hawk and Fisher, and led them away. Tiffany watched them go with wide eyes. Chance looked at the silver filigree in his hand, the delicate workmanship crumpled and ruined, and put it back inside his jerkin. "Maybe she'll want it later," he said to no one in particular.

"Humans in heat," said Chappie disgustedly. "Is there anything more embarrassing?"

Sir Vivian looked thoughtfully back at the young witch, and then at Hawk and Fisher, but he waited till they'd left the magicians' hall before raising the subject. He leaned in close, his voice low, as though he didn't want his own people to hear what he was saying.

"What was that all about? What did she mean?"

"Damned if I know," Hawk said easily. "Sounded like a prophecy of some kind, but I've never put much faith in such things."

"She mentioned the Blue Moon."

"So she did." Hawk shrugged. "She also claimed to channel Princess Julia, but since Julia is definitely still very much alive . . ."

"She's a witch," said Chance shortly. "They See too much of the world. Their minds don't work like ours do."

"I don't think Tiffany's mind works like anybody else's," said Fisher. "It's a wonder to me she can tie her own bootlaces."

"Witches are fairly low-level magic-users," said Hawk quickly. "Why do they have such a presence here?"

"The Queen puts great faith in the Sisters of the Moon," said Sir Vivian carefully. "She has officially asked the Academy to investigate the matter of the King's death. It seems she doesn't entirely trust the Magus or his investigation. Can't think why."

"And since Tiffany is quite definitely the most powerful, if not the most experienced, witch the Academy has ever produced, the Mother Witch put her in charge of the investigation," said Chance. He didn't sound too happy about it. "She's barely left the Academy; spent most of her life behind their walls. How we do things in the real world is still something of a mystery to her."

"Innocent but powerful," said Fisher. "A dangerous combination."

"Oh, yes," said Chance. "Much like me, after I left St. Jude's. Single-sex institutions have a lot to answer for."

"How does the Magus feel about this involvement of the witches?" Hawk asked thoughtfully.

"So far he's completely ignoring them," said Sir Vivian, who seemed to have forgotten he wasn't talking to Hawk. "The Magus has always been very good at not seeing things he doesn't want to see."

"I'm surprised we haven't seen him yet," said Chance. "I was expecting him to be there to greet our return. I mean, this whole journey south was mostly his idea."

"The Magus is currently attending the Court," said Sir Vivian, sharing a look with Chance that Hawk caught but couldn't interpret. "The Magus spends a lot of time at Court these days."

"How about the Shaman?" asked Chance. "Another face suspicious by his absence. It doesn't seem like the Castle without him bursting into other people's gatherings, to make a speech or pick a fight."

"No one's seen him all day," said Sir Vivian, frowning. "Which means he's plotting something again. The Shaman is always most dangerous when he's not around. That man never chooses a straight line if he can find a more devious one. If I thought I could enforce it, I'd ban him from the Castle, but . . ."

"Yes," said Chance. "But."

"He's much more than he seems to be," said Sir Vivian. "But then, that's true of a lot of people here at Forest Castle."

"Including you?" asked Fisher.

"Oh, of course," said Sir Vivian solemnly.

Hawk stopped abruptly as something on the wall to his right caught his attention. Fisher followed his gaze and stopped with him. There on the wall before them, nine feet tall, were the official portraits of Prince Rupert and Princess Julia, living legends of the Demon War. Prince Rupert stood tall and heroic, heavily muscled inside formal plate armor chased with gold. A single straight scar ran down the wrong side of his face, and he still had both his eyes. The artist had given Rupert's face a noble, almost saintly look. Princess Julia stood barely five feet tall, wearing a long flowing gown of midnight blue, with gold and silver piping. Diamonds gleamed brightly on rings and bracelets and necklaces, and her long blond hair was piled up on top of her head in an intricate style. Hawk and Fisher studied the images in silence for a long while.

"We never looked that good in our lives," Fisher murmured finally.

"Right," said Hawk, just as quietly. "No one's ever going to recognize us from these. Talk about idealized. No wonder we're such a disappointment, compared to *them.*"

"Don't worry," said Fisher. "We'll soon make our mark. In someone's forehead, if necessary."

And then they both jumped as they realized someone was standing right there beside them. He definitely hadn't been there a moment before. He had suddenly and silently appeared out of nowhere. While Hawk waited for his heartbeat to return to something like normal, it occurred to him that such a practice could quickly become extremely irritating.

"Good evening," said the new appearance. "I am the Magus."

"Of course," said Fisher. "You would have to be."

Hawk glowered at the Magus to show how unimpressed he was, but he took his hand away from his axe. Fisher pushed her sword back into its scabbard. The Magus was a few inches less than average height, with a round, calm face under a sparse mousey haircut. His eyes were a faded blue, and his mouth held a constant gentle smile. He had an almost absentminded stare, and his gaze tended to drift, as though he was always thinking of something more important. His clothes were at least thirty years out of fashion, and ruthlessly formal, topped off with a huge enveloping cloak of midnight blue, whose top rose up and over the Magus' head, as though watching over him. He was a man who knew things. Hawk knew this immediately, just from looking at him. There was a low but menacing growl from behind Hawk, and he looked quickly around to see Chappie backing away to hide behind Chance's legs, his tail between his legs.

"Bastard!" growled the dog. "You jump out of nowhere near me again, and I'll bite your bum off!"

"Chappie!" snapped Chance immediately. "Show some respect."

"He smells *wrong*," said Chappie defiantly. "High Warlock's successor, my hairy arse."

The Magus ignored both of them with the ease of long practice. "Welcome to Forest Castle, Captain Hawk, Captain Fisher. I've been expecting you for some time."

"How could you?" asked Fisher suspiciously. "No one knew we were coming instead of Rupert and Julia, and word hadn't had a chance to get ahead of us."

"How do I know anything?" the Magus asked pleasantly. He plucked a long-stemmed rose with no thorns out of nowhere and presented it to Fisher with a slight bow. She smiled slightly, charmed despite herself. Chappie sniffed loudly.

"Show-off."

"I know why you're here," said the Magus, his calm gaze drifting over to Hawk. "I can't think of anyone better suited than you to investigate poor Harald's murder."

"How could he have been killed when he was protected by your magical wards?" Hawk asked bluntly. He could tell the Magus was trying to be charming, but Hawk didn't feel like being charmed.

"That is one of the few things I don't know," said the Magus, his voice still unwaveringly calm. "Technically speaking, it should have been impossible. No doubt you'll work out the answer in time. But then, answers aren't everything. I've always been more interested in questions. The truth rarely makes us happy, or even satisfied."

"Is that why you've been unable to solve the King's murder?" Sir Vivian asked harshly.

"Nothing is as it seems," said the Magus vaguely. "But then, that's business as usual in Forest Castle. Here, there are secrets hidden inside enigmas, and false faces everywhere." He smiled at Hawk and Fisher. "I don't have to tell you that. The past is coming back to haunt and possess the present, and not all old ghosts have been laid to rest."

"You know," said Fisher, "just once I'd like to meet a sorcerer who wasn't so fond of his own voice. It always has to be riddles and mysteries. *What the hell are you talking about?* Can't you say anything open and straightforward?"

"Very well," said the Magus. "The Blue Moon is coming back."

Hawk and Fisher looked at each other sharply, and then at Chance and Vivian, but judging by their startled faces, this was news to them, too.

"Would you care to elaborate on that?" asked Sir Vivian.

"No," said the Magus. "Follow me, please. Court is still in session, and I'm sure everyone there could use someone new to shout at."

He drifted off down the corridor. Hawk couldn't help noticing that the sorcerer wasn't casting a shadow. Fisher gave a start as the long-stemmed rose she was holding collapsed suddenly into a pale pink mist and floated away. Sir Vivian smiled.

"Just another illusion. You can't trust anything where the Magus is concerned."

"But he does know things," said Chance. "From the past, the present . . . and the future. No one keeps secrets from the Magus."

"Then why can't he see who the killer is?" Hawk asked.

"Good question," said Sir Vivian.

They set off after the Magus, heading for the Court. They'd all pretty much run out of things to say, though they had a lot on their minds. Hawk was trying to figure out how he felt about the Magus. For a supposedly first-rate sorcerer, the Magus didn't have anything like the air of authority that the High Warlock had always had, even when in his cups. The High Warlock had always been a very dangerous man, and everyone knew it. The Magus, on the other hand, was quiet, serene, almost self-effacing. He didn't look like he had it in him to be threatening. But still, there was something about the man, something almost sinister. As though he knew many things he wasn't supposed to know. Knowledge can be power, particularly if blackmail is involved. Hawk pondered the implications of that all the way to the Court.

They eventually came to a halt before huge closed double doors that led into the Courtroom. By tradition no one was allowed entrance to the Court once the doors were closed, without express permission from the Throne. Raised voices could clearly be heard from behind the doors, rising and falling in angry chorus. Hawk had a sudden strong sensation of déjà vu. He'd stood here once before, as a much younger Prince Rupert, waiting to be allowed into Court, to learn what his future would be. In those days, many people had had power over him. Or thought they had. Most of those people were long dead now, but even so, Hawk felt an unfamiliar uncertainty run through him, like a cold breath of his past, from memories he'd never been entirely able to forget.

"They're all in there," said the Magus, studying the closed doors as though he could see right through them. "The Queen, the Landsgrave, the Duke . . . all the would-be movers and shakers."

"The Landsgrave?" asked Sir Vivian. "I wasn't aware he was even back in the Castle."

"He's been speaking, on and off, for some time," said the Magus. "Sir Robert always did have a lot to say. Unfortunately, so does everyone else. And they're all too busy fighting to be heard to listen to what anyone else is saying. No wonder they never get around to deciding anything. I often wonder if I should change them all into birds. At least then they'd make a pleasant noise. See if you can do anything with them, Captains. Someone has to. Before the bad times come."

"So you keep saying," growled Sir Vivian. "But until you're prepared to be more specific about the nature of this threat, you can't blame us for not taking you too seriously. If I want my future told, I'll ask a witch to read the tea leaves in my cup."

"Patterns can be seen in many places," said the Magus. "As above, so below. Nature reflects the supernature. I see many things. Luckily not all at the same time. The future is constantly shifting, shaped and determined by the decisions we make every day. But some things are inevitable. Magic is going out of the world, but that, too, could be changed. Nothing is certain in this world, not even death, in some circumstances. Right, Captains?"

Hawk and Fisher, who had died once in a bloody cellar deep under the city of Haven, said nothing but thought much.

The Magus gestured lazily at the closed doors with a limp hand, and they flew open, swinging inward as though the huge slabs of oak were weightless, crashing back against the inner walls. The great reverberating sound silenced the acrimonious roar of the Court for the moment, and the Magus led his party forward into the shocked silence. The packed crowd drew back to form a wide aisle for the Magus to walk down. It seemed no one wanted to get too close to him. Hawk and Fisher followed after him, looking about them to see how much the Courtroom had changed in their absence. The vast, spacious hall looked much as they remembered, perhaps a little cleaner, illuminated now by modern gas lights rather than the fox fire lamps of old. The last of the evening light was falling through the gorgeous stained-glass windows, most of it falling on the raised dais at the end of the hall, on which stood the ancient Forest Throne, carved in its entirety from a single huge block of oak. The Magus stopped some distance short of the Throne and slipped his cloak from his shoulders. He then walked forward, leaving the cloak hanging unsupported on the air.

"Don't get too close to the cloak," the Magus murmured to those courtiers nearest. "I haven't fed it recently."

He stopped directly before the Throne, and bowed courteously to the imperial figure sitting on it. Queen Felicity acknowledged his presence with the merest inclination of her crowned head. The Magus gestured for Hawk and Fisher to approach, and they did so, giving the hanging cloak a wide berth. They could feel the eyes of all the Court upon them in the continuing strained silence, but did their best not to show it. Regardless of what authority they might or might not have, they still understood the importance of making a good first impression.

"Your Majesty," said the Magus easily, "may I present to you Captains Hawk and Fisher, from the south, authorized by Prince Rupert and Princess Julia to investigate the terrible murder of your dear departed husband, the King."

Hawk and Fisher smiled at the Queen on her Throne,

and nodded briefly. Strictly speaking, they should have bowed low, or even knelt, but Hawk and Fisher didn't do things like that. Besides, it was important to get off on the right foot. Hawk studied the Queen openly, as she studied him.

Queen Felicity was tall, fashionably slender but with a heavy bosom, and showed the world a sharp bony face under a thick mop of blond hair, in ringlets so tightly curled, they just had to be artificial. Her face was powdered so pale, it seemed like a mask, while her lips were a vivid scarlet. Her eyes were cold and knowing, and her tight-lipped smile was openly cynical. She was smoking a cigarette in a long dark ivory holder, Southern style. Her other hand held a cut-glass goblet, half full of wine. She was dressed fashionably but formally, her long golden gown studded with pearls and polished semiprecious stones. The ancient, simple crown of the Forest line was almost hidden in the thick blond curls. Her scarlet fingernails looked long and sharp enough to rip someone's throat out. Armed guards stood on either side of the Throne. They looked tense, as though expecting a threat at any moment.

Hawk was still wondering exactly what he should say to the Queen, when there was a sudden interruption. A tiny figure, no more than nine inches high, fluttered swiftly through the Court, bobbing over the heads of the courtiers, some of whom ducked and gasped, until finally the figure settled elegantly onto the Magus' left shoulder. He smiled at her fondly as she sat down, arranging herself comfortably. Hawk gasped despite himself as he realized he was looking at a winged faerie. She was spindly thin but normally proportioned, with a cloud of jet black hair over a pinched face and pointed ears. Her wide translucent wings held all the hues of the rainbow, shifting and sliding like the colors on the skin of a soap bubble. She wore a black basque, fishnet stockings, and heavy black eye makeup. She grinned at the Magus.

"Hello, lover. Miss me?"

"Always, my dear." The Magus beamed at her and then turned to Hawk and Fisher. "Captains, allow me to present to you that darling of the dark, mystical marvel and leader of fashion, Lightfoot Moonfleet, last of the faerie kind to dwell in the world of mortal men."

"Hello, darlings," said Lightfoot Moonfleet. Her voice was quiet, but quite distinct. Her smile was impossibly wide, and her dark eyes sparkled brightly. "Always good to see new faces at Court. The old ones can be terribly dull. We haven't had a decent scandal in ages."

Hawk was delighted at the sight of her, so much so that words stuck in his throat. No one had seen one of the wee folk in years; certainly decades, maybe centuries. People were always reporting sightings, but it usually turned out to be the moon or shooting stars. It was common belief that the faeries had been extinct for ages.

"Delighted to meet you," he managed finally. "Are you really the last of your kind?"

"The very last," said Lightfoot Moonfleet. "My kind walked sideways from the sun long ago, out of history and into legend, in the place where shadows fall. Our time is over, sweetie. Magic is going out of the world, whether it wants to or not, and there's less and less room in your organized and scientific world for monsters and miracles and mysteries. And the faeries *were* magic. I only stayed behind because the Magus needs me. Whether the poor dear will admit it or not."

In a moment too fast for the human eye to follow, she suddenly grew in size, shooting up to fully seven feet tall, towering over Hawk. He would have liked to fall back, but his legs didn't feel strong enough. Full size, her blatant sexuality was overpowering, almost crackling on the air. Her dark eyes smoldered, and her crimson mouth curved in a wicked smile. Her skin was pale but perfect. She smelled strongly of rose petals and honey, with an underlying hint of pure animal musk. She reached out and took his chin in one petal-soft hand, and he felt his breath catch in his chest.

"Of course," said Lightfoot Moonfleet, "I've always had a weakness for the strong, silent type. And I do so love a hero."

And then she shrank rapidly back to her previous size, flying quickly back to the Magus as Fisher's clenched fist swept through the place where her head had just been.

Fisher recovered her balance in a moment, and glared at
the wee winged faerie, back on the Magus' shoulder again.

"We are married," Fisher said coldly. "No trespassing.
Or I'll make your wings into doilies."

The faerie shrugged prettily. "Understood, sweetie. I was
only just testing the waters. I was always taught people
should share their toys."

"You so much as flutter in his direction again," growled
Fisher, "and they'll be using what's left of you for a pipe
cleaner."

The faerie winced. "Do you think you could be a little
less premenstrual about this, darling?"

"I'm pretty sure I used to have an owl on my shoulder,"
said the Magus, his eyes far away. "Or was it two ravens?
Or perhaps a crow, from the land of the dead. I've had to
reinvent myself so many times, I sometimes confuse the
details. I am large. I contain multitudes. Especially on
Tuesdays."

"If we could return to more important matters," said
Chance, just a little desperately. He stepped forward beside
Hawk and Fisher, gesturing urgently for them to look at
the Queen again. "Captains, may I present to you Queen
Felicity, Regent of the Forest Land, protector of the King-
dom, mother of the King-to-be, Stephen."

"Good to be here," said Hawk to the Queen. "I just
know we're going to get along famously."

Chance winced.

"Why aren't you Rupert and Julia?" snapped the Queen,
leaning forward on her Throne to glare at Hawk and
Fisher. "They have to come back. It's their duty. They're
needed. I don't want to be sitting here in a dusty hall, in
front of a crowd of half-wit politicians and social climbers,
stuck on a wooden Throne while my arse goes numb, but
I'm here. Talk to me, Captains. And make it bloody convincing, or I'll have the Magus turn you into something
more aesthetically pleasing. Like a pair of throw cushions."

"Well, you could try," said Hawk pleasantly, not at all
bothered by the Queen's harsh words and manner. "But
trust me, it wouldn't get you anywhere. First, Fisher and I
are immune to change spells. Second, we'd kill you before

you got to the end of the sentence. We are Hawk and Fisher, and we don't take crap from anyone. On principle."

There were shocked gasps and mutterings from the packed Court. Those nearest Hawk and Fisher and the Magus pushed back hard against the press of the crowd, determined to get further away from any magical unpleasantness. The Queen's guards had their hands on their swords, awaiting her order to attack. Chance had his eyes shut, and was shaking his head slowly. Chappie was sniggering. The Magus studied Hawk and Fisher thoughtfully, still smiling his enigmatic smile. Surprisingly, Queen Felicity was also smiling. She leaned back in her Throne, flicking ash off the end of her cigarette.

"At last, someone with balls. I like that. You have no idea how refreshing it is to get a straight answer out of someone round here. Of course, if you're dumb enough to try it again, I'll have you executed from a safe distance. I'm not so sure I really wanted Rupert and Julia back anyway. Legends and heroes can be so . . . unsympathetic when it comes to dealing with everyday realities and people's little weaknesses. So, Hawk and Fisher, talk to whomever you have to, do whatever you have to, but find my husband's killer. I want his head on a spike. Whatever else you might discover along the way is probably best kept to yourselves. If you want to get out of this Castle alive. Do we understand each other?"

"We do," said Hawk. "I want his head on a spike, too."

The Queen glared at Fisher. "What about you? Don't you have anything to say for yourself?"

Fisher had been deliberately keeping quiet, not wanting to draw the Queen's attention. As Julia of Hillsdown, she'd never had much to do with her sister Felicity. There were eight Princesses at the Hillsdown Court, all living separate lives. Partnerships and conspiracies weren't unknown, sometimes against other sisters, but always from a distance, through intermediaries. It wasn't wise to get too close to somebody who might be your enemy tomorrow. Or who might disappear today, if the Duke took against you. The sisters followed their own interest, and led their own lives.

Sophia was very religious, and rarely left her rooms, except to go to Chapel. Althea lived and breathed politics, ignoring her sisters as mere dilettantes. And Felicity was mostly interested in men. There were rumors that the Duke had tried fitting her with a chastity belt, but she'd worn it out from the inside. As the youngest, Julia had been of least use to her other sisters, and so saw less of them than most. Which suited her just fine. She was mostly interested in finding new ways of getting into trouble, perhaps as a way of getting her distant father's attention. Until she went too far, and the Duke sent her off to die.

She and Felicity had mostly only even seen each other at a distance. Even so, Fisher was worried Felicity might recognize her, despite the intervening years and her new black hair. She carefully lowered and roughened her voice before replying to the Queen, just in case.

"I'm Fisher. I work with Hawk. We'll find the killer. It's what we do. And we're very good at it."

"And we don't need threats to motivate us," said Hawk.

"You don't speak to the Queen that way, dammit!" snapped Sir Vivian.

"Sure we do," said Hawk. "We're here to find a murderer, not bow and curtsy and kiss hands. We'll do whatever we have to to get at the truth, and we won't take piss off and die for an answer, no matter who it comes from."

"That's what I like to hear," said the Queen. "Most of this bunch take seventeen paragraphs and a non sequitur just to ask if they can leave the room. They wouldn't last five minutes in the Duke's Court. There's a lot of questions that need answering about my Harald's murder, and I haven't been able to get straight answers out of anyone. Of course, I'm just the Queen. Maybe you can do better. If anyone's evasive, feel free to give them a good slap. Two if they're a politician."

Hawk smiled and nodded, and looked slowly around the packed Court. The courtiers looked back, nonplussed. Openness and sincerity weren't something they were used to seeing in Court. If only because if everyone spoke the truth about how they felt in public, there'd probably be a bloodbath. Hawk had been away a long time, but he had no trouble spotting patterns among the courtiers. There were political groupings, family clusters, and all the usual cliques, most of them busy glaring at each other or cutting each other dead with raised noses and averted glances. Some things never changed. Hawk looked back at the Queen, who had just emptied her wineglass and was studying Hawk and Fisher with a bitter smile.

"I sent my Questor out in search of two living legends, and he comes back with a pair of scruffy-looking thugs. Typical of the way things are going these days. I need thugs, because we seem to have left the days of heroes behind us, and all we have left are . . . politicians. The way of the future, they tell me. Not much of a Kingdom for my son to inherit. The Forest Land isn't what it was. I should have stayed in Hillsdown. All right, it was a dump, but it never had any pretensions of being anything else." She raised her glass again, realized it was empty, and pouted sulkily.

"Where have all the heroes gone? Did they ever really exist? I don't suppose they'd have had much time for the likes of me, but I would have liked to have met a real hero, just once. If only because he might have seen something in me." She shook her head suddenly. "Oh, don't mind me, I'm just the Queen. And I'm having a very bad day. Someone get me another drink. Are you sure there aren't any execution warrants for me to sign? That always cheers me up." She shifted uncomfortably on the Throne. "Jesus, tonight this oak is hard on the bum. Someone bring me another cushion, right now. Who the hell's idea was it to have a wooden Throne anyway? I live in fear of splinters." She broke off, and glared ominously at the courtier heading out of the crowd toward her. "And what the hell do you want, Sir Martyn?"

The courtier came to a stop beside Hawk and Fisher and smiled dazzlingly at the Queen. He was dressed in the very latest Southern fashions, bright and gaudy as a peacock's tail, right down to the pink wig, pale blue eye makeup, and several heart-shaped beauty spots. But he still carried himself like a fighter, and the sword at his side was anything but ceremonial. He bowed to the Queen and smiled graciously at Hawk and Fisher in the most patronizing way possible.

"My apologies for intruding on your . . . soliloquy, Your Majesty, but I think I speak for all your Court in saying that we require more information on your chosen investigators' background. We don't know them. They could be anybody. One can quite understand that the legendary Rupert and Julia might not wish to return to a Land where so much has changed in their absence, but at least they were known. These, forgive me, *riffraff,* are hardly suitable for such a delicate undertaking. I mean, you can't expect the quality to answer inquiries from grubby little people like this."

"And you are . . . ?" asked Hawk politely.

"Sir Martyn of Ravenslodge. I speak for continuity. Tradition. The unbroken line of aristocratic authority and achievement. And I can assure you, no one of any substance will be answering any questions from you or your compatriot until we have strong and compelling evidence of your derived authority, and written confirmation that you will observe confidentiality where necessary."

"My wife and I were Guard Captains in the city port of Haven," said Hawk, still ominously calm. "We've investigated a great many murders in our time."

"Haven?" queried Sir Martyn, not quite openly sneering, but still pronouncing the word as though it was a small scuttling insect. "Never heard of it."

The Court muttered loudly in agreement. It was clear that while they might have sat still for questioning by living legends, they had absolutely no intention of being interrogated by nobodies. Particularly when they all had pasts, secrets, and motivations they'd prefer not to discuss at all. Hawk sighed quietly. Just once, it would have been nice if everyone could have been reasonable, but . . . When in doubt, fall back on the tried and tested ways: intimidation, sarcasm, and open brutality. He glared about him, and under that cold determined gaze the courtiers quickly grew silent again. They knew a predator when they saw one. Hawk turned his eyes on Sir Martyn, who, to his credit, didn't flinch one bit.

"Raise a hand against me, sir, and my people will cut you down," he said flatly.

"Then we'll just have to kill them, too," said Fisher easily. "We are completely impartial. We have no political, religious, or social preferences. We hate, loathe, and despise everyone equally. And you can move that hand away from your swordhilt right now, because if you don't, we'll take it away from you, and make a kebab out of you as an example to the others. We may not be living legends, but we're the most frightening thing you and yours will ever see."

"You can't threaten us all!" said Sir Martyn, but he didn't sound quite as sure as he had. There was something about Hawk and Fisher, something in their calm voices and cold eyes, that told him they meant every word. They had to know they were facing impossible odds, but everything about them clearly said they didn't give a damn.

"We can do anything," said Hawk. "Because we don't care about anything but the truth."

"And to hell with whoever gets hurt in the process," said Fisher. "You're politicians and aristocrats. You're all bound to be guilty of *something*."

"Your Majesty!" Sir Martyn turned entreatingly to the Queen. "I appeal to you!"

"No, you bloody well don't," said Queen Felicity cheerfully. "I like them with a lot more meat on. And you always were too smarmy for my tastes, Martyn. And you've got some nerve appealing to me for support, when I know damn well you and your treacherous friends have been plotting to have me replaced as Regent, so you'd have more direct influence over Stephen's upbringing."

Sir Martyn turned reluctantly back to Hawk, his hand well away from his sword. "Captain Hawk, be reasonable—"

"Sorry," said Fisher. "We don't do reasonable. Now be a good little politician and fade back into the woodwork before you lose your deposit."

"You're very good when it comes to intimidating chinless wonders like Martyn," said a new voice. "But not all of us are so easily browbeaten."

Hawk looked around quickly. He knew that voice. It had been twelve years, but he knew that voice and always would. And sure enough, a familiar figure came striding out of the crowd to confront him as Sir Martyn retreated. Still lithe and muscular despite approaching middle age, head held high and moving with a calm grace that bordered on arrogance, the man Rupert had known as Rob Hawke came to a halt before the Throne. There was gray in his hair, and age and good living had softened the harsh features, but Hawk knew him immediately.

Rupert and Rob Hawke had passed through the Darkwood together, fought demons side by side, guarded each other's back, risked their life for the other without a second thought. Rob Hawke was one of the few surviving real heroes of the Demon War, knighted afterward by King Harald for his services to the Land. A warrior who'd impressed Rupert so much, he took Hawke's name for himself when he went south. He was also possibly the only man here to have seen Rupert with his scars and eyepatch, if only briefly. If anyone here would recognize Hawk as Rupert, it would be this man. Hawk did his best to stand at ease, unmoved, and met his old companion's gaze steadily.

"And you are . . . ?" he asked.

"Sir Robert Hawke, Landsgrave. I speak for Reform. And I don't intimidate easily."

"I know," said Hawk. "I've heard some of the songs about your exploits in the Demon War."

"Believe everything you've heard," said Sir Robert. "And after the long night, there's not much left that scares me anymore."

They stood and looked at each other in silence for a long while. Two men who had once been closer than brothers, but had grown apart in such different ways. The years had not been kind to Sir Robert. Up close he looked a lot older than his age, and there was a harshness to his face, as though he had been much beaten about by life. He looked more like the father of the man Rupert had once known. Hawk couldn't help wondering if he'd changed that much, too.

"We're here on the authority of Prince Rupert and Princess Julia," he said carefully. "And we have the backing of your Queen. Do you defy them?"

"Not necessarily," said Sir Robert. "Not just now. I'll give you enough rope to hang yourselves. But tread carefully, Captains. There's a lot going on here you don't know about. There are secrets within mysteries, and not everyone's truth is the same. Not everyone is always who or what they appear to be."

Hawk and Fisher looked at each other, unsure whether that was a hint of recognition or not. Certainly nothing in Sir Robert's face or gaze suggested that he recognized Rupert and Julia. Perversely, Hawk felt almost disappointed. How could Rob Hawke have forgotten him so completely, after all they'd been through together?

Sir Vivian stepped forward to fix Sir Robert with his icy gaze. "You seem to know so much about this tangled situation, Landsgrave. Perhaps you would be so good as to suggest how it should be investigated?"

Sir Robert shrugged. "You know my feelings on the matter, High Commander. I've made no secret of them. The only way to get the truth is to question everyone, from the highest to the lowest, under a truthspell."

"That would take months," said Sir Vivian flatly. "And besides, it would be a deathly insult to all those of standing who had given their word they knew nothing of King Harald's death, sworn it on their name and their blood and their honor. And besides, who would you trust to administer such a truthspell anyway? The Magus? I don't know of anyone in this Court or out of it who trusts him entirely. The Shaman, with his well-known prejudices? Or perhaps some Academy witch, chosen at random? No, given the circumstances of the murder, no magic-user can be trusted. It's clear to me, and to anyone who's studied the matter, that the King's murder must have involved some use of magic. There's no other way the assassin could have reached him, past my guards and the Magus' wards. No, the first step to getting anywhere has to be the rounding up and imprisoning of all the magic-users currently infesting this Castle, and put them all to the question under a truthspell."

"Any magician powerful enough to get past the Magus' wards would have no trouble shrugging off a truthspell," said Sir Robert patiently. "And besides, magic has become too integral a part of our society. The Castle and the Land couldn't function without magic-users. We can't afford to antagonize them. It makes much more sense to vigorously interrogate all of your compromised guards, who continue to swear they saw and heard nothing of the King's murder, even though they were right outside the room when it happened! We could always replace them with the more independent members of our armed forces."

"You might be willing to place your trust in foreign mercenaries," said Sir Vivian. "But then, your commitment to the Throne has always been dubious at best. My people remain. They are the only ones who know the Castle and its people well enough to be able to investigate this matter thoroughly."

"As always, we remain opposed," said Sir Robert. "The old versus the new."

"Honor versus practicality," said Sir Vivian.

"Why don't we get right down to it?" asked Sir Robert. "With the King, regrettably, gone, this is the perfect opportunity to change the system. We can put aside the monarchy, which serves only itself, and replace it with a more democratic system that serves the people."

"King Harald stood fast against any real changes while he was alive," Sir Vivian pointed out. "And I support what remains of his family. Your words, however, sound more and more like a motive for murder. Did you tire of waiting for change, and decide to start the process yourself with Harald's death?"

Both Sir Robert and Sir Vivian had their hands on their swordhilts now, and imminent violence crackled in the air. Sir Vivian's guards moved quickly forward to support him, and just as quickly stern-faced courtiers emerged from the crowd to back up Sir Robert. And then Queen Felicity cleared her throat, and everyone stopped and turned to look at her.

"Harald never allowed anyone to go armed in his Court,"

she said coldly. "And it's temper tantrums like this that explain why. Sir Questor?"

Chance stepped forward. "Yes, Your Majesty?"

"Do you still serve the Throne and your Queen?"

"Yes, Your Majesty."

"Then do us the favor of killing the first damned fool to draw his sword."

"Delighted, Your Majesty." Chance had his father's huge double-headed axe in his hands, bearing the great weight as though it were nothing, and Hawk felt a sharp frisson of memory as he saw the dead Champion's cold killer's smile on Chance's lips. The dog Chappie was at Chance's side, fur bristling, growling loudly. Everyone very deliberately took their hands away from their swords, including Sir Robert and Sir Vivian. Chance nodded slowly.

"That's better. See how much more fun sanity is? Everybody calm down, right now. Or they'll be clearing up what's left of you with a mop."

"How typical of the monarchy, to settle debate with the threat of violence," said Sir Robert calmly. "Just another sign of how intellectually empty its position is. Take Hawk and Fisher, only here because Rupert and Julia declined to return. What are they but bullies with a little power? The Prince and Princess knew the days of monarchy are over, that's why they're not here."

"Bullshit," said Hawk. "They just have other responsibilities."

"Yes, well," said Sir Robert. "You *would* say that, wouldn't you?"

"In all the songs and stories I heard," Hawk said slowly, "Rupert was your friend. Your comrade in arms. Together you fought the darkness to preserve the Forest Kingdom. Do you think he'd approve of what you're doing now? Of what you've become?"

"That was a long time ago," said Sir Robert, meeting Hawk's gaze steadily. "Everything has changed since then. Rupert was a hero because of what he did, not because he was a Prince. He fought for justice, and the preservation of the Forest people. If he was here now, I'd follow him into hell itself, just on his word. But he isn't here, and I don't know you, Captain Hawk."

"Company's coming," said the Magus. And there was something in his voice that made everyone shut up and turn around.

Through the open doors of the Court came Duke Alric of Hillsdown, last in the line of Starlight Dukes, striding into the Forest Court like he owned the place. Or at the very least was thinking seriously of leasing it. Twenty armed and armored guards accompanied him. The packed Court shuffled backward to open up a wide aisle for the Duke and his guards to walk down on his way to the Throne. Queen Felicity's guards snapped to attention, and moved quickly in to stand on either side of her, glaring openly at the Duke and his guards. Alric ignored them all as he made his slow way toward the Throne.

He was an old man now, in his late seventies, not much more than skin and bone. His face was deeply lined, dominated by a jutting chin and nose. His mouth was a grim flat line, the lips pressed so tightly together, they could hardly be seen. His eyes were sunken, but still sharp and bright. He'd lost his hair long ago, save for a few white wisps over each ear. Hawk's first impression was that the Duke looked uncommonly like a vulture.

The Duke was dressed in dusty gray formal attire, and his stick-thin body was held together by a series of leather straps and metal braces, encompassing his torso like a cage, and extending down both arms and legs. Straps and hinges creaked loudly as he walked. More sounds came from within him, and he grunted now and again with the simple effort of walking. But for all the obvious frailty of his worn-out body, there was no mistaking the fire, arrogance, and determination that kept him moving. The Duke was still a dangerous man, and everyone there in the Court knew it.

"Damn," Fisher said quietly, and Hawk could hear the shock in her voice. "He's gotten *old* since I last saw him. He used to be such a fighter, such a warrior. Now look at him. Time's eaten him away. Oh sure, he's still the Duke. He'll still be deadly as a coiled snake till the day they nail his coffin lid down. But I'm not afraid of him anymore.

I don't know this man. This old man. I wonder if he'll know me."

Duke Alric crashed to a halt before the Throne and glared at Queen Felicity, ignoring everyone else. He was breathing heavily and his hands trembled, but his gaze was perfectly steady. The Queen did her best to look imperiously down on him, but it was clear to everyone how much of an effort that was.

"Well, Daughter," the Duke said finally, his voice surprisingly deep and resonant. "You've been drinking again. I can smell it."

"Well, Father," said the Queen. "To what do we owe the pleasure of your company? Found something else in your quarters to complain about?"

"Don't get smart with me, Felicity. I put you on this Throne. I can remove you from it if I have to."

"You are addressing the Queen of the Forest Land," Chance said calmly. "The correct form of address is *Your Majesty*. Do try not to forget again. I'd hate to have you dragged from this Court in chains for disrespect. Really. I'd hate it."

"Muzzle your dog, Felicity," said Alric, not looking around. "Word has come to me that you are considering accepting these Guard nobodies in place of Rupert and Julia. You can't do that. They're not fit to investigate your husband's murder. Send them away. Then send your faithful hound back to fetch Rupert and Julia, and demand they come home. Be a Queen, dammit."

"You just want me out of the way!" Chance said angrily, but the Duke still ignored him, his unwavering gaze fixed on his daughter, who was beginning to squirm under the pressure of his regard.

"All right, you have a point," she said reluctantly. "Rupert and Julia—"

"Aren't coming," Hawk said flatly, moving forward to stand between the Queen and the Duke. Fisher was quickly there at his side, glaring at her father. "Fisher and I are here, and we will investigate this murder and uncover the guilty. We're not going anywhere. We're needed here. If just because we're the only ones here without an axe of our own to grind. So back off, Starlight Duke, or I'll cut your braces."

The Duke looked at him in silence. It had clearly been a long time since anyone had dared to openly defy him. Fisher seized the advantage.

"Why would you want to see your daughter Julia again anyway, Duke Alric? Didn't you condemn her to death all those years ago?"

The Duke shrugged slowly. "She disobeyed me. She disappointed me. And since I had seven other daughters, I had to keep them in line somehow. Trust Julia not to do what was expected of her. Perhaps she's afraid to come back and face me again."

Fisher grinned. "I rather doubt that. She faced the Darkwood, the long night, and the Demon Prince. An old man held together with knotted string and sealing wax isn't much of a threat after that."

"I am the sovereign monarch of Hillsdown. You will not speak to me that way."

"Sure we will," said Hawk. "You're not the first ruler we've faced down, and you won't be the last. You have no authority over us. We're Hawk and Fisher. And we don't bend the knee to anyone."

"Damn right," said Fisher.

Duke Alric turned to his guards. "Kill them."

The Hillsdown guards drew their swords and surged forward, silent and focused. Hawk and Fisher drew their weapons and went to meet them. Everyone else watched with open mouths as swords clashed, blood flew on the air, and Hawk and Fisher wiped the floor with all twenty guards. Chance hopped around the perimeter of the action shouting, "Don't kill any of them! Please don't kill them!" The Hillsdown guards were trained, experienced men, but they were no match for Hawk and Fisher, who were shaped and trained under harsher conditions than anyone in Hillsdown had known in generations. Soon there was a lot of blood on the floor, and more on the clothes of those courtiers who hadn't stood far enough back, and there were moaning, wounded, and unconscious guards everywhere. The last few threw down their swords and surrendered, despite angry orders from their Duke. Hawk and Fisher looked around them, quietly satisfied, flicked drops of blood from their blades, and sheathed their weapons, not even bothering to look in Alric's direction. Sir Robert Hawke started the applause, and most of the courtiers joined in. Queen Felicity looked as if she would have very much liked to. Chance approached Hawk and Fisher, and sighed heavily.

"Can't you two get on with anyone?"

"We didn't kill anyone," said Hawk innocently.

"And that's your idea of diplomacy, is it?"

"Well, mostly, yes," said Fisher. "Think of it as a statement of principles. Or not. See if we care. Now, where were we, Alric?"

Chance moved quickly to stand between them and the Duke. "That's *enough*. The Duke is a guest of this Court, and as such is under my protection. Guards are one thing. I can't let you threaten the Duke."

"Spoilsport," said Fisher.

And then everything stopped as there came the sound of an awful iron bell, tolling far away. The terrible sound reverberated on the air like slow thunder, and everyone in the Court could feel it in their hearts and in their souls. The sound affected them all, like nails scraping down their bones. The awful bell rang on and on, like the Devil calling the damned to worship at his cloven hooves.

"What is that?" asked Fisher. "What is that sound? Where's it coming from?"

"It is the great bell of the Inverted Cathedral," said the Magus, raising his usually quiet voice to be heard above the din. "It hasn't been heard in centuries."

"Then why is it ringing *now*?" asked Queen Felicity, almost desperately.

"Something new has come into the Castle, something that changes everything," said the Magus. He didn't look at Hawk and Fisher.

"Who's ringing the bloody thing?" Lightfoot Moonfleet asked, her tiny hands clapped to her pointed ears.

"I don't know," said the Magus. "The Burning Man, perhaps?"

"The hell with who's ringing it," said Hawk. "How do we make it *stop*?"

The Magus had no answer. Everyone in the Court had their hands over their ears now, but it didn't help. The tolling of the awful bell of the Inverted Cathedral could have been heard by a deaf man, and a dumb man would have cried out in horror at the sound of it. People were crying now. Some were shaking or vomiting. Everywhere in the Court the light was dimming, and the shadows were growing darker. There was a sense of terrible presences moving inside the shadows. Everyone who had a weapon had drawn it. Panic was growing in the packed hall, held back only by lack of a common cause to attack or run from. And then the people on the edges of the Court, those nearest the shadows, began to sway and stumble like drunken men. The color went out of their faces and their eyes became vague, and there was something almost insubstantial about them, as though their very life was being sucked out of them. Their faces twisted with a terrible disgust, as though they were being drained by giant leeches. Some fell into the shadows, which swallowed them and consumed them like inky waters. The courtiers nearest those lost to the shadows fought each other in their desperate need to get away from the hungry darkness. The shadows grew larger, darker, deeper. The whole crowd was dangerously close to stampeding now. A few people cut at the shadows with their swords, but the steel slipped harmlessly through the darkness. Hawk and Fisher stood back to back, weapons at the ready, looking for an enemy they could fight.

The Queen stood up before her Throne. "Do something, dammit! Somebody do something!"

"The only spells I know strong enough to throw back an evil like this would probably kill the Court," said the Magus. "If the situation deteriorates further, I may have to do that, but for the moment I think we'd be better off organizing a controlled evacuation of the Court."

"If they run, half of them will be crushed and trampled to death anyway!" snapped the Queen. "Do something!"

"Alas, Your Majesty—"

"You're standing there making excuses, and people are

dying!" said the witch Tiffany, bursting out of the crowd. "Typical sorcerer. Get out of my way."

She floated up into the air, the slippers falling from her rising feet, her long red hair floating around her untroubled face like a great crimson cloud. She rose above the noise and turmoil of the panicking crowd, her hands crossed on her breast, like some old Romantic's vision of an angel. Her eyes were closed, her brow furrowed in concentration. The iron bell missed a beat. And then Tiffany spoke, but the words were huge and magnificent, as though something greater spoke through her, with her voice.

"Fiat Lux!" said Tiffany. *Let there be light.* And there was.

A bright light, shining and brilliant beyond any color, swept through the Court like refreshing rain on a hot afternoon. It bathed everyone in its blazing glory, sleeting light through their bodies in a rush of calm and forgiveness. It filled the Court, bright as mercy, vivid as justice, driving out the dark and the shadows, which could not stand against it. Those people who had been swallowed up by the dark returned, blinking bemusedly, unharmed. And then the dark and the light were both gone, and the tolling of the awful bell stopped. The Court was just a great hall again, and the shadows were just shadows. People murmured to each other, holding hands and hugging one another. And only Chance saw Tiffany fall out of the air like a stone.

He fought his way through the crowd to reach her, shoving aside personages far greater than he without a backward glance. He knelt beside the fallen witch, lying crumpled on the floor like a discarded handkerchief. He checked her breathing and her pulse, and then let out his breath in a relieved sigh as he found them both normal. He chaffed her hands and gently called her name, and Tiffany slowly opened her eyes, green as the most luscious grassy meadows of the Forest Land, and twice as warm. They smiled at each other, and for a long moment that was all they needed.

"I wasn't sure that would work," she said indistinctly. "I never tried it before. Found the spell in an old forbidden grimoire I wasn't supposed to know about. Technically, only a sorceress should have been able to power a spell like that. But somehow I knew that I could do it. Because it was needed. Am I making sense?"

"As much as usual," Chance said fondly. "Do you think you could stand up, if you leaned on me?"

"I think so, Allen," said Tiffany. "Promise me you won't go away?"

"I'll always be there when you need me, Tiff," said Chance.

They rose slowly to their feet, Chance strong enough for both of them. They smiled into each other's eyes, and neither of them noticed that rose petals were raining down around them.

"Now, that was interesting," said the Magus.

"Is that all you have to say?" demanded Queen Felicity. "You're supposed to be the official sorcerer to this Court. Why didn't *you* do that?"

"Because such a spell would almost certainly have destroyed me," said the Magus. "So much power unleashed should have burned Tiffany to ashes, from the inside out."

"Then why didn't it?" asked the Queen.

"Damned if I know. But it is interesting."

"Never mind that now! What was that bell all about? And those shadows! What does it mean?"

"I think it means that something in the Inverted Cathedral is waking up," the Magus said slowly. "But I am unable at this time to ascertain who or what that might be."

"A lot of bloody good you are," said the Queen, sinking back onto her Throne. "You couldn't save my Harald, and you couldn't save my Court. A witch from the Academy had to do it! I knew there was a reason why I let them hang around. Somebody bring that witch to me."

Chance brought Tiffany forward, and the witch curtsied low before the Throne. "I am Tiffany, Your Majesty. At your service."

"Look at you, girl," said the Queen, smiling despite herself. "I never looked that good, even when I was your age. And that's more years ago than I care to remember. You did good, Tiffany. We hereby appoint you official witch to this Court. You will join with the Questor in defending this

Court from all its enemies, without and within. Work with the Magus, or not, as you please."

"I am honored, Your Majesty," said Tiffany, curtsying again.

"Yes, you are," said the Queen dryly. "You can start work by cleaning up all those bloody rose petals." She looked out over the Court. "Everyone else, this session is now at an end. I think we've all had as much excitement as we can stand for one day, and I need to get my feet up for an hour or so, or I'm going to have one of my headaches. Duke Alric, you have our permission to retire to your quarters. We'll send you back your guards once the surgeons have put them back together again. Sir Vivian and Sir Robert, save it for another day. Hawk and Fisher, get me some answers. Court is now dismissed."

She levered herself up out of her Throne, with sudden snapping sounds from her joints, and stalked off while everyone else was still in mid-bow and curtsy. Her guards hurried after her. Hawk turned to Sir Vivian.

"We're going to need quarters here. Prince Rupert said we could have his old quarters, in the Northwest Tower."

"You can't have those!" said Sir Vivian. "They are for Royalty."

"Is anyone using them right now?"

"Well, no," admitted Sir Vivian. "We were maintaining them for Prince Rupert and Princess Julia, when they returned. But it wouldn't be proper—"

"We don't do proper," interrupted Fisher. "We can, however, get really cranky if we don't get our way."

Hawk and Fisher looked meaningfully at the wounded and unconscious Hillsdown guards, and then looked back at Sir Vivian. One of the guards close at hand chose this moment to stir. Fisher stamped on the back of his head, and he fell gratefully back into unconsciousness. Everyone watching winced, including Hawk and Sir Vivian.

"Oh, hell, have the bloody rooms!" said Sir Vivian.

Sometime later Hawk and Fisher were preparing for bed in what used to be Prince Rupert's old quarters. He was pleased to see they'd kept them just as he had left them.

There wasn't much there, just the same old bed and bare minimum of furniture. Someone had thoughtfully used a bedwarmer to take the chill off the sheets, and the adjoining bathroom was spotless. There were no frills or fancies, or anything other than the most basic of comforts. Rupert never had time for such things back then. He sat on the edge of the bed, trying to decide whether the room still felt like home. Fisher came in from the bathroom, toweling her damp hair.

"The dye's still sticking, thank God. I hope we'll be through here before my roots start to show." She looked around the room, unimpressed. "Was it always as spartan as this?"

"Pretty much, yes. Now you know why I never invited you back here." Hawk frowned. "This is where Rupert hid from the world. From the Castle, and all the people in it who wanted to hurt or use him. Can't really think of any good memories. Mostly I remember being afraid of the dark after I passed through the Darkwood. The long night put its mark on me then. I slept here with the door locked and the nightlight on. Once, I even pushed the wardrobe across to barricade the door. You know, I'm not so sure I want to sleep here after all."

"You'll be fine," Fisher said briskly. "That was all a long time ago. The dark's no threat to us now."

"Are you sure? You saw what happened in the Court when that bell was tolling. The shadows were a lot like the darkness of the long night, and the witch summoning the light was a hell of a lot like my calling down the Rainbow."

"Don't see everything in terms of our past, love," said Fisher. She sat on the bed beside him. "We're together now, and together we can handle anything the world can throw at us."

Hawk took her hand in his. "As long as we're together. Don't ever let them separate us, Isobel."

"Never," said Isobel Fisher. "Never again."

CHAPTER FIVE

Everyone's Guilty of Something

Through the eternal darkness, through the dead land where the sun has never shone, Jericho Lament came walking. Jericho Lament, the Walking Man, the Wrath of God in the world of men. He strode briskly between the rotting trees of the Darkwood, eyes staring calmly straight ahead of him. In one hand he bore aloft a blazing torch whose flame never faltered, and in his other he carried a long wooden staff almost as tall as him, weighted with steel at one end and silver at the other. He wore a dark, ankle-length trenchcoat over worn gray leathers, and the heels of his boots were worn down with all the countless miles he'd walked in the service of his God. His face was lean and deeply lined, his eyes cold and blue as the sky over a field of endless ice. His nose had been broken more than once, his slight smile was even colder than his eyes, and a lion's mane of long gray hair fell from under a battered broad-brimmed hat. He leaned forward as he walked, as though about to breast some invisible tape at the end of a race that was always somewhere just ahead of him. In the darkness all around him, demons moved silently behind the dead trees, following Jericho Lament at a safe distance. For all their numbers, none of them dared enter the small pool of steady light he walked in. Somehow they knew who and what he was, and they were afraid. Sometimes Lament felt moved to sing a hymn or two, of the more martial kind, and then his strong, sure voice seemed to carry forever in the still silence of the long night.

He could have bypassed the Darkwood if he'd chosen, but he wanted to test himself and his faith against that spiritual darkness, so he pulled his courage and his self-

control about him like a protective cloak, and walked un-
hesitatingly out of the light and into the dark. The horrid
oppression of the endless night had hit him hard, like a
physical blow, but his step never faltered and his pace never
slowed. In that place where the sun had never shone and
never would, the unearthly cold sank deep into his bones,
leeching away at his life's warmth, and the long night lay
heavily upon him, like those terrible empty hours of the
early morning, when a man cannot sleep for thoughts of
his own mortality. But the endless dark and the lonely cold
could not turn aside or even slow Jericho Lament, the
Walking Man; it was no match for the holy fire that burned
forever within him, that seared him more harshly than the
dark ever could. It is not an easy or a pleasant thing, to be
a living avatar of the good and the just.

   He had no horse, nor any other form of transport, and
never had. He was the Walking Man, and his contract with
the Lord forbade such weaknesses. He was not the first to
bear that title, to bind himself to God, to damn himself to
heaven's work. Once, years ago, he had been just another
monk, in a small quiet monastery miles from anywhere that
mattered, famed locally for a wine that did not travel well.
He worked the gardens and the vineyards, made his prayers
and did charitable work, meditated quietly in the peace of
his humble cell, and was almost content. And then the long
night fell across the Forest Land, and the demons came
hopping and scuttling outside the monastery. Neither the
monks' faith nor the monastery's high stone walls were
enough to stop the demons. They climbed the walls and
smashed down the locked doors, and blood ran freely
across the polished wooden floors. Some monks died where
they stood, rather than raise a hand in violence even against
demons. They fell with blessings on their bloody lips, and
the demons didn't care. Other monks, like the man who
had once been Jericho Lament, took up improvised weapons against the invading demons, and fought them back.
Lament crushed demon skulls with a heavy silver crucifix,
and praised his God with every blow. And when the long
night passed, and the sun returned, all the demons were
dead, and only those monks who had fought for their lives

survived. Jericho Lament stood there, breathing harshly, with blood dripping thickly from his crucifix, and took a lesson from that.

The monastery had an excellent library, from a time when the monastery had been a more central and important place. Centuries old, mostly forgotten now by the outside world, the library had books on its dusty shelves that no man had consulted for long and long. Old books, perhaps the only remaining copies in the Forest Land. Lament worked his way through the handwritten pages with almost feverish speed, searching for something he could feel but not put a name to. And finally, in a book whose silver locks he had to shatter with an iron axe from the gardens, he found what he needed. The legend of the Walking Man.

In every generation, the book said, a man can swear his life to God, and become more than a man. The pages outlined a contract between man and God, that once entered into could not be broken by either party. If that man would swear to serve the light and the good for all his life, forswearing all other paths, such as love or family or personal needs, then he could become the Walking Man. Stronger, faster, and more terrible than any other man, he would become invulnerable as long as his faith remained strong. God's warrior. More than mortal. The Wrath of God in the world of men. Everything Jericho Lament was not when the demons burst in the monastery doors and came swarming over the holy walls to slaughter good men.

Lament entered into the compact willingly, saying the words and making the terrible promises, and a holy fire came down and burned him within and without, searing away all human limits and hesitations. From now on he would walk in straight lines to go where he must and do what he had to, turning aside for nothing and no one. He could accept no human help or compromise, and he only possessed what he could carry with him. He left the monastery and never once looked back. His fellow brothers, men who had fought beside him against the demons, were now afraid of him. And so Jericho Lament went back and forth in the Forest Land, and Hillsdown and Redhart, aiding the needy and punishing the wicked, bringing to bear the terrible anger of the Walking Man on those who would dare trespass against the light. Because he followed God's law rather than man's, and never hesitated to strike down an evil man, no matter how powerful he might be, there were always warrants out for his arrest. In many places there was an impressive price on his head, and he was being pursued by a more tenacious than usual pack of bounty hunters when he came to the border of the Darkwood.

The bounty hunters didn't worry him. Their horses had to rest sometime, while he never did. Jericho Lament hadn't rested or slept or dreamed in eleven years. And it pleased him to walk where no other man would dare to follow, for fear of his soul.

There was nearly always someone on his trail. The Walking Man did what he had to, as the voice within bade him, and his uncompromising justice nearly always led to grief for some undeserving soul. Even the most evil of men could have friends or family who valued them, and were determined to avenge him. Lament preferred to leave them behind rather than kill them. Such people were misguided, not evil, and he had no business with them. He was not without compassion, though he could not allow himself pity. His most recent case had been a sad one, though necessary. The girl had been possessed, the exorcism had failed, so all that was left was to kill her and set her soul free. Her family hadn't seen it that way. The whole town turned out to pursue him. He didn't blame them. Eventually they grew tired and gave up, but the bounty hunters they hired didn't. Now they were gone, too, left behind, and Lament concentrated on his next mission as he strode through the Darkwood. The voice had been most specific, and unusually urgent.

Jericho Lament had given his life to God, over love or longing or rest. But there were times, for all his faith, when he wasn't always sure whom he'd given it to.

He studied God's word wherever he went, reading his way through testaments and gospels and epistles in libraries small and large. The older the books, the more confusing things became. The church had known many shapes and directions over the centuries, some of them impossibly conflicted. The Word of God rarely changed much, but the interpretations could vary wildly, sometimes to the point of civil wars. There were always established churches, and there were always heretics. Sometimes the heretics became the establishment, only to face new heretics in turn. Lament learned to see the varying branches of the faith as distractions from his holy purpose, and regarded them with only intellectual interest. His contract was with God, not his priests. The light may cast many reflections, but it is still the light that matters.

He had no patience for the pagan faiths that mushroomed through the countryside after the long night, and he destroyed pagan sites and ancient stones wherever he encountered them. They were a distraction from the true God. Lament took no pleasure in the destruction, especially when it was clear the pagan sites and stones gave comfort to people, but he knew his duty.

Right now, his duty was bringing him to Forest Castle.

The demons of the Darkwood kept pace with him, staying just beyond the edges of his pool of light, watching him hungrily, but still scared or sensible enough to maintain their distance. They were of the dark, and knew the light when they saw it. Lament was almost disappointed. He would have liked to kill some demons. Partly for the exercise, partly so that they would never again be a menace to travelers. But mostly because someone buried deep within him still remembered the terrible fear he'd felt as demons tore his fellow monks apart all those years ago. He knew now that the demons had been people once, but that didn't stay his hand. As far as he was concerned, demons were just the risen dead. No more worthy of sparing than a vampire or a ghoul. They were dead, and should be put to rest for their soul's sake. But his mission had precedence, and so he strode briskly along between the dead trees, following the narrow trail the legendary Prince Rupert had hacked out so many years before. Lament would have liked to kill some demons, for his own comfort and peace of mind, and so he didn't, because he was the Walking Man, and had to be beyond such personal needs.

The Walking Man, the Wrath of God in the world of

men, was heading inexorably toward Forest Castle and the Inverted Cathedral, and one final, terrible, act of faith.

The witch called Tiffany sat alone in her quarters at Forest Castle, humming a merry tune in perfect key, braiding her flame red hair in front of a tall mirror. It was a pleasant, airy room, small enough to be cozy while still large enough to acknowledge her status in the Castle. Such things had to be nicely calculated. There were flowers in earth pots everywhere. Tiffany liked flowers, but not in vases. Cut flowers in glass vases were just dying slowly, and Tiffany couldn't bear to hear them screaming. The flowers' combined perfume gave the air in the room a refreshing, lively ambiance. The bed was very comfortable, piled high with soft sheets over a deep supportive mattress, but even so, Tiffany had swung cheerfully out of it at first light. She couldn't understand lazy slugabeds, who would rather sleep on than go bustling forth to see what wonders the new day would reveal.

It helped that she was just seventeen, and full of more energy than she knew what to do with.

The servants had left her strictly vegetarian breakfast outside the door again, rather than bring it in. They were somewhat in awe of Academy witches, and her in particular. This rather disappointed Tiffany, who'd been trying really hard to fit in, but she supposed it came with the job. She realized her reflection in the mirror was frowning, so she quickly smiled to smooth the lines away. Frowns led to wrinkles. And besides, bad within led to bad without. Face the world with a smile, and it will smile right back at you. She brushed hard at her long hair, removing the last few tangles of sleep, and tried to think only happy thoughts. Tiffany tried very hard to think the best of absolutely everybody, as a matter of principle—particularly those people she didn't like. Everyone has some good in them. If you dig deep enough.

She pursed her perfect mouth at the tartness of that last thought. She tried to have positive thoughts about everyone, but some people made it harder than most. Like Captains Hawk and Fisher, for example, who seemed to her nothing more than rude, arrogant, offensive bullies. She didn't know what Allen Chance saw in them. But just possibly, Hawk and Fisher were what the Castle needed right now. Certainly her own quiet investigations into King Harald's death had gotten her absolutely nowhere. Any number of people had been happy to tell her all sorts of things they shouldn't have, once she turned her wide-eyed, emptyheaded routine on them, but she hadn't learned anything of use. Everyone she talked to had plenty of theories, and plenty of unsubstantiated gossip, but no one knew anything for sure. And those few who might, the real movers and shakers of Forest Castle, had more sense than to speak openly in front of an Academy witch, no matter how innocent and charming she seemed.

The Queen, in particular, had been most unhelpful. She'd agreed to see Tiffany more than once, but seemed more interested in exchanging the very latest gossip than in talking about things that really mattered. She was also totally and very firmly uninterested in all the things Tiffany's magic could do, even when they might have been useful to her. Queen Felicity might not have much use for her official advisers, but it seemed even she listened to them on the subject of how dangerous an Academy witch could be.

Of course, they were quite right, but still . . . Tiffany admired the Queen Regent, and would have liked to be able to help her.

She hadn't been anywhere near Duke Alric. His small army of bodyguards went pale and drew their weapons if she ever looked like she was going anywhere near his quarters, and formed a solid block around him anytime the two of them were at Court together. Which was flattering, but not particularly helpful. The Duke might be obnoxious, arrogant, and a potential threat to the whole Forest Land, but she still needed to talk to him. There were things she needed to know. About his plans and ambitions and what he was doing here at Forest Castle. And why every time she looked at him, she Saw blood dripping endlessly from his twisted hands. A witch's Sight wasn't always completely reliable, for any number of reasons, including the difficulties of interpretation, but some Sights were indisputable.

Tiffany needed to know whether she was Seeing the Duke's past, or his future. She couldn't afford to do anything drastic to him until she was sure exactly what he was guilty of.

And on top of all that, the Walking Man was coming to Forest Castle. As if she and everyone else didn't have enough problems. For someone supposed to be an avatar of the good and the holy, that man could cause more upsets, general mayhem, and high body counts than a major war and an outbreak of plague combined.

She remembered suddenly that Allen Chance was on his way to see her, and brightened up immediately. She liked Allen. He was kind and thoughtful and always treated her like a lady. More importantly, he wasn't frightened of her. And she just loved the way he went all red-faced and flustered when she took a deep breath and stuck out her bosom. Men were so easy to manipulate sometimes. It helped that Chance was very handsome, and even charming, in an awkward way. If only he wasn't his father's son. Sometimes when Tiffany looked at Chance's shadow, she Saw the shadow of a much larger and far more dangerous man.

She tired suddenly of playing with her hair. She tied the braid off with quick, careless knots, jumped to her feet, and moved over to look out of the room's only window. She usually found the view from this high up on the South Tower diverting, even comforting, but today something was undermining its ability to ease her mood. The Forest looked the same, but Tiffany knew there was a darkness coming, even without using her Sight. The Forest just couldn't help but look different. Everyone in the Academy knew something bad was coming, but not even the most advanced and experienced witches had been able to put a name to it. They were all pretty sure it had something to do with the return of the Inverted Cathedral, but those witches who had tried their Sight on the Inverted Cathedral had come to awful ends. The lucky ones had died quickly. The few survivors lay in straightjackets in isolated cells, bleeding constantly from terrible stigmata, screaming and laughing and speaking in tongues that no one understood. The Mother Witch had made Tiffany visit those poor unfortunates before she let her go to Forest Castle, so she wouldn't be tempted to try the Sight herself. She'd cried for over an hour afterward, and then never cried again. She could be strong when she had to. She could feel the Inverted Cathedral's presence wherever she was in the Castle. A harsh, hateful presence, like the endless pain of a nagging tooth. And going anywhere near the Inverted Cathedral felt like being in the presence of something awful about to give birth to something even worse.

Tiffany was potentially the most powerful witch the Academy of the Sisters of the Moon had ever produced. She knew this because her superiors had been telling her that ever since her first period, when her magic first began to manifest. The signs and portents surrounding her birth had apparently been something to see. That's why she was here, in the Castle. Because the Academy was convinced she was supposed to be here. But the more she thought about it, the more Tiffany worried she wouldn't be strong enough to face whatever it was, whenever it finally happened. For all her power, she'd never thought of herself as anyone special. Part of her wanted to run screaming from the Castle, right now, and flee back to the safety of the Academy, where she'd always felt safe and protected and secure. Where the day to day world had been comfortingly predictable, decided by those clearly superior to her. She'd cried hot tears when they told her she had to leave the Academy early, because her presence was needed at the Forest Castle. And because there was nothing more they could teach her. The world outside the Academy was so confusing. And she missed her friends. She shook her head quickly. These were a child's thoughts. She was a grown woman now, with a woman's responsibilities. And she was a witch.

She pushed open the window, put her face out into the morning sunshine, and sang. Her voice rang out on the stillness, calm and sure and quite beautiful. Her liquid, sparkling voice rose and fell as she sang a song almost as old as the Forest Kingdom itself, a simple tale of love and loss, and love regained. And as she sang, birds came from everywhere to sing with her. They came flying in from all

directions, in ones and twos and small clouds, dropping out
of the morning sky to circle and wheel before and above
and around her, dozens and dozens of them, of all sizes
and species and colors, to add their voices to hers. The
song took on a power of its own, spreading farther than
any volume could ever have carried it, till everyone in the
Castle stopped to hear Tiffany and the birds singing. And
everyone who heard it felt their hearts lift for a moment,
and the cares of the day seemed a little lighter for everybody.

And then something frightened the birds, and in a moment they all stopped singing and flew away. Tiffany faltered, then broke off, though the unfinished song seemed
to reverberate on the air a moment longer. Something new
had come into the Forest. Tiffany could feel it. She turned
her Sight on the view before her, and the Forest changed.

It was dark, and corrupt, and overhead the returned Blue
Moon glowed with the only color eyes can see at night. Its
wild malevolence crackled on the darkness, moving over all
the Forest, its irresistible influence changing everything.
Wild Magic ran loose in the world, and nothing could stand
against it, not law nor custom nor reason. Trees and foliage
had been replaced by terrible insane plant growths whose
shapes made no sense, and between them moved creatures
like living cancers, swollen and purulent. There were dark
shapes as big as houses, lurching through the transformed
Forest toward the Castle, to tear it down and grind its
stones underfoot. And demons, demons everywhere.

And then, in the middle of this Sight of things to be,
Tiffany gasped as she Saw herself. Saw her body impaled
upon a twisting tree branch, its end bursting out of her
wide-stretched mouth, its bark slick with her blood. And
she was still alive, her eyes open and endlessly suffering . . .

The door opened behind her, and she spun around, the
horror that held her bursting out of her in a scream she
couldn't hold back. And then she saw that it was Chance,
and the last of the Sight fell away. She ran forward into
his arms, and clung to him, shuddering and shaking, holding
tears back with an effort. Chance held her close, bewildered, and did his best to make soothing, comforting noises.

Slowly she calmed down, bringing herself back under control through sheer willpower. She hung on to Chance a little longer than was really necessary. She felt safe in his arms, safe for the first time since she'd come to Forest Castle. But still, in the end she made herself push him gently away, and he let go of her immediately.

"What is it, Tiff? What's the matter? Did you See something?"

"Yes. A vision of the future. Or what might be the future."

"A vision so bad it made you scream? What did you See?"

Tiffany shook her head firmly. "It wasn't certain. The future is shifting all the time. It was more like a warning, a prediction of what might happen if we don't do something to prevent it."

"Like what?"

"I don't know."

"Don't worry," Chance said firmly. "I'd never let anything happen to you, Tiff. Never."

Tiffany smiled at him, and wished she could believe him.

Hawk and Fisher ate breakfast together in Rupert's old quarters. Fisher started the day as she always did, with twenty minutes' hard exercise, followed by a full and hearty meal. Bacon, eggs, sausages, and a pint of good strong Southern coffee. There was even fried bread to go with the fried eggs. Perfect. Fisher plowed through it all with good appetite, making happy contented sounds amidst the chewing. Fisher believed in attacking the day from the very beginning, bright-eyed and alert for whatever the morning might bring. Preferably something she could hit. She was already fully dressed, her swordbelt close at hand.

Hawk, on the other hand, was still in his dressing gown. He sat slumped in his chair opposite her, trying to work up the energy for a good scratch. He hadn't shaved, and his hair was sticking out in all directions. Hawk was not a morning person. He watched bleakly as Fisher wolfed down her food, his face expressing barely concealed horror. Hawk had a bowlful of bran cereal and a small glass of fruit juice, that being all his system could tolerate first thing in the morning. Fisher chatted cheerfully about what they were going to do that day, and Hawk answered her with grunts and the occasional low groan. Hawk tended to not really wake up until he'd been out of bed for at least a good hour. Which was why they'd always done their best to avoid the morning shift in Haven. That early in the morning you could rob a bank right in front of Hawk, hit him over the head with a club, and set fire to his trousers, and he still wouldn't notice.

In Haven, Fisher usually shoved Hawk under the shower, turned the water on hard, and then joined him. That usually did the trick. However, the Forest Castle's plumbing apparently didn't extend to showers yet, which was possibly why Hawk was still in a decidedly grumpy mood when he and Fisher set out, sometime later, to start the day's round of interviews. Hawk was dressed, shaved, and awake, and looked like he hated every part of it. People tended to back away and give him and Fisher plenty of room as they strode down the branching stone corridors, following the guide the Seneschal had provided them.

Hawk had lived all his early life in the Castle, and still remembered most of the main routes, but even so, he still needed a guide to lead him through the ever-changing locations of rooms, stairways, and corridors, some of which doubled back on you when you weren't looking. The Forest Castle's internal geography had always been eccentric, if not downright willful, and things had only gotten worse since the return of the missing South Wing and the reappearance of the Inverted Cathedral. On bad days you were lucky if you woke up in the same room you went to sleep in. Or at least, that was the excuse people used. In the old days the Seneschal, or more usually one of his people, would have led the way, following their magical instincts and well-trained internal maps, but apparently these days the Seneschal rarely left his rooms. Instead he relied upon a series of magical guides, directed by his will, or his people's. Hawk and Fisher's guide was a bright glowing light that bobbed cheerfully on the air before them, like a candle flame without the candle. You told it where you wanted to go, and it took you there. Simple. Fisher was having none of it. She took the nonappearance of the Seneschal as a personal slight, and demanded the guide to tell the Seneschal to get his arse down here sharpish. There was a pause, and then the light spoke with the Seneschal's voice.

"You're not that important. In fact, at this hour of the morning no one is, except the Queen. And possibly the Duke. I don't do personal appearances anymore. I'm very busy. Don't bother me again, or I'll have the guide take you on an extended tour of the Castle's sewer systems."

And that was that.

"He hasn't changed much," said Fisher. "In fact, he's just like I remember him."

"Then he's about the only thing that is," growled Hawk. "This isn't the Castle I remembered."

"Is that good or bad?"

"I'm still deciding."

"God, you're moody first thing in the morning. Did you have a good bowel movement?"

"You always ask that," said Hawk, with some dignity. "And the answer is always yes."

"You can get bashful about the strangest things, Hawk."

"Can we please change the subject? Where are we going first?"

"We went through all this last night, Hawk. When you weren't complaining about the lumpy mattress. We're starting with a visit to Harald's tomb, remember?"

"Appropriate. I feel like death warmed up and allowed to congeal."

They followed the bobbing light through the Castle corridors, heading down into the depths of the Castle, down to the great Hall and Crypt of the Forest Kings. Fourteen generations of the Forest line lay at rest there. Hawk hadn't been there since he was a child, at the funeral of his mother, Queen Eleanor. He'd found the sheer size of the place awesome rather than frightening, but even so, it hadn't looked to him like anywhere he wanted to spend his final rest. He'd said so, and his father, the King, had hit him, and then hugged him tightly. King John took the death of his wife hard, and only held himself together

through the service by his sense of duty. Hawk understood there was a tomb for his father in the Crypt now,
even though there'd been no body to inter. Custom had to
be followed. Hawk hadn't been there for that funeral. He'd
felt it more important to get himself and Julia out of the
Castle and some distance down the road before Harald got
around to having him killed. Harald had never taken competition lightly. And now Harald was dead, too, laid out in
the family Crypt. It made Hawk feel old.

He noticed that everyone was now giving him and Fisher
lots of room, far more than could be accounted for by his
general grumpiness. He could see fear in people's eyes, and
the sudden averting of their gaze. From the highest courtier
to the lowest servant, no one wanted to be anywhere near
Hawk and Fisher. They hushed their voices and turned
their heads aside, and hurried off in different directions,
muttering animatedly to each other the moment they
thought they were at a safe distance.

"I was wondering when you'd notice that," said Fisher.

"They're scared of us," said Hawk. "Why are they scared
of us? All right, we put on an impressive performance last
night, but only the guilty have anything to fear from us.
We're here to protect the innocent. They shouldn't fear
us."

"Everyone's guilty of something," said Fisher.

Hawk thought about that for a while. "Even us?" he
asked finally.

The Crypt of the Forest Kings was located deep down
in the bedrock upon which Forest Castle was built. Entering its dusty embrace was like walking back into the past,
rediscovering the legacy and bloodright from which Prince
Rupert had sprung. The massive Hall stretched away before
the man now known as Hawk, its immense length lit by
sorcerous blue flames on the wall that would never gutter
or grow dim for as long as the Forest line endured. Standing just inside the only door, the first thing Hawk noticed
was the silence. It was like being at the bottom of the sea.
There was no sound here, except what the living brought
with them. Looking down the long reach of the Hall was

almost dizzying, like looking down the side of some plunging cliff face. The sheer scale of the Crypt might originally have been planned to be impressive, but now, fourteen generations later, it seemed simply practical. Lying quietly in their cold stone beds, in neat and ordered rows, the dead Kings and their families stretched away into the distance, protected against time and decay but not the forgetfulness of fickle descendants.

When Prince Rupert had been brought down here as a small child, to see his mother put to rest, he'd thought for a long time afterward that this was the actual afterlife, where you went when you died; a place of cold blue light and endless quiet. He thought that when everyone was gone, the dead rose up from their marble coffins and communed silently together in the endless Hall. He'd had nightmares for years. Now he found the Crypt oddly comforting. A place of peace, where no one made demands on you anymore. He was here again, after decades away, and it seemed not a bad place to sleep for all eternity, surrounded by your family.

"Damn," said Fisher quietly. "This place is huge. We've nothing like it in Hillsdown. But then, we haven't been around that long. I'll bet you could spend hours down here, just checking off the names. How many of your family are down here, Hawk?"

"I don't think anyone knows anymore," said Hawk. "Once, this would have been part of the Seneschal's rounds. He or his people would have kept detailed records on who everyone was and where, and what they did of note, and someone would have been responsible for placing fresh flowers and tidying away the old. But I suppose the place just got too crowded. Too many tombs, too much work, until one of my ancestors decided that such time could be better spent at the service of the living. No one comes down here anymore except at funerals. And no one stays except those who have to."

"The Hall seems to go on forever," said Fisher. "I can't even see the end from here. How are we going to find Harald's tomb?"

"The Seneschal's guide should take us right to it," said

Hawk. "As a recent arrival, he shouldn't be too far from the door."

They followed the bobbing light down the wide aisle in the center of the Hall, passing by countless empty marble slabs, prepared for those Forest dead yet to come. It was unbearably quiet, the only sound the soft slap of their boots on the stone floor. It seemed a very small sound in such a large place. The sorcerous light all around them never wavered, reflecting palely from the surprisingly low ceiling overhead. Fisher stuck close to Hawk's side. The sheer size of the Hall intimidated her, made her feel small and insignificant. She could almost feel the pressure of centuries of past history pressing down on her. Hillsdown was a relatively recent country, with only four generations between the current Starlight Duke and Hillsdown's original founder. Walking through the Forest Crypt was like walking back into a past she could barely visualize. Fisher kept her back straight and held her head high. Coming here had been mostly her idea. She'd needed to see Harald's tomb, if only because part of her would never really believe he was dead and gone until she'd seen his final resting place.

The first tomb they stopped beside was that of Rupert and Harald's father, King John IV. The solid stone coffin was seven feet long and covered in traditional runes and decorative curlicues, topped by a life-sized marble statue of King John, lying supine in full armor, his hands crossed on his chest, holding the hilt of a long sword that rested upon the length of his body. The carved cold marble face was idealized but still recognizable. Hawk hadn't seen his father's face in twelve years, and something very like loss tugged at his heart. Despite lives lived pretty much constantly at odds, father and son had made a kind of reconciliation at the end, fighting side by side against the overwhelming odds of the Demon War. The King's marble face had a peace it rarely knew in life, and was covered by a thin layer of undisturbed dust. No one had touched this tomb since it had been put in place.

"Fancy carving," said Fisher. "And a far better likeness than those official portraits of us up above."

"A fine tomb," said Hawk. "Of course, there's no one

in it. They never did find my father's body. Still, it's the thought that counts."

They moved on. Hawk didn't look back. Fisher shivered. The Crypt wasn't really cold, but there was a spiritual chill in the great Hall that penetrated right through to the bone. God, don't let me end up in a place like this, she thought fervently. So far from light and warmth and living things. Just lay me down under the good green grass, with maybe a small stone for my name, and a nice view. Then let me sleep till Judgment Day, and if God is kind, I won't dream.

And then, all too soon, they came to the tomb of King Harald I. Here the coffin was fully eight feet long, with many detailed elaborations carved into its sides, depicting scenes of Harald fighting the demons in the long night. The statue lying supine on top of the coffin was exactly like King John's, except for having Harald's face, and being much larger. There was a thin layer of dust covering this statue, too, and at the foot of the coffin a single wreath held dead and withered flowers. It was clear to both Hawk and Fisher that no one had come to visit Harald since his funeral. Somehow neither of them was surprised. Harald might or might not have been a good King, but he had never been the sort to inspire devotion after his death.

"Why is Harald's coffin and statue bigger than John's?" Fisher asked after a while.

"Because he designed it himself," said Hawk. "He always said he would. He cared about such things."

"Presumably that's why the statue's face is a bit more accurate," said Fisher. "Probably had it carved while he was still alive."

"Probably." Hawk looked at the oversized coffin and found it hard to feel anything. He'd said all he had to say to Harald before he left the Castle and the Forest, twelve long years ago. All their old jealousies and conflicts had been eroded away by distance and time, and now seemed like something that had happened to other people. Standing there beside his brother's tomb, Hawk felt no real sorrow, or even regret. He was there out of duty, because Harald was family. And because, truth be told, Harald would have been there for him if matters had gone otherwise. Blood called to blood, family to family, no matter how separate they might become, by time or space or emotion.

Damn you, Harald, Hawk thought tiredly. I left the Forest Land in your hands, so I could leave, and turn my back on family duty. Couldn't you do anything right?

"Nobody's been down here since the interment," said Fisher, wrinkling her nose at the dust at Harald's face. "Not even the Queen. Do you suppose that's significant?"

"Probably not," said Hawk. "According to an old book my tutors once made me read, things were very different in the early days of the Forest line. Then it was customary for the Royal family to come down here at regular intervals, to remember their ancestors, why they were and what they did. They'd hold picnics between the tombs and retell old stories of valor and courage. It was important to know the line from which you'd sprung, the history you came from, and to set an example of what would be expected of you once you came of age. But as the numbers of the dead increased, the practice declined and finally disappeared. Now the old deeds are only remembered in romanticized and probably inaccurate songs and plays that come and go according to the fashion of the day. And no one comes down here because they don't like to be reminded of the certainty of their own death. This is a place to be visited only briefly, when necessary, and then forgotten as quickly as possible."

"The Demon War might have had something to do with that," said Fisher. "We all saw too much death under the Blue Moon. We all lost friends and loved ones. Can you blame people for wanting to concentrate on life rather than death after an experience like that?"

"I don't blame anyone," said Hawk. He looked slowly around him. "I never thought to see this place again. I fully expected to die in some filthy back alley in Haven, when I got too old or too slow, and someone's sword proved just that little bit faster than my axe."

"I never really thought about it at all," said Fisher. "I expected to die in the long night. Every day since then has been a gift, a second life I had no right to expect."

"We did die in Haven, sort of," said Hawk. "And there was a place we went to."

"I barely remember it," said Fisher. "That sorcerer put a spell on us. You know you can't trust anything to do with magic."

"Dammit," said Hawk with a sudden anger that surprised them both, "Harald deserved better than this. He was a real hero in the Demon War. For all his faults, and he had many, when the time came, he went out to fight the demons in the long night, to protect and preserve the Forest Land. It never even occurred to him not to. He wielded one of the Infernal Devices, and didn't let the damned sword corrupt him. He put his life on the line for his homeland, again and again. He deserved better than to die at the hand of some sneaking assassin over some stupid piece of politics."

"I remember Harald," Fisher said slowly, looking down at the dusty marble face. "But it's hard to say who I remember. I was intimate with him for a time, you know that, but I can't say I ever really knew him. He had so many faces, to show to different people at different times. Whether the face he showed me was the real him, I couldn't say. He never let anyone get close to him. But he was always kind to me, and did his best to protect me. He tried to understand me, when no one else did. And yet whether he really cared for me or just wanted me, I never knew. Now he's gone, and I'll never know."

"I never liked him, but I always thought he'd make a good King," said Hawk. "Far better than me. He always knew the right thing to say, how to get people to do what he wanted, while still thinking it was their own idea. And he had a real gift for organization. Loved paperwork. He was the politician in the family; he should have been the perfect King for the transition between the old ways and the new. It was only because I believed that, that I was able to leave the Forest with you. I could have been King if I'd chosen. There were many who would have backed my claim to the Throne. But that would have meant civil war, and I didn't want that. I didn't want to be King. Harald looked the much better bet. But did I believe that because I wanted to? Because I didn't want all the duties and responsibilities that went with being King?"

"You did what you thought was best," said Fisher. "That's all any of us can ever do."

She let her fingertips drift slowly across the cold marble of Harald's face, leaving creamy white trails in the dust, and then snatched her hand back as a shower of brilliant sparks erupted from the carved face. Hawk and Fisher backed away, hands dropping to their weapons, and watched in amazement as the sparks circled and spun above Harald's tomb before rushing together to form a perfect image of the late King Harald. The apparition looked pretty much as they remembered him; still large and muscular and classically handsome. But his face was heavily lined with strain and care, and there were already thick streaks of gray in his hair. He looked beaten down, confused, almost bewildered. Neither Hawk nor Fisher had ever known him look this defeated, not even during the worst days of the Demon War. He stared straight ahead of him, apparently unaware of Hawk and Fisher's presence.

"Hello, Rupert, Julia. If you're seeing this, then I'm dead. No, I'm not a ghost; this is my last message to you, recorded by a spell I had the Magus prepare for me, to be triggered after my death by your return. I am threatened on all sides, and no longer know whom I can trust. There are things you must know." He paused, as though uncertain how much he could say, even to his unseen audience. "I did my best. I tried to be a good King, to preserve the Forest Land. But everyone, everything, turned against me. I should never have allowed the Magus to open the Rift. It brought prosperity of a kind, but it also brought dangerous Southern ideas into the Land. There were always factions in the Court, but at least I understood them. Knew how to play them against each other, to prevent any one cause from becoming too powerful. Now democracy has become the new religion of the people, there's more political parties than I can shake a stick at, and there's growing pressure from all sides for me to stand down and become a constitutional monarch so a bunch of damned politicians can run things. I'm damned if I'll let the Land fall into their greedy, grasping hands. All they care about is power. They know nothing of duty and responsibility. And none of them can see the big picture. Not like I do.

"As a Prince, I had to make deals with people I despised. Once I was King, I no longer had to compromise. I had so many plans, so many things I intended to do, to make the Forest Kingdom strong and great again. But always I was undermined and defeated by the bloody politicians, spreading disobedience while claiming they spoke for the people. I was King! It was my job to decide what was best for the people. Because I was the only one in a position to see the big picture. Why couldn't everyone just do what they were told, when it was clearly in everyone's best interests?

"No King ever had to deal with the problems I faced. It wasn't my fault that I inherited a Land devastated and almost bankrupt, and then had to deal with all the changes brought about by the Rift. It wasn't my fault that the Inverted Cathedral returned. My people turned against me, seduced by the false promises of democracy. It wasn't fair. No one should have to face so many problems . . . so many evils. Not after surviving the long night. I still remember the dark, and the horrid light of the Blue Moon. I still have bad dreams, sometimes. And there is no one left to stand beside me. So it was all up to me. After all the chaos, all the madness, I had to make the world make sense.

"Julia, thank you for coming back. I had no right to demand that you return, but I hoped you would. I did care for you, in my way. And you were always so very good in bed." Fisher glanced quickly at Hawk, but his gaze was fixed on Harald, as his brother spoke haltingly of things past. "I would have loved you, Julia, but I don't know if I'm capable of love. If I have it in me. None of our family's ever been much good at caring for anything other than the Forest Land. I never loved the woman they made me marry, though I did admire her strength of character. I've no doubt she'll survive me. How much you trust her is up to you.

"Rupert, if you're here, do your duty. Be a strong King. Fight off democracy. And protect my son, if you can. He was the only good thing to come out of my life. And beware our father's legacy. That's all I have to say. I'm really very tired. Avenge my death, brother. Don't let me have died in vain."

The image vanished, and the Crypt was still and quiet again. Hawk and Fisher both let out long, slow breaths. "Well, that last bit was pure Harald," said Hawk. "Manipulative as ever."

Fisher frowned. "What do you suppose he meant by beware your father's legacy? What legacy?"

Hawk shrugged. "I have no idea. No doubt we'll find out, in time. Poor bastard. He didn't look like a happy man, did he? He spent his whole life plotting and preparing to be King, invested all his hopes and dreams in it. And then his dream betrayed him by coming true."

The Magus sat at ease in his quarters, slumped bonelessly in a comfortable chair. He wore a simple white tunic and trousers, and there was no sign anywhere of his great night-dark cloak. Without it, he looked surprisingly ordinary. He watched the chessboard set out on the small table before him, frowning slightly as the black and white pieces moved back and forth on their own, darting across the board with dizzying speed. The Magus watched the patterns carefully as they developed, and when the game finished, the pieces reset themselves and started all over again.

On the other side of the spacious, airy room, a human-sized and entirely naked Lightfoot Moonfleet was admiring herself in a full-length mirror. Her arms and legs were unusually long, and she had too many ribs, and there was something subtly disturbing about the way her bones knit together; but still, she was the most beautiful woman currently inhabiting Forest Castle, and Lightfoot Moonfleet knew it. In the mirror her reflection was modeling a series of different outfits and combinations for her approval. Styles and looks and colors came and went, blinking in and out too fast for the human eye to follow, until Lightfoot finally settled on the day's look. She snapped her fingers imperiously and the image before her settled on a tight black dress that ended just above the knees, with generous cutouts to show bare flesh in interesting places. Long black boots and evening gloves finished the look. Lightfoot was in a devilish mood. Her hair fluffed out like a dark dandelion, and dark eye makeup and vivid bloodred lips sharpened her face nicely.

"A little obvious, not to mention downright sluttish," said Lightfoot crisply. "Just the look I had in mind. You can go now."

Her reflection in the mirror stuck out her tongue at her, and vanished. Immediately Lightfoot Moonfleet was wearing the outfit she'd chosen, right down to the exact shadings of color on her face. She stretched slowly, as luxurious and unself-conscious as a cat, wriggled a few times to settle her dress, and then she turned to observe the Magus at his chess.

"So, which side are you playing today?"

"Both, as always," said the Magus without looking up. "I like the outfit. Quite understated, for you. Now prepare yourself. Company's coming."

Lightfoot looked around quickly. "Who is it? Can I jump their bones?"

"It's the good Captains Hawk and Fisher. They've been down in the Crypt, and spoken with the dead King. And now they're coming here, expecting answers to their questions."

The faerie smiled. "They don't know you very well yet, do they?"

"Oh, I have answers for them. Whether they'll fit the questions, I have no idea. It's hard to see the ties of destiny around Hawk and Fisher. The Wild Magic has touched them deeply, on levels they probably don't even know about. Perhaps they will be able to understand me, after all. They are no strangers to the weird and the uncanny, or the fields beyond."

"Will they be able to get to the truth?" asked Lightfoot, striding over to stand beside the Magus. "Will they find out who killed Harald?"

"Who cares if they discover the truth?" said the Magus calmly. "What matters is that they go into the Inverted Cathedral, and face what must be faced there. Harald could have done it, if he'd been the hero he claimed to be, or the King he wanted to be. But he wasn't, and he didn't, which is why we're in the mess we're in now."

"Harald was afraid," said Lightfoot Moonfleet. "Just like everyone else would be, if they knew the truth."

"Heroes feel fear," said the Magus, watching sadly as the black pieces on his board decimated the white, moving inexorably towards checkmate. "They just refuse to be ruled by it." He leaned forward suddenly, and swept all the pieces from the board with a slap of his hand. They fell to the bare floor, and lay there twitching for long moments, before finally lying still. The Magus leaned back in his chair, his face entirely calm and composed. "Hawk and Fisher must go into the Inverted Cathedral. There's no one else left."

"What about the Questor, Allen Chance?"

"A good man," the Magus admitted. "Perhaps too good. He thinks too much. There's not enough of his father in him. Not nearly enough ruthlessness. And he has too much to live for. That can weaken a man's resolve. No, Hawk and Fisher have always been ready to do what was necessary, and to hell with the cost and the consequences."

"And if they're not up to it?"

"Then the Blue Moon will come into its power again, the Transient Beings will be released from their long confinement, and there will be hell on earth."

"Abandon all hope . . ."

"Quite. Come in!"

The knock at the door came just after he'd spoken, and there was a bit of a pause before the door opened, and Hawk and Fisher came in. They looked quickly about them, as though studying a potential battlefield, and then advanced together on the Magus. Lightfoot moved to stand a little closer to him. The Magus nodded politely to his guests without getting up, and Hawk and Fisher nodded briefly in return as they came to a halt before him.

"Nice trick with the door," said Hawk. "But it must take all the fun out of Christmas."

"I don't celebrate," said the Magus. "I find all that remorseless sweetness and light a bit trying."

Fisher looked at the chess pieces on the floor. "Bad loser, Magus?"

"I never lose. It's bad for the image. How was the Crypt?"

Hawk and Fisher looked at each other. "How did you know we were just there?" asked Hawk sharply.

"I'm the Magus. I know things. That's my job. Did Harald have anything interesting to say?"

"Don't you know?" asked Fisher.

"Oh, I don't know everything. Think how boring that would be. I'm not omnipotent, just very well informed. I set up the spell for Harald, but whatever words he left behind him were strictly between Harald and his conscience. Assuming he had one."

"He was your King," said Fisher. "Show some respect."

Lightfoot Moonfleet stirred uneasily at the sudden cold anger in Fisher's voice, but the Magus just inclined his head slightly, as though acknowledging a point. "Did the King have anything to say that might help to identify his murderer?"

"Harald didn't point a finger at anyone in particular," said Hawk. "I was more interested in what he *didn't* say. There was nothing in what he clearly intended to be his last message to suggest he thought his life was in danger. He felt under threat, but by forces in general rather than any specific person."

"I thought so," said the Magus. "If Harald had considered any person a threat to his life, he would have had them arrested and worried about obtaining evidence later. At the very least, he would have had me investigate them. Come in!"

Once again, his words preceded the knock on the door. It swung open with a crash as one of Duke Alric's men stalked in, striding across the room like he was on the parade ground. He crashed to a halt before Hawk and Fisher, ignoring the Magus and the faerie. He wore a Hillsdown guard's uniform, complete with chainmail vest, and his right hand rested on the swordhilt at his side as he barked out his message to Hawk and Fisher. His voice was like his face—arrogant, offensive, and condescending.

"Hawk, Fisher, you are hereby commanded by the Starlight Duke to attend him at his quarters, there to be ques-

tioned by him on certain matters . . . on certain matters
appertaining to . . . to . . ."

The guard slowly turned his head. It was clear he didn't
want to, and equally clear he had no choice in the matter.
The Magus was looking at him. Still talking, the guard
turned his head in slow painful jerks until his eyes met the
Magus' gaze. The guard's words trailed away to nothing.
He looked deep into the Magus' eyes, and whimpered. And
then the hold over him was gone, and he turned and ran,
fleeing the room as though all the demons in the Darkwood
were after him. He shot out the doorway, and the sound
of his departing feet quickly died away. The Magus gestured lightly, and the door shut itself. Hawk looked at the
Magus, making a point of meeting his gaze squarely.

"What the hell was *that* all about?"

The Magus shrugged easily. "He was being a bit of a
bore, so I stared him down. Of course, if you feel you must
break off our little chat, to do as the Duke ordered . . ."

"No," said Fisher firmly. "The Duke can wait. And don't
think you can impress or scare us with tricks like that. We
don't scare easily."

The Magus considered her for a moment, then smiled.
"No," he said finally. "I don't suppose you do. The Darkwood was very dark, wasn't it?" He looked at Hawk.
"Didn't your hair used to be blond? Or was that your partner? I have an excellent memory, but sometimes it's so
good, it remembers things that didn't happen. That's one
of the problems with seeing the future, when the future's
always changing."

"You can see the future?" Fisher asked.

"Through a glass, darkly. Never enough to be of any real
use, just enough to confuse and disturb me. Some things
are more inevitable than others. And people do confuse
the issue so."

The Magus rose suddenly to his feet, startling Lightfoot
into falling back a pace, and then he walked over to look
out the open window, as though forgetting they were there.
Lightfoot took a few steps after him, and then stopped.

Fisher leaned in close beside Hawk. "That blond hair
remark was a bit pointed. Do you think he—"

"If he did, he'd have said so. He loves showing off his knowledge."

Fisher frowned uncertainly. "Is it me, or did his eyes used to be gray, not blue?"

"God, I'm glad you said that. I thought so, but . . . Hold everything. Look at that."

They both looked at the Magus' feet, which were hovering a good two inches above the floor.

"Oh, don't mind that," said Lightfoot Moonfleet. "He has a lot on his mind just now, and sometimes he forgets things. Like gravity."

"What exactly are you looking for, sir Magus?" said Hawk, after the sorcerer had spent some time staring out the window in silence.

"My cloak," said the Magus absently. "It's off hunting somewhere, and I do worry about it when it's out on its own. There are dangerous things abroad in the Forest these days. It used to be the cloak was one of them, but—ah, here it comes."

He stepped back, smiling fondly as his cloak came flapping in through the open window like a great black bat. It swooped around the Magus twice, as though greeting him, and then flapped off to settle in a corner. It stood upright, trembling slightly, and then made a series of loud and quite disgusting digestive noises. The Magus shut the window.

"What exactly does your cloak hunt?" asked Hawk.

"Oh, anything that can't run away fast enough, basically," said the Magus, coming back to join them. His feet were back on the floor again.

"Including people?" asked Fisher, looking dubiously at the cloak.

"Oh, no," said the Magus. "Not anymore."

He sat down again and looked sternly at Hawk and Fisher. "We must talk. There are things I have to tell you. Some of them you may already know, but that's destiny for you. First, the Rift that links north and south. I created it. The last great spell of Wild Magic in the world of men. There will never be another to match it. Magic is going out of the world, and is flexing its muscles in a few desperate last shows of might. But as man thrives, and spreads across this world, making it his own, magic will whither away, replaced by the more useful science, which is more suited to man's nature. Science always works. Its principles are logical. Man is at heart a rational creature, and wants a rational world, where rules are always followed and everything makes sense. The Wild Magic was slowly replaced by High Magic, a more structured form that some men could tame to their use, but even that is fading now. Most people's minds just aren't flexible enough to deal with magic."

"What about this new Chaos Magic that's based on mathematics?" Fisher asked. "Supposedly that's the way of the future."

"Rubbish!" snapped the Magus. "Chaos Magic is just a pathetic halfway attempt to produce a magic that works like science. Neither one thing nor the other. It's based on a few good ideas, but it will soon be swept away by science that everyone can understand and be taught. No, within the next dozen generations or so magic will be gone, and the world will be a safer, duller place. All the myth and wonder of the world will be replaced by gadgets and mechanisms. Clever, but essentially soulless. No dragons, no unicorns . . ."

"No demons, no Demon Prince?" asked Hawk.

The Magus looked at him sharply. "Good. Yes. You grasp the point. As man learns to control his world through science, so the greater threats to his existence will be banished. You banished the Demon Prince through the Wild Magic of the Rainbow, but he can still return. He is a Transient Being, one of the never-born, the soulless, the stalkers on the edge of reality, a living personification of an abstract idea. As such, he can never be destroyed, as long as magic exists. Ideas are immortal. But replace magic with science and he cannot return, because this whole plane of existence would be closed to him and his kind. He could no longer exist here; the scientific laws of the universe would not permit it."

"The Transient Beings?" asked Fisher. "You mean there are more beings like the Demon Prince?"

"Of course," said the Magus. "For every abstract concept, idea, or myth, some magical being exists to personify it. That's part of the present magical nature of reality. Which brings me, naturally, to the Blue Moon."

"It does?" Hawk asked. "Slow this down, Magus, I'm having trouble hanging on."

"Right," said Fisher.

"The Blue Moon," said the Magus patiently. "You never did think very much about its nature and its purpose, did you? What it was, what it was for?"

"We were too busy trying to stay alive!" snapped Fisher. "The only one who really knew anything about the Blue Moon was the High Warlock. And he was usually too off his face or just plain crazy to be able to explain much."

"Ah, yes, the High Warlock," said the Magus. "Such a pity I never got a chance to meet him. A remarkable mind, by all accounts."

Hawk looked at him sharply. "Chance told us you claimed to be the High Warlock's chosen successor when you first came to Court."

"Oh, that," said the Magus easily. "I lied. I do that sometimes. And I'm sure the High Warlock would have chosen me as his successor, if we'd ever met. Now, the Blue Moon . . ."

"It unleashed the Wild Magic," said Hawk. "It spread the Darkwood across the Forest Land."

"You see? You haven't thought this through at all." The Magus suddenly looked tired. He settled back in his chair, like an old man who'd suddenly felt how cold the room was getting. Lightfoot Moonfleet moved in close beside him, and put a comforting hand on his shoulder. The Magus laced his fingers together across his chest and stared at them. "The Blue Moon. A moon orbits a world. Yes? But since the Blue Moon is not our moon, what world does it orbit? A moon reflects light from the sun. But what sun does the Blue Moon orbit that it reflects such a terrible light? Our moon and the Blue Moon exist in different planes of reality, but at certain irregular intervals their travels bring them into the same basic point in space, though separated by dimensional barriers. When the orbits coincide, and the two moons occupy the same space, certain events or people can bring the Blue Moon to this world, and then all the locks on all the doors are broken, and Wild Magic is loosed to run free in the world of men."

"We've been told the Blue Moon is coming back," said Fisher. "Is that possible? After only twelve years?"

"Of course. Times moves differently there. Once in a Blue Moon . . ."

"But what's bringing it back this time?" asked Hawk. "The Demon Prince is still banished, the Darkwood has returned to its old boundaries, and the damned fools who summoned the Demon Prince in the first place are no longer with us."

The Magus looked at him almost sadly. "The Inverted Cathedral is back. And its very existence is enough to summon back the Blue Moon. Which is why you and Captain Fisher have to go into the Inverted Cathedral, and put an end to its threat. If you can."

"Hold everything," said Fisher immediately. "We don't *have* to do anything. We're just here to solve a murder."

"The murder doesn't matter. You must enter the Inverted Cathedral. It is your destiny."

"What do you know about destiny?" Hawk asked sharply.

"More than you think."

"You can't make us do anything we don't want to," said Fisher stubbornly. "You try and pressure us, and—"

"You want answers," the Magus broke in. "And you'll only find them inside the Inverted Cathedral."

"What kind of answers?" asked Hawk.

"To everything," said the Magus.

"Including who killed Harald?"

The Magus sighed. "You will do what you have to do. Your nature will not permit anything else. Go now. I'm tired."

"We're not going anywhere till you've answered some straight questions," said Hawk. "Let's start with the obvious one. Where were you when King Harald was murdered?"

"Right here," said the Magus, as though indulging a persistent child. "I'm always here, except when I have to be somewhere else."

"Can anyone confirm that?"

"Lightfoot Moonfleet was with me."

Hawk looked at the faerie, who turned the full force of her smile on him. Her eyes were sultry and heavy-lidded. "We were both here, together, Captain. Would you like to interrogate me next? I'd just love to be interrogated by you. We could go somewhere private. I've got these lovely new handcuffs I've been dying to try out. I'm sure you could persuade me to tell you absolutely anything."

"Back off, right now," said Fisher coldly. "Your estrogen is showing. And, Hawk, if you take even one step in her direction, I will break both your legs."

Hawk looked apologetically at Lightfoot. "The trouble is, she means it."

"I should have felt my protective wards being broken," the Magus said slowly, ignoring everything else. "But I felt nothing. Alarms should have gone off in my mind if the wards had merely been tested. But I felt nothing. When I was informed of the murder, I hurried to the King's private quarters immediately, but my wards were still intact when I got there. Which is, technically speaking, impossible. The wards were set up to keep out everyone but the King's immediate family. And the Queen was nowhere near him at the time. I put a lot of work into those wards, and I would have sworn on a pile of grimoires that there wasn't a sorcerer in or out of the Land strong enough to break them. Let alone pass through them without setting off my alarms. It really is most disquieting."

"Can you think of anyone who could have done it?" Fisher asked.

"The High Warlock."

"But he's dead," said Hawk.

"That doesn't necessarily exclude him," said the Magus.

"Would you care to explain that?" asked Fisher.

"Not really, no," said the Magus. "I examined the murder scene very carefully, using every magic at my disposal, but I was unable to discover any clue or any magical residue from the site. Which again is, technically speaking, impossible. No one currently present in Forest Castle should be able to cleanse a scene that thoroughly."

"Except you," said Hawk.

"Well, yes," said the Magus. "But if I may be blunt for a moment, if I was going to kill someone, I'd have enough sense to do it in a way that wouldn't point straight in my direction. Besides, Harald was my King. I swore fealty to him and his Throne, and I do not give my word lightly."

Hawk looked at Fisher. "Can you think of anything we've missed? Then we might as well go. We've got a lot of people to see today. Thank you for your time, sir Magus, Lightfoot Moonfleet. We may be back again, if we have any more questions."

"Beware the truth," said the Magus quietly, not looking at him. "It won't make you happy and it won't set you free. Some things are hidden for a reason. Discovering the murderer won't necessarily bring the matter to a close. And justice never comes cheap."

"Am I supposed to understand any of that?" asked Hawk.

"No. But you will."

The Magus leaned back in his chair and closed his eyes, making it clear he had nothing more to say. Lightfoot Moonfleet waggled her fingers prettily in a good-bye. Hawk and Fisher left, closing the door quietly behind them. In its corner, the cloak dropped a handful of bones onto the floor. Some of the bones were quite large, with bits of meat and gristle still clinging to them. The Magus addressed Lightfoot Moonfleet without opening his eyes.

"Follow Hawk and Fisher. Go where they go, see who they see, listen to what is said, and then return. Don't be seen. And don't get caught."

The faerie grinned widely, then shrank down to barely an inch in height. Her multicolored wings burst out of her back as she shrank, and within seconds she was fluttering after Hawk and Fisher, flitting easily through the large keyhole in the closed door. The Magus sighed heavily. The Blue Moon would be here soon, darkness was already gathering in the Castle, and all the plans he had so carefully set in motion with his opening of the Rift no longer seemed as certain or as comforting as they once had.

* * *

Not for the first time Queen Felicity had woken up late, feeling terrible, and was now taking it out on all those unfortunate enough to be compelled to attend her. She strode about her receiving chamber wearing nothing but a silk wraparound robe, pursued by a small army of retainers and courtiers, all of them vying desperately for her attention. Even first thing in the morning there were papers to be signed, decisions to be made, plans to approve and assign; and as always everything had to be done right now. Nothing could wait. To hear the courtiers and retainers talk, as they pursued the Queen back and forth while she fortified herself with coffee and cigarettes, the whole fate of the Forest Kingdoms depended on the Queen paying attention to them first and everyone else second. In the past a few of the more determined souls had tried to follow her into the jakes, but that stopped after she stubbed out a cigarette on one of them. The retainers and courtiers now kept a mostly respectful distance, but that only meant that everyone raised their voices that much higher.

Queen Felicity stalked about her receiving room studying the various gowns her servants held out for her approval, and signed papers and announced decisions apparently at random. Felicity liked to make it clear who was in charge. It kept people on their toes. Sometimes literally. Eventually they ran out of important things to bother her with, and Felicity drove them all out with threats and curses and the occasional fast-moving object. The Queen's servants had learned to make sure there were always a number of useful items handy for her to throw. Otherwise she threw the expensive stuff. Felicity chose one gown and waved away the others, and then signaled for the servant hovering nearby with a coffee pot to come forward and freshen her cup. She drank deeply and sighed happily. Nothing like a good jolt of caffeine to get your heart started first thing in the morning. She waved all the servants away, and they left quickly before she thought of something else for them to do.

Felicity looked over at her young son, King-to-be Stephen, almost two years old now. He currently sat in a corner, absorbed in a pile of brightly colored alphabet bricks,

watched over by his nanny/nurse/bodyguard, Cally, a large
and muscular warrior woman the Queen had brought with
her from Hillsdown. Cally had come to Hillsdown some
years back as a mercenary sword-for-hire, and had been
appointed bodyguard to the teenaged Princess Felicity.
After a certain amount of necessary sparring, the two had
become firm friends, and it was only Cally's running inter-
ference that allowed Felicity to have as much fun as she
did. There was no one else Felicity would have trusted her
child with. Cally adored the young boy, and would have
given her life for the child without a second thought.

Tall, sturdy, and more than generously proportioned,
Cally could intimidate people just by entering the room.
She made a striking figure at Court. Felicity brought her
along now and again when she had a courtier she felt could
use a good scare. Cally's round face was disarmingly pleasant under a military-styled haircut, but it fooled no one.
She once had to kill a rather objectable person at Court,
and did it with a thoroughness that impressed everyone.
Especially those who got some of the blood on their
clothes.

The Queen hovered over her son, briskly affectionate,
but he ignored her, lost in his own little world. Felicity
snorted loudly and moved away.

"Just like his father. What he wants first, and everyone
else second. How long have we got before I have to go to
Court, Cally?"

The bodyguard put down the metal spring she'd been
squeezing to build up the muscles in her hand, and leafed
through the Queen's appointment book.

"About three quarters of an hour, Your Majesty. Time for
a bath, if you're quick about it, and don't bother with the
bubbles. Did you finish all your breakfast this morning?"

"Don't boss me, Cally. I'll have a little something about
eleven, when my stomach's woken up. Anything I need
to know?"

Part of Cally's job was keeping a discreet ear to the infor-
mal Castle gossip grapevine. Every faction in the Castle,
and a few outside, had their own paid informants on hand,
but Cally's sources were second to none, mainly because

they were composed almost entirely of servants. It was amazing how often high-placed and fairly intelligent people took servants for granted, almost like part of the furniture, and would say things in front of them that they wouldn't have dreamed of telling their own family. And all the servants reported to Cally. A bodyguard to both the Regent and the Royal heir, Cally considered the best response to any threat was knowing in advance which direction it was coming from. And it helped the Queen's image at Court no end to seem to be all-knowing. Especially on matters she wasn't supposed to know even existed.

"Nothing much of interest yet," said Cally, putting down the appointment book to study her own private notebook. "The Shaman's making a nuisance of himself again, preaching social reform and revolution in the main courtyard. Just the usual fire and damnation stuff, but the peasants are eating it up with spoons. Your father's still sulking in his quarters, after being faced down by Hawk and Fisher. Who when last seen were on their way to question the Magus."

Felicity snorted again. "And the best of luck to them. Getting straight answers out of the Magus is harder than pulling your own teeth, and about as much fun."

"True," said Cally. "I've got more useful noises out of the mouths of corpses after treading on their stomachs."

Felicity looked at her. "You didn't . . ."

"Everyone's entitled to a hobby."

"You're disgusting, Cally, you know that? I'd send you on another charm course if we hadn't run out of tutors."

"I quite fancied the last one."

"I know. He's still shaking."

Felicity dropped onto a hard chair in front of her dressing table, and studied her face dispassionately in the mirror. She hadn't an ounce of makeup on, her defiantly blond hair was curled up tightly in metal rollers, and a cigarette protruded from one corner of her mouth. "Jesus," she said tiredly. "Looking presentable gets harder every day. I'd use a shape-change spell, but you can bet one of those Academy bitches would be sure to spot it. Has that new face cream arrived from the south yet?"

"Just got through customs," said Cally. "A whole crate

of the muck. I don't know why you waste your money on it. It won't make any more difference than all the earlier muck did. You're getting old, Fliss. Get used to it."

"Never!" said Felicity. "I am in my prime! And I still look it, with a little help. I wonder if I could get away with another beauty spot."

"Any more spots and people will think you've got the plague," said Cally dispassionately. "Either that or someone will try joining up the dots to make a picture."

"It's all right for you," snapped Felicity. "You're a bodyguard. You're supposed to have a face like a bulldog licking piss off a thistle. I'm the Queen, dammit. I have to look radiant. It's expected of me." She took a hard puff at her cigarette. "Damn, these things make your head spin first thing in the morning. Have you seen my cigarette holder anywhere?"

"Where did you last have it?"

"If I knew that, I'd bloody well look there, wouldn't I? Look for it. And get me another coffee. Black, three sugars."

"You do know you're due at the dentist again, don't you?"

Felicity shuddered. "You're just trying to depress me this morning, aren't you?"

"Come on," said Cally ruthlessly. "Put on your face and get dressed if you're not going to bother with a bath. You've got to look your best for the Court, and right now you'd frighten a demon."

"Wonderful. I'm being bullied by my own bodyguard. What else can go wrong this morning?"

There was a loud knock at the door. Felicity and Cally looked at each other, surprised. Most people had enough sense not to disturb the Queen while she was dressing. People had been banished for less. Cally moved to stand beside the Queen, her hand at the sword on her hip as a servant came in, and at the Queen's nod, went to answer the door. Hawk and Fisher strode right in, sweeping past the servant, and bowed briefly to the Queen.

"Oh, bloody hell," said Felicity. "It's you. Can't this wait?"

"Not really," said Hawk. "We've a lot of people to see today." He smiled at the Queen, pulled up a chair, and sat down opposite her, politely pretending not to notice her unfinished state. Felicity was so astonished at his nerve that she let him do it. Fisher hung back. She and Hawk had decided earlier that he should do most of the talking, while she faded into the background. Julia had never spent much time with her sister Felicity, even when they both lived under the same roof. They had nothing in common save their father. It was twelve years and more since they'd last seen each other, and Fisher was a brunette now. But she still worried about being recognized. So she hung back, kept a watchful eye on the bodyguard, and tried to look inconspicuous. She had to work at it. It didn't come naturally. She and Cally exchanged glances, each recognizing a kindred spirit in the other. They both knew a warrior when they saw one. They exchanged meaningless smiles and kept their hands near their swordhilts.

"All right," the Queen said ungraciously to Hawk. "Ask your questions and then get the hell out of here." She waved for the servant to leave. "And don't think you can intimidate me, Captain, barging in here when I haven't even got my face on yet. Better men than you have tried, and run home weeping to their mothers. I grew up in the Starlight Duke's Court, and if I could survive him, I can survive any man. What do you want to know?"

"Well, let's start with your father, the Duke," Hawk said easily. "A very forceful man. I think a lot of people here would like to know just how much influence he has over you. You are Regent to the Forest Land now, and protector of its someday King. And the Duke has always had a reputation for martial adventuring whenever he sensed a weakness."

"That's a hell of a lot of inferences for just one sentence," said Felicity, entirely unruffled. "Don't you worry about Daddy. I can handle him. He's a long way from home, and separated from all his usual support. My main worries these days come from inside my own Court, damn their black and blistered souls." She took a long draw on her cigarette and threw the last of it away. "I never wanted to be the Forest Queen, you know. Never wanted to be anybody's Queen. But Daddy insisted, and I was in no position to say no then. After Julia disappeared with Rupert, the treaty between Hillsdown and the Forest meant one of the Duke's daughters had to marry Harald, or risk open war. Not that I gave a damn, but . . . Anyway, I was the next youngest after Julia, so I got to put my head on the block for the good of my country. So all of this could be said to be Julia's fault. She always was a selfish bitch.

"I didn't want to marry anyone. All I ever wanted was to party till I dropped, have as good a time as possible while avoiding dear Daddy's informers, and now and again scandalize the Court with some new fashion, style, or love affair. I once went to Court with jewelry hanging from my bare nipples, and the Duke all but had a coronary on the spot. The love affairs were all strictly for show. I kept my real romances strictly secret. I had three abortions dear Daddy never knew about. I didn't want children then, didn't want to see them grow up miserable in my father's Court, like me and my sisters. He never wanted children, either, just pawns he could use in his political games."

She broke off and rooted among the assorted garbage piled on top of her dressing table. "Ciggies . . . can't do without a ciggie this early in the morning. Best damn thing to ever come out of the south. And coffee, of course." She finally found a silver case, pulled out a black cigarette with blue rings on it, and stuck it in the corner of her mouth. Then everything had to stop while she searched for matches. Finally lit up, the Queen leaned back in her chair again, sighed contentedly, and puffed smoke at Hawk.

"Being Forest Queen was all Daddy's idea. A son of such a union could be used to unite Hillsdown and the Forest. That was all the Duke cared about. Another pawn for him to manipulate. Never asked my opinion, of course. He knew if he had, I'd just have told him to kiss my bony arse. Being Queen here wasn't much different to being a Princess at Hillsdown. Harald had all the power. My job was to run the social scene and look good on his arm. I was kept well away from all the political maneuvering. Harald didn't trust a Hillsdown woman too close to the sources of power. So we each had our separate lives, except for when we had to appear together in public for ceremonial occasions and the like."

Felicity drew heavily on her cigarette and looked moodily off into the distance. "You want to know how I felt about Harald, don't you? Well, I'm not sure I know even now. Harald wasn't an easy man to get to know. He had different faces for everyone. We liked each other well enough, I suppose. Argued morning, noon, and night, but that was just our way of communicating. And he was damn good in bed. When he was around. I used to think he had lovers, God knows I did, but if so he had them even better hidden than me. But I think he was more interested in being King and consolidating his power than he ever was in being my husband."

"All those years you were married," Hawk said carefully. "You only ever had the one child. You mentioned abortions earlier . . ."

"We only had the one child because Harald wasn't around often enough to manage more than one," said Felicity tartly. "And with anyone else I was always damned careful to use the right protective spells. A girl can't be too careful when she's Queen. And, yes, Stephen is very definitely Harald's son. He insisted on all kinds of magical tests, in private, to make sure of that. I didn't really want an heir, but I knew it was expected of me. Part of the job. And I'm fond enough of him now he's here. I'll tell you this for free: I'd kill anyone who tried to take him away from me."

They watched the small child for a while, still playing solemnly with his colored bricks. Hawk looked at the boy closely, trying to see some of his brother or the Forest line in the child, but the boy was just a boy to him. He looked back at Felicity.

"Who do you think killed Harald?"

The Queen started to laugh, and coughed suddenly on cigarette smoke. "I'm spoiled for choice, darling. He had a hell of a lot of enemies, most of them made on purpose. Either you supported the King in everything you thought and said and did, or you were his enemy. He could be charming and persuasive enough when he had to be, and he could make political deals with the best of them when his back was forced to the wall over some important issue . . . but he never forgot and he never forgave. He wouldn't delegate any of his power, either. Everything had to go through him, even when it drowned him in paperwork. Give him his due, he was always good at that side of things. No one ever got anything past him. But if you want suspects . . .

"I'd have to put the Magus at the top of the list. No one trusts him. Then there's the Shaman. Crazy old bastard, and bitter and twisted with it. Spends half his time calling for the dissolution of the monarchy and the other half trying to turn the peasants into a political power base. I'd have had him thrown out onto his smelly arse ages ago, but Harald wouldn't hear of it. In a strange kind of way I think they respected each other. Though they never met in person, to my knowledge. And finally, there's the Landsgrave, Sir Robert. There isn't a political deal or intrigue going down in this Castle that he doesn't know about or have a hand in. Never happy unless he's stirring the pot. And, of course, there's me." She smiled sardonically at Hawk, showing teeth already yellowed by nicotine. "You'll hear all sorts about me, and most of them are true. But it was always in my interest to keep Harald alive, to secure my Stephen's position and future. I'd do anything for my boy. Are we finished now? I feel naked sitting here without any slap on my face."

"Why do you think your husband was murdered?" asked Hawk, sticking doggedly to the series of questions he and Fisher had worked out over breakfast.

"Someone didn't like the way he ruled as King. I would have thought that was obvious."

"Was he a good King?"

Felicity frowned. "He thought being King meant he had to do it all himself. It was all his responsibility. His duty. He was always very big on duty. He wouldn't delegate because he never trusted anyone apart from himself. And yes, of course that included me, too. He'd listen to people at Court, and he wasn't above stealing a good idea when he heard one, but everything and everyone had to fit in around the way he saw things. That was just the way he was." Felicity thought for a moment, tapping ash from her cigarette onto the floor. "Once, in bed, he talked about his father. King John, that was. Harald said his father was a weak King, and everything that happened in the Demon War was a direct result of that weakness. That was the only time he ever talked about his father. I think a lot of what Harald did, and was, came from not wanting to be his father."

"You mentioned the two of you had rows from time to time," Hawk said carefully. "Did Harald ever . . . hurt you? Beat you?"

Felicity laughed raucously. "He wouldn't have dared. I'd have kicked the shit out of him if he ever laid a hand on me, and he knew it. We always respected each other's strength. And besides, no matter how many rows we had, we always made up in bed eventually. Sometimes I'd pick a fight deliberately, just to be sure of getting a little action later on. Harald was never easy about sex. I don't think he liked feeling emotionally naked, defenseless."

Fisher found she was nodding automatically in agreement, and quickly stopped herself. "What about your lovers?" she asked harshly, just in case Felicity or her bodyguard had noticed her lapse.

"I was always very careful," said the Queen. "You have to be, round here. Never known such a place for gossip. Makes Hillsdown's Court look like a bunch of amateurs. Harald always suspected, but as long as there was never any proof or evidence to embarrass him, he didn't care. I almost wished he would sometimes. It would have made it more fun. Of course, these days every move I make is watched and reported on, so I haven't had any fun in ages. They'd use even the suspicion of a scandal to remove me as Regent and take control of my son.

"I could always marry again. Any number of people would be only too happy to marry the Regent. You'd be surprised how charming and desirable I've become since I was widowed. Two-faced bastards. I'll not marry again. Once was more than enough, thank you. No, I'll hang on here just long enough to see Stephen safely on his Throne, and then it's a big house in the country for me, and as many pretty boys as my Royal allowance will stretch to. You're looking positively shocked, Captain Hawk. Guess whether I give a shit. You get one more question, and then I'll turn Cally loose on you. Make it a good one.''

"All right," said Hawk. "Where were you when Harald was murdered?"

"At Court," said the Queen triumphantly. "Sitting right there on the Throne, receiving a trade delegation from the south. Most of the Court was there at the time. Hundreds of people can vouch for me. Right, that's it, on your way. Cally, show them the door and then slam it behind them."

It was a good exit line, but unfortunately Cally and Fisher were engaged in a glaring contest, and oblivious. Hawk had to slap Fisher on the arm to get her attention. They bowed briefly and left. Cally locked and bolted the door behind them. Felicity slumped forward in her chair, her head hanging down, exhausted. Cally came over and massaged her shoulders.

"One of your better performances, Your Majesty."

"Yeah, but do you think they believed me?"

"Depends on what everyone else says. And let's not forget who Hawk and Fisher are. They have a reputation for getting to the truth."

"Jesus, that's all anyone needs, the truth coming out. We've got far too much to hide. And we're late for Court! Quick, you take the curlers out while I work on the face. And from the smell of it, dear little Stephen needs seeing to again. Oh God, it's going to be one of those days, I can feel it."

Hawk and Fisher strolled down the corridor, following the Seneschal's bobbing light, thinking their own thoughts. Eventually Hawk looked at Fisher and smiled.

"And I always thought you were the forceful one in the family. Are all your sisters like that?"

"We're all strong-minded in our own different ways," Fisher said defensively. "We had to be. The weak didn't last long in my father's Court. He was always looking for someone to make an example of, and sometimes I think he liked it all the better if it was someone close to him."

"And now I have a nephew," Hawk said slowly. "The Forest line continues. He looked healthy enough, if a bit on the quiet side. Why did we never have kids, Isobel?"

"I don't know. We could have found time, if we'd really wanted to. Our lives have always been full, not to mention dangerous. And just maybe it's because we both had such rotten childhoods. Both our families give new meaning to the word *dysfunctional*. This isn't something we should be thinking about now, Hawk. Concentrate on the matter at hand. One problem at a time. Otherwise, there's a really good chance we could get our heads handed to us."

"Of course," said Hawk. "One thing at a time. But there's always something, isn't there?"

They followed the glowing light in silence for a while, neither of them looking at each other.

Tiffany had to excuse herself on witchy business for the Academy of the Sisters of the Moon, so Chance went to pick up Chappie from the Castle kitchens. Chappie wasn't supposed to be there; in fact, he'd been banned several times on hygiene grounds, but when a dog is as big as Chappie, he doesn't have to observe such restrictions if he doesn't feel like it. And mostly he didn't. Chance walked into the kitchens, into the heat and steam and staff running back and forth, tending to pots and pans and large things revolving on spits, and sure enough there was Chappie sprawled out under a table, gnawing happily on an entire leg bone, and cracking it open between his powerful jaws to get at the marrow. His satisfied growls and grunts and sighs would have intimidated anyone not actually wearing full armor and carrying a battleaxe in both hands, so not surprisingly the kitchen staff had left the dog strictly alone. Chance sighed, strode up to the table, reached under it, and grabbed Chappie firmly by one great floppy ear. The dog dropped his bone to the floor and scrambled out from under the table as Chance applied merciless pressure to the ear.

"Ow! Ow! Bully! All right, I'm out, now will you let go

of my ear before it ends up twice the length? I'll report you for cruelty one of these days."

"I am not letting go of your ear," Chance said reasonably. "Because if I do, you will dive back under the tables, and I will have to spend the rest of the morning chasing you round the kitchens."

The dog grinned. "How well you know me. Ease off, dammit. You'll have it out by the roots in a minute! Where are we going?"

"To the main courtyard," said Chance, guiding the dog inexorably toward the kitchen door. "The Shaman has sent word he'd like to see me, upon a matter of some urgency."

"Do we have to? He's the only thing around here that smells worse than I do, and he doesn't roll in dead things. What does the old fool want now?"

"I don't know. That's why we're going to see him. Since he doesn't normally bother to recognize my existence except to call me a Royal lackey in his speeches, I'm just a little curious as to why he's finally decided he needs to talk to me. I'm going to let go of your ear now. If you try and run back into the kitchens, I will do something to you of a sudden, violent, and wholly distressing nature. Agreed?"

"Agreed," growled the dog. "One of these days we're going to have a long talk about which of us is in charge around here."

Chance let go of the ear. Chappie continued to trot alongside him. They headed for the main courtyard, following one of the few relatively straightforward routes in the Castle. Things tended to get much less complicated once you approached the outer layers. People smiled and nodded to the Questor as they passed, and a few of the braver souls even stopped to pet Chappie for a while. He wagged his tail vigorously but didn't ask for snacks, because he could sense Chance's hand was hovering by his ear.

"You've been to see that redheaded girl again, haven't you?" asked Chappie. "I can smell her on you. And you always sound so much more eloquent after you've been hanging around her. I keep hoping some of her courtesy and refinement will rub off on you. Have you had her yet?"

"Chappie!"

"Well, why not? You both want to—I can smell it. In fact, you are practically leaving a trail of musk behind you."

"It's not that simple."

"God, I'm glad I'm not a human," said the dog. "When I'm hungry, I eat. When I need to take a dump, I do. And when I'm feeling randy—"

"I know what you do then," interrupted Chance. "And I really wish you wouldn't. I don't want to discuss this any further. Tiffany will be joining us later, as part of our investigations into the Inverted Cathedral, and I don't want you discussing things then, either. Is that clear?"

The dog sniggered all the way to the main courtyard.

It was packed, as always; a great milling crowd that stretched from wall to wall. They were mostly peasants, come from all across the Land to worship at the Shaman's feet, and listen wide-eyed to his teachings on the perfidy of monarchs, or more importantly, the radical concept of peasants' rights. They'd erected simple tents and lean-tos all over the place, each with its own cooking fire, and its own plume of noxious black smoke. Since they'd been forbidden to cut firewood, they were burning manure. There were designated latrines everywhere, so there was never any shortage. The King had never tried sending the peasants away, because he knew they wouldn't go, and he didn't want a bloodbath in his own Castle, which would have been the inevitable result of any attempt to remove them by force. So the peasants stayed, along with their families and any amount of assorted animals. There were traders and peddlers, too, and knife-grinders, clowns, and conjurers, all competing for the limited money the peasants had brought with them. And, of course, there was the Shaman.

He lived in his own simple tent, no better than any of the others, in one far corner of the courtyard. There was an area of open space around his tent, partly out of respect, but mostly because the Shaman didn't like people getting too close to him, and wasn't above throwing things at people if they bothered him. He was standing impatiently before his tent as Chance and Chappie slowly made their way through the heavy crowd. The massed heat and smell of so many people and animals crammed together was almost overpowering. Chance tried breathing through his mouth, but it didn't help. The peasants glared suspiciously at the Questor. They would have liked to give the Royal lackey a hard time, but one look at the huge axe he bore and the large dog at his side was enough to give them pause, and every peasant decided quite sensibly to let some other poor fool start something.

The Shaman had been a hermit, living alone in the Forest for many years, and it showed. A scrawny figure dressed in filthy rags, he'd painted his face entirely with blue woad, overlaid with a stylized skull in white clay. He had a huge mane of bristling gray hair and an equally large gray beard, both of them knotted and tangled beyond any hope of redemption. What could be seen of his mouth was usually stretched in a mirthless grin, and his eyes were unsettlingly bright, like a man possessed of disturbing and unsuspected truths. His fingernails were long and pointed, almost claws, and utterly filthy. When he moved, his actions were swift and jerky, animallike. The animals who shared the courtyard with the peasants, whether as food or companions, were all strangely attracted to the Shaman, and often he seemed more at ease in their company than among the teeming humans.

He had magic. Everyone knew that.

The Shaman nodded briefly to Chance and Chappie as they finally came to a halt before him. Those peasants nearest enough crept forward to eavesdrop on whatever pearls of wisdom might drop from the Shaman's chalky lips. His response was to scoop up handfuls of animal droppings from the ground and throw them at the peasants until they retreated to a respectful distance. Chance decided immediately that he wasn't going to shake hands with the Shaman. Despite himself, he wrinkled his nose at the stench coming off the old man. Up close it really was quite appalling. Even the omnipresent flies didn't want to get anywhere near it.

The Shaman turned back from chasing off the peasants, breathing heavily, and Chance made himself produce a polite smile. He might not like or approve of the Shaman, but as Questor it was his job to listen to all sides of an argument, and to anyone with cause to complain. He felt a pressure against his leg and hip, and found Chappie had pressed in close beside him, his tail tucked tightly between his legs. Chappie had never liked the Shaman. He found the man's animal presence disturbing, even as he felt the attraction that called to other animals. Chappie could sense magic radiating from the man, and other things besides, and something that might have been insanity; or a mind pushed beyond the normal human boundaries and restrictions.

"Stop growling," Chance said quietly to Chappie, even as he struggled to maintain his polite smile.

"Don't trust him," said the dog. "He's hiding something."

"Who isn't these days? Look, just stay put and let me do the talking. And whatever happens, don't bite him. God knows what you might catch off him."

"Him? I wouldn't bite him on a bet. Besides, he's got fleas. I can see them hopping."

"Hush. Sir Shaman! Good of you to see me. An honor, as always. Now what can I do for you?"

The Shaman's voice was a harsh croak, and Chance had to concentrate to understand what he was saying. "Chance. King's Questor. Champion's son. Only the King is dead now. So whom do you answer to now, Champion's son?"

"Technically the Queen, as Regent. And King Stephen, when he comes of age. Until then I follow my honor and good sense. My business is justice. That hasn't changed at all."

The Shaman sniffed. "Heard about the newcomers. Hawk and Fisher. Come to find Harald's murderer. Are they the real thing?"

Chance frowned. "I'm sorry, I don't—"

"Can they find the killer? Whom will they support in Castle politics? Whom do they answer to?"

"They're strictly neutral, as am I," Chance said carefully. "They have a lot of experience in seeing through lies and identifying killers. They are true and honorable people. And I admire them more than I can say. They're possibly the only real heroes I've ever met. Even if their methods

are sometimes . . . regrettable. Do you want me to arrange
for them to meet with you?"

The Shaman scratched at his ribs and looked away. "I'll
find them when I want them. Don't believe in heroes.
Never have." He looked at the nearest peasants, going
about their business and carefully giving the appearance of
ignoring him. "See them. All of them. They'd make me a
hero, if I let them. They keep coming to me for help or
advice or comfort. They worship me, though I've told them
not to. Only way I can keep them at arm's length is by
yelling at them, and throwing things. Hit them, too, sometimes. But they just keep coming back. All I ever wanted
was to teach them to stand on their own two feet, and think
for themselves, to not depend or lean on anyone, even me.
But it takes time to undo centuries of deference and obedi-
ence, and I often wonder if I'll live long enough to see
them reach a point where they don't need me anymore."

He sighed and looked back at Chance. "I was happy as
a hermit. Living alone, no responsibilities to anyone but
myself. Just a man at peace with the Forest and himself. I
was a soldier in the Demon War, and I never wanted to
have to fight again. I needed the peace and quiet of the
woods, far from civilization. And slowly, over the years, I
found peace and heart's ease. But then the peasants found
me out and came to me. First for the small magics I had,
to help and heal. Then for advice, because everyone knows
all hermits are wise men. I couldn't make them understand
I only wanted to be left alone. And then I saw these people,
good people, suffering and starving and dying, because of
King Harald's new taxes and high prices, and I had to come
here and speak for them, because there was no one else."

Chance listened intently. This was the most the Shaman
had ever said to him at one time, and the first time he'd
ever volunteered any information about himself and his
past. So the Shaman had been a soldier once, during the
long night. Probably saw friends and family die. That could
explain a lot. Chance was sure the Shaman was trying to
tell him something, that he was building up to confessing
something important. Chance tried hard to look as re-
ceptive as possible. He was the Questor, and it was his

proud belief that anyone could talk to him about anything; that anyone could come to him for justice or relief. Then there was a sudden commotion to one side, and both Chance and the Shaman looked around sharply, and the moment was lost.

The Creature had emerged from the Shaman's tent, and Chappie had surged forward to back him up against the nearest wall. The two of them were snarling at each other and showing their teeth, but it was clear the much larger Creature was scared of the dog. The Creature had come out of the deep woods to accompany the Shaman. He had a wide, low-browed head squatting directly on broad, hairy shoulders, and his overlong arms fell down past his knees. His stooping body was basically human in shape, and covered in thick, dark, oily hair under a simple shift so filthy, it was impossible to guess what its original color might have been. He had a man's height even in his perpetual stoop, and great cords of muscle bulged on his misshapen frame. The Creature had a slow and crafty mind, and was quick to anger, and sometimes an almost human intelligence showed in his glaring bloodred eyes.

Like the Shaman, he ate, pissed, and crapped where he felt like, and people made allowances for him because he was with the Shaman. Chance was never quite sure whether the Creature was the Shaman's bodyguard, his pet, or even his companion, but he knew a demon when he saw one. Anywhere else such a thing would have been killed on sight, or at least driven back into the Darkwood, but in this as in so many things, the Shaman made his own rules. Presumably his mysterious magic enabled the Creature to survive the direct daylight. Chance would have liked to kill the Creature on general principles, but as long as the Shaman kept him under control, it wasn't worth making an enemy of the Shaman.

Everyone but the Shaman hated the Creature. And the Creature hated everyone but the Shaman.

Chance grabbed Chappie by his ear and pulled, but the dog wouldn't budge. All his hackles were up and he was growling steadily, like an angry roll of thunder. The Shaman kicked viciously at the dog's ribs, but Chappie dodged easily, pulling his ear out of Chance's grasp. The Creature scratched weakly at the air with his claws and howled mournfully. The Shaman raised his hand and magic sputtered on the air. Chance immediately moved forward to stand between the dog and the Shaman, his axe in his hands.

"Stop that right now, Shaman, or I swear I'll cut you down where you stand."

There was an angry sound from the watching crowd, and the peasants surged forward to protect their leader. The Shaman lowered his hand, and the magics faded away. He turned and glared at the peasants, and they immediately went about their business. Chance glared at Chappie.

"Come here. Right now."

The dog slunk reluctantly back to join him. Chance lowered his axe and looked steadily at the Shaman.

"Never try that again, Shaman. Chappie is my companion."

"And the Creature is mine."

"You control yours, I'll control mine. Deal?"

The Shaman nodded abruptly, and turned away to address the Creature. He spoke softly, his voice calm and reassuring, and the Creature came forward to crouch beside him and rub his head against him, and the Shaman patted his shoulder.

"Let me kill it," said Chappie. "It needs killing."

"Maybe," said Chance quietly. "But not now. Not here. If the Shaman didn't get us, the crowd would. And I'm not ready to kill a whole bunch of innocent people just because you can't control yourself."

He looked back at the Shaman, and the two men studied each other thoughtfully, each of them wondering if they could kill the other if they had to. Not enemies, perhaps, but two men forever separated by quite different beliefs and duties.

"It's time for you to go," said the Shaman.

"There's nothing to keep me here," agreed Chance.

He made the dog go ahead of him as they moved off through the surly crowd. Chappie growled something under his breath, but Chance didn't listen. He glanced back at the

Shaman, but both he and the Creature were no longer there. They could have just gone back into the Shaman's tent, but somehow Chance didn't think so. No one knew exactly what the Shaman's powers were, but everyone knew he'd discovered all kinds of unnatural skills during his long years alone in the deep woods. The Shaman came and went, and nobody knew how or why. Chance made the dog walk a little quicker.

The Shaman found Hawk and Fisher walking down a deserted corridor and stepped out of a side passage to block their way, the Creature crouching and snarling at his side. Hawk and Fisher had their weapons in their hands almost before they realized. It had been a long time since anyone had been able to catch them by surprise. They studied the Shaman's extraordinary appearance interestedly, but their real attention went to the Creature. They'd seen him before, long ago. Once, King John had had a longtime friend and adviser called the Astrologer. They'd grown up together, closer than brothers. The Astrologer had been a wise and powerful man, but he wanted more than that, so he betrayed the King and the Forest Land to the Demon Prince. In payment the Demon Prince transformed the handsome, intelligent man into a crafty, misshapen demon that no longer remembered what he had once been. The Creature disappeared when Rupert called down the Rainbow to banish the darkness, and everyone assumed the Creature had been banished, too. And now here the thing was, twelve long years later, like a dark and awful shadow from the past.

"I am the Shaman," said the scarecrow figure beside the Creature, in a voice so harsh, they had to strain to understand it. "This poor unfortunate has no name. He is simply the Creature, and my companion. Yes, he is a demon, but he is under my control and my protection. You are in no danger. Put away your weapons."

The Creature suddenly leaned forward, his bloodred eyes looking searchingly at Hawk's face, and then Fisher's. He frowned, thoughts moving slowly across his ugly face, and then something like memory awoke in his eyes. The Crea-

ture squealed almost pitifully, and fell back to hide behind
the Shaman, shaking and shuddering. The Shaman looked
back, startled, and then glowered at Hawk and Fisher. "He
doesn't like strangers. Though he's not usually this affected
by them. He's harmless. Mostly. I found him wandering in
the Forest years ago, half starved. A pitiful specimen, all
alone. I look after him. Someone has to."

Hawk and Fisher slowly put away their weapons. Hawk
studied the blue and white mask of the Shaman's face,
while doing his best to ignore the smell.

"Your companion looks dangerous," he said finally.
"You should be very careful around him. You never know
when he might turn on you."

"My magic protects me," said the Shaman shortly. "We
must talk, you and I. The Questor speaks highly of you, but
he is a simple soul and strives to see the best in everyone. I
know better. I see more clearly. Do you really think you
can find the King's assassin?"

"It's what we do," said Fisher. "It may take a while,
but—"

"Time is running out," said the Shaman. "Change is
coming, and they can't stop it. This place is a cesspit of
intrigue and conspiracies. Trust no one. They all lie. They
are the old way, that must make way for the new. They
know this and resent it, and will do anything they can to
hold on to power."

"According to what we've been told, you speak for the
peasants," said Hawk. "And democracy. How did that
come about?"

The Shaman snorted. "Somebody had to. Someone who
cared for them, and not just the power base they represented."

"Sophisticated thinking for a simple hermit," said Fisher.

"I've had a lot of time to think, alone in the woods,"
said the Shaman.

"What did you think of the King?" Hawk asked.

"He was a fool," said the Shaman bluntly. His hands
rose to worry at the tangles of his long gray beard. "He
couldn't see that his time was over. Change came from the
south, and he couldn't adapt. Someone sacrificed him on

the altar of necessity. You'll find there are plenty of suspects."

"Was he such a bad King?" asked Fisher.

"Put no trust in Kings," said the Shaman. "Too much power for any man. John, Harald, even Rupert who left . . . No man can be trusted with absolute power over his fellow man, no matter how good his intentions. If the King is the Land and the Land is the King, it doesn't take a fool to see the result. John was weak, Harald was a failure, and Rupert ran away. None of them were worthy. Wipe it all out. Start over. Seize the moment. Let something good come from Harald's death."

"Who do you think killed him?" asked Hawk. "Could it have been one of your followers unwilling to wait for change?"

"No," said the Shaman. "I'd have known. And neither they nor I would have been allowed anywhere near the King's chamber. He was well-protected, and with good reason. Look to his own kind for the killer. Harald must have known his murderer, to let him in. Look to the Landsgrave, Sir Robert. Always a political creature, ready to adapt his beliefs and his conscience to get the deals he thinks he needs. The King was protected by Sir Vivian's guards—why didn't they see or hear anything? Who had the money and the influence to buy their silence?"

"What about the Magus?" Fisher asked. "He's a man of great power."

"If he is a man," said the Shaman. "I'm not always sure he's human. I sense something else in him. Not all the demons look like monsters."

"Where were you when Harald was murdered?" Hawk asked bluntly.

"Alone. In my tent, meditating. I miss the solitude of the woods."

"So no witnesses?" asked Fisher.

"Only the Creature," Shaman said. He grinned widely, showing terrible teeth. "You can ask him, but he doesn't have much to say for himself."

"So you have no alibi," said Hawk.

"Suspect me if you like," said the Shaman. "I don't care.

I've said all I came to say. I'd wish you luck, but I don't care who killed Harald. All that matters is who and what replaces him. That Hillsdown woman's not fit to be Queen. Vicious, conniving slut. Sleeps around. Thinks no one knows. *I* know! I know everything that matters. Sooner she's removed as Regent, the better. Send her back to Hillsdown, where she belongs."

"And the Prince, Stephen?" Fisher asked.

"Give him a new life," suggested the Shaman. "Set him free. Give him hope and a fair chance. Don't damn him to be King."

He turned abruptly and stalked away, the Creature swaying along beside him. Hawk and Fisher watched them go till they were safely out of sight.

"In a Castle full of eccentrics and head cases, that has to be our strangest encounter yet," said Fisher. "And did you get a whiff of him? I'm surprised the hanging tapestries weren't turning brown and curling up at the edges."

"Hermits aren't known for their love of soap and water," Hawk pointed out. "Or their social graces. I'm more concerned with his Creature. You did recognize him, didn't you?"

"Of course. The transformed Astrologer. Do you think we should have warned the Shaman?"

"How could we without revealing who we are? And they seemed happy enough together. Besides, what could we do? Send him back to the Darkwood? Kill him in cold blood?"

"He was a traitor," Fisher said coldly. "He deserves to die."

"I think killing him would be a kindness," said Hawk. "There's probably just enough of the old him left in that body to remember what he used to be and can never be again. I'm more worried that he seemed to know us."

"Who could he tell?" asked Fisher.

"I can't help thinking, what else might be left over from our past? What other old, unsuspected ghosts might be watching from the shadows?"

Hawk and Fisher looked at each other, remembering

other days when they had been Rupert and Julia, and things had seemed a whole lot simpler.

There was a sudden noise to one side, and they both looked around automatically. And that was when someone hidden in the shadows set off a flare. There was a sudden blinding flash of light, so sharp and painful to the eyes that both Hawk and Fisher cried out in spite of themselves. The flare was come and gone in a moment, but to eyes grown used to the dim lighting of the Castle corridors, the bright light was overpowering. Completely blinded, Hawk and Fisher staggered back and forth, rubbing uselessly at their tear-filled eyes. And while they were blind and helpless, a weighted net was thrown over them from a side passageway. Hawk and Fisher struck out at the heavy strands enveloping them, but their struggles only tangled them further in the net. And once it was clear they were helpless, a dozen men anonymous in black hoods ran forward and attacked Hawk and Fisher savagely with heavy wooden clubs.

Hawk and Fisher heard approaching footsteps, but their eyes were still full of the flare's light. They tried to draw their weapons, but the net's close embrace wouldn't let them. A club slammed down on Hawk's shoulder with sickening force. He heard as much as felt his collarbone shatter under the impact, which drove him to one knee. His eyesight was slowly starting to clear, but he wasn't given time to recover. Clubs fell again and again, hammering against his back and his shoulders and the arm he managed to raise to protect his head. The blows fell with vicious force, and Hawk could hear the harsh breathing of his attackers. The continuing assault drove him down onto both knees. Hawk could hear Fisher crying out beside him. He fought to draw his axe, but the weighted strands had no give in them.

Bones broke in the arm and hand protecting his head. Another club slammed into his ribs, and his whole side came alive with pain. He cried out and there was blood in his mouth. He tried to crawl away from the attack, but there was nowhere to go. The clubs hit him again and again, from every direction, and the accumulated torment was almost beyond bearing. He could still hear Fisher crying out beside him. So he pulled her close to him, and covered her body with his own, denying their enemy one victim. He held her close, his body rocking to the increased punishment, gritting his teeth and refusing to cry out. Refusing to give the unknown enemy the satisfaction. His whole body burned with pain now, and still the blows fell and fell. Blood filled his mouth and spilled from his slack lips. It had been a long time since he'd taken a beating like this, since he'd felt so helpless. He hugged Fisher to him, putting himself between her and the beating. Part of him knew that the enemy wasn't here to kill him and Fisher; swords would have done the job more quickly. No, this was a warning, a punishment beating. If he held out, he would survive. Or Fisher would. And then someone would pay for this with their life's blood. A club got past his shattered arm and slammed against the side of his head. Hawk actually felt the bone of his skull give under the blow, and then the world went away for a while.

And then he came back to shouts and raised voices, and the beating stopped. There was the sound of running feet, departing and approaching, and Hawk slowly allowed himself to believe the ordeal was over. He said Fisher's name, or thought he did, but couldn't hear her reply. He could feel blood running down his face. He forced his eye open, and through tears and blood he saw Sir Vivian and his guards coming to save them. They pulled and tugged at the net, trying to untangle it, and Hawk cried out despite himself as the sudden movements shook and jerked his punished body. After that the guards moved more carefully, but in the end they had to use their swords to saw through the strands of the net. Hawk heard Fisher say his name, and tried to tell her he was all right, but there was too much blood in his mouth. Finally Hawk and Fisher were cut free from the net, and sat with their backs against the cold stone wall. Fisher took Hawk's undamaged hand in hers, and squeezed it reassuringly. Sir Vivian crouched down before them, and Hawk could tell from his expression how bad they must look. He took a breath to speak, and his left lung cried out as broken ribs pressed against it. Hawk groaned and blood came out of his mouth along with the sound.

"Don't try to speak yet," said Sir Vivian, surprisingly gently. "And for God's sake don't try to move. We've sent for a healer."

"Men . . . in black hoods," said Hawk, forcing each word past pulped and swollen lips. "Isobel?"

"I'm here," said Fisher. "You protected me. Saved me. My hero."

"Next time . . . you protect . . . me."

"Deal."

They both laughed breathlessly, wincing as the small movements hurt them. Sir Vivian shook his head in wonder.

"All right, so you're both hard cases. I'm impressed. Now shut the hell up till the healer gets here. No one dies on my shift. Captain Hawk, your partner's hurt, but doesn't look too serious. You, on the other hand, look like shit. Broken arm, busted ribs, God knows what internal injuries. And you don't want to know what your face looks like. So save the jokes. I'm amazed you're still alive."

"This was a lesson," said Hawk, spitting out a mouthful of blood so he could speak more clearly. "To show . . . we're not untouchable. And just maybe . . . to distract us. We were getting too close . . . to someone, or something."

"Right," said Fisher, peering blearily past swollen-shut eyes. "We got sloppy, Hawk. Too used to relying on our reputations to keep the wolves at bay."

"There's no telling who your attackers were," said Sir Vivian, since it was clear they weren't going to shut up and sit quietly. "They ran like rabbits the moment they saw us coming. All we got were glimpses of some black hoods. And since they had the sense to take their weapons with them, the only evidence we have is some bootprints in the blood on the floor. These guys were professionals. You've made a lot of enemies in your short time here, but my best guess would be Duke Alric's men. Punishment beatings are a way of life where they come from. And you did humiliate the Duke of Court, in front of everyone."

"And you can't touch him . . . because he's the Duke," said Hawk.

Sir Vivian scowled. "If I can put together enough evidence, I will find the men responsible and make them pay. Diplomatic immunity only goes so far. No one does this on my watch and gets away with it."

"You sound angry, Sir Vivian," said Fisher. "I thought you didn't approve of us."

"I don't. But while you're here, you're under my protection, just like anyone else. I take my responsibilities seriously. And this kind of cowardly ambush is beneath contempt. I will not stand for this. Ah, here comes the healer at last. Where the hell have you been, LeMark?"

"I got here as fast as I could," said a calm, unhurried voice. Hawk turned his head painfully slowly to see an elderly, white-haired man bearing down on him, carrying a bulging black bag and the air of competence that all the best healers have. In fact, Hawk always suspected that learning to fake that air was one of the first things all healers were taught. LeMark looked at Hawk and Fisher, and then knelt before Hawk, studying him carefully without touching him. "Damn, you look bad. I've seen men trampled by horses that were in better shape than you are right now." He felt for the pulse in Hawk's wrist, and looked closely into his eye. "Where does it hurt, son?"

"Where doesn't it?" asked Hawk. "Hit me with everything you've got, sir healer; I need to be up and about. I've got work to do."

"Lot of my patients say that," said LeMark, unmoved. "But quick fixes are nearly always a bad idea in the long run. I'm a healer, not a sorcerer. My magic won't actually mend you, just assist your body in repairing itself by speeding up the natural healing process. From looking at you, I can see a dozen broken bones and a probable concussion. The blood dripping off your chin tells me all I need to know about your internal injuries. In my professional opinion you need at least a couple of weeks in bed, recovering naturally."

"We don't have a couple of weeks," said Fisher harshly. "Do whatever you have to. We can take it."

"Any spell strong enough to put you two back on your feet will drain your life forces to dangerous levels," LeMark said sternly. "It could put you closer to death than your present injuries would. And, incidentally, it will hurt like hell. I really do recommend—"

"Do it," said Hawk.

LeMark looked at Sir Vivian. "Can't you make them see sense?"

"Probably not," said Sir Vivian. "Do your work, healer."

LeMark shook his head unhappily, and rummaged in his bag before bringing out a slender wand of what looked like pure ivory, with two green snakes coiled around it. LeMark nodded to Sir Vivian, who gestured for half a dozen guards to come forward and hold Hawk and Fisher firmly in place. The healer then bent over Hawk and Fisher, muttering under his breath. Hawk just had time to study the two snakes curled around the wand, and admire how realistic the carving looked, when LeMark stopped muttering and thrust the wand forward. The snakes' heads leaped out from the wand, and sank their fangs into Hawk's and Fisher's cheeks. They both cried out as harsh, unrelenting energies surged into their bodies, pumped through the serpents' fangs. Their whole bodies jumped and shook as the energies did necessary, painful things to them, while the guards did their best to hold them still.

Broken bones reset themselves with agonizing precision, splintered ends fitting together as torn muscles reformed around them. Bruised and damaged organs grew whole again, and Hawk's left lung reinflated itself. Blood raced through Hawk's and Fisher's veins as their hearts hammered painfully fast in their chests. The healing process hurt more than the beating they'd just taken, compressed into a few unbearable moments. And then it was over. The snakes released their grips, the green heads drew back onto the wand, and the guards let go and stood back. Hawk and Fisher were left gasping and shaking, their hands jumping and twitching uncontrollably in their laps. Their faces were slick with cold sweat instead of blood, and they could see so clearly, it was almost painful. Hawk swallowed hard and tried to slow his breathing. He felt he'd just run several marathons, back to back, all of them uphill. A bone-deep weariness pinned both of them where they were, but deep inside they felt whole and intact again, as though they'd been washed through with ice cold spring waters. Hawk and Fisher looked at each other and grinned shakily. Their faces were back to normal again, no more pulped mouths and puffed eyes, and the dripping sweat was already washing away the blood. They forced themselves to their feet, leaning on each other for support. Sir Vivian knew better than to offer help. He sniffed heavily and glared at LeMark.

"They still look like shit. A good breeze would probably blow them over."

"Well, yes," said LeMark, closing his black bag. "They've both used up a month's resources in a few moments. Their strength will return, but only slowly." He looked chidingly at Hawk and Fisher. "I'd tell you to take it easy, but we all know I'd just be wasting my breath, so what's the point? I will say this: Push yourselves too hard too soon, and you could die, just from simple exhaustion. You don't have any reserves to rely on anymore."

"Understood," said Hawk. "Thanks for your help, sir healer. Send your bill to the Regent. Technically we're her guests, so we might as well get something out of it."

"Knew I was wasting my breath," said LeMark. He turned and strode off down the corridor with an air of washing his hands of the whole affair.

"How do you feel?" Sir Vivian asked.

"Like a good sneeze would throw me off my feet," Hawk admitted, feeling his ribs gingerly. "But I can still do my job."

"Same here," said Fisher. "Whoever sent those thugs is going to have to get away with it for the time being. Revenge can wait. After all, delayed revenge is always the sweetest."

"We need to talk privately, Sir Vivian," said Hawk. "Is there somewhere secure we can go?"

"Of course," said Sir Vivian. "Are you sure I can't persuade you to do the sane thing, and rest a little first?"

"If we sit down, we'll never get up again," said Fisher. "Long as we keep moving, we'll be fine."

"As you wish," said Sir Vivian. "I have a place not far from here. My guards will ensure our privacy."

Hawk and Fisher followed Sir Vivian down a side corridor, walking slowly and steadily and no longer leaning on each other. Hawk found he had to place his feet very carefully because his head felt a long way away from the rest of him. He also felt like he could sleep for a week, but that could wait. He probed cautiously at a loose tooth with the tip of his tongue and winced. He hoped he wasn't going to lose another of the back ones. Fisher was right—in Haven their reputation had protected them and their authority as Guard Captains. In Forest Castle they were just two strangers and fair prey for anyone who thought they could get away with it. Hawk frowned. He couldn't throw his weight around and intimidate people anymore; he'd have to use his wits to outthink and outmaneuver people. Strangely, the thought did not displease him. He'd increasingly disliked the kind of man Haven had made of him. It was one of the main reasons he'd been so ready to leave.

Sir Vivian ushered them into a small room, sparsely furnished with characterless furniture and a single portrait of King Harald hanging on the wall. Sir Vivian lit the only light and then gestured for his men to stand guard outside the door. He closed the door and locked it. He yawned once, shrugged apologetically, and then sat down on the most comfortable chair. Hawk and Fisher chose to lean against the wall.

"The Magus has to be involved in Harald's death," said Sir Vivian, diving straight into what he knew they wanted to talk about. "Either he dropped the wards to let the killer in, or they were never what he claimed in the first place. It's the only explanation. And only a really powerful magic-user could have gotten past me and my guards without being seen. I had all the ways to the King's chambers sewn up tighter than a flea's arse."

"Is the Magus the only magic-user in the Castle powerful enough to have done such a thing?" asked Hawk.

Sir Vivian frowned. "Technically speaking, yes. No one knows just how powerful the Shaman is if he's pushed. He's done some very disturbing things in his time. Harald worried about him. Wouldn't see him or speak to him. In fact, I was under strict orders not to allow the Shaman anywhere near the King at any time. I tried giving the Shaman body-guards, ostensibly for his own protection, so I could keep an eye on him, but he lost them so quickly, there was no point in continuing."

"And there's no one else?" Fisher asked after a pause. "We walked through a hall packed with magic-users when we first arrived."

"None of them are worth a damn," Sir Vivian said flatly, "or they wouldn't still be in that hall. The Land has a crying need for competent high-level magicians, and the Throne pays good money for their services. If they were any good, they'd have brought themselves to our attention and they'd be out in the field earning their keep. And the Magus always has an eye for fresh competition. I know a few things about magic. You know who my father was? Of course you do. Everyone does. No, the only other name that comes to mind is Tiffany. The Academy is very proud of her. Practically forced her on the Court. And she did show up really well against the darkness yesterday. Suspicious that she never evidenced such power before."

"You don't care much for magic-users, do you?" asked Fisher. "I can hear it in your voice."

"You can't trust them," said Sir Vivian. "Their magic is always going to be the most important thing in their lives. You never knew my father or my mother. The famously unreliable High Warlock and the infamous Night Witch. A drunk and a monster. When the Blue Moon was full, and the long night threatened all who lived, it wasn't the magic-users that saved the day. It was Prince Rupert and Princess Julia. And all the rest of us, good men and true, fighting the demons with cold steel and steadfast hearts. We don't need magic to run our lives. We just think we do, because it makes things so easy, so convenient. Well, some things aren't meant to be easy; they're there so we can become strong by overcoming them. Our reliance on magic makes us weak. We'd all be much better off without it."

"The High Warlock and the Night Witch were extreme examples of their kind," Hawk said carefully. "I take it you were never close to your parents?"

"I only ever knew my father, and that from a distance.

He wanted nothing to do with the raising of us. I knew him well enough to know I wanted to be nothing like him." Sir Vivian's voice was steady, but his eyes were very cold. "Magic made him what he was, and ruined his life. He knew how to make himself a legend, but he never did learn the trick of being a man. As for my mother, she murdered young women and bathed in their blood to keep herself young and beautiful. No one knows how she and my father got together, or why she chose to give birth to me and my brother, Gawaine. When I was younger, I sometimes thought of going into the Darkwood to search for her. Though whether to embrace her or kill her I was never sure. Then the Blue Moon came, and it was all too late. She's supposed to have died in the Demon War. I can't honestly say I care much, one way or the other. She is irrelevant to who and what I have made of myself."

"What about your brother, Gawaine?" asked Fisher. She'd never heard Sir Vivian open up so much before, and she was curious to see where it might lead. She only knew him as a traitor against King John, and it was clear there was much more to him than that.

"Gawaine? As children we were inseparable, but we grew apart as we grew older. He was the real hero of Tower Rouge. He decided he would stand and fight, no matter what the odds. Just because it was the right thing to do. I only stayed because I couldn't leave him on his own. Everyone liked Gawaine. He was the charming one, the courtier. He was the warrior, the hero. I was just his companion, his brother, his shadow, following where Gawaine led. I was happy to do it. He forced me to make more of myself by following his example. I became a hero rather than disappoint my beloved brother.

"And then he married Emma. Beautiful, charming, and utterly empty-headed. She enchanted Gawaine, but not me. I knew her for what she was—a leech living off his fame and courage and potential. Just like me. We drove Gawaine to distraction, fighting each other over him. In the end there was a scandal, Emma's fault, of course, and they went away to Redhart. I heard Emma died there recently. I'm glad. Perhaps my brother will come home now. Though I hear he's become right-hand man to Redhart's new King and Queen, Viktor and Catriona."

"How did you feel about Harald?" asked Hawk, trying hard to make the question sound casual, just carrying on the conversation.

"The King?" Sir Vivian's mouth pursed. "Not an easy man to get to know. Never really liked him. He betrayed me once, but he was right to do so. I was involved in a conspiracy against King John, a stupid thing. You can look up the details if you're interested. King John could have had me executed. I certainly expected him to. But he saw something in me, gave me a second chance. He sent me into internal exile, to teach the peasants how to defend themselves against the demons. If I was still alive when the War was over, I could come back and be Pardoned. I fully expected to die out there in the long night, but I was glad of a chance to prove my loyalty and gratitude to the King.

"When the Demon War was over, I was still alive, and no one was more surprised than me. I came back to Forest Castle to find my King was dead. But Harald welcomed me, forgave me, knighted me, and made me High Commander of the Castle Guard. He trusted me so much, he put his safety into my hands. I would have died for him. Instead, I failed him."

"We won't know that for sure until we discover who killed Harald, and how," said Fisher. "If it was the Magus, or someone as powerful as him, what could you have done? Tell us about your time in exile, Sir Vivian. Everyone says it changed you."

Sir Vivian looked at her and Hawk with his cold face and colder blue eyes, and for a long moment an uncomfortable silence filled the small room. Fisher wondered if she'd pushed him too far. And then Sir Vivian smiled for the first time.

"It changed everything. King John knew what he was doing when he sent me to fight alongside the peasants. He knew I despised them. At first I saw it as part of my punishment. But fighting beside the peasants, standing firm with them against endless waves of demons, I saw their true worth. Their courage, formed by a never-ending struggle to wrest harvest after harvest from the unforgiving land and treacherous weather. I saw the strength and purpose that comes from generations of service to the land. I saw them as people, not some abstract lower order, and they won my heart and admiration because they were truer and better than I ever was. So when I returned at last to Forest Castle, I came as their champion. And I have tried to serve their interests ever since. It wasn't a difficult choice; man for man, they were all braver and more honorable than any of the nobles at Court."

"And how did King Harald feel about this?" asked Hawk.

"I never spoke with him about it," Sir Vivian said slowly. "I believe in democratic reform, slowly and from within the system. But the King would not allow even such mild arguments. He knew how I felt, but he never raised the matter, either. It didn't affect my service to him, or my loyalty."

"Where do you stand now?" Fisher asked him.

"My position hasn't changed. Whatever form of democracy we eventually embrace, the change must come slowly if we're to avoid civil war. I still serve the Throne, Felicity, and Stephen. The Court is a confused place at present. Everyone wants change of some kind, but there are so many factions and so many vested interests, all of them intent on protecting their own territory. I have never wanted power for myself, but I have to deal with those who do, to keep the peace. These days I negotiate as much as enforce the law in Forest Castle. God may know where the Land is going, Captains, but I do not. I cling to my duty, to Felicity and Stephen, because that is all that's left that is clear to me."

"One last question," said Hawk. "Where were you when the King was killed?"

"Alone, in my quarters, dealing with the day's paperwork. No witnesses, but the guards outside the door would have seen me leave."

"Your guards," said Fisher.

"Of course," said Sir Vivian.

"Thank you for your assistance, High Commander," said

Hawk, pushing himself slowly away from the wall. Fisher did the same. Hawk made himself smile easily at Sir Vivian. "You've been most helpful."

"I don't normally bear my soul so easily," said Sir Vivian in his cold voice, rising to his feet. "But I will do anything to uncover the killer of my King. The King who forgave me and believed in me. And perhaps because you remind me of someone I used to know."

He bowed to Fisher, and then to Hawk, and left the room, closing the door behind him.

Tiffany joined up with Chance and the dog Chappie outside the Court. Though she couldn't tell Chance, she'd been conferring with her sister witches on the nature of the vision she'd Seen, of a future Kingdom overrun by the darkness and the Blue Moon. Not only had they not been able to reassure her, but the more they discussed it, the more scared and alarmed her sisters became. A certain amount of tears, hysterics, and communal hugging had followed before they were able to control themselves again. The Sisterhood encouraged releasing your emotions, as long as you were careful to do it in private, so as not to disillusion the populace. But when all was said and done, they were only witches, and very young, and they knew their limitations.

Tiffany communicated her vision to the Academy so that more experienced witches could examine it, wiped her eyes and hugged her sisters a few more times, then went in search of her other source of comfort, the Questor, Allen Chance. She found him waiting patiently outside the closed doors of the Court. The day's Session was finally underway, the Queen was on the Throne and in a really bad mood, and the day's business had already descended into bickering, name-calling, and the occasional head-butting. Chance was in no hurry to make an appearance before the assembled Court, not least because he had nothing new to say of any importance. He smiled happily at Tiffany as she appeared, her beauty and charm a breath of fresh air in a dark and gloomy place. Chappie wagged his tail furiously as Tiffany bent over to make a fuss of him.

"Any idea where Hawk and Fisher are?" she asked finally, straightening up to fix Chance with her direct green gaze.

"Last I heard, the Shaman was on his way to talk to them," said Chance. "Two immovable objects on a direct collision course. Since none of them are noted for backing down or being in the last diplomatic, we can only hope it won't all end in bloodshed."

Tiffany frowned. It looked out of place on her pretty, unlined face. "I don't like Hawk and Fisher. Violent, brutal people. It wouldn't surprise me if they were trying to force confessions out of people."

Chance hesitated, torn between his desire to defend Hawk and Fisher and his inability to explain why. "I'm sure they're only interested in discovering the truth," he said finally, somewhat lamely.

Tiffany sniffed. "And how many people will they intimidate or brutalize along the way? There's something disturbing about Hawk and Fisher. There's definitely more to them than meets the eye, but I can't See what. Even though I should be able to. I can't help feeling I'm missing something where they're concerned. Something important."

Chance decided it was well past time he redirected the conversation. "They have their ways of uncovering the truth, we have ours. What matters is finding the killer, and making him pay for what he's done."

Tiffany smiled. "That's so you, Allen. Always the reasonable voice."

"Well, that's my job. Though I do sometimes admire Hawk and Fisher's directness. Getting straight answers out of anyone is increasingly difficult these days. With so many intrigues and conspiracies and clashing political factions in the Court, almost everyone has something to hide. And the nobility object to being questioned at all, on principle. Since they've already given their oath they know nothing about the murder, questioning them any further is tantamount to doubting their word and their honor. All we need is for some overproud fool to declare his honor has been slighted, and challenge the questioner to a duel. God alone knows where that would end. Particularly if he was dumb enough to do it to Hawk and Fisher. And an awful lot of the aristocrats have taken to looking me straight in the eye and asking pointedly if I'm as loyal to the Throne as my father was. The point being that the Champion was always unquestionably loyal."

"You're not your father," said Tiffany, instinctively knowing what he needed to hear.

"No, I'm not. In person or in position. As Questor I'm supposed to see the virtue of every side of the argument and base my decision only in the service of truth and justice. But it's so hard to see the truth here, and with Harald dead, no one seems to care about justice anymore. All anyone cares about is their own chances for advancement, and to hell with what the Land might need."

"So who are you loyal to?" asked Tiffany guilelessly. "The Queen? The Throne? The Land?"

"To the people," Chance said firmly. "The Queen and even the Throne may fall, but the people go on. They are the Land. And it's my job to protect them from whoever or whatever threatens them. I admire the Queen. I'd like to uphold the Throne. But times are changing, and the Land will have to change with them. How about you, Tiff? Can you tell me where your loyalties lie?"

"Of course not," said Tiffany. "I'm a witch. We're supposed to be creatures of mystery. But I'm always loyal to my friends."

Chance and Tiffany smiled at each other, and for a moment they didn't need to say anything at all.

"All very illuminating," growled Chappie, curled up and forgotten at their feet. "Personally, I'm loyal to whoever feeds me. Are you two going to have sex soon? The musk you're giving off is almost overpowering. And it can't be good for you, putting it off like this. What's the matter? Why are you looking at me like that? Chance, why are you making that funny noise?"

Sir Robert Hawke, bladesmaster, former hero, and last remaining Landsgrave, sat at his desk in his modest but comfortable quarters, reading a letter for the second time. He should have been at Court, but he was pretty confident that the first hour or so would be spent jockeying for position, so he could afford to be late. If anything of importance was even addressed before midday, it would be a miracle. With Harald gone, there was no central authority left to rule on who had precedence, so of course everyone tried to speak at once. And since no one would back down for fear of appearing weak . . . Robert sighed and turned his attention back to the letter.

It was his divorced wife, Jennifer, as usual, demanding to know where this month's bank draft for maintenance was. Apparently his two children were growing out of their clothes again and there were school fees waiting to be paid. Funny how they were always *his* children when money was needed. Robert tried to find a smile for that, but it was hard going. He should never have married Jennifer. He was just a guardsman, newly knighted, and charmed by a pretty face. She was minor nobility, dazzled at the prospect of marrying a hero from the Demon War, rather than some chinless wonder chosen by her father. They got on fine in bed, but out of it they were hard-pressed to find anything to talk about. They had nothing in common and her attempts to make a real noble out of him had driven them both to distraction. She left eventually, and took the two boys with her. Robert didn't really mind. He'd never been able to talk to them, either. He didn't miss any of them. He found politics much more interesting.

He was tempted to file her letter on the forget-about-it spike. He could always claim he never got it. She only wrote when she wanted money. However much he sent, it was never enough. Jennifer either couldn't or wouldn't understand that one could be a knight, and a landowner, and a presence at Court, and yet still not be rich. Or anywhere near it. The land he owned was poor and over-farmed, not to mention overpopulated, and Robert just didn't have the heart to authorize the cruel and brutal methods necessary to collect all the rent he was owed. He knew times were hard for everyone. He'd already mortgaged the land twice, with bankers sufficiently far away that they hadn't heard how bad a risk it was. Of course, he could have been rich if he'd accepted even half the bribes he was offered every day for this political favor or that, but

Robert still had his pride and a little honor left, however tarnished. He might take the occasional commission, money for advice or introductions, but only when he was reasonably sure nothing would come of it. Robert sighed heavily and let the letter fall back onto the desk. He'd write to her later, send her something. For the boys.

Robert pulled open a drawer in his desk, unlocked the secret compartment, and took out a bottle of blue-gray pills. He spilled two out onto his hand and swallowed them down with a mouthful of wine. Just a little something to give a tired man a boost. Keep his wits about him. Keep him sharp. He breathed deeply as the rush hit him, snapping him awake and alert like a bucket of cold water in the face. His heart hammered painfully in his chest and his fingers tingled. He felt like he could take on anybody. There was a time when he hadn't needed pills to feel this way. But he was younger then, in his prime. Now he was . . . not old, no, not old. Just not young anymore. So he took a pill now and again to give him a bit of an edge. Everyone needed something to lean on.

There was a polite knock at his door, right on time, and Sir Robert called out for his visitors to enter. The door swung open and in they filed, the three miserable creatures with whom he was currently forced to deal. Politics made for strange bedfellows at the best of times, and when you were playing from a weak hand, you had to take all the support you could get. Sir Robert smiled and bowed without getting up, and everyone murmured polite greetings. Sir Robert waved a hand at the chairs set out for his guests, and watched sardonically as they sat down and did their best to look comfortable. No one here was his friend, but they could all be useful to each other, so they all pretended.

Sir Morrison and Lady Esther represented what was left of Gold and Silver interests in the Forest. Once, they had been great powers in the Land, but that was over, and everyone knew it except for Gold and Silver. Sir Robert represented them at Court, as the Landsgrave, which meant that from time to time he had to take instructions from his putative superiors. Sir Morrison was tall and slender, dressed always in formal black, with a shaved head and a pencil-thin mustache. Calm, sophisticated, capable of dry humor on occasion. He saw democratic reform as a route back to power, and was quite prepared to trample over absolutely everybody who got in his way.

Lady Esther was a short, almost tiny woman who dressed well but carelessly, and wore far too much makeup. Her long dark hair was piled up on top of her head in an intricate style held together with delicate Silver combs and pins. Lady Esther was cold, calculating, and always to the point. Ruthless and quite without conscience, she would have been dangerous if she'd been more focused. She was on her third husband. Gossip had it she'd worn out the first two.

And finally there was Franz Pendleton, representing certain aspects of the business community, which saw big profits to be made from an enfranchised, more prosperous working class. And while business on the whole was buoyant, with goods flowing in from the south, much of the money spent on those goods went straight back to the south instead of to local established businessmen. So certain of these people wanted laws passed to control Southern imports, and since they weren't going to get them passed by the aristocracy, who enjoyed the new luxuries from the south, and didn't want anything to happen that might interrupt their flow, the current business thinking was that a democratic power base might be more open to influence. And finally, business people were looking for a cause that would stabilize the Land. Too much politics was bad for business. Democracy seemed to be their best bet. The Queen had little business acumen and cared less, the nobility couldn't or didn't want to see the dangers of unrestricted Southern trade, and absolutely no one wanted Duke Alric managing things from behind the scenes, for fear he'd asset-strip the Forest in favor of building up Hillsdown.

So Pendleton, a square-set, portly, blustery type convinced everyone had their price, was supporting democratic reform for now. Pendleton saw himself as an arranger, a fixer, a man who worked behind the scenes to make things happen. He thought he could do this by throwing money at people or problems until they went away. And given the state of the Forest these days, mostly he was right.

The conspiracy's current and rather unpleasant plan of action called for Sir Robert to set up a small and very secret intrigue, whereby the Shaman would be persuaded to kill both the Queen and the Duke, using his mysterious magic. Sir Robert would then use his skills as a bladesmaster to kill the Shaman. Though a strong supporter of democracy, it was felt by the conspirators that the Shaman was too unstable and too unpredictable to be left running loose afterward. A coalition of business interests would then propose Sir Robert as the new Regent; he was, after all, a famous hero of the Demon War, and he would have been seen to kill the terrible assassin who killed the Queen and the Duke. Nothing could be simpler. And Sir Robert would then, of course, oversee the passing of laws sufficient to weaken the aristocracy and advance the cause of Forest businessmen.

That was the plan that these three had previously brought to Sir Robert. There was, however, a small problem with this plan, as far as Sir Robert was concerned, and that was that the plan was complete and utter garbage. It was stupid, it wouldn't work, and would quite definitely get them all arrested and beheaded. However, Sir Robert couldn't just come out and say that. These people were, technically speaking, his superiors. And he'd already taken quite a lot of their money.

"So, how goes our plan?" asked Lady Esther. "How long before we can strike?"

"You can't rush a conspiracy, my lady," Sir Robert said smoothly. "The elements must be carefully assembled and examined for flaws."

"You've been paid enough money already," Pendleton told him. "It's about time we got something to show for it. Not getting cold feet, are you?"

"Certain problems have arisen, which I feel should be discussed," said Sir Robert.

"Then by all means lay these problems out before us," said Sir Morrison. "So that we can put your mind at rest."

"Well," began Sir Robert carefully, "first, we have a

problem with the Shaman. Which is that he's crazy. Barking mad and strange with it. While I might be able to persuade him to kill both the Duke and the Queen, by playing on his known populist sympathies and his well-known hatred of the monarchy, and whilst he may have enough magic to take out both targets from a distance, I have a strong feeling he might not stop there. The Shaman hates everyone who isn't actually a peasant, and once we start him off on a crusade of murder and retribution, God alone knows where he might stop. Presumably the Magus would be able to take him out eventually, but we could be hip deep in dead aristocrats by then."

"It will be your business to control the Shaman," said Lady Esther. "If he doesn't do as he's told, kill him. You're a bladesmaster. You passed through the Darkwood with Prince Rupert. You fought in the last great defense of the Forest Castle."

"The Shaman is something else," said Sir Robert. "And no one seems at all sure what. My researches suggest he is a much more powerful magician than we suspected. All my swordsmanship won't do any good if I'm sitting on a lily pad somewhere, gulping down flies and croaking a lot."

"On the other hand," said Sir Morrison calmly, "the Throne has never been weaker than it is now. It would be a pity if we failed now through lack of nerve."

"And there's all the money we've poured into this!" snapped Pendleton.

"Let us assume we find some way to control the Shaman," said Lady Esther. "Using the Magus or Sir Vivian. Do you have any other objections?"

"Well, yes," answered Sir Robert. "I can't help feeling bribes aren't going to be enough to ensure their compliance, before and after the assassinations. The Magus has never shown any interest in riches, and we don't have anything else he wants."

"We will offer him power and a high place in our new regime," said Sir Morrison.

"He already has that," Sir Robert pointed out.

"Sir Vivian believes in democracy," said Lady Esther.

"He's often spoken publicly of the need for political change."

"Sir Vivian failed to protect King Harald from his assassin," said Sir Robert. "And he took it very hard. I can't see him betraying his duty to Harald's widow, whatever the political reasoning. Sir Vivian is a famously honorable man these days."

"Then you must kill Sir Vivian!" demanded Pendleton. "Remove him from the gameboard before he can threaten us!"

"Ah," said Sir Robert. "So as well as killing a possible rogue sorcerer in the Shaman, I am also supposed to kill the legendary hero of Tower Rouge? And for an encore, presumably, I will kill the Magus as well. Lady, gentlemen, I fear you've been listening to those terrible songs and sagas about my exploits in the long night. They're really not all that accurate, you know."

"If you're not the hero we paid for," murmured Sir Morrison, "then what good are you?"

"You're paying for my experience," Sir Robert said flatly. "I have survived more death and violence and horror than you can imagine, and I didn't do that by being stupid. If you wish to proceed with your plan, that's up to you. I can set it in motion. I'm just pointing out my carefully considered opinion as to why it will almost undoubtedly go horribly wrong and get us all killed. Let us all be very clear about this, lady and gentlemen: We're only going to get one shot. If we fail, we won't live long enough to put together a second attempt. It therefore behooves us to make damn sure our plan is waterproof before we begin."

There was a long, uncomfortable silence.

"Very well," said Lady Esther finally. "Do nothing for now. We will consider your words and put together an amended plan. In the meantime we wish you to keep a close eye on Hawk and Fisher. They're an unknown quantity, and therefore dangerous. We need to know whether it would be best to make a deal with them or have them killed. I take it you could arrange the deaths of two simple Guard Captains?"

Sir Robert shrugged. "They handled the Duke and his

thugs easily enough. Let me talk to them before you decide anything. As long as they concentrate on their investigation into the King's death and show no interest in current politics, I think we can safely ignore them." He stopped and raised an eyebrow. "I trust I can take it you had no part in Harald's death?"

"Of course we didn't!" Pendleton answered hotly. "We might have discussed it occasionally, but Harald was more use to us alive than dead. Alive we could have struck a deal with him. It's his death that produced the very chaos that makes our desperate measures necessary."

"Well, quite," said Sir Robert. "Now, if you will all excuse me, I must be about my business. Can't have the Court wondering where I am, can we?"

After they were gone, Robert sighed heavily, and poured himself a very large drink. Idiots with their idiotic conspiracies. This was the seventh plan they'd come up with, and it was no obvious improvement on the previous six. He'd known lemmings that were less determined to get themselves killed. Still, as long as he kept shooting down their plans, they'd go on paying him. And he liked to think he was doing his little bit to protect the Throne and the Land along the way. He glanced at the clock on the wall and gulped down his drink. He still had to look in on an old comrade before he got to Court. And whilst he didn't care for any of his conspirators, Robert would have died before he let down Ennis Page.

Sir Robert strode through the narrow corridors of the servants' sector of the Castle, and the men and women there bowed respectfully to him as he passed. There had been a time when he could have walked among them unremembered, no different or better than any of them. Sometimes he thought he'd been happier then, as just another guard, with no more concerns than his next week's wages. But the King knighted him after the Demon War, in recognition of his services, and for a time Sir Robert had been very happy to be a noble and a hero, adored by all. He'd thought the good times would last forever. He should have known better. As a knight, he'd had to put his old friends

behind him, and making new ones among his new circle
had not been easy. Hero or not, the established aristocracy
had little time for arrivistes. You were nobody in their eyes
unless your ancestors had been somebody for generations.
But having bitten the poisoned apple, Sir Robert couldn't
go back. Once a noble, always a noble, forever separated
from those of the lower orders.

Prince Rupert had never cared about such distinctions.
But then, Prince Rupert had been a real hero.

Ennis Page had been one of the few other men to fight
beside Robert Hawke and Prince Rupert, and still survive
to see the end of the long night. He'd fought well, never
once buckled under the pressure of the darkness, and killed
more than his fair share of demons. A good man, a hero.
Mentioned in quite a few songs. But afterward things
hadn't gone at all well for Ennis Page.

Sir Robert finally came to a halt before the door to a
servant's quarters, no different or better than any of the
others. He knocked politely, and the door was opened by
a small careworn woman who nodded familiarly to Sir Robert. She was just forty, but she looked ten years older. Her
clothes were simple and much worn, and her hands were
rough from hard work. She beckoned for Sir Robert to
come in, and then shut the door quickly behind him.
Strictly speaking, he shouldn't have been there, and both
of them knew it. Inside, it was typical servants' quarters:
one fair-sized room, with a bedroom leading off. Simple
furniture, few frills, and no fancies.

"Hello, Rob. Good of you to come. He's been restless
all day."

"Hello, Maggie. I would have been here sooner, but I
got held up. Has he been asking for me?"

"Sometimes. Sometimes it's you, sometimes me. Now
and again he wants Prince Rupert."

And then they both looked around, startled at a knocking on the door. Sir Robert's hand dropped to his sword.
No one ever came to see Ennis Page but him, which could
only mean they were looking for Sir Robert. And why look
for him here, unless they wanted to be sure of catching him
where no one else could see? Maggie looked at Sir Robert

questioningly, catching his mood. There was no other way
out. Sir Robert drew his sword, then gestured for Maggie
to open the door and then stand well back. She did so, and
there framed in the doorway were Hawk and Fisher.

"Looking for me?" asked Sir Robert, not lowering his
sword.

"We asked the Seneschal's guide to find you, and it
brought us right here," said Hawk. He looked at the sword
in Sir Robert's hand, but made no attempt to draw his axe.
"I do hope we're not intruding . . ."

"Not at all," said Sir Robert. He put away his sword and
everyone relaxed just a little. "Come in, Captains. There's
someone here I think you ought to meet."

Hawk and Fisher came in, and Maggie shut the door
behind them. Sir Robert introduced her to Hawk and
Fisher, and she bobbed her head quickly. She didn't get
many visitors. Hawk recognized the name of her husband
immediately, but did his best not to show it.

"Ennis Page," he said, carefully vague. "I think I've
heard his name in songs about the Demon War. Fought
beside Prince Rupert himself, didn't he?"

"Oh, yes," said Sir Robert. "He was there. But he didn't
get knighted, like I did. His heroics weren't conspicuous
enough. King Harald granted him some land, off in the
back of beyond, but Ennis had to sell it off over the years.
He's been ill ever since the Demon Wars, and healers' bills
don't come cheap."

"What's wrong with him?" asked Fisher.

"Demon War Syndrome," said Sir Robert. "Which is
typical of healers. Put a name to something, and they think
that means they understand it. They don't. It's been twelve
years, and they're still no nearer finding anything that will
help him. Come and see for yourself."

Hawk looked at Maggie. "With your permission . . ."

"Oh, yes. Of course. But don't expect too much from
him. He has his good days and his bad days, and
sometimes . . . sometimes I think not all of him came back
from the Demon War. Maybe the best part of him is still
lost in the long night."

They went through into the adjoining bedroom. It was a small room, just big enough for a bed and a chest of drawers. Ennis Page was sitting on a chair by the bed, wearing a gray nightie and a woolen shawl, rocking quietly back and forth. Hawk remembered Page as being about the same age as himself, but the man sitting on the chair before him looked a hundred years older. He'd been a big man once, but he'd been eaten away by time and hurt. His face was heavily lined, his hair was gray, and his hands trembled constantly. He didn't respond to his visitors. He was staring at nothing, or perhaps the past he could never forget. A thin line of drool hung from one corner of his mouth, and Maggie hurried forward to wipe it away with a cloth.

"Dear God," said Hawk.

"There are a lot of people like him," said Sir Robert. "People who were hurt by the long night and never got over it. Ennis was a trained fighter, but nothing could prepare him for the horrors he encountered under the Blue Moon. He saw terrible things, and did worse just to survive. The dark of the long night was a spiritual darkness, as well as a physical threat, and in the end it broke him. Broke his body and his mind and his spirit. He was a good man once. Just the sort you'd want watching your back in a scrap. Brave and honorable; a canny warrior with a great booming laugh. Now this poor shadow is all that's left of him. A lot of men who followed Prince Rupert to be a hero got lost in the dark and never came home."

"I never knew," said Hawk.

"No reason why you should. But there are a lot like him, in homes all across the Land, looked after by their loved ones. People who never recovered from the oppression of the long night. Old before their time, wandered in their wits. Demon War Syndrome. Never mentioned in any of the songs or sagas."

"They still sing songs about my Ennis," said Maggie, almost defiantly. "My Ennis, who fought beside the Prince. And the late King provided us a pension after he heard our money had run out." She looked fondly, sadly, at her husband sitting rocking on his chair. "Some days he's quite bright. Knows who he is, who I am, takes an interest in my day. I clean, you see. Now and again we go for short walks, up and down the corridor. Never outside. He only feels safe inside walls, well away from the Forest he remembers. He hasn't seen sun or moon in twelve years. Sudden noises panic him. He doesn't like being alone. I get someone to sit with him when I'm out."

"He's become your child," said Fisher.

"A child would be more independent," said Maggie. "And he'll never outgrow this. If anything, he's a little worse each year, drifting further away from the world, and me. You should have seen him when he was in his prime. A fine, big, handsome man. Could have had any woman he chose, but he only ever wanted me. Now he's afraid of the dark, and he has bad dreams and cries out in his sleep. Not much of a legacy for a hero."

"Do you . . ." Hawk's voice was rough, and he had to start again. "Do you blame Prince Rupert for taking your man off to fight the demons?"

"No," said Maggie. "Ennis was proud to have served with the Prince. Said he was the best man he ever knew. He was proud to have done his bit to save the Land."

She broke off sharply, and they all turned to look when Ennis Page tried to speak. His head had risen, and his eyes were clear as he gazed at Hawk.

"My Prince . . ." he said slowly. "You've come back."

Hawk looked quickly at Sir Robert. "What—"

"He thinks you're Prince Rupert," said Sir Robert. "Your voices are somewhat similar. Talk to him!"

Hawk moved forward and crouched down before the old man in his chair. "Hello, Ennis. I hear you've not been well."

"The war took a lot out of me. I sleep a lot now. It's good to see you back home again, Rupert. Where you belong. You'll put things right. You look a bit battered yourself."

"I'm fine. Are you comfortable here? Is there anything I can get you, do for you? Better quarters, perhaps?"

"No, thank you. I know this place. I'm happy here. My Maggie looks after me. She's a good lass. I know how ill I am. I'm just seeing out my time now."

"Are you ever sorry that you served with me?" asked Hawk. "I led you into the Darkwood. Set you fighting against impossible odds. I'm responsible for what you are now."

"No!" said Ennis sharply, and for a moment his voice and gaze were that of the man he'd once been. "Don't you ever think that! I knew my duty. I was proud to follow you, Rupert. We all were. You were the only real hero in the whole damned war. Because I helped to bring you home safely, you were able to call down the Rainbow that saved us all. I was proud to fight beside you, proud to be a part of your legend. Proud . . ."

His eyes grew confused again, all the fire and animation going out of him. Maggie came forward as Hawk straightened up, and pulled Ennis' shawl more comfortably around his shoulders.

"He's gone again," she said calmly. "Thank you for pretending, Captain. He hasn't been that sharp for ages. But he'll want to sleep now. You'd better go. He's tired out."

"I'll come and see you both tomorrow, Maggie," said Sir Robert.

He led Hawk and Fisher back into the other room, closing the bedroom door behind him. Hawk and Sir Robert looked at each other for a long moment.

"That was kind of you," Sir Robert said finally. "Pretending to be the Prince. I knew Rupert well. Rode beside him, fought beside him. I'm probably one of the few people left alive who knew him well."

"If he were here," said Hawk, "is there anything you'd have liked to say to him?"

"If he were here, I'd just say what Ennis said. That I was proud to fight alongside him, proud to be the friend of a real hero. I never got the chance to tell him how much he meant to me. And if he'd stayed . . . I think he'd have made a much better King than Harald ever was."

"But he had to go," said Hawk. "And in such a hurry, he never got the chance to say how much those friends had meant to him."

"Yes," said Sir Robert. "He had to go." He smiled suddenly. "There are things we need to discuss, Captain Hawk,

Captain Fisher. There's a rather good coffee shop not too far from here. Does that sound good to you?"

"Coffee sounds very good," said Hawk.

A few minutes' walk took them to an altogether more salubrious area, much frequented by artists, actors, musicians, and other feted parasites of the Castle. There was an ornate square fronted by fashionable eating and drinking establishments surrounding a small interior arbor. People in their very best came here just to promenade, to see and be seen. In particular, Southern-style coffee shops had become all the rage since the Rift opened, and the most popular, most expensive, and certainly most exclusive was the Southern Comfort. Sir Robert was recognized immediately by the beaming proprietor, and welcomed in with much bowing and gushing of praises. He ignored Hawk and Fisher completely, which only amused them. The proprietor seated them at the very best table, and brought menus printed on cards fully two feet tall. Sir Robert ordered a large pot of coffee, with all the trimmings. Hawk found chocolate gateau on the menu and got quite excited, but Fisher wouldn't let him order it. Hawk grumbled, and would have sulked if Sir Robert hadn't been there.

Nothing more was said about Prince Rupert.

"Couldn't any of the magicians help Page?" asked Fisher when their coffee arrived.

"The Shaman tried," said Sir Robert. "But the long night put its mark on Ennis' soul, and repairing a soul is sorcerer's work. The High Warlock might have been able to do something, but he's gone. And the Magus didn't want to know. There are any number of magic-users here in the Castle ready to help Ennis, but surprisingly enough, the cures they offer are all very expensive, with no guarantee of success."

"Did any of Princess Julia's female warriors survive?" asked Fisher, trying hard to sound casual as she sipped her coffee.

"Sure. The only one I've heard of recently is Jessica Flint. She's a Ranger now. Doing well, or so I understand." Sir Robert frowned. "Once, I could have named all the great heroes of the Demon War and told you where they were, what they were doing. But they've all scattered over the years. Only a very few were able to profit from their valor and their fame. Most went back to their old, everyday lives, while the same people stayed in power. No one cares about the heroes now, except in some drunken tavern songs. And they'll stay forgotten, anonymous, until the Land needs them to be heroes again."

He smiled suddenly. "I, of course, played the hero card for all it was worth. As an arriviste, despised on all sides, I had to use what advantages I had. Now I'm something of an elder statesman. People pay for my advice on all kinds of things. And as long as I keep playing one side off against another, they'll keep coming to me for my very expensive advice."

"But you're the Landsgrave," said Hawk. "Doesn't that position hold any power or prestige these days?"

"Unfortunately, no. Not since they wasted the last of their influence trying to fix the choice of Questor. No one minded that they tried, only that they failed so ignominiously. A failure has no friends. A lot of the Forest's Gold and Silver goes straight to Redhart and Hillsdown these days. I am all that remains of Gold and Silver's voice at Court. I do what I can, and pocket my retainer."

"Are you happy?" Hawk asked suddenly.

"Happier than most," said Sir Robert after a moment. "I was a hero once, and that's once more than most people manage their whole life. And if the life I have now isn't exactly what I hoped or planned for, well, that's true of most people. I have my memories of my time with Prince Rupert, when everything I did was important, and my life mattered . . ."

"If Rupert and Julia were here now," said Fisher quietly, "what would you advise them to do?"

"I'd tell them to do the right thing—whatever it costs, whoever gets hurt. Be the heroes they used to be. Because God knows the Land needs all the heroes it can get right now."

"What about you?" asked Hawk. "You were a hero once. You mattered."

"Politics corrupts," said Sir Robert. "And I lost my way long ago. You can't mortgage your soul as many times as I have and still call it your own. Let us change the subject. Let us talk of King Harald's death."

"Are we going to have to pay for this consultation?" asked Fisher.

"Advice costs money. Information you get for free."

"Who do you think killed Harald?" Hawk asked bluntly.

"He had a lot of enemies," said Sir Robert, pouring himself another cup of coffee. He stared down into the cup as he added two teaspoons of sugar and stirred slowly, slowly. "Many of his enemies he made by choice. He was a hell of a politician when he was just a Prince, but once he became King, he seemed to just throw all his old skills away. He could have made deals, compromises, for the good of the Land, but he wouldn't. He was King, and he was determined to be King. A lot of people had good reasons to want to kill him. Particularly his Queen, Felicity. She had a lover. No one knows who, which in a Castle like this is nothing short of a minor miracle, but everyone knew there was someone. Harald had to have heard. And the last thing he needed, personally or politically, was any shadow of doubt over the parentage of Prince Stephen. Especially after they'd been childless for so long. But apart from that, you could point a finger anywhere in the Castle and find an enemy of Harald's on the end of it."

"Including you?" Hawk asked.

"I remember Harald fighting in the last great defense of Forest Castle, when the dead piled up so high, we used them as barricades," said Sir Robert slowly. "He fought well. He was a hero then. Saved my life once, though I don't know if he noticed, or ever remembered. I would have followed that man. But King Harald was someone else. It was as though he'd put all his effort into becoming King, and didn't know what to do with it once he got there. All I ever saw was a man determined not to give up one ounce of power to anyone else, and to hell with the rights or needs of his people. I believed in democracy. That made me his enemy in his eyes."

"Where were you when the King was killed?" asked Fisher.

"Meeting with a pro-democracy group who'd expressed an interest in hiring me. Turned out they couldn't afford me."

"I thought you believed in democratic reform," said Hawk.

Sir Robert smiled. "I'm a professional politician. I have no personal opinions anymore except those I'm paid to have. But democracy of some kind is coming. Everyone could see that except Harald. The idea is in the air, and it's not going to go away. The monarchy was doomed from the moment Harald allowed the Magus to open the Rift." He looked steadily at Hawk and Fisher. "I'll give you one piece of advice for free, though it goes against my nature. Watch your backs. There are a lot of people in this Castle with good reasons for wanting Harald's death to remain a mystery."

Hawk and Fisher smiled slightly, painfully. "We know," said Hawk. "Trust us, we know."

Sir Vivian Hellstrom, the feted hero of Tower Rouge and High Commander of the Castle Guard, sat alone in his quarters reading a book that didn't interest him. He'd always been alone, even as a child. People were afraid of him because of who his parents were, and what he might become in time. His only friend was his brother, Gawaine, and Vivian always envied Gawaine's easy charm that turned aside fear and made friends out of enemies. But Gawaine wasn't there to look after him anymore. So Sir Vivian did his job, commanding guards who admired and obeyed him but never liked him, and when he wasn't needed, Sir Vivian went home to his sparsely furnished quarters, and sat there alone, waiting to be needed again. Because being needed was the next best thing to being wanted.

The book was yet another treatise on the one bright moment in his life, the holding of Tower Rouge. The publishers had sent him an advance copy, respectfully asking if he'd check the facts for accuracy, and perhaps write them a recommendation. He was halfway through and wasn't impressed. They had the bare facts right, but they obviously had no real understanding of the people or the powers involved. Not surprising, considering that none of the major protagonists, including Gawaine and Vivian, had ever agreed to be interviewed. Sir Vivian thought the past should stay in the past. Let the people have their songs, and their legends. For one brief day he'd been a hero, and he would share those memories with no one.

The light in the room was growing dim. Sir Vivian looked at the candle on the desk beside him and it burst into flame. Magic came easier to him all the time now, as he got older. He'd never studied it, never wanted it; he'd even denied it to be the one thing he really wanted. A soldier. When he and Gawaine were cornered in Tower Rouge, the magic had been so deeply buried in him that Vivian had been convinced he and Gawaine were going to die. So he fought his enemy with guts and cold steel, standing firm against what seemed like a whole army, and when it was over, and he and Gawaine were still somehow alive though cut to ribbons, they held Tower Rouge, and magic had no part in it at all.

It had always been important for Vivian to prove himself as a man, unaided by the legacy of his infamous parents. So he became a warrior and a hero. And still no one really liked or trusted him.

It was at a time like this that Sir Vivian wished he had been a drinking man.

Until he remembered his father.

Sir Vivian had a certain amount of faith in Hawk and Fisher. They seemed determined to get to the truth, and more to the point, they didn't take any nonsense from anyone, including him. Which made them a breath of fresh air in the current Court. Sir Vivian scowled. He tried to like the Queen, but it wasn't easy. Felicity never let anyone get too close to her. But still, he would see her husband's murderer found and punished, whatever it took. He had sworn this on his name and on his honor. He tried to be supportive, to protect the Regent from all her many enemies, even when one of them was her own father. Sir Vivian admired the Queen's strength of character, even if the character wasn't a particularly likable one. He didn't know if she knew this, or how she felt about him. He'd never known how to talk to women. What to say. What they liked to hear. That had always been Gawaine's specialty.

Sir Vivian still missed Queen Eleanor, wife to the late King John, though she was dead and gone these many years. She was beautiful and charming and very graceful, even to a tongue-tied fool like the young Vivian Hellstrom, who worshipped her from afar and would have died for her. She smiled on him once, upon his return from Tower Rouge. Of course she smiled on Gawaine, too, but even so, there had been something special in that smile, just for him. He carried the memory of it with him always. It warmed his heart, even on the coldest of days.

He looked around his room, and everywhere candles sprang into flame, filling the room with light. Magic. Useless magic.

He looked at his door, and a moment later there was a confident but respectful knock. Sir Vivian called for his visitor to enter, and the door swung open to reveal the Questor, Allen Chance. He nodded briefly to Sir Vivian, who nodded briefly in return without getting up. Chance shut the door and then stood at parade rest before Sir Vivian. At least he didn't have his dog with him this time. Sir Vivian had never been able to look at Allen Chance without seeing the ghost of his father, the Champion. Another son cursed with the weight of a famous father. Sir Vivian had never liked the Champion; a cold-hearted killing machine and borderline psychopath whose only saving grace had been his ferocious loyalty to the Throne and the Land. Fortunately Chance seemed to take more after his mother. Whoever she was.

"You wished to see me, High Commander?" Chance asked finally.

"Yes," said Sir Vivian. "Take a seat."

He waited while Chance settled himself in the chair opposite, then put aside his book and fixed Chance with his best steely gaze. "Talk to me about Hawk and Fisher. You've spent the most time with them. Can they do the job? Can they succeed where we have failed and uncover Harald's murderer?"

"I have every confidence in them, High Commander."

"They're outsiders, ignorant of the complicated politics of our Court."

Chance shrugged easily. "Sometimes outsiders can see things we can't because we're too close to them."

"Good," said Sir Vivian. "Good. Did you come here alone?"

Chance blinked, thrown by the sudden change of subject. "Chappie's waiting outside. I know you two don't get on. Your guards are making a fuss of him."

"And the witch?"

Chance didn't bother to hide his surprise. "Tiffany? She's talking with the Queen at present. Why do you ask?"

Sir Vivian templed his fingers together and stared over them at Chance. "I'm worried about you, Questor. You mustn't let that witch get too close to you. A soldier can never trust a magic-user. And who knows what hidden agendas the witches of the Sisterhood follow? Their Academy is closed to men. No one knows what goes on behind their closed walls. What oaths they take, what powers they secretly worship. There are rumors—"

"There are always rumors," said Chance angrily. "I went to St. Jude's, remember? You should hear what some people say about us. Tiffany doesn't have any secrets. I don't think she even knows what hidden depths are, let alone possess any. That's part of her charm. We work well together, High Commander. We complement each other."

"I knew your father," Sir Vivian said slowly. "A strong man. Strong, because he stood alone. Nothing to distract him or compromise his loyalty."

"He was lonely and a monster," Chance said flatly. "He had no life of his own, only a role to play. Never any time for friends or family or human feelings. I won't live like that. I'm not my father. I'd have thought you, if anyone, would have understood that."

"I do," said Sir Vivian, struggling to find the right words, feeling the conversation slipping away from him. "My mother was the Night Witch. Everyone knows what she did. You can't trust a witch, Questor. Any witch. They live differently from us."

"We're all different," said Chance. "That's why it's so important to reach out to other people. You should try it sometime, Sir Vivian. Instead of trying to infect other people with your own paranoia. Thank you for your advice, High Commander. May I go now?"

"Yes. Go!" Sir Vivian gestured sharply at the door. Chance bowed briefly and left, closing the door firmly behind him.

Well, thought Sir Vivian. That went well.

He sighed heavily. As always, he did the most harm when he tried to help. And now his harsh words had probably alienated the only real ally he had at Court. He looked down at the book he'd automatically picked up again. The wonderful and marvelous history of Tower Rouge. The one moment of worth in his life. Sir Vivian threw the book aside. Like too many men, he'd made the mistake of outliving his own legend. Perhaps all that was left to him now was to find some enemy's sword to throw himself onto, to redeem his useless life with a good death. Like the Champion.

He sat in his chair thinking dark thoughts, alone.

And deep within him the magic churned and boiled, promising to put everything in the world right if he would only set it free.

Hawk and Fisher settled down comfortably to tea and cakes with the Seneschal. His apartments were marvelously luxurious, everything padded and cushioned to within an inch of its life. The man himself was heavier and older than Fisher remembered, and crippled with gout. One heavily bandaged foot lay propped up on a padded footstool. He'd been surprisingly happy to meet Hawk and Fisher, and soon had his plump and red-cheeked wife running back and forth with pots of tea and little delicacies on doilied plates.

"I don't get out much these days," said the Seneschal, chewing contentedly on a toffee cake. "My apprentices can handle most things, and those little magical lights the Magus created for me mean I can send my presence anywhere, so I'm free to spend time with my family, and curse this gout. My healer recommends red wine and red meat, but I can't say I've noticed any improvement."

"You look pretty healthy otherwise," said Fisher. "I'd heard you were pretty badly mauled by demons in the South Wing."

"Oh, I was," said the Seneschal. "I was. Bastards made a real mess of me. But the High Warlock's brood are hard to kill. You did know he was my grandfather? Of course; everyone does. Anyway, my life's been a lot easier since I learned to delegate. Used to be I was the only real guide the Castle had, and I spent my whole life trying to be everywhere at once. Now thanks to the Magus' lights, I *can* be everywhere at once. And I got married late in life. Three kids. That did a lot to calm me down, and make me take an interest in things other than myself." He stopped, frowning unhappily. "Everything was going really well. And then King Harald was killed, and the whole place has been buzzing with intrigue ever since."

"I notice you haven't mentioned the Inverted Cathedral," said Hawk.

"I try very hard not to," snapped the Seneschal, with just a little of the bile Fisher remembered so well. "Hate the bloody place. Impossible damned construct, right in the middle of the Castle. My magic means I know where every part of the Castle is at any given moment, no matter how things move or twist around. But not the Inverted Cathedral. I can't see that at all. It's like a hole in my mind, or an itch I can't reach. I've never tried looking inside it. Don't even like getting close to it. It scares the crap out of me, to be brutally honest, which I never am unless I'm forced to it."

"According to what I heard, you were never scared of anything," said Fisher, almost accusingly. "You rediscovered the missing South Wing when everyone else was too scared even to talk about it much."

"You don't understand," said the Seneschal. He sank back in his chair, the fire going out of him. "No one understands, though God knows I've told them often enough. The Inverted Cathedral isn't just a physical structure, it's

an outgrowth of Hell itself. The one time I went to see the
Inverted Cathedral in person, to test my gift against it up
close and personal, all I saw was a dark pit, falling away
forever. I turned and ran and never went back. Let us
change the subject. I understand you've been talking to my
uncle Vivian?"

"The High Commander, yes," said Hawk. "A strong-
minded man."

"Bloody-minded, more like. He lets his duty run his life,
the way I used to. I keep trying to open him up but it's
hard going. We're pretty much the only family we have
here in the Castle. I've been encouraging him to adopt my
family as his own—inviting him to dinner, having him sit
with the kids. I think he's softening toward them, but it's
hard to tell with Vivian. Always was a cold sort. Nothing
like his brother, my father. My mother, Emma, died not
long ago, in Redhart. King Harald wouldn't let me go to
Redhart for the funeral. Said I was too valuable to be
risked. Bastard. I kind of hoped my father would come
back, but apparently he's very close to the new King Viktor, and can't be spared. He writes now and again, when
he remembers. So I make do with Vivian.

"And now to the real purpose of your visit. No, I don't
know how King Harald died or who killed him. I never
liked the man, but if everyone who disliked Harald was a
candidate for murder, you'd have a line of assassins stretching from here to Redhart. And back again. I have an alibi.
I was right here with my wife and children at the time he
was killed. There's only one thing I can tell you that might
be of any use. As Seneschal, I could feel the presence of
the Magus' protective wards in my head, like a background
hum. They never fell, not even for a moment, and they
weren't broken. I would have known."

"Tell us more about the Inverted Cathedral," said Hawk.

"Oh, Jesus, do I have to?"

"What is it, exactly?"

"All right, if we must. Technically, it's a large building
that's been turned upside down. Once you enter it, everything should seem perfectly normal, but the higher you ascend inside the Cathedral, the deeper into the pit you go.

And at the peak of the Cathedral is perhaps one of the legendary doors into Hell that can only be opened from this side. I've studied the writings of my Seneschal predecessors, in the Castle Libraries. There have always been Seneschals of one kind or another for as long as there's been a Castle. There's evidence the Cathedral was constructed centuries ago, in the time of the first Forest King. He had the Castle built *around* the Inverted Cathedral, specifically to contain it and seal it off from the world. Its presence is the cause of the Castle's unusual spatial characteristics. The interior is so much larger than the exterior because the heavy magical gravity of the Inverted Cathedral warps space around it. And perhaps its malicious presence is also responsible for the darkness and tragedies that have always followed the line of the Forest Kings. Who knows what subtle influence it had on all the people who lived unknowingly in such close proximity to it for all those centuries? How many lives has it damned or blighted over the long years?

"Records no longer exist to tell who planned or funded or designed the original Cathedral, or how it became Inverted. A lot of the records for that time are listed as destroyed. Deliberately destroyed. The only thing I can say for sure is that this is the first time the Inverted Cathedral has reappeared in the Castle. Don't ask me what brought the bloody thing back. The reappearance of the lost South Wing? The Astrologer's spell that first summoned the Demon Prince out of the darkness? The long night? The Blue Moon? All of the above? I have no idea. We're talking about magic, not history. My own gifts are very limited, and some of the relevant books can only be opened by a sorcerer. My grandfather could probably have told you more, but he's gone. You could ask the Magus. God knows I have. But if he does know anything, he's keeping it very close to his chest. Enigmatic bastard."

"You mentioned the Blue Moon," said Fisher. "We've been told it could be coming back."

"Yes," said the Seneschal. "I've heard those rumors, too. From usually reliable resources. It doesn't seem fair we should have to face such evil and such horror more than once in our lifetime. But man proposes, God disposes, so let's all hope He knows what He's doing. If you're asking me whether the Blue Moon is returning because the Inverted Cathedral is back, or vice versa, I have no idea. But I'll tell you this: Whoever buried the secret of the Inverted Cathedral buried it deep. This could only have been done with the connivance of generations of Forest Kings. They really didn't want anyone to know about this until they had to. I found a book. A strange book. It wasn't listed in any of the library indexes. In fact, the Chief Librarian swore it had never existed until I found it. The book is handwritten in half a dozen languages, some of which no longer exist in the real world. It's more full of hints than actual information, as though the writer was afraid to say too much, for fear of being noticed. There's definitely a connection between the Inverted Cathedral and the rise and fall of Wild Magic. You know how Cathedrals were constructed originally to resonate as spiritual tuning forks? Yes, well, this Cathedral was supposed to be particularly potent because it contained wonders."

He stopped and was silent for a long while, staring off into space. Finally Fisher prompted him. "What *kind* of wonders?"

"The Grail, perhaps," said the Seneschal. "Furniture that the Christ made with His own hands, when He was learning to be a carpenter with His earthly father. The crown of thorns, with His dried blood still on it. An Ossuary, a museum containing the bones of saints, some of them carved and crafted into objects of great power. Opinion was divided as to whether these were reliquaries or blasphemies. And then there's the Burning Man ringing the great and awful iron bell of Hell.

"And you wonder why I want nothing to do with the place?"

"Let's change the subject," said Hawk. "Who do you think killed King Harald?"

"I never follow politics. I have to be seen to be impartial, my services freely given to all. But there's something very wrong about the Magus. And I'm sure Felicity had a lover, though I couldn't tell you who. Beyond that, I'm as much in the dark as anyone."

"If we set up an expedition to enter the Inverted Cathedral, would you come with us?" Fisher asked.

"What? Why the hell would you want to do a crazy thing like that? Haven't you listened to a word I've told you?"

"I've got a horrible feeling it may become necessary," said Hawk. "The Inverted Cathedral's reappearance seems tied to so many things, including Harald's death. So, would you join us if we had to do it?"

"My gout . . . I don't know. Give me some time to think about it. You don't know what you're asking. Go away. I'm tired. I'll send word when I've made my decision, one way or the other."

And then the door burst open, and in came his merry wife, Jane, with scones and jam and fresh cream. Three small children came running in after her, clustering excitedly around the Seneschal to tell him all the things they'd done that day. Hawk and Fisher let themselves out.

And finally, like intrepid hunters braving the bear in his den, Hawk and Fisher went to see Duke Alric of Hillsdown. They'd deliberately left him until last, partly because he'd tried to pressure them while they were with the Magus, partly because they were mostly convinced their ambush and beating had come at the Duke's orders; and mostly because Fisher desperately wanted her despised father to be the murderer. So they left him until last to allow themselves to get a better view of the various theories and motivations. And not at all because he was the most dangerous of the suspects, and they still felt weak and broken inside.

The Duke's guest apartments were the finest in the Castle, outside of the Royal suites; big airy rooms stuffed with every luxury and modern convenience from the south. Hawk and Fisher had to pass a number of armed guards just to get to the Duke. At every stage guards demanded that Hawk and Fisher hand over their weapons, and at every stage Hawk and Fisher calmly made it clear that wasn't going to happen. The threat of imminent violence hung heavily in the air, never quite materializing.

Eventually they were ushered into the Duke's presence. He sat in a very comfortable chair in the exact center of the room while servants moved silently around him, hurrying to follow the endless series of orders barked in the Duke's rough voice. *Bring me a footstool. Bring me a drink. Bring me a different drink. Close the curtains on that window.* Hawk and Fisher were clearly supposed to wait on one side until he summoned them, so they could be impressed by the Duke's power and authority. Unfortunately for the Duke, Hawk and Fisher weren't easily impressed. They just marched forward, scattering the servants like frightened birds, and planted themselves right in front of the Duke. They stood straight and tall, with no betraying hint of the bone-deep weariness that still filled their bodies.

"Nice place you've got here," said Hawk.

"Far too small," said the Duke. "Not at all what I'm used to. If it wasn't for Felicity and the child, I'd leave this dump so fast, it would make people's heads spin. But my daughter needs me, whether she wants to admit it or not. She needs my support. Those back-stabbing courtiers would walk all over her if I let them. They want to replace Felicity as Regent so they can get their hands on my grandson. I'll see them all dead first."

"You're talking about war between the Forest and Hillsdown," said Fisher.

"Wars are expensive," said the Duke. "Something you only turn to when everything else has failed. That's why I'm here, so far from home and real comforts. By protecting my daughter, I protect my interests here. Harald's death ruined everything. I could talk to him. We understood each other. We might have had a few border disputes, just to see who could be pushed or pressured by a little military action, but never anything serious."

"Serious enough for the men who died in those disputes," said Fisher.

"Soldiers," said the Duke. "Just soldiers. They're paid to fight—and die, if necessary."

He lifted a glass of wine slowly to his mouth. The leather

straps and steel cables surrounding and supporting his arm made soft creaking noises as they moved. There were even delicate strips of bone and metal on each individual finger, hinged at the joints, like some exotic exoskeleton. The Duke caught their eyes on his supports, and laughed lightly, a dry, breathy sound.

"Arthritis. Every move I make is agony. Without my carefully designed cradle and the subtle magics that hold it together, I'd be a helpless cripple confined to my bed. But I'm not ready to give up my life to illness yet. There's still far too much for me to do."

"There are magics that could help," said Hawk.

"Put my life and well-being into the hands of magic-users? I think not. I will be my own man, whatever that costs me. I use only the magics I must, and no more."

"You see that polished black stone on a chain round his neck?" Fisher said to Hawk. "That's the Candlemass Charm. Very old. Some say it came to Hillsdown with the first Starlight Duke, looted from the Forest Castle treasury. It's a protective agent against all physical and magical attacks. But as long as he wears it, he can't be affected by any spell that comes from outside, not even ones that might heal him. Of course, he could give up the Charm and be cured, but then he'd be vulnerable to attack. And you do have so very many enemies, don't you, Duke? So you stay safe behind your Charm, safe from attack or help, a crippled old man crawling toward death, condemned by his own past deeds."

"You're very well-informed, Captain," said the Duke, his face as calm as ever. "But then, there are always those ready to tittle-tattle in a place like this. Yes, I have many enemies, and I regret none of them. Everything I have done had at its heart the purpose of making Hillsdown strong, and keeping it safe and secure. I have given my life to the service of Hillsdown. That's what it is to be the Starlight Duke."

"And the Starlight Duke is Hillsdown," said Fisher. "So what's good for the Duke is good for Hillsdown."

"Exactly," said the Duke. "Politics is my lifeblood, now I'm too old and brittle to defend my country on the battlefield. Politics is just war by different methods, when all is said and done."

"What about your family?" asked Hawk. "Couldn't you delegate some of your power and responsibilities to them?"

The Duke smiled, but there was no humor in his eyes. "My last wife died ten years ago. My daughters have all been disappointments to me. None of my wives proved capable of giving me a son, and the chances of my fathering one at this late date would seem to be very remote. So when I die, there's no direct heir to Hillsdown. God knows I tried hard enough. Someone must have cursed me. Rather than see Hillsdown split up among whatever strangers eventually marry my daughters, I have chosen my grandson, Stephen, as my official heir. Half Forest blood, but still of my line. It has to be him. All my other daughters produced only daughters. Apart from Sophie, who became a nun just to spite me."

"And that's really why you're here?" asked Hawk. "To protect your daughter and your grandson?"

"And because the Blue Moon is coming back. Don't look so surprised, Captains. We have witches in Hillsdown. They See things. The last time the Blue Moon came, I had no magic-users among my defenders. I never trusted them. The first we knew about the long night, it had already covered the whole Forest Kingdom, and demons were pouring across my borders. The Rainbow put an end to the long night in time to save us, but it was still a hell of a shock. I was determined never to be caught napping again. Now my newly installed and very expensive magic-users tell me the Blue Moon's coming back again. They can't See when or where, but they know it's tied to Forest Castle somehow. So here I am, where I need to be, right at the heart of things. My army is massed on the Forest borders, waiting only for my call. If the long night comes again, and the demons rise, my army stands ready to do what is necessary."

"Of course, you could always call them in if you just suspected the long night might be coming," said Fisher. "You could even use them to take control of the Forest Kingdom—for its own good and protection."

"My grandson will rule both the Forest and Hillsdown,"

said the Duke. "He will combine them into one country, as it was once, long ago. I'll be here to see he's raised right. To be strong and mighty, and to stamp out all this Southern democracy nonsense. I will do whatever's necessary to see that nothing threatens that."

"We need to talk to you about Harald's death," said Hawk, deciding he'd had enough of standing around and listening while the Duke talked. "Where were you when the King was murdered?"

"Right here, with my people. My arthritis was particularly bad that day. Don't seek to put the blame on me, Captain. I had no wish to see Harald dead. Fliss was far more use to me as a Queen than as a Regent. And Harald's death has stirred up this democracy nonsense more than ever."

"Who do you think killed him?" asked Hawk.

"You want me to do your job for you?"

"You're as much an outsider here as us," said Hawk. "But you've been here longer, and you're much better connected. Perhaps your people have seen things, heard things, that we might find useful?"

"The Magus has to be your best bet," said the Duke slowly. "He's even more powerful than he lets on, he's mysterious as all hell, and he knows far too much for anyone's comfort. And who better to get through magical wards than the man who set them up? I did wonder about Fliss for a while, but she hasn't the gumption."

"There are rumors about a lover," said Fisher.

"Just rumors. There was no one. I'd have known."

"Could Harald have had a lover?" Hawk asked.

"No. I'd have known that, too. And I wouldn't have permitted it. No one insults my daughter and gets away with it. There's always the Hellstrom, of course, Sir Vivian. Once a traitor, always a traitor. Harald should have killed him when he turned up alive after the Demon War. And of course, there's Sir Robert, the Landsgrave, and the democratic scum he represents. The only way they'll ever come to power is by assassination. Dig there, and you'll find dirt."

"But with Harald gone," said Fisher, "you'll find it that much easier to pressure Felicity into doing what you want.

Like you tried at Court yesterday. And you just said you had your own ideas on how Stephen should be raised. With your army massed on the Forest borders, you could pressure the Court into making you Regent, and then you'd be in effective control of both Hillsdown and the Forest Kingdom."

"You think well," said the Duke approvingly. "If any of my daughters had half your brains, I wouldn't be so depressed about my legacy."

Fisher swallowed an angry retort. She wanted her father to be the killer, but as yet there just wasn't the evidence to justify accusing him. And she was too good a cop to let her emotions cloud her judgment. She wanted to ask the Duke more questions, just for the feeling of power over him it gave her, but it was hard to take satisfaction from browbeating a crippled old man. Hawk saw the conflict in her eyes.

"Time to be leaving," he said quickly. "Thank you for your cooperation, Duke Alric."

"Don't bother getting up," said Fisher. "We can find our own way out."

"You're not going anywhere just yet," said the Duke.

Armed guards suddenly appeared all around Hawk and Fisher, their swords already in their hands. Hawk and Fisher moved quickly to stand back to back, but made no move to draw their weapons. Exhausted as they were, they didn't want to start something they might not be able to finish.

"I haven't forgotten how you humiliated me at Court yesterday," said the Duke. "I never forget a slight. I think you should both apologize to me before you leave."

Hawk looked quickly about him. There had to be forty armed guards in the circle around him and Fisher. Big, professional-looking men. Bad odds, even if they weren't so drained by the healing spell. There was only the one door, and it seemed a very long way away.

"All right," said Hawk. "I'm sorry we offended you. Can we go now?"

"Captain Fisher hasn't apologized yet," said the Duke.

"Go to hell," said Fisher.

"Say it," Hawk said quietly. "We're in no position to stand on our pride. It's only words."

"I'm sorry," said Fisher, just loud enough to be heard.

"I really don't think that's good enough," said the Duke. "It didn't sound like you meant it. I think you need to do it properly. I think both of you should kneel down before me and bow your heads till they touch the floor, so that I can put my feet on your necks. So that there will be no misunderstandings about who's in charge here."

"Sorry," said Hawk. "We don't do that. We'd rather fight and take our chances."

"But your chances really aren't very good just now," said the Duke. "Not in your present weakened conditions. And you can't attack me, because of my charm. It's really very simple. If you don't do exactly what I say, Captain Hawk, I'll have my men kill Captain Fisher. And vice versa, of course. Either way, at least one of you will bow down to me."

"You'd never get away with killing us!" said Fisher.

"Oh, I think I will. Remember my army waiting at the borders? You're not important enough to be worth fighting a war over."

"You'd start a war just over your own hurt pride?" said Hawk.

"Oh, he would," said Fisher. "Nothing's ever mattered more than his pride."

"My reputation is all I have left to savor in my life," said the Duke. "No one speaks to me as you did and gets away with it."

Hawk and Fisher turned and looked at each other. They both knew that if they tried to fight, they'd lose. And probably die. Hawk remembered dueling the Champion all those years ago in the main courtyard of Forest Castle, remembered how that terrifying warrior had beaten and humiliated him, and left him lying in his own blood. He'd promised himself then that he'd never allow anyone to treat him that way again, but he couldn't risk Fisher's life.

It wasn't such a big thing. He'd suffered worse, for her sake.

"All right," he said finally. "We kneel, we bow, and then we leave. Agreed?"

"Of course, Captain Hawk. You have my word."

"We can't do this, Hawk," said Fisher. "I can't. Not to *him.*"

"We have to. It won't kill us." Hawk lowered his voice to a murmur. "There will be time later, for revenge."

"Hawk—"

"We have to."

Hawk walked forward, knelt down before the Duke, and pressed his forehead to the cold marble floor. He was trembling with suppressed rage, and the taste of humiliation was bitter in his mouth. He would never have done this for himself, but this was for Fisher. He heard her kneel down beside him. There was a pause, and then a quiet creaking of straps and cables as the Duke lifted his feet and set them on Hawk's and Fisher's necks. And then he laughed quietly before he took his feet away again. Hawk and Fisher scrambled to their feet. Fisher's face was scarlet with shame and barely controlled rage, her hand shaking beside her holstered sword. Hawk's face was cold and composed, and his single eye burned with a cold and deadly fire. The Duke looked at him thoughtfully.

"Interesting. You did it, but you still plan to defy my will. It didn't break you. What will it take, I wonder . . . Ah, yes. That's a very pretty axe you have there, Captain. Very pretty. I think I'll take it, for a keepsake, so we'll both always remember this moment. Give me the axe, Captain. Now."

Hawk looked down at the axe on his hip. He drew it slowly, the great weight dragging his tired arm down.

"Don't do it, Hawk," said Fisher. "Oh, God, don't do it."

"The High Warlock gave me this axe," said Hawk, his voice calm and thoughtful. He looked at the Duke, and smiled slowly. "It has a singular, very useful property. It cuts through magical defenses. Very probably including the Candlemass charm of yours. Fisher and I are leaving. Because if anyone tries to stop us, I swear I'll take this axe you want so much and bury it right between your eyes."

The Duke started to say something, then stopped. Hawk

and Fisher turned and walked toward the door. The guards fell back out of their way. The only sound in the quiet, airy room was Hawk's and Fisher's departing footsteps. They left the Duke's apartments, and for a long time neither of them had anything to say.

Lightfoot Moonfleet, barely half an inch tall but still perfect in every detail, buzzed along the corridor after Hawk and Fisher. Her head was still spinning with all the suspects and theories they'd turned up, and she decided it was time to return to the Magus to tell him what she'd learned. She worried about him when he was out of her sight. She stayed with him because she loved him, even though she knew what he really was. And that the day would come when she'd have to leave him, because she couldn't be part of what he was planning to do. She fluttered off down the corridor, dive-bombing a slow-moving mouse along the way.

CHAPTER SIX

Explorations into the Soul

Jericho Lament, not in the least tired after many days traveling on foot, walked out of the Forest and strode steadily across the great open clearing toward Forest Castle. He didn't hurry. He wanted the Castle guards watching the clearing to have plenty of time to see him coming, recognize who he was, and panic. Lament had no wish to face an organized resistance. Practically speaking, they couldn't keep him out of the Castle if they lined up in ranks before him with a sword in each hand. He was the Wrath of God, and could not be stopped by anything in the mortal world. But Lament preferred to keep innocent casualties to a minimum wherever possible. For all his reputation, Lament still liked to think of himself as a kindly man, doing only what was necessary; like a surgeon cutting away diseased flesh so that the body as a whole might thrive. There was no anger or malice in what he usually did. He did God's work, killing only when he had to, and it grieved him that not everyone could see it that way.

Still, his reputation did come in handy sometimes. All the Castle guards had to do was lower the portcullis, raise up the drawbridge, and station a whole bunch of archers at strategic points on the wall, and he'd have a much harder task getting in. But he was already halfway to the Castle, and the only guards he could see were running frantically back and forth on the battlements, and trying to hide behind each other. They knew who was coming. Probably passing the buck further and further up the chain of command, rather than have to decide for themselves what to do about the imminent arrival of the dreaded Walking Man. With any luck they'd still be panicking, wetting themselves, and running around in circles by the time he got to the entrance Keep.

And so it proved. Jericho Lament strode unhurriedly across the drawbridge, the thick wood trembling under his heavy tread, and whatever currently occupied the Castle moat took one quick look and then wisely decided to keep their heads well down until he was past. Lament walked through the great stone passage of the Keep, not even glancing at the still-raised portcullis, and entered into the main courtyard beyond. And there he stopped for a moment, leaning on his long wooden staff, to study the huge crowd arrayed before him, silent and staring. They were mostly peasants and traders, with a few guards, standing well back. Everyone present knew who and what Lament was. Even those who didn't know his face or his description knew him the moment they saw him. Knew him on some deep, instinctive, *spiritual* level that could not be denied. Lament smiled on them, and something like a shudder ran through the packed crowd.

He started slowly forward and the crowd drew back to form a wide central aisle for him to walk through. No one said anything, and the silence now was so strained and heavy that it had an almost tangible presence. Lament walked unhurriedly forward, looking straight ahead, and on either side of him men and women sank down on one knee or two, crossing themselves, clutching crosses and rosaries and the sign of the fish, mouthing quiet prayers and pleas. No one tried to touch Lament's clothes or beg for favors or even bid him welcome. People might crowd to holy men for advice or wisdom or even instruction, but no one wanted to be noticed by the Walking Man. He might be an avatar of the good and the just, but it was not a forgiving aspect, and everyone knew there was no mercy to be found in Jericho Lament.

So he was more than a little surprised when a tattered old man stepped out of the crowd to block his way. Lament stopped and studied the defiant figure with the woad and clay-marked face, and knew who this had to be. He'd heard of the Shaman, the hermit and holy man who'd made politics his religion. There wasn't much to the Shaman, but he had a certain bitter charisma. Lament inclined his head courteously, one servant of God to another.

"I know you," said the Shaman, his voice a harsh, almost painful sound.

"And I know you," said the Walking Man.

"Have you come for me?"

"No. I know who you are. I know what you've done. But it's not for me to judge you. God has a use for you, holy man. And it's not the one you think."

"I'm not afraid of you," said the Shaman.

"Yes, but that's because you're crazy," said Lament kindly.

"These are my people," said the Shaman, gesturing widely at the watching crowd. "I won't let you hurt them."

Lament could have said something cutting, but in the end he settled for a milder answer. "The innocent have nothing to fear from me."

The Shaman snorted. "Everyone has cause to fear your heartless ideas of justice."

"I go where I must, and do what I must," Lament said patiently. "I am the Wrath of God in the world of men."

"Which God?" asked the Shaman.

"There is only one."

"Shows how much you know. Why are you here, Walking Man?"

"To punish the guilty and redeem the fallen."

"Then why don't you start by killing off all the damned aristocrats, the privileged few who live off the sweat and blood of the many?"

"I deal in God's laws, not man's," said Lament, just a little sternly. "Think about it, holy man. Would you really want someone with all my power taking an interest in politics and wars?"

The Shaman opened his mouth but realized he had no answer to that, and had to close it again. Lament started forward and the Shaman fell back, out of his way. Those peasants nearest the Shaman formed a protective wall around him, clapping him on the shoulder and on the back, and even daring to murmur words of support and admiration. There were few indeed who dared stand up to the Walking Man, and even fewer who lived to tell of it.

Lament entered the Castle proper, and no one tried to stop him. He walked purposefully through the corridors, unaffected by the strange twists and turns of the Castle's unique inner structure. He had never been in Forest Castle before, but his inner voice told him where he must go, as it always did. Everyone hurried to get out of his way, including the Castle guards. Lament had no doubt that increasingly urgent messages were being sent to whoever was in charge of Castle security, but as yet no one showed any interest in interfering with his mission. Instead, a few guards followed him at a very respectful distance, hoping fervently they wouldn't be called on to actually do anything, while others went running ahead of Lament to spread the news and clear the way.

And then Jericho Lament stopped suddenly and turned to look at the hall of the magic-users. They'd closed the door against him, as though that made any difference. The usual deafening babble of voices was stilled, but Lament could almost hear the strained breathing of the magic-users massed on the other side of the closed door. They would have known he was coming, but not the details of his mission. Such information came from God, and could not be Seen or known by mere magic-users, however skilled or talented. Lament stepped forward and tried the door handle. They'd locked it and reinforced the lock with binding spells. Idiots. Lament lifted his staff and pounded on the door with the end tipped in cold iron. The heavy wood split apart under the first knock and the second threw the door inward, torn free from its hinges. The door hit the floor like a thunderclap, and Jericho Lament stepped into the hall of the magic-users.

They stared back at him, wrapped in their gaudy robes and cloaks, surly and rebellious, but already just a little shocked at how easily their first defense had been swept aside. Lament could feel magic building in the great hall, like the pressure of a coming storm. The fools were going to make a fight of it. He looked unhurriedly about him, taking in the witches and hedge-wizards, conjurers and magicians of varying calibers, but none of them were a threat to what he was. Jericho Lament had put down sorcerers in his time. Everyone in the hall was scared. He could feel it. No magic-user rises to power without making questionable deals and compromises and sacrifices somewhere along the line. Every man and woman in the hall had every right to feel guilty. But if Lament were to pursue every sinner he came across, he'd never get anything important done. Only one man here interested him today.

Lament opened his mouth to speak, and the magic-users' nerve broke. They hit him with everything they had, all at once. Magic crackled and spat on the air, lightnings flared, and unnaturally colored fires warred about him. Holes opened up in space, and horrid voices spoke, and there were new and awful presences in the hall. Hands gestured with unearthly skill, and strained voices chanted incantations in tongues never meant for humankind. And none of it could touch the Walking Man. All the various magics, Wild and High and Chaos, broke harmlessly against him, or earthed themselves through his staff. Potent energies shattered against him, and all the summoned presences fled rather than face his gaze. And when all the spells and curses were exhausted, Jericho Lament still stood there, untouched and unharmed. He was God's warrior, and nothing in this world could have power over him. The magic-users stared dumbly at him, not used to feeling helpless. Not used to feeling frightened.

"I am here for only one of you," said Lament, his voice clear and distinct in the strained silence. "Russel Thorne, come forth!"

There was a disturbance at the back of the crowd as someone tried to run, but those magic-users nearest him grabbed him and thrust him forward, happy to do anything that might turn aside Lament's wrath from them. Eventually a small, nondescript man was pushed out of the crowd to stand unhappily before the Walking Man. Wrapped in a dirty gray cloak, his hands hidden inside greasy bandages, he looked more like a merchant than a magic-user; the kind who'd let his thumb rest on the scales as he weighed out your purchase. He was trying hard to look defiant, even innocent, but his trembling mouth betrayed him.

"That's not my name!" he said loudly. "Ask anyone here!"

"It was your name," said Lament. "When you lived in the small town of Shadetree. You should have settled in a city, Thorne. Your practices might not have been noticed so easily there. I know who you are and what you are, and all the evil things you did in that unfortunate place. You escaped their justice by running for your life and hiding here, but you shall not escape God's justice."

"You came all this way just for me?"

"Don't flatter yourself, necromancer. You're not that important. You're just something I have to deal with on my way to my real work."

"What right have you to judge me?" asked Thorne, glancing about him in hope of support. "I don't believe in your god or his laws! And as Walking Man you've broken every law there is in pursuit of your victims! How many people have you murdered over the years? Everything I've done is nothing compared to your crimes!"

He gestured suddenly with both hands, and blasted black and twisting energies straight at Lament, only to see them fade away long before they reached him. Thorne whimpered and tried to force his way back into the crowd, but they wouldn't have him.

"You can't harm me," said Lament. "You can't touch me. I am under God's protection."

"We all know about the contract you made," Thorne said breathlessly. "But are you sure who you made it with? Are you sure where all your power comes from? Think of all the things you've done, all the blood you've spilled, all the lives you've ruined! All that, to serve a loving and merciful God?"

"Even God has to take out the garbage now and again," said Lament.

"Everything I did, I did for knowledge," said Thorne desperately. "Your god wants to keep people ignorant so they'll never become powerful enough to challenge him!"

"Innocents paid the price for the foul knowledge you

gained, necromancer. How many children died horribly, screaming for help that never came, in that awful cellar under your house? You savored their screams and washed yourself in their blood. Do you even remember their names?"

"They didn't matter, they were just peasants. Leading squalid little lives, of no importance to anyone, even themselves. I saw a chance to become a god and I took it! Anyone else would have done the same!"

"No one else would have done what you did," said Jericho Lament. "I was there when they brought the bodies out. Those terribly small and broken bodies. There's nothing more to be said. Now everyone here knows your crimes and your guilt. It's time for justice."

He put aside his staff and it stood on its end, alone. Thorne tried to run, but there was nowhere to go. Jericho Lament quickly caught him, and then calmly and deliberately beat the necromancer to death with his bare hands.

Chance, Tiffany, and Chappie heard the screaming three corridors away. The raised voices of horrified men and women, and above that the screams of one man, dying horribly slowly. The three of them had already been hurrying toward the magic-users' hall, warned by half a dozen panicked guards that the Walking Man had stopped there, but on hearing the awful screams, they broke into a run. Chance had never heard anything so dreadful in his life. All kinds of hideous visions filled his mind as he led the way down the last corridor and burst through the doorway into the magic-users' hall. The screaming stopped suddenly, and Chance realized sickly that he'd got there too late. Jericho Lament was kneeling beside the bloody broken wreckage of a man, blood dripping thickly from his hands. The dead man's face was crushed and broken beyond recognition, and from the twisted way he was lying, it was obvious most of his bones were broken. Lament made the sign of the cross over the dead man, drops of blood flying from his fingers with every movement, and then he rose unhurriedly to his feet and turned to face Chance. Tiffany and Chappie arrived a moment later, moving quickly in to stand on either side of Chance.

All the other magic-users in the hall had backed away as far as they could. Some were crossing themselves, some were crying. A few were vomiting. Most were just trying hard not to be noticed. Chance stood glaring at the dead man, his breathing harsh and strained. Jericho Lament produced a handkerchief from his coat pocket and began calmly cleaning the blood from his hands. His long staff stood on end beside him. Chance took a step forward, and Lament turned his head slightly to look at him.

"What have you done, Lament?"

"God's work," said Lament, unmoved by the open rage in Chance's voice.

"I am Queen's Questor," said Chance, so angry, he didn't even notice Lament's normally overpowering presence. "I am responsible for justice in this Castle. These people are under my protection! If you have a problem with anyone, you come to me, and I take care of it!"

"His name was Russel Thorne," said Lament. "He raped, tortured, and murdered small children in pursuit of forbidden knowledge. He made the cellar beneath his house into a place of horror, and took children there one by one. When their bodies were finally brought out, their own parents couldn't bear to look at what had been done to them. I did what I did partly as a warning to others, and partly so that word of this would get back to those parents, and they would know justice had finally been done."

"I didn't know any of this about Thorne," said Chance.

"Of course not. But God knows everything," Lament looked Chance steadily in the eye. "Does it make you feel any better about what I did now that you know about him?"

"No, it doesn't," said Tiffany.

"Not everyone has the stomach for justice," said Jericho Lament.

"This was revenge, not justice," Tiffany said hotly. "You deal in violence and death. The God you serve is the God of Cemeteries."

"I killed Thorne so that no other child would suffer and

die at his hands," said Lament. "I protect the innocent. Don't seek to judge me, witch. You have secrets, you and your Sisterhood. Pray that God does not send me to investigate what they are."

"I thought you just said God knows everything," said Chance.

"He does," said Lament. "But He only tells me what I need to know."

Tiffany and Lament studied each other silently for a long moment. The witch was using all her power to try and See the Walking Man's plans and future, but all her witchy gifts were useless against the sheer power of the man before her. Using her Sight on him was like looking into the heart of the sun, a light so fierce and intolerable, she had to look away or be blinded. She shut down her Sight and glared at Lament, who was still staring calmly back at her.

"Something bad is coming to the Forest Land," she said sharply. "I've Seen it. The long night come again. Demons spilling unchecked through a foully transformed Forest, with a full Blue Moon hanging overhead."

"Something bad is already here," said Lament. "That's why I've come to Forest Castle. Didn't you See that?"

"I thought *you* were the bad thing," Tiffany said reluctantly. "There's enough blood on your hands."

"Don't get in my way, little pagan," said Lament, not unkindly. "I am here to save you all."

"You're the kind who'd kill us all to save our souls," snapped Tiffany. "Be warned, Walking Man. I will defend this Castle, with my power and my life, if need be."

Lament actually smiled then, surprising everyone. "Well said, witch. Innocence is the only weapon I can't overcome." He turned to look at Chance, who'd been watching the conversation with a bemused fascination. "Questor, I need to see the Queen. Now."

"That's not possible right now," said Chance. "She's at Court. If you'd like me to take her a message—"

"Take me to see her right now, or I'll find my own way," said Jericho Lament.

"I won't let you threaten the Queen," Chance said slowly. "I'll fight you right here if I have to. I might not have your magic, but I have my father's axe, and the oath I swore to stand between my Queen and all harm."

"A brave oath," said Lament. "Relax, Questor. I haven't come to judge your Queen. I mean her no harm. I just need to talk to her." •

"Will you give me your word on that, Walking Man?"

"I do, Questor. And my word is God's word, which is never broken."

"Then you'd better follow me. Though I can't imagine what the Court is going to make of you. Chappie, would you please get out from behind my legs?"

"Don't like him," growled the dog, his head down. His hackles were raised, and his tail was tucked tightly between his legs. "He smells like a grave."

"Don't be frightened of me, boy," said Lament. "You're a fine-looking dog. Won't you say hello to me?"

He reached down to pat Chappie's head, but the dog backed quickly away, growling loudly. Lament looked at him sadly.

"I think you'd better stay here and look after Tiffany, Chappie," said Chance, and the dog nodded quickly in agreement. Tiffany bristled.

"Why should I stay here? I want to be at Court when Lament meets the Queen!"

"We have a whole room full of traumatized magic-users here," Chance said quietly. "And God knows what they might get up to if someone isn't here to calm them down. Someone with enough magic to shut them down, if necessary. Get them settled, and you can join me later. All right?"

"I suppose so," said Tiffany ungraciously. "I hate baby-sitting."

Chance decided he'd settle for that, and gestured politely for the Walking Man to follow him. They left the hall together, and every magic-user there let out their breath in one great sigh. A babble of bewildered and outraged voices broke out, some of it bordering on hysterical. A few sat down with their backs to the walls, and held their hands tightly together to stop them shaking. No one looked at

the broken and bloody corpse of Russel Thorne, not even
Tiffany and Chappie.

At Court the courtiers' reaction to Lament's arrival was
even more extreme than that of the magic-users. Chance
let Lament in, announced who he was, and before he'd
even finished speaking, every courtier in the hall headed for
the nearest exit at top speed. They ran in every direction at
once, shouting and screaming and cursing at those who
didn't get out of their way fast enough. A few avoided the
crush at the doors by throwing themselves out the open
windows, trusting the moat below to break their fall. Lament watched it all unmoved. He was not unfamiliar with
such reactions. The Queen's private guards hurried forward
to form a wall between the Throne and the Walking Man,
swords at the ready, and then they looked into Lament's
eyes and turned and ran with the rest. Felicity sat stiffly on
her Throne, looking steadily at Lament as he looked at her.

All too soon, everyone was gone except for the only two
of the Queen's guardians who would never run. Her bodyguard Cally, and Sir Vivian. They stood together before the
Throne, facing Lament with swords in their hands, putting
their bodies and their lives between the Queen and danger.
They looked into Lament's eyes and shuddered, but they
would not turn away, and their swords were steady in their
hands. Cally grinned mirthlessly at Lament.

"Old Man Death. Always knew you'd come for me one
day. But I've never been afraid of you."

"I'm not here for you," said Lament.

"You'll have to get through me to get to Felicity," said
Cally. "And I'm even better with this sword than people
think."

"You don't remember me, do you, Cally?" the Walking
Man asked.

Something in his voice made Cally frown and lower her
sword. She stepped forward and looked closely at Lament's
face, then her eyes widened. "Jesus, it's *you*."

Sir Vivian looked on uncomprehendingly as Cally backed
away from Lament. He didn't understand what had passed
between them, or why the Queen was just sitting there, but

it was clear he was the last defense for the Queen. He'd heard about the Walking Man, the Wrath of God. The living legend. Sir Vivian didn't know if he could hope to stand against such a powerful figure, but he'd been a living legend, too, in his time. So just maybe Lament wasn't everything he was supposed to be, either. Sir Vivian hefted his sword. Cold steel wasn't going to be enough this time, or Chance would have stopped the Walking Man long before this. But he couldn't let the Queen be hurt, not after failing to protect her husband—and that left only one option. The one weapon he'd never wanted to use.

He was Vivian Hellstrom of the Tower Rouge, and he knew his duty.

So he let the magic run loose within him. It surged forth, free at last, crackling on the air around him, a new and potent presence in the Court. Everyone there could feel it, and looked in astonishment at Sir Vivian. He seemed suddenly larger, more solid, almost as impressive as the Walking Man himself. He was the son of the High Warlock and the Night Witch, possibly the two most powerful sorcerers the Forest had ever known, and he had finally come into his inheritance.

He gestured sharply, and lightning bolts flashed through the air, crackling loudly, heading straight for Lament. The Walking Man put his long staff before him, and the bolts grounded themselves through the staff, discharging harmlessly. Sir Vivian gestured again, and fires blazed up around Lament, a great circle of flames whose heat was so intense that Chance had to throw up an arm to protect his face, and fell back several steps. The floor of the Court blackened, but Lament stood calmly inside the ring of fire, untouched by the vicious heat. Sir Vivian scowled, and the flames were gone as swiftly as they'd arisen. Sir Vivian pulled his magic out and around him, enclosing himself in a liquid silver armor that covered him from head to toe. He moved forward like a living statue, and there was something about him that had the inevitability of an avalanche or an earthquake. His power beat on the air like giant wings. His sword glowed so brightly, it was painful to look at. And Jericho Lament went forward to meet him.

Their magics went out before them and grappled on the still air. It was like two huge icebergs slamming together, two unstoppable forces stopped at last. Reality itself seemed to ripple around the two men as they slowed to a halt facing each other. Sir Vivian raised his sword and the Walking Man raised his staff. Unseen forces warred in the Court, old and potent. And slowly, inexorably, Sir Vivian Hellstrom was forced down onto his knees. The silver armor disappeared abruptly, and Sir Vivian was thrown back to lie gasping and trembling on the floor. Cally moved quickly forward to kneel beside him, sword ready to protect him if necessary. Lament studied his fallen foe dispassionately.

"God is my armor, Warlock's son."

"You shan't have her," said Sir Vivian, struggling to his feet with Cally's help. "While there's breath in my body, I'll defy you in the Queen's name."

"You inspire brave defenders, Your Majesty," Lament said to the Queen. "But I am not here to judge you."

Sir Vivian looked at him, confused but still determined. "Swear you mean the Queen no harm."

"Of course he doesn't," said Felicity.

"I'm not here for her or you, Warlock's son," said Lament. "Stand down. I'm just here to talk with the Queen. In private."

Chance looked at him, startled. "You must know that's not possible—"

"Leave us," said the Queen. "All of you."

"You can't trust him, Your Majesty," Sir Vivian said stubbornly. "The Walking Man serves only his God."

"He would never hurt me," said Queen Felicity. "Go. Leave us. We have much to discuss."

Chance, Cally, and Sir Vivian looked at another, shrugged pretty much simultaneously, bowed to the Queen on her Throne, and left the Court, Sir Vivian leaning just a little on Cally's supporting arm. The Queen and the Walking Man stared at each other for a long moment, and then the Queen rose to her feet and stepped down from the Throne on its dais. She stood before Jericho Lament and they both smiled.

"Lament wasn't always your name," said Felicity.

"It is now," said Lament. "Now and forever. That was the deal I made."

"Is there anything left of the man I remember?"

"Of course. I'm more than I was, not less. And I could never forget you, Fliss."

"Then let us walk awhile," said the Queen. "And talk of old times, when we were young and foolish, and still had hope."

They strolled together around the great Hall, companionably close but not touching. Felicity drew a cigarette case and her long holder from a pocket in her sleeve, and lit up. Lament shook his head.

"You know those things are bad for you."

"Everything I like is bad for me," said Felicity cheerfully. "But I'm still here. And you look at least two meals short. Are you eating properly?"

"I only eat and drink when I think of it," said Lament. "And I haven't slept in years. When I swore myself to God, He put me beyond all physical weaknesses. I can't die anymore. God wouldn't allow it."

"I've always excelled at physical weaknesses," said Felicity. "They're what I do best."

"I know," said Lament. "I remember."

Felicity looked at him fondly. "How much do you remember, Lament?"

"I remember that I was never happier than when I was with you. Or more miserable. That's love for you, I suppose."

They walked awhile together, in silence. Thinking, remembering. "So much has changed," Felicity said eventually. "When we were younger, and still together, the Forest Kingdom was the enemy. Now I'm its Queen, and you've come here to save it. I take it you have come here to save it?"

"That is my mission. You are all in great danger. Fliss, how long have you known I was the Walking Man?"

"Some time now," said Felicity. Still looking straight ahead, she put an arm through his. "As Queen, I have a great many agents spread throughout the Forest Land who

report to me on important matters like that. You've made
quite a reputation for yourself. Some of the things I've
heard . . ." She looked at him almost accusingly. "The man
I remember was never so harsh, so judgmental. You've
killed a lot of people, Lament. Most of them needed killing,
from the sound of it, but—"

"God, and the world, changes us all," said Lament. "I
became who I had to, to do what I must. You never tried
to contact me . . ."

"I didn't want to meet the kind of man you seemed to
have become. I was happier with my memories of the man
you used to be. The man I loved."

They stopped before an open window and looked out
at the peaceful view before them. The empty Court was
very quiet.

"I see Cally's still with you," said Lament. "I always
approved of her. Even though she scared the crap out of
me in the old days. She never took any shit from anyone,
even your father. Do you feel threatened here?"

Felicity laughed shortly. "Only every bloody day, darling.
I have so many enemies now, they have to line up to plot
against me."

"Would you like me to do something about them?" Lament asked politely.

"Can you?" asked Felicity, just a little surprised. "I
mean, are you allowed to get involved with mere worldly
matters like politics?"

"No," said Lament. "But they don't know that. A good
hard stare from me should be enough to make most of
them back down. Sin is sin, and all politicians are guilty
of something. Just the knowledge that you are under my
protection should be enough to scare off all but the most
determined. And I will kill anyone who tries to harm you,
Fliss. For my heart's sake."

They walked on again, not saying anything. They had a
lot of catching up to do, but they were in no hurry.

"We were happy at my father's Court," Felicity finally
said. "In those long summer days that seemed to go on
forever. When you had another name, and I was just another Princess. You've changed so much. You were always

so frivolous then. Always ready for a party, or dressing up for a costume ball, always there when I wanted to go dancing or hunting."

"Mostly I was happy," said Lament. "But often I just pretended. Keeping myself busy because it passed the time and kept me from thinking disturbing thoughts. I didn't know it at the time, but even then I was looking for someone or something to give my life to. I thought I'd found it in you, but I was wrong."

"Are you happy now?" asked Felicity, not looking at him.

"Sometimes," said Lament. "At least my life has meaning now. Purpose."

"But you're so alone."

"God is with me."

"And is that enough?"

"Sometimes."

"We were so happy then," Felicity repeated. "I'd never had a lover like you. Someone who cared so much about even the smallest things."

"But you always cared more about being a Princess than you did about us," said Lament. "No matter how close I held you, you always kept me at a distance. And then there was the baby."

"I had to abort it. I *had* to. The scandal if my father had found out about us, about the baby . . ."

"You didn't even tell me about it until it was too late. Until it was over and done with."

"You would have tried to talk me out of it. And I didn't want to be talked out of it. You were never supposed to know."

"But someone talked," said Lament. "Someone always talks. The abortion was the last straw for me. I kept telling myself you'd change, that I could change you. But you were always your father's daughter. We were always separated, by royalty and religion. You never understood how important my faith was to me, my beliefs. Or you couldn't have done what you did."

They walked on, not looking at each other. Felicity's hand gripped Lament's arm a little more tightly.

"Did the Duke ever know about us?" asked Lament.

"Of course, dear." Felicity blew a perfect smoke ring and watched it sail away on the air before them. "Daddy made it his business to know things like that. He had more spies inside his Palace than outside. As long as we weren't public knowledge and a threat to his reputation, he didn't care. And he never saw you as a threat. A very minor noble, more interested in the priesthood than politics. The perfect chaperone in Daddy's eyes."

"But he never knew about . . ."

"The pregnancy? No. He'd have had you killed slowly and horribly if he even suspected."

"You knew the abortion would hurt me when I found out."

"I had to be strong," said Felicity. "For both of us."

"Was it a boy or a girl?"

"I never asked." Felicity threw aside the last of her cigarette and chose another one. Her hand shook just a little as she fitted it into the elegant holder and lit it. "I never thought it would drive you away from me. Never thought you'd leave me, and the Palace, and everything we had."

"If you had known that," said Lament slowly, "would you still have done it?"

"Yes," said Felicity. "I've always been able to do what is necessary."

"And now you are a Queen, and I am the Walking Man, and we are further apart than ever." Lament sighed heavily. "We had such hopes and plans, you and I. We never foresaw anything like this."

"Well, you were the one who ran off to join a monastery!" said Felicity sharply. "Gave up your title, your lands, and your money, just to wear out your knees with a bunch of God-botherers. You never even looked in to say goodbye! I had to find out about it from the gossip sheets!"

"You would have talked me out of it," said Lament, repeating her words. "And I didn't want to be talked out of it."

Felicity sniffed. "You wouldn't catch me in one of those places on a bet. All ritual and discipline and cold baths at unnatural hours. If God had meant us to pray that much, he'd have put padding on our knees."

"I went there looking for peace of mind."

"Did you find it?"

"I think so, yes. Sometimes. Until the long night fell and the demons came. I'm sure you know the rest of the story. Everyone does."

Felicity stopped walking and Lament stopped with her. She turned to face him, and they looked into each other's eyes for a long time. "You were the only man I ever really loved," Felicity said quietly. "The only man who ever meant anything to me."

"But not enough to marry me," said Lament.

"I couldn't! Daddy would never have allowed it. He would have exiled you. Or had you killed."

"We could have run away together."

"No," said Felicity. "I couldn't. I couldn't give up the life I thought I valued so much."

"I know," said Lament. "I understood that, even then."

"Your hair is gray," said Felicity, almost wonderingly. "And your face is so much older than mine, though there's only a few years between us." She dropped her cigarette holder to the floor and used both hands to push aside his long coat to get at the shirt beneath. Lament stood stiffly as she undid the shirt buttons one by one, and then opened his shirt to look at his bare chest. "Your hair is gray here, too. And so many scars, so much pain. My poor dear. You had such a beautiful body once."

"Every scar tells a story," said Lament. "Medals in God's wars. I have been very busy in my Lord's work."

"Jesus, what have we done to ourselves?" asked Felicity. "This isn't how the story's supposed to end. Me, the widow of another man, and you, married to your religion. Doesn't what we want matter anymore?"

"God has a plan for all of us," said Lament. "I have to believe that, or I'd go mad. The darkness is real, so the light has to be."

Felicity turned away, her eyes bright with the tears she refused to shed. Lament buttoned up his shirt again.

"After you left, did you ever think of me?" Felicity asked finally.

"I gave myself to God."

"That isn't what I asked."

"Of course I thought of you, Fliss. I always will. But I have given myself to something bigger, to a cause that means more to me than life itself. I am the Walking Man now, the Wrath of God in the world of men. And the man you knew can only be a small part of that."

"So," said Felicity, looking back at him, eyes dry and mouth firm. "What brings you to Forest Castle after all these years?"

"Fliss . . ."

"Why did you come here!"

"The voice within me told me I was needed here. That I must go into the Inverted Cathedral and reclaim it for God. Make it clean again. Felicity, we have made our own lives by our own choices, and the love we once had, or might have had, is no part of either of them. You are the Forest Queen and I am the Walking Man, and that is all we can ever be."

"Would you give up being the Walking Man for me?" asked Felicity, so quietly, he could barely hear her.

"Would you give up being Queen?" Lament asked. "Would you give up your son's chance to be King?"

"Go away," said Felicity tiredly. "Leave me alone." She turned her back on him. "There's a private room just to your left. You can wait there while I send for a guide."

There was a long pause and then he said quietly, "I never meant to hurt you, Fliss." And then there was only the sound of a door opening and closing behind him as he left the Court, perhaps forever.

Felicity hugged herself tightly to stop herself from falling apart. She could cope with this. She'd coped with worse in her time. Nothing could destroy her anymore. And if she'd become hard over the years, well, she'd had to become hard, because the only other alternative was to be torn apart by all the opposing forces in her life. She pulled the authority of the Queen about her. It was a cold comfort, but better than none.

The Court's main doors swung slowly open and Cally and Sir Vivian peered cautiously in. On seeing the Queen alone, they entered the Court, and a collection of the braver courtiers filed slowly in behind them. Felicity went back to her Throne and seated herself carefully, her head held high, her chin firm, her gaze cold and forbidding enough to discourage all but the most polite and general of questions. Cally took up her usual position beside the Throne without saying anything, for which the Queen was quietly grateful. Sir Vivian took up a position standing before the Throne, while roughly a third of the normal number of courtiers spread out behind him, unusually quiet and subdued. There was a certain amount of craning of necks as they looked worriedly about them for some trace of the Walking Man.

"Welcome back, my loyal attendants," said the Queen icily. "Perhaps in future we should forget all about your solemn oath to protect the Throne, and just issue you all some running shoes. For now, you will no doubt be happy to hear that I am entirely unharmed and in no danger. Neither are any of you, as long as you behave yourselves while the Walking Man is here. He has given me his word he is here solely to deal with the problem of the Inverted Cathedral. So unless any of you are stupid enough to bring yourselves to his attention, you should be safe. Any of you with really guilty consciences should consider locking yourselves in your rooms till he's gone. Hiding under the bed might not be a bad idea, either."

The courtiers murmured quietly among themselves once she'd finished. Her stock had risen dramatically just for having survived a meeting with the dreaded Walking Man, let alone with such aplomb. Though every one of them would have given good money to know just what he and she had talked about for so long. A Queen Regent backed by the Starlight Duke was worrying enough; a Queen backed by the Walking Man was enough to make them want to change their underwear urgently. A great many plans would have to be reconsidered and possibly dropped, at least until the Walking Man was safely gone from Forest

Castle. The Queen let them mutter, and turned her attention to Sir Vivian, still standing at parade rest before her.

"Our thanks to you, too, Sir Vivian. You were ready to put your life on the line to protect me. I won't forget that. Though I suppose I should have expected nothing less from the hero of Tower Rouge. But your methods came as something of a surprise. I never knew you were a magician of such power."

"It's not something I'm proud of, Your Majesty," said Sir Vivian, his voice and face as cold and formal as always.

"Thank you anyway, High Commander, for staying when everyone else fled. I have never doubted your courage, but it is good to know I can depend on your honor as well." She turned to Cally. "Not a word now. We'll talk later."

Cally nodded and then looked at Sir Vivian, surprising him with an approving smile. He nodded stiffly back. He wasn't used to such praise from women, and honestly didn't know how to react to it. Truth be told, it made him feel more nervous than facing the Walking Man had.

Among the returned courtiers, various cliques and factions were already forming to mutter animatedly with each other, and discuss the ramifications of the Walking Man's presence and Sir Vivian's new powers. The whole balance of power in the Castle was up for grabs now, and everyone knew it. The Queen watched them talk themselves into a major panic, and smiled sardonically. Cally watched the Queen watching the Court, and frowned thoughtfully. She remembered the man who'd gone on to become the Walking Man, remembered how he broke Felicity's heart by leaving. Right now he was a complication the Queen didn't need. Cally's frown became a scowl as she looked ahead and saw nothing but trouble. There was nothing like the return of an old love for screwing up your life.

And Sir Vivian stood stiffly before the Throne, his thoughts moving furiously behind the cold mask of his face. His secret was out now. Soon the whole Castle would know. For all his efforts on the battlefield, for all his attempts to be a hero as other men, for all his endless restraint, he had become the only thing he never wanted to be—the Warlock's son, in fact as well as name. No one

would ever see him as anything else now. And what worried him most of all, and squeezed his heart with a cold
fist, was how natural it had felt to wield such powerful
magics. How natural and how good, how very good. Like
something he was born to do. Sir Vivian fought a desperate
battle to control his feelings and the new ambitions rising
slowly within him, and wondered what he would do next.

Hawk and Fisher sat together in a small, quiet antecham-
ber, and compared notes on their day so far. They were
both bone-deep weary, but they stubbornly put their heads
together and plowed through what little useful information
they'd gathered. Because they knew that if they put their
feet up and relaxed, even for a moment, they'd probably
sleep for a week. Unfortunately even after all their interviews, they still didn't have much worth discussing. Practically everyone had some motive to kill Harald, but no one
had the means, the opportunity, and the motive. Or at least,
not in any combination that made sense. Fisher still wanted
it to be her father, on general principles, but had to admit
there was no real hard evidence against him. Their arguments went in circles for some time without getting anywhere, until they were suddenly interrupted by the sound
of a large number of heavy feet heading in their direction.
Fisher moved over to the door and looked out, then
stepped back and shut the door quietly. She looked at
Hawk, who'd already risen to his feet.

"Duke's men," said Fisher. "Twenty of them, heading
straight for us. What do we do?"

"There was a time ten to one odds wouldn't have bothered us much," said Hawk. "But in our current state . . . I
don't think they'd kill us. But they might well work us
over again."

"Should we run?" asked Fisher.

"Do you want to?" countered Hawk.

"I couldn't bear to see you hurt again," said Fisher.
"You know the Castle better than them. We could lose
ourselves till they get tired of looking."

"No," said Hawk. "We don't run. Not ever. Not for my
sake, or ours. Because if we run, everyone will know we're

weak. That those bastards have broken our spirit, as well as our bodies. The news would spread all over the Castle. No one would talk to us anymore. And besides, we're Hawk and Fisher. We don't run. That's part of who and what we are."

Fisher smiled slowly. "Of course. I forgot that for a moment. Better to stand and fight and maybe die, because if we don't, we wouldn't be ourselves anymore."

"Couldn't have put it better myself," said Hawk.

He drew his axe and Fisher drew her sword, and they stood together in the middle of the room, watching the door. It took all their strength just to hold their weapons steady. The door soon burst open, slamming back against the wall as twenty of the Duke's men stamped into the room. They came to an abrupt halt and stared at Hawk and Fisher a little uncertainly, taken aback by the drawn weapons. The Duke's men looked at one another for a moment, and then their leader stepped forward. A big man with muscles on his muscles. He tucked his thumbs into his swordbelt and did his best to fix Hawk with an imperious gaze.

"I'm Hogg. I speak for the Starlight Duke. He gives you a deadline. Either produce a viable suspect for King Harald's murder by midday tomorrow, or he commands you to leave Forest Castle, never to return. The Duke will then merge Hillsdown and the Forest Kingdom by force of arms, in the name of his grandson, Stephen. The Duke will of course rule this new country, until Stephen comes of age. If you stay, or seek to interfere in any way, you will be killed. You are also commanded to stay well away from the Inverted Cathedral, also on pain of death. That is all."

"Very nicely memorized," said Hawk. "Ten out of ten for content, but you need to work on the menace more. It's all in the delivery."

Fisher looked at Hawk. "Why would he care about the Inverted Cathedral?"

"Because whatever weapons, treasures, or powers are to be found there, the Duke presumably wants them for himself," Hawk said easily. "Or at least, he wants only his people, or people under his control, getting their hands on

uch things. And he doesn't want us in particular getting
nvolved, because either we'd give what we found to the
Queen so she could be more independent of her father, or
we might keep them for ourselves and become even more
of a danger to him."

"Yeah," said Fisher. "That sounds like the Duke. Now,
are you going to give this arsehole the bad news or am I?"

"Me first, then you," said Hawk. He smiled at Hogg, the
Duke's spokesman. It was a confident, happy, and really
rather unpleasant smile. "I notice Duke Alric didn't come
himself. That's because he wasn't dumb enough to deliver
such a speech in person. He knew Fisher and I would take
turns kicking his arse until he could use his buttocks for
earmuffs. You can go back to your master and tell him that
Hawk and Fisher don't give a damn what he wants. We
will go where we choose, do as we will, and make fillets
out of anyone who gets in our way. Now, I know what
you're thinking. You're thinking there's twenty of you, versus two people who recently got the crap kicked out of
them. Well, we may not be exactly all that we used to be,
but you will observe that all our injuries are gone. And ten
to one odds or not, we're better than you'll ever be. If you
rush us all at once, there's a chance you'll bring us down
in the end. But we'll kill a hell of a lot of you along the
way. So, which of you are willing to die so that some of
your fellows might win out? How much does the Duke pay
you guys? Does it include funeral expenses?"

"Enough talk," growled Fisher. "I feel like killing someone."

Hawk grinned his old wolf's grin, his axe steady in his
hand. Fisher was grinning, too, and there was no humor at
all in her unrelenting gaze. Hogg swallowed hard and fell
back a step. And then he turned and almost ran from the
room, his men hurrying out after him. Hawk and Fisher
waited until they'd heard the Duke's men retreat a fair way
down the corridor, then they lowered their suddenly very
heavy weapons, staggered over to the nearest chairs, and
sat down.

"Damn, we're good," said Fisher.

"Oh, yeah," said Hawk. "Of course, it helped that we

weren't bluffing. We were ready to fight, and they knew it. They just couldn't believe we'd be ready to take on such odds if we weren't up to it."

"We have got to do something about this, Hawk," said Fisher. "Before we run into someone who's too dumb to be fooled."

"There is another way," Hawk said slowly, reluctantly. "I've been thinking more and more of all the good I could do if I were to reveal who I really am. If I declared myself Prince Rupert. I have the Royal seal. Chance would back me up. As Prince, I'd have the authority to order the right things done. The people would flock to me as they did before. The Duke would think twice about leading an army against forces led by the legendary Prince Rupert. I could put that legend to good use for once. Do I have the right to deny my duty, just because I don't want to take up my family responsibilities? I was always frustrated by my lack of authority back in Haven, by the lack of power to do something about all the evil I saw every day. As Prince Rupert and Princess Julia, we could make people do the right thing, force them to do what's necessary by sheer Royal authority."

"Isn't that what Harald tried to do?" asked Fisher.

"I'm not my brother. As Prince and Princess, our physical weakness wouldn't matter. We could just order people like Chance and Sir Vivian to do the hard work for us."

"You're not thinking this through," said Fisher. "Once you put the crown on, you could never take it off. To get the kind of authority you're talking about, you'd have to put aside the Queen Regent and your nephew, Stephen, and become King Rupert. Ruler of the Forest Kingdom. Our lives would never be our own again. And isn't that why we left here in the first place?"

"I know, but perhaps it's my duty to be King."

"What about your duty to me?" Fisher asked.

Then the window behind them burst open, and rain came pouring into the room. It sprayed through the window in an almost horizontal blast, as though forced into the room by some unimaginable pressure, only to stop short barely halfway across the room. As Hawk and Fisher watched open-mouthed, the water pressed together to form a solid pillar, blue and glistening, before slowly shaping itself into a human form. The spraying rain cut off abruptly, and there before Hawk and Fisher stood a woman made all of water. Six feet tall and clear as crystal, she wore a long dress, but it and her form were entirely fluid, with long, slow ripples flowing through her. The long hair that fell to her shoulders ran constantly away, constantly renewing itself. Beads of water ran steadily down her face like endless tears and dripped from her chin. She turned her head slowly to look at Hawk and Fisher, and her pale blue mouth moved in a gentle smile.

"All right," said Hawk. "You win the prize for the weirdest thing I've seen today. Who might you be?"

"I am the Lady of the Lake, an elemental protector of the Forest." More ripples spread across her face as her lips moved, and her voice was like the gurgling of a running stream, given shape and meaning and a human warmth. She walked slowly around the room, studying it. A fire in a grate steamed when she got too close to it, and she left a wet trail behind her. With no sign of feet beneath the long dress, she seemed to glide more than walk, like a watery spirit. She turned back to face Hawk and Fisher. "I have come to protect the Castle once you have gone into the Inverted Cathedral."

"Hold everything," Fisher said firmly. "We haven't decided we're going to do that yet. We still have a murder to solve."

"You will go into the Cathedral," said the Lady calmly. "Because you have to."

"Lady," said Hawk politely, "who, or what, are you, exactly?"

"I was created around the spirit of a woman who drowned herself," said the Lady of the Lake. "She wanted to escape from a world she found intolerable, but the world wasn't finished with her. There had been an earlier Lady of the Lake, but she was gone, and a new protector was needed. And so a mortal soul became immortal, as the spirit of the waters. But not long after my creation, while I was still weak and inexperienced, the Demon Prince used

Wild Magic to contain me in my Lake, and I became a helpless captive. I knew what was happening to the Land as the long night spread, but I was unable to intervene.

"After the Demon Prince was banished, I emerged, took on my full powers, and I have spent my time since slowly helping and encouraging the regrowth of the Forest. The Land was badly damaged during the long night, and I fear parts of it may never recover, even with my help. Now a dark time threatens us again, and I have come here to warn you. I have avoided human contact until now, partly because I didn't want to meet people who might have known me while I was still alive, and partly because I'm not human anymore. I remember what it was like, but I must take a larger view now."

"Why choose us to reveal yourself to?" asked Hawk.

"Because I knew I could trust Prince Rupert and Princess Julia. I am the Lady of the Lake, and nothing is hidden from me."

"Oh, great," said Fisher. "Another complication. Try and remember we're Hawk and Fisher these days if you have to talk to anyone else."

The Lady of the Lake didn't seem to be listening. She was looking around the room again. It was hard to read the expressions of her watery face, but Hawk thought she looked sad. She brought her hand to her mouth, and for a moment her fingertips merged seamlessly with her lips. "It's been a long time since I was last here," she said quietly. "When I was still alive. It hasn't changed much. That's the Castle's strength, and its weakness."

"Do you really live in a Lake?" said Fisher bluntly.

The Lady smiled at her. "I *am* the Lake. Wherever water flows in the Forest, I am there. I exist in every stream and brook, every waterfall and rainstorm. I am a part of the Land now. I've been watching you ever since you entered the Forest. Everything here has been waiting for your arrival. Now you are here, destiny can finally begin to unfold. It is your fate to enter the Inverted Cathedral and do what must be done there."

"We don't have to do a damn thing we don't want to," said Fisher just a little testily. "And what the hell is so important about us going into the Inverted Cathedral anyway? Seems like everybody wants us to go in there."

"The Blue Moon will be here soon," said the Lady. "Full and potent, to reign over a word of unleashed Wild Magic. An endless nightmare for whatever humans survive in it. Only you can prevent this. It's why you came back here."

"We came back of our own free will, to discover Harald's murderer!" said Hawk.

"You already know who killed him," said the Lady. "You just don't want to admit it yet."

Hawk looked at her for a long moment. "I know you from somewhere, don't I?"

"I'd like to think so," said the Lady. She smiled at Hawk and he smiled back, strangely drawn to her, though he didn't know why. Fisher watched all this and felt a bit left out.

"I can cure you both," said the Lady, suddenly all business again. "I know what has happened to you and how weak you are. I can make you whole and strong again."

"Is that a bribe?" Fisher asked. "Conditional on us going into that damned Cathedral?"

"No," said the Lady. "It is my gift to you. Whatever you decide to do." She held out her hands to Hawk and Fisher, and water fell from her palms and fingers like splashing waterfalls. "Come to me, and drink of my waters, and be whole again. The strength of the Forest Land flows through me. Drink of the Land, and be its champions again."

Hawk and Fisher looked at each other. They both wanted to ask what the catch was, but the words wouldn't come. They knew they were in the presence of something bigger than themselves, as though some aspect of the Land itself was in the room with them. They bowed their heads to the Lady of the Lake, and drank of the water flowing from her hands. It was cold and fresh, like water from a mountain spring, and as they swallowed, they could feel it coursing through their bodies like a tidal bore, slow but irresistible, washing away all the detritus of their lives. Strength filled their arms and legs, and straightened their backs. All their pains were gone, and their minds were suddenly, almost painfully, clear. The Lady of the Lake withdrew her hands, and Hawk and Fisher grinned at her, feeling fit and well and wholly alive for the first time in ages. The door opened behind them, and they both spun around, weapons at the ready, to find themselves confronting Chance and Sir Vivian standing, somewhat startled, in the doorway. Hawk and Fisher put away their weapons and smiled radiantly at their visitors.

"Sorry to intrude," said Chance, looking with interest at the smiling Lady of the Lake. "Are we interrupting anything?"

"I am the Lady of the Lake," said the watery spirit. "Don't worry about the carpet, it'll dry out. I am an elemental champion of the Land, come to protect it in its hour of need. It is good to meet you at last, Sir Questor, Sir Vivian."

Sir Vivian looked at Chance. "I don't know why we bother having any security in this Castle. People come and go as they damn well please these days."

"Be that as it may," said Chance, turning back to Hawk and Fisher, "Jericho Lament, the famous, or infamous, depending on which version you listen to, Walking Man, is here in the Castle. And he wants to talk to the pair of you. Right now. And even sooner than that, if possible."

"I've heard of him," said Hawk. "But I thought he was just some sort of rural legend."

"Oh, he's real enough, unfortunately," said Chance. "And altogether far more powerful than I feel comfortable contemplating. Please come and talk with him, before he starts looking for more evil people to punish."

"If we must," said Fisher. She looked at Hawk. "Want to bet he wants us to go into the bloody Cathedral as well?"

"No bet," said Hawk. "Though if truth be told, right now I feel strong enough to dismantle an entire Cathedral with my bare hands, brick by brick, if I had to. Or kick the Walking Man's arse round to the front, if it came to it."

"Please don't even consider it," said Chance earnestly. "I hate to think how much damage the two of you could cause if you really got into it."

Sir Vivian had been looking closely at the Lady of the

Lake, and he took a sudden step forward. "I know you. I know who you are."

"Of course you do," said the Lady. "But you mustn't tell."

She smiled at him and he sank on one knee before her. She put a hand on his shoulder, as if in blessing, and water ran down his arm. He didn't notice. He looked up at her with earnest, almost tearful eyes, and something passed between him and the Lady that the others saw but couldn't comprehend. The Lady raised Sir Vivian up from his knee, and the two of them left the room together. Chance looked at Hawk and Fisher.

"Do you know what that was all about?"

"Haven't a clue," said Hawk. "But then, I feel that way about a lot of things these days."

"Oh, good," said Chance. "I'd hate to think it was just me. I used to understand what was going on in the Castle. Hell, keeping on top of things was part of my job. But just lately, I might as well be walking around with a bag over my head, and a sign on my back saying 'Kick me, I'm stupid.' " He shook his head slowly. "Look, we need to talk about the Walking Man. *Please* don't do anything to upset him. He is immensely powerful, utterly devoted to his cause, and has about as much sense of humor as a dead frog. If you irritate him, he'll probably kill you—and anyone else who happens to be around at the time. He says God talks to him, and tells him to kill people. In my experience, the best thing to do with people like that is just nod and smile and go along with it, in the hope he'll move on somewhere else."

"We used to know this guy in Haven who used to hear God talking to him," said Fisher. "Apparently God told him to recite bad poetry in public and expose himself to nuns."

"Until he tried it on the Street of Gods," said Hawk. "And the Little Sisters of the Immaculate Razor turned him into a jigsaw, right there on the street."

"We know about the Walking Man," said Fisher. "He's a legend, even down in the Southern Kingdoms. But we're legends, too. We can look after ourselves."

"The problem is, unlike most legends, the Walking Man is even more dangerous than most people think he is," said Chance. "He's killed a hell of a lot of people in his time. Not always for reasons the rest of us could understand. I was there at the end of one of his cases. The Dead Hand Abominations and the Wolves of September. Lament had been gone for over an hour, and they were still carrying bodies out of the town."

"And he wants to talk to us," Hawk said slowly. "Just as a matter of interest, does anyone know who he's come here to kill?"

"No," said Chance. "But he's already beaten a magic-user to death with his bare hands, and that was just something he did along the way."

"He could be after us," said Fisher. "We've killed a hell of a lot of people, too, in our time. Always for what we thought were good reasons, but I suppose that's what everyone says."

"We'd better go see him," said Hawk. "Try not to worry about us, Chance. If Lament gives us any trouble, Isobel and I will send the Walking Man to talk to God in person to explain what went wrong."

Chance shook his head slowly. "I wish I thought you were joking."

Sir Morrison, Lady Esther, and Franz Pendleton, those notable would-be traitors, waited impatiently outside Duke Alric's private quarters while the Duke decided whether he wanted to see them or not. Half a dozen armed guards watched them closely with unsympathetic faces. Morrison and Esther sat calmly on their chairs while Pendleton paced nervously up and down before them.

"This is taking too long," Pendleton said finally. "Something must have gone wrong. He knows why we're here. He should have made up his mind by now. What's taking him so long?"

"He's just making us wait to demonstrate how important he is," said Morrison. "The more important the person, the longer the wait. We'll be lucky if the Duke sees us at all today. Now sit down and stop making an exhibition of yourself. Look at the nice portraits."

"Stuff the portraits!"

"Shut up and sit down," said Lady Esther firmly. "If the Duke gets the impression we're weak and uncertain, he'll walk all over us. It's vital we persuade him that we represent powerful interests he can't afford not to deal with. You embarrass us in there, Pendleton, and I'll kill you myself. Now *sit down.*"

Pendleton sat down on the very edge of a chair, wringing his hands together. "This is bad. Coming here in person. We've always dealt through intermediaries before."

"And that's why we haven't gotten anywhere," said Sir Morrison calmly. "Our message gets diluted. Our intensity goes unrecognized. Sir Robert was our last hope, and he proved dangerously soft. Didn't have the balls for the kind of direct action needed to grasp power. So we will proceed without him and his expensive advice. If we can persuade the Duke to our cause, we'll be halfway home."

"That's a hell of a big if," muttered Pendleton.

Then the doors swung open and the guards gestured silently for the conspirators to go in. They got up and walked into the Duke's private chambers, doing their various best to look calm and collected and people of power and destiny. The Duke was sitting in a chair in the middle of the room, held upright by his straps and braces and supports. He didn't even bother to look at his visitors until they were standing right in front of him, and then his gaze was cold and almost openly contemptuous. Morrison and Pendleton bowed low to him, and Esther curtsied. The Duke barely nodded.

"You wanted to talk to me," he said flatly. "So talk. And keep to the point, or I'll have my guards beat it out of you."

Pendleton flinched. The guards had already demanded they give up all their weapons before they were even allowed to wait outside the Duke's quarters. Morrison smiled politely and addressed the Duke in tones of perfect reasonableness.

"We are here to present a simple proposition to you,

Your Highness. My associates and I represent the Landsgraves of Gold, Silver, and Copper, and other assorted business interests in the Land. We are not as mighty as we once were, but we could be again, with your help. We have extensive information-gathering operatives spread throughout the Land, which could be put at your disposal. We're talking about the kind of information—people, places, and troop positions—that would be invaluable to you if you found it necessary to invade the Forest Kingdom for its own good. We have no faith in the current regime, who have always failed to recognize our true worth. In short, we offer you vital intelligence in return for your support after you come to power. Our interests are purely economic, not political. All we want is for things to be as they were, when the Landsgraves were a force to be recognized and valued. Not much to ask for a trouble-free invasion by your armies."

"We can even provide armed men to fight beside yours," said Lady Esther. "Mercenaries, but good fighters. And we also command assassins within the Castle. We could kill anyone for you. Anyone at all."

"Good plan," said the Duke. "I admire ambition. And ruthlessness. But I don't need you. Guards, kill them."

The three conspirators gaped at him, shocked, and then looked quickly about them as the Duke's guards moved smoothly forward to cut them off from the Duke and any escape route. Sir Morrison struggled to find his voice.

"You can't do this! We are people of influence and power!"

"You are traitors," said the Duke. "And no one will miss you."

"At least give us back our weapons," demanded Sir Morrison. "Let us fight and die like men!"

The Duke laughed breathily. "Do I look stupid?"

Sir Morrison snarled a curse and threw himself forward, trying to plow through the guards to reach the Duke. The guards cut him down before he was even close. Pendleton broke and ran, and the guards killed him easily. Lady Esther watched her allies die, then pulled a nasty-looking steel pin from her piled-up hair. She held the long pin like a knife, and the guards nearest her hesitated. Lady Esther shot the Duke one last look of defiance, then turned the pin on herself and thrust it through her heart, robbing him of the kill. The Duke watched her body crumple lifelessly to the floor.

"Dead is dead," he said finally, unmoved. "And I never did have any time for traitors. Guards, take away the bodies and dispose of them where they won't be found. And clean up the mess. These people were never here."

Chance took Hawk and Fisher to meet Jericho Lament in the Queen's private chamber adjoining the Court. No one would disturb them there. No one would dare. Along the way Chance persevered with his efforts to try and impress on Hawk and Fisher how they should act around Lament. As God's chosen warrior, Lament had no doubts or uncertainties. That made him extremely dangerous and very narrowly focused. You couldn't argue or reason with him, and if you tried to get in his way, he'd just kill you.

"Sounds like our kind of people," said Hawk, and Fisher nodded solemnly. Chance wondered if he had time to stop off and update his will.

When Chance finally ushered them into the small chamber, Hawk and Fisher were immediately impressed by Lament's sheer presence. Just standing there, he looked large and holy and altogether menacing, like one of God's nastier angels slumming it in the mortal realms. Hawk wondered for a moment if this was how other people felt when they met him and Fisher. Or Prince Rupert and Princess Julia. Hawk felt like he should kneel and ask for a blessing, or at least absolution, but he didn't. Partly because he answered to no other conscience than his own, but mostly because if he was going to have to work with this man, it was important he should see Hawk and Fisher as at least potential equals. So he bowed politely to Lament, and glared at Fisher until she did, too. Lament bowed politely in return, and gestured at the chairs set out. Everyone sat down and pretended they were comfortable.

Hawk looked at Lament and wondered what it must be like to always be sure you were doing the right thing. To never have doubts or hesitations, before or after. Hawk had always had doubts, even back when he was Prince Rupert. Perhaps especially then. He looked at Lament looking at him, and wondered whether such certainty made the Walking Man more or less than human.

"The Blue Moon isn't finished with the Forest Kingdom yet," Lament said abruptly. "There is a voice within me, the voice of God, and it tells me things. Things you now need to know. I have read certain books from church libraries, old books forgotten or forbidden to those with less authority than I, and what I learned from them has not comforted me. When the Magus opened the Rift, joining the north to the south, he upset the balance of Wild Magic in the world. The Rift is maintained by a *continuing* spell using appalling amounts of Wild Magic to keep the Rift open. It is this growth in magic that has led to the return of the Inverted Cathedral and made it possible for the Blue Moon to manifest itself again.

"Have you never considered the nature of the Blue Moon? What kind of sun the Blue Moon must orbit that it reflects such a terrible light? What kind of world it must orbit that needs such a light? Scholars have been considering these questions for centuries, and nowhere have I found an answer that satisfies me. All I have is a name, perhaps the name of the Blue Moon's world: Reverie."

He stopped for a moment to be sure they were taking in what he'd said, and then he continued in the same grim voice. "There is only one way the Blue Moon can be prevented from manifesting in our sky again, and that is why God has brought me here. I shall enter the Inverted Cathedral, cleanse it of evil, and make it holy again, reclaiming it for God. I will bring the Cathedral back into the world of men, and it shall spread its sanctity across the Land, as was originally intended, canceling out the influence of the Wild Magic forever."

"Hold everything," said Hawk, leaning forward. Lament raised an eyebrow at being interrupted, but Hawk pressed on. "Are you talking about reinverting the Cathedral? Make it rise up instead of down?"

"Essentially, yes."

"Can I just point out that this Cathedral is right in the middle of the Castle? If it suddenly goes shooting up instead of down, what is that going to do to the surrounding structures? There are whole floors above it!"

"I don't know what will happen," said Lament. "It isn't important. God's will must be done."

"People could die!"

"People die all the time," said the Walking Man. "How many will die if the Blue Moon returns and the long night establishes itself in the world again? I have no wish to see the innocent harmed, but I will do what I must to prevent the triumph of the dark."

"All right," said Hawk, just a little heavily. "Let's try this from a slightly different angle. What exactly is it that you're going to do inside the Inverted Cathedral that will cleanse and reclaim it?"

"I don't know yet," said Lament. "All I have been told is to enter the Cathedral and then proceed as my voice and my experience suggest."

"You're not much of a one for forward planning, are you?" asked Fisher.

"With God guiding my steps, how can I go wrong?" countered Lament.

"We used to work the Street of Gods in Haven," said Fisher. "We met a lot of people who claimed to be doing the work of one god or another. Some of them were nasty bastards, and we had to shut them down. And sometimes we killed them to stop them doing what their gods told them to. You say you hear a voice, Lament. That's fine, but Hawk and I don't, so we just have to do as our consciences dictate. You've got an impressive reputation, Walking Man, but so have we. And we will stop you if it looks like you're threatening the Castle's safety, or the Land's. So I think Hawk and I will join you on your little excursion into the Inverted Cathedral. Just to keep an eye on things."

"I knew you would," Lament said easily. "The voice told me so."

Hawk decided to change the subject slightly, before Fisher's blood pressure hit a dangerous level. "The Seneschal said he looked at the Inverted Cathedral with his augmented Sight, and saw a vision of Hell."

Lament shook his head firmly. "No. The Cathedral has become a dark and evil place, but it is not itself a province of the inferno. It does, perhaps, contain a gateway to Hell. And if it does, I will close or banish it. I have always done what I must, for the greater good."

"I used to think that way once," said Hawk. "I'm not as sure as I used to be. So whatever you do inside the Inverted Cathedral, we're going to be right there with you. And Lament, if you do turn out to be just another crazy bastard, we will shut you down."

"Right," said Fisher. "Suddenly and violently and all over the place."

"I knew putting the three of you together in one room was a mistake," said Chance. "I am now officially changing the subject, and I don't want to hear any arguments. Tell me, Sir Lament, there are all kinds of rumors that the Inverted Cathedral contains hidden treasures and forgotten wonders. What do you think is in there?"

"The Grail, perhaps," said Lament, quite seriously. "Fragments of the True Cross. The mummified heads of saints, still alive and speaking strange truths. The whip that scourged Jesus' back, with the holy blood still dried on it. Even some of the furniture He made for His earthly father. To touch something the Christ touched with His own hands . . ." Lament smiled suddenly. "I haven't found two books that can agree on the subject. But one thing they all seem sure of, the Inverted Cathedral contains a true wonder, a thing of great power. Perhaps the source of the Cathedral's magic, or the key to its re-creation. Or its destruction. I am the Wrath of God, and if I cannot save the Cathedral, I will unmake it."

"All right, that does it," Chance said firmly. "I am going into the Inverted Cathedral with you people. Somebody has to be the quiet voice of reason, and I don't see any other volunteers."

"You can't go," said Hawk, just as firmly. "I need you here to protect the Castle in our absence. There's always the chance something nasty might break loose from the

Cathedral while we're inside. Remember the killing shadows in the Court? And if we don't come back, and nothing's changed in the Cathedral, someone will have to be here to lead in the next team."

Chance gestured for Hawk to join him. The two men got up and moved to the other side of the room, where they could speak quietly and privately. Chance put his head close to Hawk's. "If the powers that be knew who you really were, you wouldn't have to go in alone. You'd have a whole army at your back, ready to follow you into hell itself."

"Maybe," said Hawk. "But I have a strong feeling an army would just get in the way. A small force might go unrecognized for quite a time, and we can use all the advantages we can get. Besides, I don't think this is a struggle that can be won by force of arms. I'll go that far with Lament. I don't know what we'll find when we go all the way down. Which is all the more reason not to endanger anyone we don't absolutely have to. And if worst comes to worst, all three of us are expendable."

They broke off as Lament turned suddenly, and his hand snapped out to snatch something from the air. The tiny captive buzzed angrily inside his great fist, and then Lament's fingers were forced apart as Lightfoot Moonfleet expanded rapidly to full human size. She glared at Lament, then flapped her translucent wings vigorously to make sure they hadn't been crumpled.

"Honestly," she said. "Some men are all hands."

"I have no use for spies," Lament said coldly.

"Then you won't go far in politics. Someone's always listening in Forest Castle," said the faerie tartly. "You should know that. How did you know I was here?"

"God sees all," said Lament. "Now leave. I will not tolerate the presence of your kind. Soulless tricksters, godless immortals. The faeries have never been a true friend of man. Go back to your master and tell him to wait until I come for him."

"The charm school just took your money and ran, didn't they?" asked Lightfoot Moonfleet. "See you around, people."

She shrank back down to insect size and flew out the door as it opened, just missing a startled Seneschal's head. He blinked a few times, ran a hand through what was left of his hair to make sure nothing was caught in it, then he entered the room and shut the door behind him. He nodded to Hawk and Fisher, and hefted a long cloth-wrapped bundle in his hands.

"I've decided I'm going in there with you. It is undoubtedly a bad idea, and it will all inevitably end in tears, but you wouldn't get ten feet without my gifts to guide you. Let me make it very clear that I am only here because of emotional blackmail, and that this time I expect to get my fair share of whatever treasures we might find along the way. I didn't care so much about such things when I rediscovered the missing South Wing, but I have a wife and children to support now. I wouldn't mind if I got a pension. I did ask, but apparently no Seneschal has ever lived long enough to claim one before, which tells you something if you're paying attention."

"You must be the Seneschal," said Lament dryly. "You're just as I imagined you. I understood you were crippled with gout."

"Oh, I am," agreed the Seneschal. "But I had a healer slap a temporary spell on it so I can't feel it. Can't risk anything stronger, or the magic would interfere with my directional gifts." He glared at Fisher. "No doubt I will pay for this later with suffering beyond your ability to imagine, but I couldn't let you go into that awful place without me. If only because if this mission fails, the whole Castle could be endangered. So here I am. Ready and willing and not at all resentful." He looked at Hawk. "I brought something for you. Thought it might come in handy if we run into trouble."

He gave his cloth bundle over to Hawk, who looked at it uncertainly for a moment. The bundle seemed unusually heavy, but it was a familiar weight. He unwrapped the cloth with increasingly hurried fingers, and his heart beat faster as he looked at the long sword in its battered scabbard.

"The Rainbow sword," said Chance, his voice soft and reverential.

"I thought someone on this mission should have it," said the Seneschal. "Since everyone's been talking about the Blue Moon coming back. And Captain Hawk seemed the most suitable person to wield it."

"Of course," said Chance, tearing his gaze away from the sword. "Of course it should be you, Captain."

"I am God's representative," said Lament. "If anyone should have that sword—"

"I wouldn't even give it to you as a suppository," snapped the Seneschal. "I don't trust your motives, Lament. Never have. I want that sword in the hands of someone I can trust."

"Thank you, Sir Seneschal," said Hawk. "I hope we won't need it, but having it makes me feel a whole lot better."

He strapped the sword on his hip, opposite his axe. The weight was immediately comforting, and somehow right. As though the Rainbow sword belonged there and always had. Then Chance produced the Hand of Glory he'd used to open the Rift outside Haven, and Lament nearly hit the roof.

"What the hell is that infamous thing doing here!"

"The Magus created it a while back," said Chance. "I thought the Seneschal could use it to find or force a way into the Inverted Cathedral."

"Good thinking, Questor," said the Seneschal, taking the mummified Hand and inspecting it closely. "I'm glad someone here is thinking ahead."

"That is an evil thing," snapped Lament. "A product of unholy magics and an offense of God!"

"Stuff and nonsense," said the Seneschal. "It's just a magical tool, no different than any other. Unpleasant to manufacture, I'll admit, but then so is jugged hare."

"It is made from the hand of a dead man!"

"You should see what they do with the rest of the body." The Seneschal stopped a moment to consider. "Actually, no, you shouldn't. It would put you off tripe and onions for life. Now stop arguing and let's get a bloody move on. You can lead the way, Sir Lament, since you're so eager."

He looked thoughtfully at Lament. "What do you think we're going to find inside the Cathedral?"

"A journey down through the circles of the damned," said Lament.

"Right, that's it—I'm not talking to you anymore," said the Seneschal.

"I'd better get back to the Court," Chance said tactfully. "I hope by now they'll have recovered from Sir Lament's little visit earlier. Last I heard, they were still fishing politicians out of the moat. Good luck to you all."

He smiled and left. Everyone looked expectantly at Lament, who shook his head slowly. "Perhaps I should do this alone."

"Not a hope," said Hawk.

"Not in my Castle," said the Seneschal.

"Let's go," said Fisher.

They left the room and made their way down the corridor. Fisher found herself beside Lament, and groped for some kind of small talk. "I notice there's a lot more Christian worship going on these days. I suppose the long night put the wind up everybody."

"Children kneel in Jesus till they learn the cost of nails," said Lament.

"I'm not talking to you anymore," said Fisher.

In a deserted corridor some distance away, Lightfoot Moonfleet was flying back to the Magus as fast as her wings could carry her. He had to be told what was happening. He hadn't foreseen the arrival of the Walking Man, or that he would choose to descend into the Inverted Cathedral. Which could mean all the Magus' careful planning had been for nothing. She strained for more speed and hoped she'd reach the Magus in time.

CHAPTER SEVEN

Going Down, Down

•

They could feel the pressure of the Inverted Cathedral long before they could see anything. Approaching the warded-off site was like heading toward a dentist with blood dripping from his hands, or a surgeon holding a bone saw caked with dried-on gore. A mixed feeling of alarm and horror, and the foreknowledge of unavoidable pain. The last few corridors were deserted, silent, and filled with uneasy shadows. There were no human guards. Nothing human could bear the proximity of the Inverted Cathedral for long and still stay sane. The small group heading determinedly into the shadows were four very special people, all with some claim to be just a little more than human. But even they could feel something terrible waiting ahead of them, pulsing with considered menace and awful intent.

When the four of them finally reached the chamber that held the entrance to the Inverted Cathedral, it came as something of a disappointment. It was only a medium-sized room, maybe twenty feet across, with a six-foot-square trap-door set right in the middle of the floor. Nothing else. No furniture, no paintings or hangings, and certainly no sign of life, human or otherwise. Only a vague feeling of pressure on the air, like pushing against some unseen barrier, prevented them from walking straight into the chamber. The four of them stood together in the open doorway, the only entry into the silent room, and looked carefully around the bare and empty chamber.

"You are sure this is the right place?" Hawk finally asked the Seneschal.

"Of course I'm sure!" snapped the Seneschal without turning around. "My sense of direction is never wrong. And besides, according to my extensive knowledge of Forest Castle's layout, this whole room shouldn't be here. This is supposed to be one long, uninterrupted corridor. And up until twelve years ago, it was. It's an interesting thought: Does this room really exist, does it have an actual history, or has it just manifested here to provide an entrance to the Inverted Cathedral? Was the room built long ago by human strength and skill and sweat, or is it just a magical construct?"

"What's the difference?" asked Fisher.

The Seneschal gave her a pitying look. "If this chamber was actually built by human means, it won't necessarily disappear once the Inverted Cathedral's magic shuts off. After all, no one knows what might happen once we start messing about inside the Cathedral."

"Thanks a whole bunch," said Fisher. "Now I have a new threat to worry about."

"Just doing my job," said the Seneschal.

"What's this pressure I can feel?" asked Hawk, quickly changing the subject.

"The Magus' protective wards," said Lament. "He's set up an avoidance spell. Quite a powerful one. Only the strong-willed and those with certain purpose could even look into this room. If we try to enter, the pressure against us will grow stronger. The harder we try to get in, the harder the wards will push us out. How's your willpower these days, Captain Hawk?"

"Oh, he's stubborn as hell," said Fisher. "And I've been known to be pretty bloody-minded myself."

"I'd never have guessed," murmured Lament. "All right, you two go in first. See how far you can get. The Seneschal and I will observe you from here and take notes."

"Just in case you don't come back," said the Seneschal helpfully.

Hawk and Fisher looked at each other, shrugged simultaneously, hefted their weapons, then stepped cautiously forward into the room. The sound of their boots on the bare wooden floor was almost painfully loud. Everything still looked the same, but the sense of pressure was immediately much worse. Hawk's instincts were yelling at him to turn and race out of the room, and his heart beat frantically in his chest as his breathing became harsh and hurried. He just knew something bad was going to happen. His hand tightened on the hilt of his axe until his knuckles went white. He glared quickly about him, but the room remained still and quiet and empty. Close beside him, Fisher advanced step by unwilling step. Her face was strained and pale, and her eyes were almost painfully wide. Hawk and Fisher looked at each other and shared a humorless smile before pressing on, leaning forward slightly like two runners breasting an invisible tape.

They were only half a dozen feet into the room, and already Hawk's legs were shaking violently, while his stomach muscles clenched in sympathy. The sense of threat was so real now, he could almost touch it. Sweat ran down his face and dripped from his chin. He couldn't even look around to see how Fisher was doing anymore. He had to concentrate all the willpower he had into taking the next step, and the next. His whole world had narrowed into the room ahead of him, and the trapdoor straight ahead. So he was very surprised when all the lights went out and darkness engulfed him.

The pressure was suddenly gone, and he stumbled forward a few steps before recovering himself. The darkness was absolute, no matter which way he turned his head. For a horrible moment he thought he was back in the Darkwood, alone and abandoned. Panic threatened to overwhelm him before he fought it ruthlessly down. He wasn't scared of the dark anymore. He wasn't. He called out to Fisher, and then to Lament and the Seneschal, but there was no reply. Hawk wondered if he was even in the same chamber anymore. Perhaps he and Fisher had triggered some hidden spell of the Magus', and they'd been transported somewhere else. He had a feeling of space around him, but no way of knowing how great that space was. His breathing speeded up again as he had to consider the possibility that he was indeed back in the rotten heart of the long night and the Darkwood, where it was always dark, dark enough to break anyone.

And then he knelt down and touched the ground beneath

him, and relief flooded through him as he felt bare wooden boards with his hand. He was still in the room. He straightened up, angry at how close he'd come to losing control, and moved cautiously forward, his empty hand stretched out before him. He had a box of matches on him, but lighting one would mean putting away his axe, if only for a moment, and he didn't feel like doing that just yet. Besides, who knew what light might attract in a darkness like this?

And then there was a light, some distance away, right in front of him. A silver glow formed, eerie and unnatural, and out of the growing light came a face from Hawk's past, when he had another name and another legend. Out of the silver light a dead man came walking, the late King John IV, once ruler of the Forest Kingdom, once Hawk's father, when he had been Prince Rupert. The King looked just as he had in the final few moments before the last great battle to defend Forest Castle from the imminent demon army. He wore full armor, the breastplate etched and traced with defensive runes, and in his hand he carried that great and awful sword *Rockbreaker,* one of the ancient and powerful Infernal Devices. When *Rockbreaker* spoke, the world trembled. The King's hair was gray, and his face was lined with age and pain and loss, but still he held himself well, standing tall and proud and utterly royal. Hawk had always found it sad that his father had only really learned to be a King at the very end of his life. He held his ground as his father approached and finally came to a halt before him. King John looked his son up and down, his gaze openly contemptuous.

"I know who you are," said the King.

"Of course you do," said Hawk. "I don't suppose much is hidden from the dead. What are you doing here, Father?"

"Your disgrace has raised me from my grave," said the King harshly. "You have disappointed me, Rupert. You failed me, you failed your brother, and you have failed in your duty to the Land. I brought you into this world, and so I have a responsibility to remove you from it."

He lunged forward, swinging *Rockbreaker* with both

hands, and at the last moment Hawk brought his axe up to block the blow. They circled each other slowly.

Fisher was lost in the darkness for a while, too, before pushing the fear and the panic the same way Hawk had. She also saw the silver light form, and a familiar face walking out of it toward her. She took up a fighting stance, her sword held out before her, and the late Prince Harald came to a halt a respectful distance away from her. He looked just as she remembered him; tall, well-muscled, classically handsome. He was clad in rune-scored armor and carried in his hand the Infernal Device known as *Flarebright*. When that terrible blade spoke, the world burned. Harald looked her over slowly, his face cold and emotionless.

"What are you doing here?" asked Fisher, almost angrily. "I went to your Tomb. I heard your message. I'll find your killer."

"You should not be here," said Harald, his voice little more than a whisper. "Your curiosity and trespass have brought you to a place where the dead walk. Here old slights can be avenged, and old hurts eased. If you'd stayed at the Castle, Julia—if you'd loved and stayed with me, I'd still be alive. I should never have trusted you."

He attacked her then, the long deadly blade of the Infernal Device sweeping in a wide arc. Fisher met it with her own sword, and sparks flared in the darkness as Fisher held her ground. The two swords swung and clashed as Fisher and Harald circled each other, launching attacks that held no mercy on either side. And all the time Fisher was thinking, This can't be Harald. He wouldn't do this. And more importantly, Harald never trusted me. He never trusted anyone in his life. And since the Infernal Device should have shattered my ordinary sword by now, this isn't Harald.

She stepped back, not lowering her guard, but unwilling to continue the fight until she was sure just who and what she was fighting.

Hawk was also beginning to wonder just who and what he was fighting, when the King suddenly disengaged and backed away from him. Hawk didn't go after him. This

couldn't be the King. He and his father had made their
peace with each other long ago. Someone was trying to pull
his strings, and he'd never believed in playing someone
else's game. And there'd been something damnably familiar
about the skills of the person he'd been fighting. The answer was on the tip of his tongue when a hand grabbed his
elbow firmly from behind and pulled him out of the dark
and back into the light.

Hawk and Fisher stood together, blinking dazedly in the
sudden light of the chamber. Lament held them both by
the elbows until he was sure they knew where they were,
then he let them go and stepped back to study them
thoughtfully. The Seneschal was still in the doorway, looking confused. Hawk rubbed at his eye, and realized he was
right back by the chamber door again. He looked at Fisher
and then at Lament.

"We were fighting each other, weren't we?"

"Yes," said Lament. "You both reached a certain point,
stopped dead, muttered a few words, and then attacked
each other. It was quite a sight. You're both excellent
fighters. And then you both suddenly stopped, so I seized
the moment and hauled you back here."

"You didn't see the darkness?" Fisher asked.

"There was no dark," said the Seneschal. "What happened?"

"The avoidance spell," said Hawk. "It made us see
things. People from our past. Tricked us into attacking
each other."

"Damn," said Fisher. "I hate being suckered that easily."

"I have to wonder what other levels there are to the
warding spell," said Lament. "Perhaps I should go in alone
after all."

"Hell with that," said the Seneschal. "No one tells me
where I can and can't go in my own Castle!"

And he strode forward into the chamber before anyone
could stop him.

He felt the building pressure, too, but brushed it briskly
aside. The Seneschal was used to being in places where he
wasn't supposed to be. In fact, he took pride in it. He

strode on, his head thrust bullishly forward, his hands clenched into fists. He fiercely resented the very existence of the Inverted Cathedral in his nice familiar Castle, and he was in the mood to take out his anger on someone—or something. Darkness blossomed suddenly around him, and he stopped. Out of the silver light came his grandfather, the legendary High Warlock. A short, slender man in black sorcerer's garb, with frighteningly intense eyes.

"I'm very disappointed in you," said the High Warlock.

"Oh, piss off," said the Seneschal. "You're not my grandfather. He never gave a damn about me. He died still owing me seven birthday presents. Now get the hell out of my way."

He strode forward, walking right through the image of the High Warlock, and both the image and the darkness disappeared. The chamber reappeared around the Seneschal, who smiled triumphantly. The trapdoor was only a few feet ahead of him. The relentless pressure was as strong as a gale wind now, and the Seneschal had to lean well forward as he pressed on, but he was damned if he'd be stopped now, so close to his goal. And that was when his heart stopped beating, his lungs stopped breathing, and he fell to the floor, dead as any doornail.

Once again Lament had to go into the chamber and pull out the lifeless body of the Seneschal. Lament laid him out on his back by the doorway, and Fisher knelt beside him to do mouth to mouth while Hawk did vigorous compressions on his chest. You picked up a lot of emergency medical procedures, working in the Haven Guard. The Seneschal jerked suddenly as he started breathing again, and Hawk and Fisher backed away from him. The Seneschal sat up slowly, and coughed and spluttered for a while, clutching at his bruised chest with one hand. It was a while before he was able to explain what had happened, and the Walking Man nodded thoughtfully.

"The next level of the avoidance spell," he said finally. "Presumably only the illusion of a heart attack rather than the real thing, which is why you were able to recover so quickly once I dragged you back here."

"It was a bloody convincing illusion," said the Seneschal, scrambling awkwardly to his feet while waving aside offers of assistance. "I am going to have strong words with the Magus about this. So what do we do now? That layer of the spell will stop anyone who gets too close to the trapdoor."

"Not necessarily," said Hawk, giving Lament a hard look. "I can't help noticing that you walked in and out of this room twice without even hesitating. Didn't you feel anything?"

"No," said Lament. "As the Walking Man, I walk in straight lines to go where I must and do what I must, and because this is God's will made manifest, nothing can stand in my way or delay my journey. Including, it would appear, the avoidance spell of a certain Magus. I see no reason why I shouldn't be able to walk right up to that trapdoor, unaffected by anything the wards can throw at me."

"You knew that all along," Fisher said accusingly. "So why did you let us go in first and trigger the defenses?"

"Because I wanted to see what they would do," said Lament calmly. "I wanted to know what the Magus was capable of."

"Don't hit him, Isobel," Hawk said quickly. "We need him."

Fisher growled something under her breath and glared at Lament. He smiled back, entirely undisturbed.

"It seems to me," he said mildly, "that if we were all to walk into the room together, with all of you sticking very close to me, your proximity to my holy nature should be enough to protect you from the wards."

"And if it doesn't?" asked the Seneschal, just a little testily, still rubbing at his chest.

"Then I'll drag you back out, and you get to say I told you so," said Lament. "And I will continue this quest alone." He paused to look at the others in turn. "I would prefer company."

"Yeah," said Fisher. "Just like the miner who takes a canary in a cage in with him to check for bad air."

"Exactly," said Lament. "I couldn't have put it better myself."

"Isobel . . ." Hawk warned.

*   *   *

They walked into the room together, Hawk and Fisher and the Seneschal pressing as close to Lament as they could get without actually climbing into his pockets. This time there was only the briefest feeling of an opposing pressure, which burst like a soap bubble against the Walking Man's certainty. They crossed the empty chamber unopposed, and finally knelt beside the trapdoor in the floor, studying it carefully from different angles and what they hoped was a safe distance. Somewhere far away, something screamed once with rage.

"What the hell was that?" asked Fisher, glaring about her.

"The Magus, perhaps," said Lament, not looking at her, all his attention focused on the trapdoor. "Having his wards broken so abruptly was probably rather unpleasant for him. Or possibly the scream could have come from somewhere inside the Inverted Cathedral. Which means that whatever's in there knows we're coming, and that we won't be easily stopped."

"I wish I had your confidence," said Hawk. "It must be wonderful to always be so sure of things."

"Oh, it is," agreed Lament. "You have no idea. Faith means never having to say you're uncertain."

He leaned out over the trapdoor, studying it closely, but still careful not to touch it. Hawk watched him do it, momentarily distracted by a new thought. Harald's killer had walked right through the Magus' strongest wards to reach him. But Lament hadn't been in the Castle then. As far as anybody knew. Hawk frowned. The Lady of the Lake had said he already knew who killed Harald but didn't want to admit it. Hawk smiled sourly. If so, it was news to him. Anyway, that would all have to wait until they'd finished their business inside the Inverted Cathedral and returned. Assuming any of them did return. He made himself concentrate on the trapdoor, six square feet of unpolished wood held shut by a simple steel bolt. It looked straightforward enough. If anything, too straightforward. In fact, everything about it set off Hawk's worst instincts.

"I have a really bad feeling about that trapdoor," said Fisher, close beside him.

"You are not alone," said the Seneschal. "There's magic in that trapdoor, I can sense it. Strong magic, soaked into the wood itself. Entirely separate from the avoidance spell."

"A booby trap," said Lament, nodding. "Presumably set to be activated by whoever is foolish enough to open the trapdoor. Let's see what happens when I push back the bolt from a safe distance."

He stood up and stepped well back, and everyone hurried to get behind him. Lament slowly pushed back the bolt with the steel tip of his long staff. Nothing happened until the bolt was all the way back, then there was a loud bang, a flash of something moving too quickly to be seen, and then another loud bang as the trapdoor, ripped free from its hinges, slammed against the ceiling overhead with vicious force. The ceiling's plaster cracked jaggedly from the impact, and flakes fell slowly to the floor. The trapdoor stayed where it was. The four members of the investigating party craned their necks to get a good look at it.

"If any of us had been leaning over the trapdoor when we opened it," Hawk said slowly, "part or all of us would have ended up as the meat in a very nasty sandwich."

"Ouch," said Fisher. "The Magus really did want to stop people getting in." She looked at the Seneschal. "Can you sense any more booby traps?"

"No," said the Seneschal, frowning as he peered dubiously at the newly revealed gap in the floor. "But this opening is positively crawling with magic. There's so much power radiating from it, I can feel it in my bones. And I mean old magic, far beyond anything I'd expect the Magus to be capable of. I'd say we've found our entrance to the Inverted Cathedral. And it gives me the creeps something fierce."

They all crowded around the open space, working up the nerve to peer in while trying very hard not to think about the trapdoor overhead, still stuck to the ceiling. When they did finally look, all they could see was six square feet of drifting clouds. And not nice, fluffy, white cotton clouds, either; these clouds were dark and threatening, boiling and churning like a fast-building thunderstorm. There was a low rumbling deep within the clouds, like something growling. Lament dipped the steel end of his staff into the clouds, and nothing happened. He slowly thrust the staff further and further in, until he was kneeling beside the square, with his arm fully extended and his hand nearly touching the clouds. He stirred the staff around for a while, to no obvious effect, and then stood up again, withdrawing his staff. It seemed unaffected, though beaded here and there with drops of water.

"Well," he said easily, "the next step requires a volunteer."

"Why do I just know it's going to be me?" asked Hawk.

"Because we need Lament for his power, the Seneschal for his magic, and I've got more sense," said Fisher. "Guess who that leaves?"

"If anyone thinks I am just going to jump blindly into those clouds . . ."

"No, of course we don't think that," said Lament. "Far too many things could go wrong, and if you just disappeared, we'd have no way of knowing what. Since the Cathedral is Inverted, it could drop away into the earth for several hundred feet. Or more. I have a coil of rope with me. We'll tie one end round your ankles, and then lower you headfirst into the clouds. All you have to do is yell back once you've ascertained what's beyond them."

Hawk shook his head slowly. "I never did like heights."

"Think of them as depths," suggested Fisher.

"You're not helping, Isobel."

"You'll be perfectly safe with all of us on the other end of the rope," said Lament with the easy assurance of someone who wasn't going. "If you see anything at all worrying, just yell out and we'll pull you back up."

"If it's so safe, why aren't you doing it?" snapped Hawk.

"Because you're the hero. Sit down, and I'll tie your ankles together."

Hawk growled something that everyone pretended not to understand, then sat reluctantly down beside the open space. Lament's knots turned out to be excruciatingly tight but comfortingly professional. Hawk waited until he was sure everyone had a good grip on the rope, then swung his feet out over the drop. He knew there was an awful lot of nothing beneath his feet. He just knew it. Back in Haven there'd been a group of extreme sportsmen who climbed to the top of tall buildings, tied themselves to something secure, and then jumped off, just for the thrill of it. Hawk had always considered them to be complete and utter lunatics.

He took a deep breath and pushed himself off the edge and into the clouds. His head and feet quickly changed ends, and soon he was diving through the clouds, his hands held uselessly out before him. The violent air buffeted him back and forth as he fell through the clouds, which were bracingly cold and wet, and billowed all around him until he had no sense of direction apart from the falling feeling in the pit of his stomach. And then suddenly he was through and out the other side. Bright light hit him like a thunderclap. He cried out in shock as he found himself plummeting headfirst into a huge structure that seemed to fall away forever. He had brief glimpses of huge marble walls plunging by on either side of him, marked here and there with splashes of color, all details blurred by the speed at which he was falling. Vertigo sucked the breath out of his lungs as he fell on and on into something too large for him to comprehend.

And then he was jerked to an abrupt halt as the rope at his ankles snapped taut. His neck creaked painfully. His eye bulged from its socket. He flailed about with his arms, but there was nothing in reach. He turned slowly back and forth, fighting for breath. There were details all around him, but he couldn't make sense of any of them upside down. He could see colors, mostly red, and the air was foul beyond description. And the walls, the great walls, gleaming white marble falling away forever, like a glimpse of heaven. He tried to shout up to his companions, but it was all he could do just to get his breath. He couldn't think straight with the blood pounding in his upside down head. There was something about the walls . . . There was a yank on the rope, sending him spinning back and forth again, and then he was pulled back up, foot by foot. The whole length of the rope couldn't have been more than forty feet, but the trip up seemed endless.

They pulled him back up through the clouds, and hauled him out of the floor of the chamber. Hawk scrambled away from the open space, and Fisher held him while he waited for his head to stop spinning and his stomach to settle. Everyone was very patient, which was just as well, as Hawk was in no mood for nonsense. He'd never liked heights. Finally he pulled vaguely at his clothes, tugging them back into place again, and glared at Lament.

"Well, there's definitely a building down there. And a bloody big one, too. Marble walls. Some kind of decorations. Place stinks, though. Probably because it's been deserted for so long."

"No sign of any occupants?" asked Lament.

"Look, I was upside down and fighting not to puke," said Hawk. "There could have been an orgy going on down there and I wouldn't have noticed. Still, if there was anyone there, I think they would have made some sort of comment at me bursting up out of their floor and hurtling toward their ceiling, and I didn't hear a damn thing. I'm assuming there was a ceiling somewhere, but I never even got close to it. This Cathedral has got to be one hell of a size. Big as a mountain. Bigger."

"Perhaps it's been growing, deep in the earth," said Lament. He didn't sound like he was joking.

"So, what do we do now?" asked Fisher. "Lower everyone through on a rope? Then who gets to stay behind?"

"I don't think that will be necessary," said the Seneschal, scowling thoughtfully. "If you remember, I encountered something like this before, on my journey to rediscover the lost South Wing of Forest Castle. I found a doorway leading into a Tower that was upside down to its surrounding structure. When I passed through, I became upside down, too—or rather, the right way up as far as the Tower was concerned. The magic here feels very similar to what I encountered then."

"Then why didn't I turn right way up?" Hawk asked.

"Because you were still physically connected to this room by the rope."

"Hold everything," said Fisher, just a little ominously. "Are you seriously suggesting we all just jump into the clouds feet first, and trust that everything will turn out all right?"

"Well, basically, yes," admitted the Seneschal.

"You first," said Fisher. "And we'll all listen for a scream."

"I'll go first," said Lament. "You just have to have faith."

And as easily as that he stepped off the edge of the square, and dropped into the roiling clouds. Everyone listened intently, but there was no scream. A few moments later, Lament's voice came back to them from surprisingly close at hand.

"Come on in. The Cathedral's very interesting."

The Seneschal jumped in immediately, and disappeared into the clouds. Fisher took Hawk's hand in a firm grip, and they jumped in together.

They burst through the cloud cover, somersaulted disconcertingly fast in midair, and the next thing they knew they were standing on a bare marble floor at the foot of an immensely tall gallery. There was no trace in the floor of the gap they'd just jumped through. That worried Hawk and Fisher for a moment, but they were quickly distracted by the sheer scale of the Cathedral around them. They'd appeared in the central gallery, a huge open space bounded by sheer white marble walls that shot up for hundreds of feet before finally disappearing into a vague blue beyond the human eye's reach. The gallery would have seemed serene, even spiritual, if it hadn't been for the thick rivulets of dark red blood that ran endlessly down the marble walls. The blood collected in great pools on the gallery floor, creeping slowly around the rows of dark oaken pews.

The whole place stank like a slaughterhouse.

"Where the hell is all that blood coming from?" Fisher asked quietly.

"Just as much to the point," said Hawk, just as quietly, "who or what is it coming from?"

The whole floor was awash with blood, but never more than an inch or so deep, despite the never-ending crimson flow down the walls. Fisher stepped gingerly through it to inspect the nearest pew. The solid wood was clean, but the cushions and embroidered knee pads were soaked with blood. A single prayer book sat on a wooden seat, its leather cover dappled with dried blood. Fisher picked it up and opened it at random. The text was handwritten in a clear copperplate and consisted of the phrase *We all burn* repeated over and over again. Fisher flicked through the pages, but everywhere it was the same. *We all burn.*

"Blasphemy," said Lament, and Fisher jumped, startled. She hadn't heard him come up and look over her shoulder. He reached out for the prayer book, and Fisher was only too happy for him to take it. She rubbed her hands vigorously on her hips, as though they might be contaminated. Lament opened the book, and then made a quick, surprised sound. Fisher looked at the pages open before him. The handwritten text now said *Welcome, Jericho Lament. We've been waiting for you.* Over and over again.

"Interesting," said Lament, his voice calm and apparently unmoved.

"Is that all you've got to say?" asked Fisher. "A book that's been sealed away here for centuries, and it knows your name?"

"Whoever's responsible for this little parlor trick, they don't know everything. They don't know my true name. I only adopted Lament as my name when I became the Walking Man."

"But Jericho Lament is your true name now," said a distant, rasping voice. "The old you is dead. You killed him to become what you are. Lament is all you'll ever be now, Walking Man."

Everyone looked quickly about them, but there was no one else in the great gallery. Fisher and Lament moved away from the pew to join the others, leaving the prayer book behind them. Hawk already had his axe in his hand, and he and Fisher stood back to back, ready to take on any threat. The Seneschal was trying to look in every direction at once. Lament leaned on his long staff and frowned thoughtfully.

"It would appear we are not alone here," he said matter-of-factly.

"Get away," said the Seneschal. "You do surprise me. Of course we're not bloody alone! If the Cathedral was uninhabited, we wouldn't have had to come here! No, there are presences here. I can feel them. Can't you feel them?"

"A lot of people died here," said Lament. "A blood sacrifice, perhaps."

"Then why is the blood still running?" asked Hawk.

"Good question," said Lament.

He had nothing more to say. Everyone looked back and forth, tensed for an attack that never came. There were wonderful mosaics on every side, carvings and tapestries, all of them beautiful, all of then fouled and disfigured by the running blood. The single pulpit looked like something large had been butchered in it. There were many standing statues in various attitudes of grace. All of them were missing their heads. The air was close and very hot, and everyone was sweating now. There were no windows anywhere, no release from the overpowering coppery stench of freshly spilled blood. Hawk spat several times, but the taste stayed in his mouth. There was a horrid oppressiveness to the place, a pressure on the soul, like a weight too heavy for mortal frames to carry.

"It's like being back inside the Darkwood," said Fisher after a while. "It drags at your soul, weighs you down. Till you feel stained, inside and out."

"Yes," said Hawk. "I remember."

"I wasn't aware you'd passed through the Darkwood," said Lament.

"Yeah, well, you don't know everything," said Hawk. "It was a long time ago. The point is, we can't stay here too long. Not even you, Walking Man. If this place is some cousin to the Darkwood, it'll eat our souls. This isn't the kind of place humans were ever meant to be."

"Something's coming!" said the Seneschal. "Something . . ."

The dead materialized around them, fading into reality like dark shadows staining the air. Rows of men, women, and children, hanging on the air in great circles surrounding them. Dressed all in black, with white faces, their eyes and mouths little more than dark smudges. Blood dripped slowly from their hanging feet. They were utterly, inhumanly still, and waves of pain and loss and horror hit the four living souls from every direction at once. They cried out, even Lament, and then were silenced by the sheer scale of what they were feeling. Unbearable pain, terrible loss, horror beyond imagining. This was nothing like the quiet, ineffectual ghost Hawk and Fisher had found in Haven. These were the spirits of the murdered dead, ripped untimely from their lives, condemned to remain in the place of their death. In the place where all life and love and hope had been cruelly stolen from them. Trapped between this world and the next, in a never-ending moment of despair.

"Dear God," said Hawk shakily.

"Oh God, oh God," said the Seneschal. "How many of them are there?"

"Hundreds," said Lament. "And they've been here a long, long time."

"Poor bastards," said Fisher. "Poor bastards."

A ripple moved slowly through the dark crowd, and a silent voice beat in the heads of the living. *Free us. Free us.*

"Isn't there anything you can do?" demanded the Seneschal of the Walking Man. "You're supposed to be the Wrath of God, the avenger of wrongs. If anything ever deserved avenging, this is it. There are children here! Do something, damn you!"

"I can't give life to the dead," said Lament. "Only one man was ever able to do that, and I am not He. The best I can do is free them from this place and send them to their rest. Vengeance will have to wait till we find their murderer."

He reached for his holy power, and found it wasn't there. The power he'd called on so freely in the past, the embodiment of God's will in the world of men, was no longer his. He called out to the voice within him, and there was no answer.

"Well?" said Hawk. "What are you waiting for?"

"I am much less than I was," Lament said slowly. "I am the Wrath of God in the world of men, but I don't think that's where we are anymore. We're somewhere else."

"I always know where I am," said the Seneschal. "That's always been my gift, my power. But I don't anymore. I feel lost. I never felt lost before. Never. How do you people stand it?"

His voice moved rapidly through uncertainty to fear to hysteria, and only stopped when Fisher grabbed him by the arm and gave him a good shake. "Take it easy. You'll adjust. Concentrate on what's happening now. I've always found the presence of death concentrates the mind wonderfully."

"Something's happening with the ghosts," said Hawk. "They look agitated."

The dark figures were moving now, gliding sideways in a great circle around the living, circling faster and faster till the individual shapes were lost in a great blur of black and white. Their whispering voices rose again, trying desperately to communicate something important, but all that could be understood were three ominous words: *The Transient Beings.* Lament sucked in a sharp breath, startled, and the others all turned to look at him.

"That's a name I wasn't expecting to hear," he said. "The Transient Beings are immortal creatures of great power, the physical manifestations of abstract concepts or ideas. They exist outside of time and space until some fool summons them into the walking world. Never born, they cannot die. Ideas distilled into mortal form, they can never be destroyed, only banished. The Demon Prince was a Transient Being. He alone nearly destroyed the mortal world. If there's more than one of his kind in this place, we are all very definitely out of our depth."

And then the dead screamed shrilly, an awful sound that filled the great gallery and echoed back from its blood-stained marble walls. Their cry faded suddenly away, along with their ghostly forms, and in moments only the echoes of their horror remained to show they had ever been there. And yet there was still a presence in the gallery, so strong, they could all feel it, a sensation of being observed by malignant eyes. Hawk and Fisher were back to back again, their weapons held out before them. Lament glared angrily about him. The Seneschal cocked his head slightly to one side, listening.

"Something else is coming," he said finally. "Something bad."

And then there he was, right before them, a man wreathed in flames. Hawk and Fisher fell back a step, driven away by the blazing heat. The Seneschal stood behind Lament, who put his staff between him and the man on fire. The flames rose and fell, but did not consume him. His skin started out a painful red, and then it burned and blackened and split, glowing bloodred in the open cracks, before darkening further like a living cinder, only to crack and fall away, revealing fresh new skin underneath. Over and over again, in an endless agonizing cycle. The crackling flames rose and fell, and his body burned forever. Wreathed in flames, endlessly tormented.

"The Burning Man," said Jericho Lament softly.

"Welcome to my creation," said the Burning Man in a dry, rasping voice. Flames danced on his tongue, inside his mouth. "All this is mine. I designed it. And because of it I made all those people die, in pursuit of something greater. Because of me, and what I did, they are captive in this place forever. They come and go as I please. I let them manifest for a time, to talk with you, that you might know of my power."

"If you're so powerful," said Fisher, "why are you on fire?"

"Because I died and was damned," said the Burning Man. "And then I was summoned up out of Hell to be the guardian of this place. Still burning, for all eternity, inside and out, endlessly consumed and regenerated, wreathed in the flames of the pit, that my punishment should not end just because I am briefly out of Hell."

"How long have you been here?" asked Hawk, trying not to turn his head away from the choking stench of roasting flesh.

"Centuries," said the Burning Man. "Centuries of torment, and never a moment's ease. You'd think you'd get used to it eventually, but you never do. The pain is as horrible now as it was the first day I was dragged down into the inferno. I can't even cry. My tears turn to steam."

"You dare ask for our pity?" questioned Lament. "After admitting you murdered all those poor imprisoned souls? Explain yourself! Who are you? What happened here all those centuries ago?"

"What makes you think I'll reveal my secrets to you, Walking Man?"

"Because sinners love to boast of their sins. It is all they have in the way of accomplishment or comfort."

"You think you know so much," said the Burning Man. "You know nothing. Nothing at all. While I can tell you things that will blast your reason and damn your soul. I am Tomas Chadbourne, architect and creator of this Cathedral. Everything here was born in my mind. I supervised its construction, agonized over every detail, and drove my workforce to distraction because I would accept nothing less than perfection. And there was my first sin. Pride. Because I came to love my Cathedral more than the God it was meant to venerate. I thought myself a man of power and distinction, and I wanted more. Much more. And while studying certain ancient books in search of ways to make my creation even greater, I came across an old, old compact that would transform me and make me as a god. Following its instructions I walked into the Darkwood unafraid, and none of the demons there opposed me. They knew I was expected, invited. In the rotten heart of the Darkwood I found the Demon Prince, sitting on his rotten throne. He told me what I had to do to become as powerful as him, and I did it. But of course, he lied. They all lie, the Transient Beings. Our mayfly lives are nothing to them, save entertainment. They hate humanity for being real.

"The price of power was surprisingly simple. A mass sacrifice. My Cathedral was finally completed, and so I called its first congregation to attend. I promised them a special ceremony they would never forget. They all came, those who had worked so hard and so long to build this Cathedral, and brought their families. They sang hymns and praised the Lord I no longer believed in, and all the while I stood within a disguised pentacle and said the words I'd been taught. And in a moment every man, woman, and child turned upon each other in a terrible mad fury, and tore each other to pieces. Fathers and mothers murdered their children and then slaughtered each other. It was a most marvelous, if bloody, spectacle, and I laughed and laughed and laughed. They're still here, of course, the poor murderers and their victims, bound together by horror and loss and dreadful crimes unwillingly committed. Contained here for all eternity by the spell their deaths powered.

"The whole Cathedral shook as the sounds of murder and dying built into a howl of outrage that resonated through the whole structure, amplified and concentrated according to my design. And in a moment that never really ended, a building that once rose up toward the heavens was instantly Inverted, and plunged down toward the pit. Space itself was corrupted at my command. Something that should have been God's, a joy and a wonder in the world of men, had been given into the hands of the enemy."

"You bastard," said Hawk.

"What?"

"You heard me," said Hawk. "Did you think we'd be impressed by your story? Even scared? We've seen worse than you in our time, little man. All you've done is sicken me to my stomach. All those people sacrificed for your ambition. Still here, in this awful place, because of what you did. I saw children among the dead. Children, you bloody bastard! I won't stand for that. Whatever it costs, I'll tear you down and see those poor souls set free. You hear me, Burning Man? Whatever it costs!"

"What will you do?" asked the Burning Man. "Kill me? I died long ago, Captain Hawk. I have been sentenced by the judges of Hell, and my torment is already worse than anything you could ever do to me. The spirits of the dead are trapped here forever, by my will, and there's nothing you or any other living soul can do about it."

Hawk lifted his axe and started forward. Fisher grabbed him quickly by the arm and stopped him. "No, Hawk! That's not the answer. Even the High Warlock's axe couldn't hurt something like him. We have to wait, and hope for a better chance."

"She's right," said Lament. "Contain your anger, Captain. He seeks to provoke you. Continue your story, murderer."

"It all went wrong," said the Burning Man. "Such massive necromantic force generated by such a monstrous blood sacrifice should have made me a power and a domination in the earth. I had such wonders and horrors planned. I would have been the father of a whole new monstrous age. But I was only safe from the effects of my spell while I remained inside the pentacle. When the Cathedral was Inverted, so was I, and I found myself outside the pentacle. Such a stupid mistake. I was torn apart by the victims of my own spell. I died, and damned myself to Hell, for *nothing*. For being stupid. The Demon Prince could have warned me, but of course he didn't. He must have laughed for years at the thought of my burning in the inferno because of him."

"What's Hell like?" Fisher asked.

"Knowledge of your own guilt forever," said the Burning Man. "I'm not allowed to say any more. Except . . . even after all that's been done to me, for all my never-ending torment, I still won't repent. I'm still proud of what I did and what I almost achieved. And I still have hopes. That's why the four of you are here now. You're part of a plan you don't understand, a plan formed in the vast intellects of beings older than mankind. To throw down the restraining laws of order, reshape reality, and bring about hell on earth."

"What makes you think we'd do anything to help scum like you?" asked Hawk, still gripping his axe tightly.

"Don't be so high and mighty, Captain Hawk. Hell waits for you, and your woman, too. I can always smell another killer." He turned to Lament and smiled broadly, his blackened lips splitting apart. "Murder has a savour all its own, doesn't it, Walking Man?"

"You haven't finished your story," said Lament, his voice flat and unaffected. "Why are you here and not in Hell, where you belong?"

The Burning Man shrugged, and flames danced on his shoulders. "The first Forest King tried to reclaim the Cathedral by calling on many a powerful sorcerer, but what I had done could not be so easily undone. And so the King had a great Castle built upon and around the site of the Inverted Cathedral, to contain it. And then the King had his most powerful sorcerer, an enigmatic personage called the Magus, summon me up out of Hell to be the guardian of this place, bound by Wild Magic to prevent anyone or anything from getting in or out. The final irony. The architect of all this, trapped as a slave inside his own creation. So I now burn here instead of in Hell. It hurts just as much."

"But if Forest Castle contains the Inverted Cathedral, why does it need a guardian?" the Seneschal asked. "I mean, who'd be crazy enough to come in here if they didn't have to?"

"Because of the Gateway," said the Burning Man. "And the power it promises."

"A Gateway to Hell?" asked Lament.

"No, to somewhere worse. And I'm going to lead you there. All the way to the top of my Cathedral, and deep into the earth. And either you'll fail and die for my amusement, or you'll come at last to the Gateway; and I'll watch as you open it, and go to a place that's worse than Hell for humans. It's called Reverie. You can be damned there forever while you're still alive. You will know pain and horror and despair in a place that has no ending."

"You do like the sound of your own voice, don't you?" Fisher asked.

"Reverie is not a part of the material world," said Lament, ignoring Fisher as the Burning Man had. "How can this Gateway lead us there?"

"Because of what I did, the Inverted Cathedral is no longer a part of the material world. My blood sacrifice thrust it outside the world of mortal men. Surely you've noticed that you're no longer everything you used to be, Walking Man. You have no authority here."

"God is everywhere," said the Walking Man.

The Burning Man shrugged. "The space the Inverted Cathedral now occupies forms a connecting bridge between the world of men and the world of Reverie. An unsuspected back door through which Wild Magic shall come again to rule all that is."

Lament and the Burning Man then began to argue about this in increasingly technical and abstract terms, and Hawk and Fisher quickly tuned them out. They moved a little way off to talk quietly together. The Seneschal went with them, rather than be left alone.

"How much of this are you buying?" asked Hawk.

"I don't know," said Fisher, frowning. "It all ties together, but it's all based on the word of a confessed murderer."

"Why would he lie?" the Seneschal asked.

"Why would he tell the truth?" countered Hawk. "He's got no reason to help us."

"Maybe he needs us to open this Gateway," suggested Fisher.

"Could be," said Hawk. "I think we have to go along with this bastard, for the time being at least, if only in the hope we'll find some chance to free the spirits trapped in this awful place. The Burning Man deserves to be here. They don't. I'll do whatever it takes to set them free."

"This is a bad place to make promises," said the Seneschal. "We don't understand everything that's going on here."

"Right," agreed Fisher. "Let's just try and make sure we're not doing someone—or something—else's dirty work." She glared about her. "I really don't like this place. In its own way, it's darker than the Darkwood ever was."

"The Burning Man mentioned a sorcerer called the Magus," said the Seneschal. "You don't suppose . . ."

"That was centuries ago," said Hawk. "How could it be the same man? Even sorcerers don't live that long. Besides, I've seen nothing to indicate the Magus is that powerful."

The Burning Man spun around suddenly to face them. "The Magus still lives? I should have known he'd still be around. Still working his plots, manipulating everyone to serve his own ends. We have to get moving. Now. Before he comes in here after you."

"You're frightened of him," said Hawk. "Why? You're dead. What more could he do to you?"

"He could send me back to Hell," said the Burning Man. "After all, he summoned me up out of there." He hugged himself with his flame-wrapped arms, as though trying to hold himself together, and then glared angrily at Lament. "Why aren't there more of you? I was expecting more. Why isn't the Queen here? This is her Castle, her Kingdom. She has a duty to be here. Or is she too scared?"

Lament smiled for the first time. "If Felicity was here, she'd probably just light a cigarette off you. She doesn't need to be here, we represent her."

Fisher chuckled suddenly, and everyone looked at her. She shrugged defensively. "I was just wondering, if we brought the Lady of the Lake in here and put her together with the human candle, would she put him out?"

There was a pause. "Your sense of humor picks the weirdest times to surface, Isobel," said Hawk.

"The Lady has manifested?" asked the Burning Man. "That's it. We are moving right now."

"Hold everything," said Fisher. "Lament, you're supposed to be the Wrath of God. Can't you do anything to help the souls trapped here?"

"I was wondering about that," said the Seneschal.

"My power here is much diminished," said Lament. "In this place of lies and deceptions, I can no longer hear the voice of my God. With no divine guidance to lead me, I have only my own wits and experience."

"You're a fine one to talk about deceptions, Lament," said the Burning Man. "You've been lying to yourself for years. There never was any voice of God within you. All you ever heard was your own voice, the part of you where your magic comes from. Your magic, your power—not God's. Never God's. All you are, and all you ever were, is a sorcerer with delusions of grandeur. There is no God, Lament. Do you think your good God would allow a torture chamber like Hell to exist? There is only the dark, and what waits there. The light is just a passing thing."

"Liar," said Lament. "Hell is built on lies, and you are a part of Hell. Everything you say is suspect."

"Why lie, when the truth can be so much more harmful?" questioned the Burning Man.

He laughed at Lament, and the Walking Man struck at him with his silver-tipped staff. He put all his strength behind it, but at the last moment the staff jerked away, unable to touch the Burning Man. Lament was thrown off balance, and had to step quickly aside to avoid the flames before him. He seemed to have forgotten that he was supposed to be invulnerable. He recovered himself quickly and began a service of exorcism in a loud trembling voice, until the Burning Man's rising laughter drowned him out. Lament broke off in mid-sentence. He looked lost, and for the first time confused and uncertain. And perhaps a little afraid.

"I am here because it is willed for me to be here—by a power far greater than yours, sorcerer," said the Burning Man, grinning. "Your whole life has been a lie, Lament. All you are is a magic-user whose powers remained latent until late in life, when they were finally activated by the trauma of seeing your fellow monks die in the long night. You were afraid of your long-suppressed magic, so you found someone else to blame it on. Everything you've done is the result of religious mania focused through your own sorcery." The Burning Man laughed again as Lament cried out in wordless rage. "All the terrible things you've done, in the Lord's name! Smiting the sinners with your holy rage! We know all about anger in Hell, Lament. Did no one ever tell you rage is a sin? Even holy rage. And murder is always murder. Every day, Jericho, since you took up your false cause, you damned yourself in your God's name. They're going to enjoy you in Hell. There's a specially hot corner of the Inferno for false prophets."

"Lies," muttered Lament. "It can't be true. It can't—"

"That's enough!" Hawk broke in sharply. "Give me one good reason why we should follow you anywhere, murderer. You obviously don't have our best interests at heart."

"The answer to all your questions and all your problems lies on the other side of the Gateway," said the Burning Man. "You risk your lives and your souls, but if by some miracle you can pass through the Gateway and return, you can put right everything that's wrong in the Forest Kingdom. Everything."

"How is that possible?" asked Hawk.

"I told you. There's power there. Power to change everything for the better. Or the worse, if you fail."

"And you'll lead us to the Gateway? Even though you were put here to prevent just that?"

"I have been here a very long time," said the Burning Man. "And the geas that bound me is not as strong as it was. I'll take you all the way to the very top of my Cathedral, and the Gateway there. All the way up, or all the way down, if you prefer."

"All the way down," said Lament quietly, his eyes unfocused. "To see something awful squatting on its terrible throne."

"Been there, done that," said Hawk briskly. "The Demon Prince was pretty impressive, but we still kicked his arse. And it's not a Gateway to Hell, remember? It leads to Reverie. Whatever that might be."

"Hell, like religion, takes many faces," said Lament. And then he turned away so they couldn't see his face.

"Why is it so important that we should go through this Gateway?" the Seneschal asked after a pause.

"There are forces moving now," answered the Burning Man. "Influences vast and powerful, pressing against the other side of the Gateway. They want to be free, and they think they can use you. And if you fail, I shall at least see you fall and suffer, this side of the Gateway or that."

"Is that all there is left to you?" asked Fisher, wrinkling her nose. "Spite and vindictiveness?"

"The damned must take their comforts where they can," said the Burning Man.

"What will happen if we go through this Gateway?" Hawk asked.

The Burning Man shrugged, and his flames jumped and flickered. "Probably you'll all die. No man or woman has ever returned alive from Reverie. It's not a place where humans, or even human thought, can survive. Too limited, you see. So, are you ready to die, my brave heroes? Ready to lay down your lives for a chance to save the Forest Kingdom? After the way this Land has treated you all? Can any of you really say the Forest has treated you fairly?"

"I could destroy the Gateway," said Lament, not turning back. "Seal Reverie off forever from the world of men."

"No you couldn't," the Burning Man told him. "The Gateway is an important part of reality; one of the cogs in the great wheel around which everything turns. If you were even to attempt to destroy it, you risk unraveling everything. No, your only choice is whether to try and enter the Gateway or not. Live or die. Be the heroes you think you are, or abandon the Forest to its fate."

"I know my duty," said Hawk. "I've always known my duty."

"Some things you just have to do," said Fisher.

"That's what gives life purpose and meaning," agreed the Seneschal.

The Walking Man turned back to face them all, smiling slightly. "Thank you. For a moment, I forgot myself. All my life, for whatever reason, has been given to protecting the innocent and avenging the injured. Nothing has changed my faith in that. We go on—to the Gateway and beyond."

"Oh, I'm impressed," said the Burning Man. "Maybe, just maybe, you'll prove strong enough to survive the transition through the Gateway. And if you can, you could make a deal with the Beings on the other side. The Transient Beings. If you can find the right price to offer them, they just might re-Invert the Cathedral for you, and free the spirits contained here. There's a small part of me that would like to see the Transient Beings thwarted in their plans, because one of them betrayed me. But what price could you offer them, greater than the domination of reality itself? They're very powerful now, grown horribly strong on all the Wild Magic generated by the Rift, and collected and focused down through my Inverted Cathedral. With or without your intervention, I don't know how much longer the Gateway can hold them back. They hunger to become real. Once they manifest in our world through the Blue Moon, Wild Magic will have dominion over all, and there shall be hell on earth forever."

"They sent the killing shadows into the Court, didn't

they?" asked the Seneschal. "The ones the young witch stopped."

"A test of their power," said the Burning Man. "A taste of things to come."

"Everywhere we turn, I see the Magus' hand," said the Seneschal. "I never trusted him. He created the Rift and did nothing to stop the invading shadows. And now the Burning Man knows his name. Could the Magus be behind everything that's happened, from the Inverting of the Cathedral right up to the Kingdom's present troubles? And if so, dare we leave him unopposed in the castle in our absence?"

"I don't see we have much choice," said Hawk. "The Gateway must come first. If we survive that, maybe we can make him shut down the Rift, and put a stop to the building Wild Magic."

"That's a big if and maybe," said Fisher.

"It doesn't matter," said Lament. "We have to go to the Gateway. Everything we ever believed in depends upon that."

"We're all going to die," said the Seneschal. "I just know it."

"One last thought," said Fisher to the Burning Man. "What happened to the earlier investigating teams that came in here? Why haven't we seen them anywhere?"

The Burning Man grinned widely. "I ate them."

To go down, they had to go all the way up. The Gateway to Reverie was situated at the very top and tip of the Cathedral, and could only be reached by climbing a narrow stairway built directly onto the inner wall of the Gallery. It wound up and up, out of the main gallery and on up through all the many floors and layers of the Cathedral, until it ended in the solid gold spire at its peak. The Burning Man led them over to inspect the stairway, and smiled at their obvious distress. The steps were barely eighteen inches wide, jutting directly out from the wall, and there was no railing. The only thing between a prospective climber and an increasingly long drop was plenty of not-so-fresh air. The Burning Man pointed out the way with a flame-wrapped finger, and the others craned back their necks painfully, trying and failing to make out the ceiling of the gallery so very high above them.

"How many floors are there above this one?" asked Hawk, fighting down a sudden surge of vertigo. He had an irrational and thoroughly unpleasant feeling that at any moment gravity might invert itself again, his feet would leave the floor, and he'd go falling up toward the ceiling. His eye started to glaze over, and he had to look away. Fisher took him unobtrusively by the arm.

"More floors than you can comfortably imagine," said the Burning Man.

"How long will it take to reach the top?" Fisher asked.

"Who knows?" responded the Burning Man. "No one's ever climbed all the way to the top before. Apart from the dangers of the climb itself, for this was intended to be a pilgrimage, I feel I should warn you that there are wonders and terrors in my Cathedral—veils and mysteries beyond anything you've ever seen or dreamed of."

"Don't put money on it," said Hawk. "We've been around, Isobel and me."

"Right," agreed Fisher.

"Who goes first?" asked the Seneschal, eyeing the narrow steps uneasily. "Normally I'd lead, but without my power . . ."

"You can follow me," said the Burning Man. "No one knows the layout of this place better than I do."

"And that's why you're *not* going first," said Lament firmly. "I wouldn't put it past you to deliberately lead us into danger, just for the fun of watching us fight for our lives. I'll go first."

"I don't think so," said Hawk. "No offense, Walking Man, but you said yourself you've lost most of your powers. If we do run into anything nasty, the man at the front is going to have to bear the brunt of it. You may have lost your powers, but I've still got my axe. So I go first."

"With me right behind you," said Fisher immediately. "Seneschal, you tuck in behind me."

"I don't mind bringing up the rear," offered the Burning Man.

"I don't trust you there, either," said Lament. "Who knows what you might get up to behind our backs? No, you go next, and I'll bring up the rear. And if you even look like you're thinking of doing something treacherous, I'll boot you right off the edge."

"O ye of little faith," said the Burning Man. "So much cynicism in a holy man."

And so they started up the narrow stairway, pressing their right shoulders firmly against the inner wall, to ensure they wouldn't drift too close to the open edge on their left. The steps were solid marble, pale and perfect, and reminded Hawk uncomfortably of so many teeth jutting from the wall. The steps were spaced just far enough apart to stretch and tire the legs, and Hawk paced himself carefully. There was no telling how many rest stops they'd be able to take. The group moved slowly up the inner wall of the gallery, trying not to look down too often at the increasing scale of the drop below. It sucked at the eye, pulling them away from the wall with almost physical force. Hawk kept his gaze fixed firmly on the steps directly ahead of him, and advised the others to do the same.

The Burning Man walked alone in his own space, a careful distance between the Seneschal in front and Lament behind, because his flames were too hot to tolerate close up. The pain bothered him more when he couldn't distract himself by talking. Now and again he had to stop and hug himself until he had it under control again and could carry on. He left black, sooty, sticky footprints on the pale steps. Lament watched all this, and was quietly disturbed. More than once he had damned an evil man to burn in Hell for the suffering he'd caused in life, but to see the effects of Hell close up was upsetting. Even after all the Burning Man had done, Lament still felt a little sorry for the man.

They climbed and climbed, like insects crawling up a wall, and the great domed ceiling slowly formed itself out of the distance before them. It was covered in one great painting of a blue sky with clouds, almost unbearably real.

They stopped there for the first real rest. They sat down carefully on the steps, shoulders still pressed to the wall. No one was really out of breath yet, but already they were feeling the strain in their back and leg muscles. They leaned against the wall, trying not to imagine how far there was still to go, or what might be waiting for them once they got there. It was one thing to be brave and heroic and certain down on the floor of the gallery, but it didn't come quite so easily sitting on a narrow step above a drop you didn't even like to look at. Hawk let his fear and uncertainty move through him and watched it from a distance, acknowledging it but not letting it get to him. He'd been through this before. A thought struck him out of nowhere, and he looked down at the Burning Man.

"Why did you ring the bell in here?"

"I didn't."

"Someone did. Everyone in the Castle heard it."

"There is no bell," said the Burning Man. "Only the sound of a bell. It's a warning. Part of the Cathedral's original design. It's there to warn the surrounding countryside of imminent danger. I created the whole warning system, back when I was still a holy man, and a fool. It still rings, despite me."

"Hold everything," said Fisher. "How can you have the sound of a bell without the bell to make it?"

"Magic," said Hawk.

"That just makes my head hurt. Something has to create the sound in the first place, doesn't it?"

"Think of it as a mental exercise," said the Seneschal. "Like the sound of one hand clapping. One of those religious riddles with no obvious answer."

"Exactly," said the Burning Man, looking back at Lament. "How many angels can dance on the head of a pin, holy man?"

Lament smiled. "Depends on the tune."

The Burning Man sniffed, and then beat his blazing hand against the wall as though trying to distract one pain with another. "I built a lot into this Cathedral. Most of it's been forgotten over the centuries. What it can do, as well as what it contains. No one remembers now, all the many innocent people impressed by force to build it, all the materials requisitioned from unwilling owners, all the peasants put off their land so the Cathedral could be built in the most propitious spot."

"More lies," said Lament, unmoved. "It was never like that. I've read old reports in church libraries. People traveled for miles just to be a part of such a marvelous project. No one was ever forced, and all materials were freely given, for the greater glory of God. Everyone knew good could not come from evil beginnings. This was to be a place of joy and celebration, and no stain of any kind could be allowed on its construction."

The Burning Man laughed softly. "All right, so maybe I exaggerated. You're so easy to manipulate sometimes. But you shouldn't believe everything you read in a church library. History is always written by the winners."

"Keep your petty nature to yourself," said Lament. "We are here to put things right at long last, and nothing will stop us now."

"Never say things like that," warned Fisher. "It's when you start getting all confident and cocky that everything suddenly goes pear-shaped, and nasties start jumping out of the woodwork at you. Usually with bloody big teeth."

"You understand nothing of what's happening here," said the Burning Man spitefully. "You're here because the Transient Beings want you here to open the Gateway. You're just pawns in a larger game."

"Why would they need us?" asked Hawk. "I thought you said they'd soon be powerful enough to force the Gateway open from their side."

"They're impatient," said the Burning Man. "They can feel their time coming round at last."

Fisher stirred unhappily, hefting her sword in her hand. "I'd almost feel happier if we actually had something physical to fight. This place wears you down, like fingernails scraping over your soul."

"It would be something of a relief," said Hawk. "To have something to strike back at. But I think the threats here are more spiritual in nature. We have to concentrate on who we are, and what we believe in."

"What do we believe in?" asked Fisher slowly. "I mean, after everything we've seen, everything we've been through, all the different people we had to be at different times, what is there left to believe in?"

Hawk looked at her and smiled. "We believe in each other."

"Yes," agreed Fisher, smiling back at him. "There is always that."

"Their legendary love," said the Seneschal, so softly no one else heard him.

Hawk looked cautiously down at the long stretch of steps they'd climbed, and then up at the long trail of steps still to go, and remembered another set of steps, from years ago. He'd been much younger then, a second son that nobody wanted, determined to prove his worth by climbing Dragonslair Mountain, to kill the dragon in its cave at the summit. He'd expected to die facing the dragon, but the climb alone almost killed him. The ascent was brutally hard, and the weather punishingly harsh, and the last part of the mountain had to be climbed by hand, over treacherous loose rocks and shifting scree. He could have turned back many times, but he didn't. And when he finally reached the cave at the very top, he found a friend in the dragon, and a love in the dragon's captive, the Princess Julia.

He smiled, remembering. Every now and again he got something right.

They started climbing again. Back and leg muscles ached viciously, and finally screamed in protest, but still they all pressed on. Hawk slowed his pace even more, but it didn't help. Time seemed to pass at a crawl. Their heads hung down, and they were too tired even to look down at the increasing drop. They finally reached the wide, gently sloping dome of the ceiling, and passed through the single trapdoor in the painted blue sky, climbing through into the next floor. There were more steps along the inner wall. And more floors above that one. They trudged on, trying hard to think only of the steps immediately ahead of them.

There were wondrous works of art everywhere now, magnificent and glorious, unseen by mortal eyes for untold centuries, all of them stained and disfigured with the blood of the slaughtered innocents. The Burning Man's treachery had put his mark on all the Cathedral, and he laughed to see it.

They'd just reached the ninth floor when Lament suddenly called a halt. Of them all, the Walking Man had felt the strain of the climb the least, and since it was the first time he'd called for a pause, everyone stopped and looked at him. He didn't seem tired, or even out of breath. Instead, he was staring thoughtfully at a simple, ordinary-looking door set directly into the wall they were passing. Lament reached out to touch the door, and let his fingers trail lightly across the pale brown wood.

"What lies beyond this door, murderer?"

"Treasures and horrors," said the Burning Man easily. "Dreams and nightmares in physical form, long lost to the world of men. Many precious things were brought and stored here, to add to the splendor of the world's greatest Cathedral. You can take a look if you like. None of these doors are locked. But remember, here you open doors at your soul's risk."

"Oh, shut up," snapped Fisher. "Why can't you talk like normal people?"

"I don't think we really have the time to go treasure hunting," said the Seneschal testily, mopping sweat from his face with his sleeve. "Maybe on the way back . . ."

"There is a wonder that's supposed to be here," said Lament. "A glory from the life of Christ."

"Oh, that," said the Burning Man. "If it's reliquaries you're after, you've come to the right place. Beyond that door lies the Ossuary, the Museum of Bone. We were brought all kinds of religious shit while we were building the Cathedral, so I had it all put in here on display. Take a closer look at the door, Walking Man."

Lament leaned in closer, until his nose was almost touching the pale brown door. His keen eyes slowly made out a fine network of interlocking lines or cracks, as though the whole door was one great jigsaw puzzle. He scowled thoughtfully as he tried to make out the patterns. It was all fitted so perfectly together. Then, finally, he recognized the shapes that made up the door, and he jerked his head back in shock and outrage. He spun around dangerously fast on the narrow step and glared at the Burning Man.

"What have you done, abomination? This is bone! Human bones! The whole door is constructed from human bones!"

"So it is," said the Burning Man. "Why else do you think it's called a Museum of Bones? Go in, go in. You haven't seen anything yet."

The door opened easily at Lament's touch, and he went in. The others followed him in, giving the Burning Man plenty of room, as always. The long narrow room leading off from the door was composed entirely of human bones. No pains had been taken inside the room to conceal its nature. Arm and leg bones had been forced together to form the walls, with fingerbones packed in to fill the occasional spaces. The ceiling was a sky of skulls, gazing down with empty eyes at their first visitors in centuries. Two rows of commonplace glass display cases stretched away down the room, holding assorted objects within. At the very end of the Ossuary stood a blasphemous bone altar, with grasping hands for candleholders and a skull for a drinking vessel. The very floor rose and fell beneath their feet in waves of closely packed ribs.

"Where did you get so many bones?" asked Hawk, his voice hushed, not sure whether he was in a chapel or a graveyard.

"It wasn't easy," admitted the Burning Man. The bones under his feet blackened slowly from the heat. "I tracked down the burial grounds of every saint and holy man in the Forest Kingdom, every priest and hermit and religious nut, and had them all dug up so that their bones could be brought here to increase the Castle's sanctity. The bones of saints have always been venerated, things of worship for the common herd. I just extended the concept. In the end, there were so many bones, I felt I ought to do something useful with them, so I had them made into this Ossuary. Isn't it splendid? So much beauty that was only wasted in the cold earth."

"How many?" asked Lament softly. "How many people did you drag from their graves, and from their rest?"

"Oh hell, I don't know," said the Burning Man. "I lost track after a while. My attitude then was, you can't have enough sanctity. I had a lot of people working under me, locating the bodies, checking for frauds, paying off the right people so the holy corpses could be disinterred and brought here. Some of the people who did that for me are still here, down in the gallery with all the other sacrificed souls. Do you feel the same about them now you know what they did?"

"This is sacrilege!" said Lament.

"Nonsense. The church has always collected holy relics, so they could show them off to the faithful, for a small fee, as physical proof that what they were teaching was true. I thought you'd be more sophisticated than that, Walking Man. Bones are just bones."

"They'll all have to be returned," said Lament. "So that the families of the desecrated dead can at last be comforted. You never gave a thought about the distress your grave-robbing would cause to the families of the holy men, did you? No, of course not. What was a little human suffering, compared to the glory of your Cathedral?"

"You see?" said the Burning Man. "You're beginning to understand. But these bones aren't going anywhere. What I did to them here can't be easily undone."

"I will see them all put at rest," said Lament. "Whatever it takes."

The Burning Man grinned. "Oh, I love it when you talk like that. Hell loves nothing more than to see a good man fail to keep his word."

Lament ignored him, studying the ranks of display cases suspiciously. "What have you got here? More horrors, or the wonder you promised?"

"Depends on your definition," said the Burning Man, leaning casually against a wall. The bones blackened and cracked under the heat of his flames. "What kind of wonder did you have in mind?"

"Well, the Grail," said Lament, and then stopped as the Burning Man laughed again.

"Oh dear, are you still looking for that? And all the other religious paraphernalia? Rubbish, rather than relics.

Most of it's fake, anyway. If all the supposed splinters from the True Cross displayed in churches were ever assembled in one place, you'd have enough wood to build a new Ark. Junk is junk. But there are a few genuine wonders here you might like to see. One of the Transient Beings, The Engineer, passed through here briefly, and was much taken with my collection. He paused awhile to manufacture killing tools from the bones of saints. The holiest of bones to make the deadliest of swords. The ultimate perversion, the most delicious blasphemy. The Engineer only made six of these blades, but they went on to become very famous, over the centuries. You know them as the Infernal Devices.

"The Engineer took three with him when he left. They ended up in the Armory of the Forest Kingdom. Three swords remained here, waiting patiently for someone to come and put them to use. What do you think? Do you dare awaken them and take them for yourselves? You're going to need powerful weapons when the time comes to face the powers and dominations beyond the Gateway."

He gestured with a flame-wrapped hand, and as though a curtain had been swept from their gaze, the others suddenly saw the three Infernal Devices standing together in their own little alcove in the bone wall. Three great longswords, in chased silver scabbards. Fully seven feet tall, and six inches wide at the crosspiece, their foot-long hilts were bound with dark leather. There was nothing graceful or elegant about them. They were killing tools, designed for butchery and slaughter and the ruining of lives. And yet still, somehow, there was a dark glamour to the swords; something that called to the darkest places in a man's soul and promised satisfaction for his most private, bloody dreams. The Seneschal was already moving toward them when Hawk grabbed him firmly by the arm.

"Don't get too close," Hawk warned quietly. "You might wake them."

Fisher shuddered suddenly, a cold feeling of utter revulsion running through her. For a time in the darkest part of the Demon War, she had wielded the Infernal Device known as *Wolfsbane*. The sword had proved to be alive and aware and utterly evil. It had sought to corrupt and possess her until she gave it up. And sometimes she thought giving it up had been the hardest thing she'd ever had to do. Even now a part of her wanted to walk over and claim one of the Infernal Devices, take its dark power for herself again. To kill and kill, until all the world ran red with blood. She fought the feeling down, crushing it mercilessly, but was shocked at the effort it took.

"Magnificent, aren't they?" asked the Burning Man. "*Soulripper. Blackhowl. Belladonna's Kiss.* With three Infernal Devices at your command, you could conquer the world."

"Or destroy it," said Hawk. "Those damned swords have their own desires. Let them sleep here forever."

"I've heard the stories and the songs," Lament said. "Could whatever's inside those blades be the souls of saints, captive and corrupted?"

"Unfortunately, no," said the Burning Man. "Whatever's in them, The Engineer brought out of Reverie with him. A little bit of the dark world, free in the world of men. Sometimes you need more than one serpent."

Hawk turned his back on the Infernal Devices, and after a painfully long moment, the others did the same. They all breathed a little more easily. Lament glared at the Burning Man.

"You said there was a wonder in here. A genuine wonder. Where is it?"

"On the altar," said the Burning Man, reluctantly.

They all turned to look, and together they moved forward to stand before the altar constructed from human bones. In the middle of the altar lay a small wooden casket, six inches by four by two. Simple polished wood, with no obvious markings. Just two silver hinges for the narrow lid. It looked perfectly ordinary at first, but as they drew closer, drawn by some deep, primal attraction, they realized it was more than just a box. The casket had a presence to it, a feeling of enhanced, almost overwhelming existence, as though it was the only real thing in the room, or perhaps even the world. Just being in its presence was strangely comforting, the first time any of them had felt at ease since they'd entered the Inverted Cathedral. They felt welcome, like finally coming home after a long journey. And yet none of them wanted to pick it up or open it. None of them dared.

"What . . ." said Lament, then had to stop and clear his throat, and start again. "What is this box? What's inside it?"

"They know of this box even in Hell," said the Burning Man. He was still back standing with the Infernal Devices, his gaze averted. For the first time he sounded uncertain. "The box is older than anything here. Christ made it when He worked as a carpenter with His earthly father, Joseph. It is said that within the casket is the original spark, from when God said *Let there be light,* and the universe began. The single spark of light that was the source of all creation, preserved forever in a small wooden box. Is that enough of a wonder for you?

"It's said a man brought the box out of the Deadlands soon after their creation. Perhaps it was what the two sorcerers were fighting over. No one knows who the man was, though there are rumors. Some say it was the surviving sorcerer, much diminished. Some say he was called the Magus. No one knows for sure, even in the inferno. Someone gave the box to the first Forest King, who commanded this Cathedral be designed and built to honor it. Did the Magus give it to him? I don't know. But he was right there when the King needed someone to undo the dreadful thing I'd done. Now he's back at Forest Castle while matters threaten to come to a head at last, and the fate of the world shall be decided. Who is the Magus? What is he? I don't know. All I can tell you is that he frightens me, and I have known the horrors of the pit."

"Why are you keeping your distance?" asked Hawk. "Can't you feel the peace there is here?"

"I can't even look at it," said the Burning Man bitterly. "Peace and hope are for the living."

"Has anyone ever tried to see what's inside the box?" asked Fisher.

"A lot of people have thought that, by all accounts," said the Burning Man. "Why don't you try?"

Fisher started to reach for the box, and then stopped abruptly. She couldn't touch it. Deeper than knowledge, deeper than instinct, she knew that the box was a holy thing and she was not worthy. She said as much, and Hawk and Seneschal nodded. And then they all looked at Lament.

"I have given myself to God," he said slowly. "If He wishes it, I shall take His casket out of this awful place."

He reached out his hand, paused briefly, and then picked up the box with no trouble at all. He smiled, almost shyly, and held the casket up before his eyes, studying the workmanship at close range. "To touch something that Christ touched . . ." He smiled again, then put the box in one of his coat's inner pockets. Everyone stirred unhappily as the feeling of peace and comfort diminished, and was gone.

The Seneschal sniffed loudly. "If you ask me, there's far too much religion in this quest. Religion should keep its distance from real life. It's far too distracting."

"Come on," said Fisher. "Your grandparents were the High Warlock and the Night Witch. You should be used to weird shit in your life."

"Well, yes, but that's just *magic*. Magic's everywhere. This is *religion*. If I actually believed in any of this, I think I'd be getting very worried."

They left the Ossuary behind them and continued the long climb up the gently curving wall of the Cathedral. They were all tired now, that bone-deep weariness that's worse than pain. As they passed from floor to floor, and from level to level, increasingly slowly now they were finally nearing the top, they began to feel changes, in the Cathedral and in themselves. Pressures and influences came and went like tides. Distances varied, coming closer and backing away, all without moving. They all felt like crying or laughing, and didn't know why. The base of the Cathedral seemed impossibly far away now, and they felt that if they should by some chance fall from the narrow stairway, they would drop and tumble forever, and never reach an end. They began to wonder if they would climb forever and never reach the spire. Or if they had always been climbing, and everything else had just been a dream along the way. Sometimes it seemed there were more than five people climbing the narrow steps, and sometimes less than five, and both perceptions seemed entirely normal until they were over.

As they finally drew near their destination, climbing doggedly on past pain and tiredness and everything else the Cathedral could throw at them, the Burning Man began to taunt them, saying that when the Transient Beings broke loose, this time the Wild Magic wouldn't be limited to just a long night. This time not just the Demon Prince and his demons, and not just the Northern Kingdoms. When the Gateway opened, the Blue Moon would shine forever, and Reverie would swallow all of reality, making reality a part of itself. Wild Magic would finally run free, unchecked by such human concepts as logic and order, cause and effect. It would be Chaos Unleashed. Everything would be possible. Every dream they'd ever had, especially the bad ones. Hell on earth, eternally.

"Personally, I can't wait," said the Burning Man, and they all winced at the harsh sound of his laughter.

"You are testing my faith," said Lament. "I won't listen to you, liar."

"What use is faith in a place like this?" asked the Burning Man. "In the end, you're just a man, and the Transient Beings are so much more."

"Why are you so happy about these monsters breaking loose?" Hawk asked him. "What's in it for you?"

"When Reverie is all there is, all restraints will be broken, all the locks on all the doors shall shatter, and every demon in Hell will be liberated. The dead and the damned will walk the earth again, and I will be there with them, finally no longer burning."

"You see," said Lament. "You still know hope. You still have faith in something."

The Burning Man stopped on the stairs and looked back at Lament, and his words came fast and viciously. "You say you gave yourself to God, Lament, but did you really do so of your own free will? Did you ever really have a choice in the matter? Or did God direct those demons toward your monastery? Did He send them there to kill your brethren, destroy their innocent lives and your simple happiness, just because He needed a new Walking Man?

Would a good and loving God do a thing like that? Or is everything you are, and everything you've done, the result of a compact you made not with God, but the Enemy?"

Lament cried out, a terrible pain-wracked sound. The others looked back as Lament buried his face in his hands, his shoulders shaking. None of them knew what to say to him. The Burning Man went back down to the step above Lament, and leaned down to pat him comfortingly on the shoulder.

"There, there. Let it go. It's not so hard to give it all up. Better to have no faith at all than to believe in a lie. Throw away your tyrannous conscience; you won't feel nearly so bad when it's gone."

The shoulder of Lament's coat burst into flames as the Burning Man took his hand away. Lament slapped at the fire with his bare hand, beating out the flames, trying to use the pain to center himself again. It was only when the flames were out, and he looked at his scorched and blistered hand, that he realized the truth. He should have been invulnerable to the Burning Man's touch, but that strength was based in his faith. As doubt undermined belief, he became human and vulnerable again. Lament took a deep breath and pulled the tatters of his faith around him. He had to believe. Or everything he'd done, all the people he'd killed, was nothing more than a monstrous lie. He tried to remember when his faith had been as much a part of him as the air he breathed and the blood in his veins, but that seemed impossibly long ago now. He should never have come here. Never allowed his pride to bring him to this terrible place.

Then he remembered the box in his inner coat pocket, and was ashamed. All he'd been through was nothing compared to what Christ had suffered. Lament let out his breath in a ragged sigh. He would believe because he chose to believe. Because the things he'd fought for were worth fighting for. Because for all the losses and hurts of his life, he still believed in love and justice and hope. No one ever said the Walking Man would have an easy job. He straightened his back and looked up at the Burning Man.

"Keep going, murderer," he said calmly. "We're not at the Gateway yet."

"If you knew what really lay beyond the Gateway, you wouldn't be nearly so keen to get there," said the Burning Man, starting up the steps again.

"You don't know any more than we do," said Hawk.

"I know you'll meet an old friend there," said the Burning Man spitefully. "When you banished the Demon Prince, he returned home, to Reverie. He's waiting for you there. I'm sure there's a lot he wants to discuss with you."

"Hell," said Fisher. "We kicked his arse once, we'll kick it again."

"Right," agreed Hawk. "And I've got the Rainbow sword again."

And then they both looked quickly back at the Seneschal and Lament, to see if they'd heard that. But both of them had their heads down, lost in their own thoughts. Hawk sighed tiredly.

"I came back to solve a murder," he said plaintively. "No one said anything about having to save the world. Again."

"Life's like that," said Fisher. "Our life, anyway."

CHAPTER EIGHT

True Colors Revealed

Queen Felicity sat alone in her empty Court and thought how small it made her feel. The great Hall had been built centuries ago, to house a great host of knights and heroes and warriors, but they were all long gone. Even the Land's last few heroes, those brave men and women who fought in the Demon War, were mostly gone now. Fill the Court with a few hundred politicians screaming their heads off, desperate for their voices to be heard, or at the very least to be sure of drowning out their opponents, and then the Court seemed alive and vibrant, even powerful. But more and more that seemed to Felicity to be nothing more than an illusion. And all the raised voices did was give her a headache.

Felicity was isolated. No one even wanted to plot with her anymore. She only held on to the Regency because no one felt strong or secure enough to take it away from her.

So now she sat alone in an ancient Hall, on a carved wooden Throne that had once been the seat of legends, planning one last desperate throw of the dice. One last reckless gamble, to find out who her true friends and enemies were, and perhaps reestablish her authority. She'd never wanted to be Queen. Marrying Harald had always been her father's idea. Felicity had never wanted the responsibility. But now she had to be Queen because someone had to save the Land before warring factions tore it apart and soaked the earth in innocent blood. Felicity sighed tiredly, and gently massaged her aching temples with her fingertips. She'd never wanted to be anybody's savior. Why did it have to be her?

Because there's no one else, said a quiet voice that just

might have been her conscience. *Because you're the one on the Throne. Because you accepted the job, and now you have to prove yourself worthy of it.*

The great double doors swung slowly open, and the warrior woman Cally entered the Court. She had to struggle with the doors by herself. The usual guards had been dismissed. This particular Court session was strictly private. Cally pushed the doors shut behind her and approached the Throne. She was wearing her best leather armor, all buffed and shining, and her hand rested on the pommel of her sheathed sword.

"Everyone we can reach has been contacted," she said crisply. "All the messengers have been bribed to complete secrecy, and promised a horrible death by me personally if they screw this up. Even so, it won't be long before word gets out. You can't hold a special invitation-only Court at this late hour of the evening and not have someone notice."

"They can suspect what they like," said Felicity, stirring uncomfortably on the wooden Throne as she tried to find some sitting position where her buttocks wouldn't go to sleep. The Forest Throne had been designed to be impressive, not comfortable. "By the time people have realized what's going on here, this meeting will be over, and I'll know where I stand. And, I hope, what to do next." She started to fit a cigarette into her long holder, then gave up because her hands were shaking too much. She couldn't afford to look nervous. "Do you think they'll all come?"

Cally shrugged. "Curiosity should bring most of them. But whether you can make them listen is another question. What will you do if this doesn't work out? Would you resign as Regent?"

"Would I hell," said Felicity. "Give my son over into the hands of some damned politician? No, I'd grab Stephen and a box full of jewels, and head for the horizon first. Leave the Forest to stew in its own messes. But I won't do that until I absolutely have to. As long as there's even a hope we can work things out, I'll stay. It's a good Land. It deserves saving. It has such potential, certainly more than Hillsdown ever had under my father. So let's try to be optimistic. At least some of the people coming are sup-

posed to be my friends, or at the very least loyal to the
Throne. And those who are my enemies can perhaps still
be made to see sense."

"You really think so?" asked Cally, taking up her usual
position at the Queen's right hand.

"They have to listen," said Felicity. "There's too much
at stake for us to indulge our egos anymore."

"Never thought I'd hear you say that," said Cally dryly.

Felicity laughed briefly. "Times are hard indeed if I'm
the Land's last hope."

She stretched slowly, arms above her head, and groaned
loudly as she let them fall back. "Christ on a crutch, I feel
tired. My corset's the only thing that's holding me upright.
And I've still got the day's paperwork to go through after
this is finished. There are people in the salt mines who
work less hours than I do. Of course, they don't get to
wear such pretty clothes." She rubbed at her eyes.

"Coming here was never my idea, but if I have to be
Queen, I'll be a Queen they'll never forget. I can't let my
authority be undermined any further. Someone has to take
charge of the Court. Right now there are too many politicians chasing too many causes, and they're tearing the Land
apart. No decisions are being made, and nothing that needs
to be done is being done. The whole infrastructure of the
country is breaking down, just because no one at the Court
can agree on how to share out the toys in the sandpit!"
She looked at Cally. "That's what I'm going to hit them
with. Does it sound convincing?"

"Very convincing, very concise, very sharp," said Cally.
"You're a natural, Fliss. Should have been a politician."

"Mind your language. Still, I didn't spend all those years
in my father's Court and not learn anything. I could teach
this Court a lot about the subtle arts of conspiracy. Dear
Daddy would have had me exiled or killed, like Julia, if
he'd suspected even half of what I was up to. And I learned
a lot from listening to my father's speeches. Say what you
like about him, he understood the value of a good speech.
Always hired the very best writers. I could do with a few
of them here. Harald always wrote his own. Wouldn't be

helped in anything. Typical of the man. Who do you think will support me, Cally?"

"Sir Vivian is loyal to the Throne, and to you," Cally said slowly. "Same with Allen Chance. Hawk and Fisher are close with the Questor, so they'll probably follow his lead. Tiffany's a witch, so her main loyalty is always going to be to the Sisterhood. She'll probably have to check back with the Academy before she can commit herself to anything. But since she and Chance are so sweet on each other, odds are she'll side with him unless or until she's instructed otherwise. Ah, young love. The three so-called Landsgraves, Morrison, Esther, and Pendleton, are vicious little back-stabbing toads who don't give a damn for anyone's interests but their own. But just maybe you can bribe or intimidate them into doing the right thing for once. Your father will do what he will do. As for your last choice . . ." Cally shrugged unhappily. "Who knows what the Magus will do?"

"We need him," Felicity said firmly. "He's our only defense, our only weapon against the growing forces that threaten the Forest Land. If we can get him to commit to the Throne . . ."

"That's a hell of a big if."

"Then no one else would dare attack us directly. And if the Blue Moon really is on its way back, you can be sure that bunch of self-abuse experts in the magic-user's hall won't be enough to save us."

"I don't know that the Magus is necessarily up to it, either," said Cally. "All right, he created the Rift, but in all the time he's been here, he hasn't done a single damn thing about the Inverted Cathedral."

"One problem at a time," said Felicity. "I have to concentrate on one thing at a time or I'll go crazy. Sometimes I wonder if I'm strong enough to be Queen."

"You have to be," said Cally. "Because all the alternatives are worse."

Felicity smiled humorlessly. "How the hell did I end up here? I spent all my youth fighting authority, and now I'm Queen. Do all children become their parents?"

"Now there's an idea!" said Cally. "Take a leaf from

your father's book. Declare war and invade Hillsdown! Or Redhart. Nothing brings a country together like a good war!"

Felicity shook her head. "You're really not helping, Cally."

Sir Robert Hawke, once a bladesmaster and a hero famed in song and legend, but now only a minor politician with a largely discredited background, sat alone in his quarters, and cursed the world quietly with tired but explicit venom. It had been a long, hard day, and it showed no signs of being over yet. His desk was piled high with assorted crumpled papers, information his carefully chosen and bribed sources thought he ought to know about.

The Duke was a threat, Hawk and Fisher were intimidating, but Jericho Lament was genuinely scary. Everyone had heard a story about the Walking Man's never-ending vengeance, and everyone in the Castle had something to feel guilty about. People were talking anxiously in private and in public, and preparing for the worst. No one believed he was just in the Castle to deal with the Inverted Cathedral. Lament came after guilty men. Everyone knew what he'd done in the hall of the magic-users. Conspirators were gathering together and saying now or never. Strike now, or we may never get another chance. No one was actually saying civil war yet, but it was in everybody's thoughts.

Sir Robert scowled. If civil war did break out in the Forest, there'd be so many sides, so many factions, the fighting would drag on for years. It would tear the Land apart, split up families, set neighbor against neighbor. The Land would be reduced to burnt-out villages and blood-soaked fields. And God alone knew who'd be left alive to see the end of it. Sir Robert swore angrily. He hadn't fought in the Demon War all those years ago, putting his life on the line again and again, to see the Land he loved and fought for destroyed in a stupid, needless war. There had to be a way to stop this insanity, before it all got out of hand. There had to be something he could do . . . if only he wasn't so damned tired . . .

He needed some sleep. Even a nap would help. To just

lie down, stretch out, and relax, if only for a while, but he couldn't stop thinking, planning, plotting . . . His mind was working at frantic speed even as he sat there, urged on by all the uppers he'd taken. You couldn't be just a man in Forest politics these days; there was too much to do, to process, to cope with, to be only, merely, human.

Sir Robert unlocked and opened the secret door in his desk, and looked at all the assorted colored pills laid out before him. All the colors of the rainbow to help him sleep and to wake him up, to make him eloquent and to keep him sharp. But where was he, in the midst of all this chemical brilliance? Was all he had left the choice of which pill to take next? He sighed, and selected three black pills. Just a few downers, to help him sleep, help him rest, soothe the clamoring thoughts in his head. In the end he took four, washing them down with the last of the good brandy.

He sat down heavily on the edge of his unmade bed and slowly pulled off his boots. A delicious languor seeped through his body, sweeping away the cares of the day, as he lay back on the bed, not bothering to undress any further. It felt so good to not have to care for a while. But still, tired as he was, with sleep tugging at him like a determined child, thoughts swirled sluggishly through his head. The three would-be Landsgraves had disappeared. Which just had to be bad news. It meant they'd gone to ground, and were even now busily plotting something he just knew he wouldn't approve of. But when all was said and done, they were amateurs. They shouldn't have been able to disappear so completely that even his network of spies and informers couldn't find them.

There was always the possibility something had happened to them. The three Landsgraves had many enemies in Forest Castle. Well, if he was lucky, they were just dead. If he was really unlucky, they'd been handed over to Sir Vivian, that paragon of duty and honor, and were even now telling him everything they knew under intense interrogation. And there were all kinds of things they could be saying to incriminate their good friend and confidant, Sir Robert Hawke.

And they owed him money.

He supposed he should be worried, but he couldn't seem to make the effort. Why look on the dark side? They'd probably turn up eventually. They always did. Like bad pennies, or a case of the crabs that wouldn't go away. Maybe he should just cut them loose. He didn't need their money that badly. Well, actually, he did, but there had to be somewhere else he could find it. Somewhere without so many risks involved. It wasn't as if he had any expensive tastes to support. He'd never had the time or the inclination to develop any really interesting vices. Most of the money he collected went straight to the various democratic causes he supported. Democracy was about the only thing left he still believed in. Even when he wasn't sure he believed in *himself* anymore.

It had been a long time since he'd considered himself anyone worth believing in.

His thoughts were floating now. Slowly drifting apart. The black pills were really kicking in. His old bed seemed luxuriously soft, and his body was too heavy to move. Some days this fleeting moment of ease and pain between waking and sleeping was the only thing he had to look forward to all day. Sleep beckoned with a languorous finger, promising relief from all the cares of the day, and he was almost there when some bastard knocked loudly on his door.

Sir Robert's first clear thought was to ignore whoever it was, and hope they'd take the hint and go away, but whoever it was knocked again, almost immediately, and twice as loud. It had that urgent, arrogant sound of a messenger whose message was so important, he was prepared to go on knocking until hell froze over, or a merciful and sympathetic God struck him with a bolt of lightning. Since neither event seemed particularly likely in the immediate future, Sir Robert groaned loudly and forced himself up and off the bed. It took him a while. His body now seemed to weigh a ton or more, and his feet seemed a long way away from his head. Fighting to keep his eyes open, he lurched across the room toward the door and leaned against it before unlocking and pulling it open. He was still leaning on the doorframe as he gave the messenger before him his best scowl.

"This had better be important, or I swear I am going to rip out your spleen and eat it right in front of you."

The royal messenger looked back at him, entirely unmoved, and handed Sir Robert a scroll closed and sealed with the Queen's personal seal. He accepted it automatically and looked at it numbly as the messenger looked him over with a critical eye.

"I am required to wait for your answer, Sir Robert," he said formally.

"Keep your voice down," growled Sir Robert. "If you wake me all the way up, we'll both regret it." He turned his back on the messenger and stumbled over to his desk. He had to grab the edge of the desk at the last moment to stop himself from falling, and lowered himself carefully into his chair. He fumbled at the scroll's wax seal, his fingers numb and clumsy. He should never have taken that many blacks. He scrabbled at the wax seal for embarrassingly long moments, then finally was able to break it, tearing the thick paper in the process.

The messenger watched it all from the doorway, stonily silent.

Sir Robert made himself concentrate on the handwritten note. It was a summons from the Queen. He was commanded to attend a special Court. Right now, if not sooner. No excuses accepted. Since it was written in Felicity's own hand rather than that of a Court scribe, it meant this was a private summons. Secret. Sir Robert felt stupidly pleased that he was able to follow all the implications of that. A special, secret Court session meant that important things would be said. Things he needed to know. So of course he had to go. Except . . . was this good news or bad? A commendation or an accusation? Just how much did the Queen know about all the things he'd said and done in his time?

His thoughts were whirling all over the place now, and he had no idea how long he sat there, staring blankly at the torn scroll, until the messenger in his doorway cleared his throat loudly. Of course, a reply was expected. He had to say something.

"Tell Her Majesty . . . I'm delighted to . . . be delighted

to accept her kind invitation. I'll be there." His tongue felt like it was drunk, and his words were so slurred, even he could hardly make them out. Sir Robert could have wept. It wasn't fair. He was in no shape to deal with this. Why did the Queen have to send for him now? He needed to sleep. He swayed in his chair.

"Jesus, you're a mess," said the messenger, and there was as much disappointment as contempt in his voice. "Come as you are. If you can."

He turned and left, and the sound of the door slamming shut behind him was almost unbearably loud. Sir Robert fumbled out his keys with numb fingers, searching for the key that would open the secret door in his desk. He needed more pills. Something to wake him up, to make him sharp again. Something to make him the man he used to be.

Sir Vivian was talking with the Lady of the Lake. He'd brought her to one of his favorite and most secret places, an indoor Forest glade deep in the heart of the North Wing. It was a long way off the beaten track, so far off that only a few people even knew it existed. Sir Vivian was happy for it to stay that way. The glade was entirely self-sufficient, an oasis of greenery inside the cold stone of the Castle. There were trees and shrubs, grassy lawns and mossy banks around a slender chuckling river that ran to and from nowhere, all centered around a delicate stone fountain whose gushing waters rose high into the air. Rich scents of earth and grass and growing things hung heavily on the air, and all the trees' branches hung down with the weight of summer greenery. The glade was a peaceful place, the only sound the gurgling of the fountain. Sir Vivian came here when he needed quiet, a place to clear his thoughts and listen to his own heart. He'd been a bit shy of revealing his special place to the Lady, but she loved it immediately. She was currently manifesting within the fountain's waters, standing tall and proud as water streamed down from her outstretched hands.

"This is a wonderful place," she said happily, her voice giving shape and meaning to the sounds the fountain made. "I don't remember it from when I was last here."

"You wouldn't," said Sir Vivian. "It's only twelve years old. During the Demon War goblins came to live in the Castle for a while, after their home, the Tanglewood, was destroyed by the encroaching long night. They created this place from cuttings they brought with them. This is all that's left of the Tanglewood now. The goblins are long gone, and given their obnoxious nature I can't say anyone really misses them. But they left this behind, and anyone who could fashion and appreciate a small miracle like this couldn't be all bad."

The Lady laughed, and suddenly it was raining. A soft, gentle sprinkling of rain that fell out of nowhere like a delicate haze on the air, just cool enough to be refreshing. The glade blossomed as the rain touched it, and the grass became almost unbearably green, and flowers were bursting out of everywhere in bright and glorious colors. Sir Vivian looked about him, awed and wondering and happily enchanted, and laughed quietly.

"That's more like it," said the Lady approvingly. "You look quite handsome when you smile. You were always a grim and brooding one, as I recall, but that was many years ago. Haven't you found anything to be happy about since?"

"Not really," said Sir Vivian, and his smile was gone as quickly as it had come.

"How did you recognize me?" asked the Lady of the Lake. "I am much changed from what I once was."

"I'd know you anywhere," said Sir Vivian. "I recognized your smile. You were always very special to me. I would have died for you."

"I'd much rather you lived," said the Lady. "My true and gallant hero. I've heard a lot about you."

Sir Vivian grimaced, and half turned away from her. "Then you know I was a traitor. I betrayed my King."

"And was Pardoned by another King," the Lady said gently. "Look at me, Vivian. You have done many remarkable things. You were a hero at Tower Rouge, and a hero again to the peasants you fought beside in the Demon War. They still sing songs about your exploits. The Forest Land still stands, in part because of you. You should be proud of what you have achieved."

"I always wanted to be a warrior," said Sir Vivian. "To prove myself worthy by my own actions. But now even that is being taken away from me. I thought the Walking Man had come for Queen Felicity. I couldn't trust my swordsmanship to stop him, so I used magic against him. The magic I inherited from my notorious parents. It didn't stop Lament, of course. I doubt even the Magus could stand against the Walking Man. But I had to try to protect my Queen, and now the magic I never wanted runs loose within me, a constant burning temptation. It's almost a physical need to use that power to make the world make sense, by force if necessary. To shake some sense into the world whether it wants it or not."

"And into people, too?" said the Lady.

"Especially people," said Sir Vivian.

"I feel the same way sometimes," said the Lady. "I felt it when I was alive, and even more when I was reborn in this form. When I see people abuse the Land or each other, and the anger rises within me, I could make it rain for fifty years, cause the rivers to break their banks and flood the fields, and drive the people from the Forest. But I don't. My role is to protect the Land, and those who live in it. It would be wrong for me to interfere too much, for then people would grow dependent on me, and learn nothing. And so I do the most good I can, quietly, from a distance, with the minimum of magic. I wouldn't have revealed my existence even now, but events here are drawing to a climax, and at the end, I will be needed to do what no one else can."

"Your life, or after-life, has purpose and meaning," said Sir Vivian heavily. "I'm still looking for mine. By my age most men have found a shape or direction to their lives. They have a job they're good at, an end to aim for, or at least the simple pleasures of wife and family. I have none of those things. I was a hero once, but it wasn't at all what I thought it would be. I found something to fight for when I was defending the peasants against the demons, but it didn't last. I left them for what I thought was a greater cause. But defending them against the Court proved too much for my limited diplomatic abilities. And the one thing

I'd always set my heart on, becoming High Commander of the Castle Guard and personally responsible for the safety of my King, turned out to be the one thing that damned me. I failed, and in failing I betrayed another King. He died because I wasn't up to the job he gave me.

"My life is so empty, Lady. So cold. Nothing and no one to care for, or care for me. This isn't the life I hoped and fought for when I was young and still had dreams. You've been dead, Lady. What was it like? Would I find peace there at last?"

"You know your trouble?" asked the Lady of the Lake. "You need to get out and meet some girls." She laughed at the almost shocked expression on his face. "I'm sorry, Vivian, I know you were expecting something more mystical, but sometimes the obvious answers are the right ones after all. You need to open your eyes and look around you, Vivian. The answer could be closer than you think. Now stand up straight and make yourself look presentable. There's a royal messenger on his way with something important to tell you."

As he scrambled to his feet and tugged more or less randomly at his uniform, the Lady merged into the waters of the fountain, her shape disappearing until there was only water, pouring smoothly from stone mouths. The gentle rain stopped. A messenger knocked on the closed door, and entered uncertainly at Sir Vivian's command. His eyes widened as he took in the green glade, and then he saw Sir Vivian and marched smartly forward to stand before him. They exchanged formal bows and then Sir Vivian gave the messenger his best glare.

"I thought I gave orders I wasn't to be disturbed."

The messenger nodded, unmoved by the glare. He was used to people not being pleased to see him. "Sorry to intrude, High Commander, but I bear a personal message from the Queen. I am to wait for your answer."

Sir Vivian nodded grimly, and all but snatched the scroll from the messenger's hands. He broke the wax seal with a quick twist, and quickly scanned the message. Special Court . . . your earliest convenience . . . matters of urgency . . . no exceptions. Just what he didn't need right now. He rolled up the scroll and stuck it in his belt. A summons from the Queen in her own handwriting was unfortunately too important to be ignored, or even put off.

"Tell the Queen I will be with her directly."

The messenger nodded before leaving as quickly as dignity allowed. Even Royal messengers had more sense than to hang around Sir Vivian when he was in one of his moods. The Lady of the Lake reformed in the fountain as the door closed behind the messenger.

"You're frowning again, Vivian."

"With good cause. The Queen wouldn't be sending for me this urgently unless things were really getting out of hand. Why did you vanish like that?"

"Because the less people who know of my presence here, the better, for the moment."

"Why are you here?" asked Sir Vivian. "Why return now, after all these years?"

"Because I'm needed," said the Lady. "Just like you, Sir Vivian. Go and see Felicity. She needs you now more than ever. I can't come with you. And you mustn't tell anyone who I am—or, rather, was. And try not to worry so much; things aren't nearly as out of control as they might seem."

Then she was gone again, and the fountain was just a fountain. Sir Vivian headed for the door. He somehow knew she wouldn't be reappearing anytime soon. The sense of her presence was gone from the glade. He sighed. It had been good to see her again, talk with her, but . . .

"Just when you think things can't become any more complicated," he said gruffly, "fate starts dealing from the bottom of the deck. Maybe I'll just use my magic after all, turn everybody into frogs, and take a long holiday somewhere more peaceful."

He laughed briefly, surprising himself, and then left his precious private glade to attend his Queen and his duty one more time.

Elsewhere in the Castle, the young witch Tiffany was taking the dog Chappie for a walk, and it would be difficult to say who was the more embarrassed. She had gone to the trouble of conjuring up a leather collar and lead for him, but he took one look, snatched them out of her hand, and ate them, and that was the end of that. But Tiffany was still determined that a walk was in order, and her iron will wore Chappie down to the point where he went along with it just so she'd stop talking at him. They went for a walk, side by side, each grimly determined to outlast the other.

Chappie stared straight ahead and pretended she wasn't with him, which was difficult because she insisted on keeping up a stream of happy chatter, and asking him the same question over and over again until he had to answer her. Tiffany could find topics of good cheer in practically anything, and usually did. Chappie limited himself mostly to grunts and the occasional quiet curse, and glared at everyone they met along the way. People took to shrinking back against the walls as they passed. Some even turned and ran. Particularly when Tiffany tried to stop and chat with them.

"Honestly," Chappie said emphatically for the fifth time, "I don't *need* to be taken for walkies. I agreed to protect you because Chance made me promise, but we could do that just as well behind a locked door. Preferably somewhere not too far from the kitchens. Right now I'm so hungry I could eat an entire horse, including the hooves and the liver. And I hate liver. So would you, if you thought about what function it serves in the body. Why is it that everything that's supposed to be good for you always tastes absolutely foul?"

"Same reason that medicine does," said Tiffany. "How else could you be sure it was doing you good? Everything in the world has to balance out, even symbolically. Perhaps especially symbolically."

"It's thinking like that that makes my head hurt," said Chappie. "Look, can we please stop for a minute? I need to have a good scratch and lick my balls."

"Chappie! You can't do that in front of me!"

"Sorry," said the dog. "Didn't know it was your turn."

He sniggered as Tiffany groaned loudly, and then they both stopped so they could glare at each other thoroughly. Tiffany could feel her voice rising in spite of herself. "Every day, Chappie, I pray none of you is rubbing off on Allen."

"Funny. Every day he prays that part of him could be rubbing— "

"Chappie!"

"I do wish the two of you would just have sex and get it over with. You'd both be a lot less frustrated and distracted, and maybe then you'd stop taking it out on me. You do both know about sex, don't you? I mean, you don't need me to explain the ins and outs to you?"

"I can't believe I'm having this conversation," said Tiffany to the ceiling. "This kind of thing was very definitely not covered in the briefing on the outside world I was given before I left the Academy."

"A pity they didn't teach you more about self-preservation," said the dog, scratching thoroughly at his ribs. "Then I wouldn't have to be here at all."

"I don't need protecting," Tiffany said icily.

"Humans always say that," said Chappie. "And they're always wrong. Show any one of you a path sign-posted DANGER, EVIL FORCES, and SUDDEN DEATH THIS WAY, and there you go charging straight down it. Usually shouting some nonsense about duty and honor, and all those other things that get you killed at an early age. Any truly rational creature would do the sensible thing and head for the nearest horizon in the opposite direction. Personally I'm surprised any of you have the sense to come in out of the rain."

"Look," said Tiffany, "let's not quarrel. I hate quarreling."

"Probably because you're so bad at it. If you really want to make up, find me something to eat. I'm not fussy. Animal, mineral, or vegetable—I'll scarf the lot and gnaw on the bones. Hell, I don't even care if it's still kicking a bit."

"No snacks," Tiffany said firmly. "You're already far too heavy for your size. When I've got a minute, I'll work out a nice diet plan for you, with lots of healthy roughage—"

"Oh, God," said Chappie. "Chance, please come back! All is forgiven! Just come back and save me from this terrible woman! I don't know what he sees in you anyway." He paused and looked at Tiffany's chest. "Well, I guess I do, but frankly it baffles me."

"You care about Allen, don't you?" asked Tiffany.

"Of course," said the dog gruffly. "I approve of him. He'd make a good dog. If I could just wean him off this duty and honor crap, we could probably have a really good life together."

"You understand duty," said the witch. "You said yourself you're only looking after me because you promised Allen you would."

"That's different."

"How?"

"It just is, all right!"

This was a really bad moment for the royal messenger to appear suddenly out of a side passage, right in front of them. Furious at letting himself be distracted from a potential threat, Chappie launched himself at the startled messenger, knocked him flat on his back, stood on his chest, and growled straight into the man's face. All the color went out of the messenger's face, and he actually whimpered, which did a lot to cheer Chappie up.

"You have thirty seconds to tell me who you are and what you want," he said conversationally. "And then I'm going to bite off your nose and swallow it."

"I'm a messenger for the Queen! I've got the scroll right here! Oh, Jesus, I think I've wet myself."

"This is *so* embarrassing," said Tiffany.

"Now you know how I feel," said Chappie.

Sir Vivian got to the Court first, and was surprised and not a little shocked to find that none of his people were present to guard and protect the Queen. The great double doors were locked, but the only person there to open them was the Queen's companion, Cally. Sir Vivian nodded briefly to her as she let him in. He'd never had much to do with Cally. The warrior woman was part of Felicity's inner circle, to which he had very definitely never been privy. Sir Vivian had always been King Harald's man. Still, he approved of Cally in a distant sort of way. She was very protective of the Queen, and the infant King, and took no nonsense from anyone, least of all Harald's people. He gave her plenty of room as he advanced quickly on the Throne and bowed to the Queen.

"Your Majesty, please allow me to send for some of my people. You are not secure here."

"Hardly anyone knows I'm here," said Felicity. "Secrecy has always been my best protection. Besides, I've got you and Cally. I'm sure I can rely on you two to keep order. Now we can't start till everyone's here, so be a good High Commander of the Guard, and go and do something protective somewhere else for a while, so I can think in peace. I've got a lot on my mind."

Sir Vivian sighed resignedly. "Could Your Majesty at least tell me what this is all about?"

"Not really, no. Be patient with your Queen, Sir Vivian. She's making this all up as she goes along. Go and talk with Cally. She's as nervous about this as you are. So go and annoy each other and let me concentrate. That's an order."

Sir Vivian swallowed several icy and cutting remarks that would have made him feel much better, but which somehow he knew would do nothing to improve the situation. He settled for a resigned sigh, bowed formally to the Queen, and walked stiffly back to join Cally by the closed double doors. They stood side by side for a while, not looking at each other.

"You know," Cally said finally, "there are times when I feel Her Royal Majesty's disposition could be greatly improved by a swift kick to the behind."

Sir Vivian laughed briefly, in spite of himself. "I think that's probably true of most royalty. They're never more trouble than when they start thinking. I take it she hasn't discussed this special Court session with you, either?"

"Not so you'd notice. And she usually runs most things by me, even when she knows I won't approve. Perhaps especially then. She knows I always have her best interests at heart. But she put this particular piece of insanity together by herself. All I know for sure is that she's sent out personal invitations to a few select movers and shakers for a private little chat. You're one of them. Though what good she thinks more talking is going to do at this late date . . ."

"Exactly," agreed Sir Vivian. "We're well past the point where talking can change anything. Everyone's drawn their own line in the sand, and now they're just waiting for the first person to put one foot wrong. I wish the Queen would confide in me more. How can I protect her properly if I don't know which directions the threats are likely to be coming from?"

"Don't take it personally," said Cally. "She must trust you, or she wouldn't have called you here to be her defender. There are a lot of other people she could have called who are noticeable here by their absence."

"Does she trust me?" asked Sir Vivian, looking at Cally for the first time. "I've never been sure. After I failed her husband— "

"Of course she trusts you," said Cally, meeting Sir Vivian's cold eyes directly. "You're one of the few people left in the Castle she knows she can depend on. You're the hero of Tower Rouge, the peasants' defender; last I heard there were twenty-seven ballads and eight plays about you. No one blames you for the King's death. Even the Magus couldn't protect the King from whoever killed him. No one in the whole Castle thinks you failed, except you. Believe me, the Queen trusts you. And so do I." She smiled at him suddenly. "I'm something of a fan, you know. Even before I came here with Felicity, I'd read all the books on the Tower Rouge siege. They're best-sellers in Hillsdown. You're as well known there as Prince Rupert and Princess Julia."

Sir Vivian shrugged uncomfortably. "I'm surprised I'm not seen as a villain in Hillsdown."

"We admire warriors," said Cally. "And you've always been one of my special heroes."

Sir Vivian could feel his cheeks warming just a little. "You don't want to believe anything you read in books," he said gruffly. "And the songs are even less accurate. The real hero of Tower Rouge was my brother, Gawaine. I just stayed to keep him company."

"Balls," said Cally. "I've read the accounts written by Hillsdown survivors of that siege. They said you were unstoppable with a sword in your hand. That you never wavered, despite the impossible odds. That they did everything but hack you to pieces, and still they couldn't get you to retreat or surrender. Your name is another word for courage and duty and honor in Hillsdown."

"Just shows what distance can add to a legend," said Sir Vivian.

"Why do you run yourself down like that?" asked Cally. "There are heroes with ballads to their names who haven't done half the things you've done. You held Hob's Gateway when all but you and your brother had fled. No one would have called you a coward if you'd left, too. Any general would have said the Tower couldn't be held against such odds. But you two stood against a whole damned army and would not be moved."

"It wasn't like that."

"All right, what was it like? Really? Tell me. I've always wanted to know."

"It all happened so quickly," said Sir Vivian. Held by Cally's intense gaze, he never even considered not answering. "Everyone else was running. On horse or on foot, leaving behind anything that would slow them down, even their armor and weapons. They called themselves soldiers, and they ran like rabbits. It was the sensible thing to do. Even our commander agreed. One small company couldn't hope to stand against the army that was coming. But Gawaine wouldn't leave. He never even considered it. Because he knew that if the Tower fell, the Hillsdown forces would sweep right through Hob's Gateway and on into the undefended heartland of the Forest Land. Hundreds of small towns and villages at the mercy of a Hillsdown army baying for blood to avenge their recent string of defeats. The slaughter of helpless civilians would have been horrific.

"Gawaine was convinced we could hold the Tower, and whoever held Tower Rouge controlled access to Hob's Gateway. I tried to talk him out of it, but he wouldn't be moved. He knew his duty. So I stayed with him. Because he was my beloved brother, and I couldn't leave him to die alone. And perhaps because I was looking for a good death, a death that mattered, even then. We rigged Tower Rouge with all kinds of deadfalls and booby traps so that there was only one way they could come at us, and then we waited. The waiting was the hardest part.

"And then the Hillsdown force arrived, and it was even bigger than we'd anticipated. The Hillsdown generals had bet everything on one unexpected thrust while the main Forest army was occupied elsewhere. They hadn't allowed for two honest fools who thought duty and honor were more than just words. Gawaine and I said good-bye to each other in case there wasn't time later, and he said he was proud of me. I was always proud of him. And then we took up our positions to meet the first charge with our swords in our hands.

"I don't remember much about the actual fighting. It all blurred together after a while. All the blood and the dying, and the screams. There wasn't time to be brave or to think about what was at stake. We just did what we had to. We'd made sure they could only come at us a few at a time, and we held them off for what seemed like forever. Sometimes I wonder if I'm still there, still fighting, and everything since has been a dream. Gawaine and I fought side by side, even after the ground grew slippery with our own blood. I felt every sword and axe that hit me, but the pain was just something else to fight. I sometimes wonder if I would still have stood my ground if Gawaine had been killed and there was only me left; but I think I would have. In my own way I have always tried to be an honorable man.

"You know the rest. Inspired by word of our stand, the Forest reinforcements broke all records racing across the Land to get to us in time. They threw back the Hillsdown army and the Land was saved, and no one was more surprised than Gawaine and I to find we were still alive at the end of it, and we'd held Tower Rouge and Hob's Gateway. We never thought of ourselves as heroes; just soldiers doing the job we had sworn to do.

"Some years later the King ceded Hob's Gateway to Hillsdown as part of a diplomatic deal to rationalize the border. So what was it all for, really?"

"Duty and honor and courage," said Cally. "What else is there?"

Sir Vivian smiled at her. "I wish I saw things as simply as you."

"Real heroes never see themselves as anything special," said Cally. "That's part of what makes them a hero in the first place. I've been waiting for a chance to talk to you ever since I came here, but what with one thing and another it never seemed the right time. And I didn't want to just seek you out like some simpering fan. I'm sure you've seen enough of that kind in your time."

"I wouldn't have minded," Sir Vivian said slowly. "You have a reputation, too, as a brave and canny warrior, and a selfless defender of the Queen. I'm sure we would have found something to talk about."

"You've always been my hero," said Cally. "Only unlike most of the heroes in the songs, you really did do most of the things they said you did."

"I've done other things, too. Less worthy things."

"I know. Harald told Felicity, and she told me. But even your betrayal arose out of your honor, your need to protect the Land. Harald knew that. That's why he Pardoned you, made you High Commander. Because he needed someone he could trust to care for the Land and protect it. Even from him."

For a long moment Sir Vivian looked at Cally, seeing himself through her eyes. And through her words, allowed himself some of the comfort he had never felt able to justify giving himself. He looked into her steady gaze, approving but not hero-struck, and thought suddenly that she was attractive, in an unconventional way. And her smile, free and open, touched him in a way no other's had since he was a young man being smiled on by Queen Eleanor. He smiled back at Cally, an unexpected warmth from a cold man, and something stirred in both their hearts, and both of them knew it.

"The magic," Cally said finally. "The magic you wielded at Court. That was something new. Impressive. Unexpected. Have you always had it?"

"Perhaps," said Sir Vivian. "But I wasn't able to use it until fairly recently. I never wanted it, you see. I was afraid it would make me like my parents. Most people inherit weak eyes or receding hairlines. I got magic. But magic corrupts. Makes it too easy to get your own way. With magic you never have to earn anything, so you never really value anything. Magic makes it far too easy to treat people as pawns, as things. So I made myself into a soldier, a warrior, and what I won, I won honestly, by my own efforts. So that people would see me for what I was, and not what I was expected to be."

"I know how you feel," said Cally. "I always wanted to be a warrior, ever since I first heard songs of valor as a child, sitting by the family fire. I wanted to be someone, to make a difference in the world. To be important because I earned it, not because of who I happened to be married to. To be someone in my own right, and not what others thought I should be, just because I was a woman. We've both had to fight all our lives just to be seen as ourselves."

"And that's why we've both been so alone," said Sir Vivian. "Because we insisted on living the life we chose, and not what others tried to choose for us. Because we wouldn't compromise, either in what we thought we should be, or in how we wanted others to see us."

"I knew you'd understand," said Cally. "We don't have to be alone, you know."

"No," said Sir Vivian. "Not anymore."

They were both smiling now, their faces so close, they could feel each other's breath. And then they both looked around, startled, as someone knocked loudly on the other side of the closed double doors. They both stepped back and drew their swords, professional soldiers again. Sir Vivian made sure he had room to work in if need be, and then nodded for Cally to unlock and open the doors. She did so, and Sir Robert Hawke almost fell through the gap.

He caught his balance with an effort, drew himself up to his full height, and nodded cheerfully to Sir Vivian. His face was flushed and his eyes were very wide. Sir Vivian knew immediately what was wrong with him, and Sir Robert knew that Sir Vivian knew, and he really didn't care. He was flying. He was dressed in his best, but the loud colors he'd chosen clashed hideously, and his jerkin was buttoned wrong. There were beads of sweat on his forehead, and his hands moved back and forth uneasily until he noticed and stuck them firmly behind his belt.

He'd taken a handful of wake-up pills to counteract the downers he'd taken, and right now the various drugs were fighting it out to see which could screw him up the most thoroughly. He was holding himself together through sheer willpower, ignoring what the pills were doing to his body so he could concentrate on keeping his thoughts clear and focused. He met Sir Vivian's disapproving glare and giggled briefly despite himself. He didn't trust himself to bow successfully, so he just nodded to Sir Vivian and set off across the wide open Court. He held his head high and kept his gaze fixed on the Queen on her Throne. If he could just get to her and find out what this meeting was all about, he'd have something specific to concentrate on, to center his whirling mind. The Court seemed impossibly vast as he stumbled on, like those rooms in uneasy dreams where the far wall seems to recede endlessly away. It was getting hard to tell left from right or forward from backward, and his eyes were so intent and focused now that they ached.

He stopped at what he hoped was a respectful distance from the Throne, and managed a fairly normal bow, though the effort brought fresh beads of sweat popping out on his brow. He smiled at the Queen, hoping it looked more normal than it felt. He was scared. He'd never felt so out of control before. He'd taken far too many pills, and his body was too weakened by long abuse to be able to cope. It was like trying to ride a horse that had suddenly gone mad. And all the time his chemically stimulated thoughts were dashing frantically back and forth inside his head, bouncing off the walls of his skull, producing and discarding desperate plans over and over again, while his mouth struggled with a simple greeting to the Queen. He felt horribly helpless, trapped inside a body that no longer obeyed him, while his thoughts felt like somebody else's. His mind was slowly slipping its moorings, and drifting away on a dark, dark sea.

"Thank you for coming on such short notice, Sir Robert," said the Queen. Her voice sounded far away, as though it were underwater. "I have also sent for your associates, the three putative Landsgraves, though I'm not sure if they'll be able to join us. Apparently no one's seen hide nor hair of them in some time."

"Don't know where they are myself just now," said Sir Robert, swaying slightly on his feet. "Still, they're no great loss. Dangerous, treacherous scum. Always plotting something. You wouldn't believe what they wanted me to do. Completely untrustworthy. Unlike me, of course. Work my balls off for the Land. For the people. Even deal with those I can't stand, like those Landsgraves. If you only knew what I saved you from by dealing with those scumbags. Taking their money, listening to their stupid, treacherous plans . . ."

He heard his voice running on, and couldn't stop it. His mind was lagging dangerously behind his mouth. By the time he realized he was admitting not only to links with traitors but knowledge of their plans, it was already too late. He forced his mouth shut, his hands clenching into fists as he fought for self-control, his fingernails digging deep enough into his palms to draw blood. The pain helped to steady him a little, until the shock hit him. He'd just given the Queen enough cause to have him dragged away and examined under truthspell. And once they started digging for secrets, they'd never stop. Why had he come here? He should never have come here. Not in this condition. He'd betrayed himself, and all the people who believed in him, through his own damned weakness. The Queen leaned forward on her Throne and looked at him closely. Sir Robert wondered if he'd have the strength of will to take his own life rather than betray his cause.

"Go home, Sir Robert," Felicity said finally. "Go home. You're not well."

Sir Robert flushed with shame, and couldn't bring himself to do anything more than nod in agreement.

There was a new knocking at the double doors, and Cally opened them to admit the witch Tiffany and the dog Chappie. Tiffany brushed straight past Cally and Sir Vivian, striding across the Court with Chappie at her side. She took up a determined stance right before the Queen, completely ignoring Sir Robert, and launched right into the speech she'd been preparing all the way to Court.

"I got here as fast as I could, Your Majesty. You mustn't stay here. It's not safe for you. Powerful magics are stirring somewhere in the Castle. I can feel them, though as yet something prevents me from Seeing their actual location or nature. You must guard yourself. I sense danger, terrible danger."

"She's right," growled Chappie. "Something bad's coming. I can almost smell it."

"Calm yourself, my friends," said the Queen. "I'm as safe here as anywhere. And I have summoned the Magus to attend this Court, too."

Tiffany sniffed loudly. "I don't trust him."

Felicity smiled. "No one does, dear, but he is terribly useful. Especially at moments like this."

Another knocking was heard, and the doors opened to admit Allen Chance, the Questor. Tiffany cried out his name and ran back across the Court to take him in her arms, wrapping him in a happy hug that squeezed all the breath right out of him. Chappie romped around them, tail wagging furiously, jumping up at them both until Chance freed a hand to pat him on the head and tug at his ear.

"I was so worried about you!" said Tiffany. "I could feel you drawing closer and closer to horrible danger, but you were too far away for me to be able to warn you!"

"It's all right, Tiff," said Chance, carefully disengaging himself from her while very conscious of the Queen's amused gaze. "We'll talk later. Right now I have important information for the Queen."

He approached the Throne, Tiffany and Chappie sticking close beside him, bowed formally to Felicity, and ignored Sir Robert after a quick glance. "Your Majesty, I have to report that Jericho Lament, the Walking Man, together with Captains Hawk and Fisher and the Seneschal, have broached the Magus' wards and entered the Inverted Cathedral."

"I knew something bad was happening!" said Tiffany. "Oh, Allen, how could you have let them do something so stupid?"

Chance looked at her. "One doesn't say no to the Walking Man, Tiff. Trust me, one just doesn't. Besides, someone had to go inside and take a look eventually, and personally I'd back Lament and Hawk and Fisher against anything up to and including a demon army. In fact, I think I'd feel sorry for the demons. No, Tiff, whatever they find, I'm sure they're eminently qualified to deal with it."

"Is this the magical upheaval you were sensing?" the Queen asked Tiffany. "Is this the threat you were worried about?"

The young witch scowled, shaking her head slowly. "No, I don't think so. If feels closer than that."

The Queen looked sharply at Chance. "You should have consulted with me before allowing Captains Hawk and Fisher to enter the Inverted Cathedral. I needed them here. I'm going to need all the support I can muster for this meeting, considering whom I've invited."

"I am Your Majesty's protector now and always," said Chance. "And I see Sir Vivian's here, too. I assure you, you will be quite safe in our hands."

"Hey, don't forget me!" said Cally.

"I wouldn't know how," Chance said generously.

The Queen could see where that was going, and butted in quickly. "I have heard that Captains Hawk and Fisher were actually attacked earlier even though they were under my express protection. Do you know anything of this, Sir Questor? In particular, who might be behind such an outrageous attack? Hawk and Fisher represent my authority while they are investigating my husband's death, and an attack on them is an attack on me. I also require to know why you didn't inform me of this outrage as soon as it happened. Well?"

There was a pause as everyone looked at everyone else. No one wanted to be the first to say what they were all thinking. In the end Sir Robert spoke up, on the grounds that he couldn't be in more trouble if he tried.

"We all knew, Your Majesty, but nobody wanted to be the one to point the finger. Given that there is no real evidence—"

"Who did it?" demanded the Queen, leaning forward angrily. "Who would dare strike at me in this way?"

"I'm sorry," said Sir Robert, "but the hand behind the attack had to be your father's. No one else could, or would, have dared such an affront to your authority."

Felicity sank slowly back into her Throne. "Damn. I didn't want to think he'd be that blatant. I have sent for him. In fact, he was the first name on my list. I'm surprised he's not already here. He does so hate to miss out on things."

"Perhaps he feels he is no longer bound to obey Your Majesty's instructions," said Chance carefully.

"Right," said Sir Robert, hanging on to clarity by his fingertips. "If he was going to be here, he'd be here by now."

"Who else is there still to come?" asked Tiffany.

"Just the Magus." Felicity scowled, and drummed her fingers on the arm of her Throne. "Where the hell is the man when I need him?"

"Right here," said the Magus reproachfully. "There's no need to shout, I'm not deaf."

Everyone jumped a little, startled by the Magus' sudden appearance before the Throne. He was standing right beside Sir Robert, who was too out of it to be shocked and just stared at the Magus owlishly. Chappie growled loudly, and Chance had to grab him quickly by the ear to hold him back. Tiffany raised one of her hands in a warding gesture that the Magus didn't even bother to acknowledge. Cally and Sir Vivian left the double doors and hurried forward, swords in hand. The Magus smiled amiably about him. He looked much as he always did, except that perhaps his face and eyes were just a little less vague than usual.

"What is it this time, Your Majesty?" he asked mildly. "I'm really very busy just at the moment."

"Busy at what?" asked the Shaman, appearing suddenly beside the Magus, the Creature crouching at his side. Everyone except the Magus jumped again. Cally and Sir Vivian moved quickly to stand on either side of the Throne, glaring at the new arrivals with their swords at the ready. It was getting rather crowded around the Throne now, but no one had any intention of backing down to anyone else. The Magus and the Shaman regarded each other coldly while the Queen glared at both of them.

"I didn't summon you to my Court, Sir Shaman."

"I go where I choose," said the Shaman in his rough, cracked voice. "You know that. I'm here because it's necessary. Nothing less would bring me to this place."

By now Chance, Tiffany, and Chappie had taken up positions before the Throne, too. Chappie and the Creature snarled at each other.

"That abomination is dangerous," Sir Vivian told the Shaman. "I demand that you remove it from this Court. Or we'll do it the hard way."

"You don't object to the Magus' cloak," said the Shaman.

"Well, that's not alive," said Cally.

"Shows how much you know," said the Shaman. "That cloak is just as alive and twice as dangerous as my poor Creature. It doesn't matter anyway. Wherever I go, the Creature goes, too. I'd feel far too vulnerable in this Castle without my protector. Everyone needs someone they can depend on. He's quite safe as long as I am."

"Don't anyone mind what I think," said Felicity. "I'm only the Queen."

"Exactly," said the Shaman. He turned his clay-marked face to glare fiercely at the Magus, who didn't so much as bat an eye. The Shaman's voice was cold and measured and very dangerous now. "You're the reason I'm here, Magus. You and that bloody Rift you opened. You have to shut it down. Right now. It's a danger to the whole Forest Kingdom. All the time it's operating, it's leaking Wild Magic into the world."

"Yes," said the Magus. "It is."

"You admit it?" asked the Shaman. "Your monstrous creation is undermining the very structure of our reality!"

"Quite correct," said the Magus, entirely unmoved by the Shaman's fury, and the shocked and startled faces around him. "Such leakage from the Rift is a necessary by-product. The only alternative would be to shut down the Rift. Permanently. But is everyone here ready to shut down something so massively useful? Is the Forest Kingdom ready to go back to being just a backwater cousin again? To give up all its new comforts and scientific advances? Are the people willing to be cut off from the current flow of political beliefs and philosophies?" He looked unhurriedly about him, taking in their torn, undecided faces. "You've all come such a long way since I opened the Rift and made trade between north and south practical. Surely you don't really wish to become barbarians again, based on the fears of a scaremongering hedge wizard with a grudge?"

"I thought you believed in the people!" Sir Robert said angrily to the Shaman, forcing the words past numb lips. "Shut down the Rift and you cut off all democratic support from the south! You'd have us betray everything we believe in over a little magical pollution? There's always been *some* Wild Magic in the Land."

"Never this much," said the Shaman, matching Sir Robert glare for glare. "If the Rift's continuing pollution isn't stopped, Wild Magic will grow and spread until it's powerful enough to undermine and then destroy all the world. And anything we might recognize as reality. Have you all forgotten the horror of the long night so soon? Would you have the Blue Moon back again, shining its awful light over all the Kingdom?"

"The Blue Moon's return is just a rumor," said the Queen slowly. "And there's no sign of the long night spreading. The Darkwood's boundaries haven't moved an inch in twelve years. I have people stationed there, watching the Darkwood constantly."

"She's right," said Chance. "I was there just recently. Nothing's changed. The long night is quiet, and there's no sign anywhere that the demons are on the move. And none of our magic-users have produced any evidence that the Blue Moon is coming back."

"I Saw the Darkwood return in a vision," said Tiffany.

"There could be many interpretations to such a vision," said the Magus smoothly. "Don't concern yourself over dreams, my child."

"Wild Magic has always been bad news for the Forest," said Sir Vivian in his coldest voice. "Wild Magic, High

Magic, Chaos Magic, none of it worth the problems it brings. The Wild Magic of the long night would have destroyed us all had it not been for Prince Rupert and Princess Julia. In the end it's always people who solve problems, not magic."

"Try and concentrate on the matter at hand, Vivian," snapped the Shaman. "The Rift is unbalancing the natural order in the world. I can feel it. Something awful is sitting at the threshold of our world, waiting to come through and trample on everything we believe in and care for. I lived through the long night. Saw good men and women die, over and over. I won't stand aside and see that happen again. If you won't shut down the Rift, Magus, I will."

"Will you really?" asked the Magus softly. "Now that is interesting. I hadn't realized you were so powerful. But then, there's a lot about you that people don't know, isn't there, sir Shaman?"

The Shaman said nothing, his fierce eyes locked on the Magus'. Everyone else backed away a few paces, even the Creature. They could all feel a magical presence building right there in the Court between the Shaman and the Magus, a rising potentiality of magic and violence and power building, building, ready to be unleashed. The two men seemed suddenly larger, realer, than they had been only moments before. Sir Vivian could feel his own magic stirring within him, eager to be let loose, and he fought it down.

"So you're finally ready to reveal yourself," said the Magus to the Shaman. "Do you really think you can stop me?"

"I learned much in my long years as a hermit," responded the Shaman. "You'd be surprised what I can do if I set my mind to it."

"It's not too late to stop this," said the Magus, his voice the very epitome of calm and reason. "Wild Magic isn't necessarily a bad thing except to the established order. It doesn't take sides. Maybe the Forest Kingdom could do with a little chaos, to shake things up, to bring about social and political change. You of all people should know that real, lasting change is only ever brought about by sacrifice."

"Your words are just a distraction," said the Shaman. "Wild Magic is a threat to human reason. To rationality itself. What's coming has nothing to do with how we live, it wants to change all the rules and create a new world where humanity might not even be able to exist. I've felt the effects of Wild Magic during the long night. Seen its horrors close up. You weren't here when the Darkwood came flooding over all the Land . . . or were you?"

"Was the Blue Moon really such a bad thing?" the Magus asked. "Look at all the heroes the Demon War produced. All the deeds of courage and self-sacrifice. Having a common enemy to fight against brought out the best in people. All right, a lot of people died, but people always die. For some people the long night was the making of them, a second chance they might never have found for themselves. Isn't that right, Sir Vivian?"

Sir Vivian looked briefly at Cally, then looked away. "Things were clearer then," he said thoughtfully. "You knew where you were. There was good and bad, light and dark . . . Our every decision took on mythical proportions. Everything's been so confused since then. And the darkness did make heroes out of men who might otherwise have just stumbled through their lives, but the price was too high. No amount of heroes was worth all the innocents who died horribly at the hands of demons. The long night must never come again, while we have strength in our bodies to prevent it. No matter what it costs us."

"King John would have shut down the Rift," the Shaman pointed out. "He knew all about poisoned gifts."

"Yes," said the Magus. "He did, didn't he? Such a pity he's not here now. But then, all he ever really knew was how to die for his country. Not how to put things right."

"You don't talk about the King," snapped Sir Robert, lurching forward to glare right into the Magus' face. "You know nothing about him. He led us against the demons. He was a hero."

"Only because he died," said the Magus. "Heroes are so much more convincing when they're dead. Mostly because it's so much easier to forget the faults of the nobly fallen. Look at you, for example, Sir Robert. A hero in the Demon

War and a savior of the Land, but what are you now? A minor functionary with a title that no one respects, chasing dreams of democracy. Relying on pills to wake you up, pills to get you through your day, and more pills so you can sleep at night. How far have you fallen, Robert Hawke? But you could still be what you used to be. Would you like that? Of course you would. Allow me to demonstrate, Queen Felicity, that the Wild Magic can be put to good use, as well as evil. Observe . . ."

He gestured grandly at Sir Robert, who bent over suddenly, convulsing and crying out in pain and shock as magic shot through his veins and exploded in his blood. All the drugs he'd dosed himself with over the years seemed to come shooting forth all at once as he vomited violently, his whole body shaking with the power of it. Sweat burst out of his pores, smelling rank and acid, as all traces of his drugs left his body by the quickest route. Everyone before the Throne drew back to give him plenty of room as the unpleasant purge proceeded. At the end he was on all fours before his Queen, wiping at his wet mouth with a shaking hand, feeling and smelling absolutely foul, but clear-eyed and sharp-minded for the first time in a long time. He was still panting roughly with the strain of what he'd been through as he rose slowly to his feet, but all his old authority and command was back in his voice as he glared at the Magus.

"What have you done to me?" he demanded.

"What you didn't have the strength of will to do for yourself." The Magus gestured casually and all the foulness Sir Robert's body had thrown out was suddenly gone. "The unpleasantness is only fleeting, I assure you. You are now pure in body, if not in spirit, and all your old strength is yours again. What will you do with it, I wonder? Well? Aren't you going to say thank you?"

"I don't know," said Sir Robert. "I haven't seen the price tag yet. Is this a gift, or a bribe?"

The Magus shook his head sadly. "Still so cynical. Perhaps a further demonstration is in order to show what wonders the Wild Magic can perform. Let me turn back the clock for you, right before your eyes. Let me make whole again what time has broken. Observe."

He clapped his hands once, and Sir Robert's old comrade in arms, Ennis Page, was suddenly standing beside him. Old before his time, trembling in every spindly limb, Page blinked confusedly about him, and then cried out as Magus gestured sharply. The years fled Page's face in a moment, and his body filled out into the muscular bulk of his prime. The bones in his back cracked loudly as he straightened up for the first time in years. His eyes were sharp and clear again, his mouth firm, all the confusion swept from his thoughts like so many clinging cobwebs. His old sword hung from his hip, and he looked quickly around the Court with his old warrior's clarity. Sir Robert saw his old friend returned, and his heart was so full, he thought it would burst. He tried to say something to Page but was stopped with a look.

"Explanations can wait," Page said crisply. "Just point me at the villains."

"Hell," said Sir Robert, grinning fiercely. "Just pick a direction."

They laughed briefly together, two fighting men in their prime again, ready for anything.

"You see?" said the Magus mildly. "This is what the Wild Magic can do, to heal as well as change. The Wild Magic is a thing of wonders and miracles as well as darkness."

"No need to bother with the sales pitch," said Sir Robert. "We're convinced."

"Then you must stand with me," said the Magus. "Stop these people from trying to close down the Rift. I am very powerful, but even I need someone to guard my back. I can't be everywhere at once, so I require allies. Heroes such as yourself and Ennis Page. You know I'm right, Sir Robert. Your politics, your dreams of a better future for all, derive from the Rift. If the Queen forces its closure, everything you believe in will be lost to you forever."

Sir Robert looked at him for a long moment. "What do you want me to do, sir Magus?"

"Stop anyone who tries to stop me."

"You mean kill them?"

"If necessary, yes."

"Starting with the people here? Sir Vivian and the Questor, and Cally?"

"I can handle the magicians," said the Magus. "Surely you and your friend can handle the others. Or is your reputation merely legend after all?"

Sir Robert looked at Ennis, who shrugged easily. "I haven't got a clue what's going on here, Rob. You decide and I'll follow."

"Just like old times," said Sir Robert. He turned to the Magus. "And if I won't do what you want? If I decide I must follow my heart and my conscience, as I have always tried to do? What then, sir Magus?"

"Then you should consider that what the Wild Magic has given, it can also take back."

Sir Robert smiled mirthlessly. "Somehow I just knew you were going to say that. That's all you understand, isn't it, sorcerer? The carrot and the stick. Reward with one hand and threaten with the other. You'd have made a fine politician, sir Magus. But this isn't a time for politics. If you'd appealed to my patriotism, asked me to defend the Rift for the good of the Land and its people, I might just have gone along with you. There's a part of me that's really missed being a hero. But you don't understand about things like heart and conscience, do you? All you understand is threats and power.

"Well, thanks to you I'm the man I used to be, and my mind is wonderfully clear. And I say to hell with you. The Wild Magic is, was, and always will be a threat to everything that men of good will hold dear. I lived through the long night while many of my friends and comrades did not. I'll do whatever it takes to stop the Blue Moon coming round again. If the Rift really is doing what the Shaman claims, it's a sword hanging over all our heads. Shut it down, Magus, or we'll make you shut it down. And to hell with your gifts and your threats."

"That's my old Hawke," said Ennis Page. "I'm a little confused as to how much things have changed while I was not myself, but the present situation seems clear enough.

Typical sorcerer, thinking it all comes down to power. A soldier knows better. A man either has his loyalty and his honor, or he is not a man. The Throne is the Throne no matter who happens to be sitting on it, and I have sworn my life to defending it from all enemies. And especially from vicious little shits like you, Magus. So take back your gift if you wish, sorcerer; but you'd better be bloody quick with your spell, or I swear I'll hang on long enough to spill your tripe on the floor."

"Damn right," said Sir Robert. "We're Prince Rupert's men, and no one messes with us and lives to boast of it."

"Ah, well," said the Magus. "It was worth a try."

"How dare you?" thundered the Queen, and the cold, fierce fury in her voice drew all eyes back to her. "How dare you treat my people like this, sorcerer? They are my subjects, under my protection, not your playthings! Threaten harm to any one of them again, and I'll—"

"Oh, shut up," interrupted the Magus. "Or I'll do something amusing to you."

And in that moment of unchecked temper he lost whatever influence he might have had. Chance, Sir Vivian, and Cally moved quickly together to form a living shield between the Queen and the Magus. Chappie crouched before them, growling fiercely at the sorcerer. Sir Robert and Ennis Page drew their swords. Tiffany raised her hands in a gesture of summoning. The Shaman raised his hands, too, while the Creature crouched beside him, flexing his claws. The Magus considered them all and smiled tiredly.

"You never learn, do you? What is steel and conjuring and numbers against the Wild Magic? You have no idea of what I am and what I can do. What I have had to do in years gone past. I have seen things that would blast the reason from your eyes and done things you would never dare to consider, even in your worst nightmares. I am the Magus, and only I know what is truly necessary. I have come a long, hard way to reach this place and this time, and I will not see my long-laid plans thwarted by a few small-minded people. You know nothing. You are nothing. I am the Magus, and I will do what I will do."

Tiffany drew her power about her, and it snapped and

crackled on the air as she rose up above the Magus. Lightning flashed about her hands as she hung high in the air,
then the Magus looked at her and all her rising magic was
snuffed out in a moment, like a doused candle flame. She
fell out of the air like a stunned bird, and Chance was
quickly there to catch her. The impact drove them both to
the floor, and Tiffany clung to Chance, wide-eyed and shaking, all her power ripped from her in a moment. The Magus
laughed softly.

"Poor little Tiffany. So sure in her power that she never
thought to wonder where it might be coming from. Ever
since you came to the Castle, little witch, you have been
channeling another's power. You're quite gifted in your
own right, and someday you might be powerful indeed. But
right now you're just another witch, and I always knew
there was no way you could wield the power you showed
without burning yourself up in the process. Only a sorcerer
could have driven the killing shadows from the Court that
day. Once I realized that, it was easy to uncover the hidden
link connecting you to the Mother Witch of your Academy.
The sorceress who founded it and runs things from her
hidden cell. It was her magic you were channeling, all unknowingly, and now that I have severed that link, you're
just another witch. And your little magics aren't nearly
enough to stop a creature like me. So be a good little girl
and sit this one out. Or I'll hurt you."

Chappie was suddenly there, standing defiantly between
Tiffany and the Magus, showing all his teeth in a terrible
grin. "Don't touch her, you bastard."

"Oh, please," said the Magus. "I don't have time for
this."

"I swore to protect her," said Chappie. "And I will. To
get to her, you have to get past me."

"I have always found you a very tiresome animal," said
the Magus. "Pets should know their place."

A bolt of black lightning blasted from his hand, only to
fade away to nothing before it could get anywhere near the
dog. Chappie laughed nastily.

"I'm the High Warlock's dog, idiot. You might wield

magic, but I *am* magic. And now I'm going to bite your balls off."

"What an edifying spectacle to come across in a Royal Court," said Duke Alric. "You really have let things go to the dogs, Felicity."

Everyone looked around sharply as the Starlight Duke walked slowly toward them. Behind him the double doors stood wide open, and a small army of soldiers filed quickly through, fanning out past the Duke to take up strategic positions covering the whole Court. There were dozens of them, all wearing Forest uniforms, but they all looked to the Duke of Hillsdown for their orders. By the time they were all in, they filled half the Court, swords and axes at the ready in their hands, silently watching the Duke as he made his painful way across the Court to confront his daughter, the Queen. He stopped a respectful distance short of the people clustered before the Throne, and ignored them all to fix his daughter with a steady gaze. The creaks and shiftings of his metal and leather bracings sounded loud in the strained quiet of the Court.

"You see, Felicity?" asked the Duke. "I told you it would come to this. You're not in control anymore. Even your closest defenders squabble amongst themselves. These armed men were once your soldiers, but now they are mine. They're all mercenaries, you see, serving the Forest Throne for money, not loyalty, and I have made them a substantially better offer."

"You've turned my own people against me?" the Queen asked.

"They were never really yours. A mercenary will always go where the money is. And they've rather lost faith in your ability to pay them. So I am now taking over for the good of everyone. I never intended to launch an invasion from outside the Forest Kingdom. Far too many people would have died—on both sides. No, I came here into the hands of my enemies and simply waited for the right moment. And now my newly bought army will put me into the seat of power with a minimum of bloodshed. Get off that Throne, Felicity. I need to sit down. My back's killing me."

"Not all my army are mercenaries," said the Queen. "Most are still loyal to the Throne and to me."

"By the time they discover what's happened, it will all be over," said the Duke easily. "And I will be installed as the new King of the Forest and Hillsdown. Technically I'll just be Regent here, ruling in Stephen's name until he comes of age, but it all amounts to the same thing. I shall rule here and make the Kingdom strong again."

"The people will never accept this," said Chance. "They'll never accept you."

"Which people?" queried the Duke. "The Forest people or the Hillsdown immigrants or the Redhart communities? They might have risen up in support of Harald, that hero of the Demon War, but not, I think, for a foreign-born Queen. In the end the people will do what the army tells them. And the army will follow whoever's in charge. That's their job. Of course, certain subversive elements will have to be purged from my army; there are always a few fools determined to be heroes or martyrs. But my mercenaries will weed them out quite efficiently. A few mass public executions should make my position quite clear. And after that, things will go on as they did before for most people, and they will learn to do as they're told by a strong King. Bring the child forward."

One of the soldiers came to stand beside the Duke. In his arms he carried a sleeping child, his small form wrapped in a blanket, and the Queen cried out and half rose from her Throne as she recognized the child.

"Stephen! That's my son! What have you done to him?"

"Calm yourself, daughter. And sit down. You don't want to make my mercenaries jumpy, do you? That's better. The child is fine. Do you think I would harm my own grandson? He's just been given a little something so he'll sleep till this is over."

"But I left him guarded! How . . . ?"

"The gentleman at my side with my grandson in his arms is called Snare. My very own personal magic-user. Not actually a sorcerer, but well on his way. I brought him here disguised as just another soldier, and no one noticed. He killed your guards with a single spell and took your son away. And now he guards Stephen against any physical and magical attempt to retrieve him. Stephen is mine now, and I will raise my grandson to be a real King. A true ruler of the Forest and Hillsdown, united again into one great country as it was always meant to be."

"You didn't do such a good job of raising your daughters, did you?" asked Cally. "They all turned against you in the end. What makes you think you'll do any better with a boy?"

"I have learned from my mistakes," said the Duke. He looked coldly at Felicity. "You couldn't protect Stephen; that in itself is enough to prove you are not worthy to be Queen. You should have had all my people checked out for hidden treachery. Did you really think I would deliver myself into the hands of my enemies unprotected? You're not fit to rule, Felicity. It's as simple as that. I will silence all the squabbling in your Court and put an end to all this democracy nonsense. Power belongs to those strong enough to take and hold it. My grandson will be King, and by the time he comes into his power, I will have seen to it that his enemies are dead."

All the people before the Throne, who had been at each other's throats only moments before, now stood shoulder to shoulder facing the Duke, united in a common cause against a common enemy. Whatever their varying beliefs, causes, or intentions, none of them had any intention of bowing down to the Starlight Duke. Everything else could wait. A few quick looks among them was all it took to confirm that, but politician that he was, Sir Robert still felt the need to put it into words.

"This is our Court and our Land, Duke Alric, and we will all fight to the death in their defense."

There was a general murmur of agreement from the other defenders. The Shaman stepped forward to glare directly at the Duke. "This is my home, and I will not see it threatened. Stand down, Alric, or I swear I'll see your head stuck on a pike."

The Starlight Duke just sniffed briefly. He looked unhurriedly from one determined face to the next, settling at last on the Magus. "Well, sorcerer? Do you have no brave

speech to make? No last words of defiance? No? I thought
not. I never did believe all the things they said about you.
But then, I've always known the value of a good bluff.
You've done nothing of note since you opened the Rift.
My spies' reports were very clear on that. Could it be you
burned yourself out casting such a magnificent spell? It
doesn't matter. I am protected from all magical attacks by
the Candlemass Charm. And I have enough armed men
here to drag even you down. So." The Duke looked back
at his army of mercenaries, poised and waiting for his word.
"Kill them. Except for my errant daughter Felicity, kill
them all."

The mercenaries surged forward, hundreds of armed men
yelling battle chants and war cries. And Allen Chance went
forward to meet them, his father's great double-headed war
axe in his hands. He swung the massive blades as though
they were weightless, and the first mercenaries to reach him
died immediately, thrown back bloody and broken. Chance
swung his axe with both hands, and the blades sheared
through flesh and bone and armor, killing every man who
came against him. The sound of steel chopping through
flesh was the sound of simple butchery, and the floor ran
thick with blood. The Questor's eyes and his wide smile
were both very cold now, and to those there who remembered, he looked very much like his late father indeed.

But he was only one man, and the tide of mercenaries
swept past him like the sea crashing past a stubborn rock.
Chappie stayed with Tiffany. His heart ached to be with
his friend, but he had sworn to protect the witch. Tiffany's
faith in her magic had been crushed by the Magus' casual
words, but faced with an immediate threat to all she held
dear, her old Academy training reasserted itself, and she
forced a calm upon her thoughts. She reached deep inside
for her magic, her old familiar power, and it responded
immediately. Not nearly the powerful force she had grown
used to wielding, but a sharp and potent magic all the same.

Tiffany sent out her will against the advancing mercenaries, and those nearest fell immediately asleep, crashing to
the floor. More and more fell as they entered her field of
influence, piling up before her. A sharp stabbing pain began

in Tiffany's left temple, and a thin trail of blood ran from one nostril. Cut off from her unexpected power source, she was just a witch now, and the forces she was wielding took a harsh toll from her. It didn't matter. She had a job to do, and she would not be found wanting.

A handful of mercenaries stopped outside the reach of her spell, and drew throwing daggers. Chappie charged forward and hit them like a battering ram, scattering the soldiers and throwing them to the floor. And then he was among them, ripping out their throats with his terrible jaws. He glared about him, shaking his head angrily, blood drops flying from his crimson mouth as he looked for more threats. A dozen mercenaries came at him with swords and axes, and he howled happily as he danced among them, tearing at their legs and bellies, moving impossibly quickly for a dog of his great size.

Tiffany called to the Magus to restore her link to the Mother Witch, but he was standing to one side, still and silent, watching the bloody fury about him but not interfering. His cloak stirred restlessly, but the Magus cast no spells, even as the first mercenaries drew near him. His thoughts seemed to be elsewhere, concentrating on something else, something that mattered more to him than the simple struggle of humans.

Cally and Sir Vivian fought side by side, wielding their swords with the deadly skills of long experience. They worked well in concert, as though they belonged together. Hardened mercenaries came at them in waves, and not one of them could get anywhere near the warrior woman and the hero of Tower Rouge. Cally and Sir Vivian stamped and thrust, their blades whirling in shining arcs too fast for the human eye to follow, and no one could stand against them. The dead and the dying piled up around them, and still they fought, cutting down their enemies with terrible ease. Cally grinned fiercely as she fought, happy to be doing what she was born to do, and even Sir Vivian was smiling. It had been a long time since they'd faced a threat worthy of their expertise, and after struggling with the shadowy enemies of politics for so long, simple violence like this was a relief and a happy release. For all the odds against him,

Sir Vivian felt strangely at peace. It had been far too long since he'd fought beside someone he could count on to match his skill. Not since his brother, Gawaine, in fact. He glanced across at Cally, and she grinned back.

"So, Vivian, what are you doing after the massacre?"

"Taking you out for a very large drink," said Sir Vivian, surprising himself.

"Sounds like a plan to me," said Cally. "And afterward, I'll jump your bones till they rattle."

"Where have you been all my life?" asked Sir Vivian, and they both laughed as they slaughtered more mercenaries.

Two soldiers burst past the defenders and threw themselves at the preoccupied Magus. The Duke had armed them with ancient silver arthames, long, slender witch daggers with powerful runes etched into the blades. But before they could reach the Magus, his huge black cloak detached itself from his shoulders and flapped through the air like a bat. It fell upon the mercenaries, enveloping them in its dark folds. The two men screamed as the cloak crushed the life out of them with one powerful constriction. Blood and other things dropped out of the bottom of the cloak as it briefly fed, and then it dropped the ruined bodies on the scarlet floor and flapped back to hover beside the Magus, ready for more prey to approach.

Sir Robert Hawke swung his sword with unmatchable skill and cut a wide path through the mercenaries. In his younger days he was literally unbeatable with a sword in his hand, and with his strength and health restored there wasn't a man in the Court who could stand against him. The mercenaries tried to bring him down through sheer force of numbers, but his sword was seemingly everywhere at once, parrying and thrusting and cutting, beating down the most powerful defenses as though they weren't even there. He was laughing as he fought, even in the face of such appalling odds. It felt good to be himself again, fighting a clear enemy for obvious reason; and these odds were nothing to those he'd faced in the Demon War. And Ennis Page, young and strong and whole again, guarded Sir Robert's back and cut down those few who managed to get past him.

"Just like old times," Page said cheerfully. "Overwhelming odds, an impossible situation, and the whole fate of the Kingdom in our hands. I love it!"

"Hell, this is amateur hour," said Sir Robert. "We fought demons in those days."

"After we've finished here," said Page, pausing to run through one mercenary, jerk his sword free, and gut another, "what say we kill the Magus? Just on general principles."

"Let's," said Sir Robert. "I never liked him."

The Shaman stood beside the Throne, scowling thoughtfully as his Creature fell upon the attacking mercenaries with horrible glee. The Creature fought like an animal, claws and fangs dripping blood, and now and then he used his unnatural strength to tear a man literally limb from limb. Swords and axes cut at him, but he never seemed to feel them, and his wounds never bled for long. The Shaman watched the tide of battle closely. Even now he was reluctant to reveal the true extent of his powers, but when a handful of mercenaries came rushing toward the Throne, the Shaman sighed briefly and called the power of the Forest about him. He shaped it and thrust it against his enemies, and the mercenaries screamed shrilly as they stumbled to a halt, the Forest already moving within them. Bark swept over their skin, and thorny branches thrust out of their eyes and mouths, tearing through their insides. Soon there were only a dozen spindly trees standing before the Throne, lightly rooted in the wooden floor. The Shaman took no pleasure in the sight. He'd seen too many men die in his time. He reached over to pat the Queen reassuringly on the arm.

"Don't worry, my dear. We'll see you're safe. Scum like this are no match for such as us."

"Please," said Felicity. "Help my son. Your magic is different. Can't you get my son back from Snare?"

"I already tried," said the Shaman, frowning. "Snare appears to be warded against any form of magical attack. And I am really not much more than a glorified hedge wizard with a few nasty tricks. You need the Magus."

"You try talking to him," said the Queen disgustedly. "He won't listen to me."

"When the battle's over, and you and your Throne are safe," said the Shaman, "you can be sure I intend to have some very sharp words with him."

All across the Court the fight was slowing down. The mercenaries had realized they were losing, and that an awful lot of them were dead. They began to fall back. The Duke had promised them a simple, relatively bloodless coup, with hardly any risk. Nothing had been said about facing magic and heroes out of legend. But they couldn't afford to lose. As traitors, they'd probably all be hanged. None of them trusted the Duke to protect them. So they turned to Snare and the plan they'd quietly arranged earlier, just in case. Because mercenaries are an inherently suspicious and practical breed. Snare got the nod and brought the whole fight to a halt by holding the sleeping child Stephen above his head and shouting, "Stop! Everyone stop fighting right now, or the boy King dies!"

Everyone stopped. In ones and twos they disengaged, lowered their weapons, and backed away from each other. All eyes were on the magician Snare now as he slowly lowered the child and cradled him in his arms again. Snare looked about him and then smiled unpleasantly.

"That's better. Everyone be sensible now. I hold the trump card, and I'm not afraid to sacrifice it. I want to see all the Queen's defenders put down their weapons, surrender, and kneel to me. Or I'll kill the boy . . . inch by inch."

Felicity looked in horror at the Duke. "You'd allow the murder of your own grandson?"

"No," said the Duke. "No, I wouldn't. Snare, give me the child! This was never part of my plan."

"It was always part of *my* plan," said Snare. "I knew I couldn't count on you to be strong when it mattered. Now tell everyone to do what I say. The child means nothing to me. I will kill it if I have to."

"Give me the child!" said the Duke. "That's an order!"

"Oh, be quiet," said Snare. "You're getting soft, old man. Let me handle this and we can still win."

Sir Vivian summoned up all his magic, compressed it into a single deadly bolt, and threw it at Snare, hoping to catch him off guard. But his magic just rebounded from Snare's

wards, and flew back to strike at Sir Vivian. He was thrown
to the ground by the impact of his own magic, and lay
there groaning, unable to rise. Cally was immediately there,
crouching at his side, sword in hand, putting her own body
between him and further harm.

"Don't anyone try that again," Snare said easily. "I may
not be a sorcerer yet, but I've got defensive wards you
wouldn't believe. Anyone else throws magic my way, I'll
kill the child. No more time to think, Your Majesty. Surrender yourself and your people now, or watch your precious
son die."

"I think he means it, Your Majesty," said Sir Robert.
"But it's your decision. If you want to bet he's bluffing,
we'll follow your lead."

"No," said the Queen. "It was never really my Throne
anyway. Lay down your weapons, my people. We surrender."

Her defenders looked at each other, then Sir Robert and
Ennis Page dropped their swords to the floor and moved
back to stand before the Throne. Chance laid down his
great axe, took Tiffany by the arm, and led her back to the
Throne. Chappie slunk back to join them, still growling
under his breath. The Creature loped back to crouch beside
the Shaman, licking blood and gore from his hands. Cally
threw aside her sword and sat down beside Sir Vivian.

Tiffany glared at the Magus. "This is all your fault! Do
something!"

"Hush," said the Magus. "I'm thinking. Something is
happening. Something I hadn't planned on. I can feel it."

"It's happening right in front of you, you idiot!" said
Tiffany.

But the Magus wasn't listening. His eyes were lost in
deep contemplation, and his frown was slowly deepening
into a puzzled scowl. Snare laughed softly.

"I always thought he was more bluff than anything else.
Leave him to his dreams and fancies. Now, Your Majesty.
Come here and collect your child."

"Don't do it, Fliss!" Cally said immediately. "You can't
trust him!"

"I know," said the Queen. "But I have no choice. He
has my son."

She stood up from the ancient wooden Throne and stepped slowly down from the dais. She looked at her helpless defenders, smiled gently to show them she didn't blame them for anything, and then walked slowly across what had been her Court to stand before the grinning magician Snare. It was very quiet now, as though everyone was holding their breath. Felicity looked at her son, Stephen, in Snare's arms, but didn't dare to reach out and touch him.

"Very good," said Snare. "Now you just stand there like a good girl and let me kill you quickly and easily, and I swear no harm will come to your child. I have to kill you, you know."

"Yes," said Felicity. "I know."

"Alive you'd always be a rallying point for patriotic rebels. Can't have that. And don't look to your father for help. I'm running things now. It was time he stepped aside anyway. Those who rule by force should never grow old, and weak. And besides, I've always wanted to kill a Queen."

"Felicity!" said the Duke, and everyone's head whipped around as his voice rose, strong and powerful as it had always been. "Catch!"

And he took off and threw to her the Candlemass Charm, the powerful amulet that protected him from all magical attacks. Time seemed to slow as the whole Court watched the magical charm flash through the air to slap into Felicity's waiting hand. Snare's eyes widened, but even as he opened his mouth to speak, Felicity drew the slender dagger she always kept concealed in her long sleeve and cut Snare's throat with one expert slash.

All the magics that might have protected him were nothing against the power of the Candlemass Charm. He started to fall backward, hands rising uselessly to his severed throat, knowing he should never have allowed the Duke's daughter to get so close to him. Felicity snatched her still sleeping son out of Snare's loosening grasp and stepped quickly back, but Snare was dead before he hit the floor. From all around the Court came the sound of the mercenaries' weapons hitting the floor. They were a practical breed. Felicity looked down at the dead Snare and kicked him in the head.

The Starlight Duke smiled. "That's my daughter."

Queen Felicity returned to her Throne, cradling her son in her arms. Her defenders quickly took up their weapons and formed an honor guard before the Throne. Sir Vivian was back on his feet but leaning on Cally, his eyes clear and the sword in his hand perfectly steady. The Duke moved slowly forward and bowed formally to his daughter, the Queen.

"Stephen will wake up in about an hour. The dose I gave Snare was carefully measured."

"Why?" said Felicity. "Why did you give up the Charm and put your own life at risk?"

"He would have killed you," said the Duke. "I lost one daughter through my stubbornness and pride, and always regretted it."

"And Snare was threatening to replace you as ruler of Hillsdown," said Sir Robert. "I just mention that in passing."

The Duke smiled. "There was that, yes. But when all is said and done, family is family."

Tiffany put her arm through Chance's. "Don't you just love a happy ending?"

And that was when the wee winged faerie Lightfoot Moonfleet came hurtling into the Court through the open double doors, flying as fast as her wings could propel her. She grew rapidly to full human size and dropped out of the air before the Magus.

"Magus! They've gone into the Inverted Cathedral!"

"I know," said the Magus, snapping out of his trance. "Hawk and Fisher, with the Seneschal, as I planned."

"And Jericho Lament!"

"What?" The Magus looked shocked, then alarmed. He spun on Chance. "The Walking Man has come to Forest Castle? Why didn't you tell me!"

"You weren't around," said Chance. "What difference does it make?"

The Magus' face was bright red now, and his eyes were almost bulging out of their sockets. He swept his arms about him distractedly as though he didn't know what to do with them. His cloak wrapped itself around his shoulders, but he didn't even notice. Everyone else was watching him very carefully, and working out which way to jump if he lost control.

"I knew about Hawk and Fisher," said the Magus to no one in particular. "I always intended they should enter the Inverted Cathedral. I had hopes of Harald, but he was too weak. And I had a feeling the Seneschal's presence would be useful, given his lineage. But I couldn't See, couldn't predict, that the Walking Man would come here and involve himself! He could ruin everything! I have to stop him!"

He screamed, a terrible sound of rage and horror and loss, and vanished, taking his cloak with him. There was a long moment of silence, and then everyone turned to look at Lightfoot Moonfleet. She shrugged prettily.

"Don't look at me. He never tells me anything."

CHAPTER NINE

In the Land of Reverie

And so they came at last to the summit and spire of the Inverted Cathedral, buried deep in the dark, dark earth. Hawk and Fisher, the Seneschal, the Burning Man, and the Wrath of God in the world of men. Spent and weary now, dragging their exhausted bodies up the last few steps protruding from the blood-dappled inner wall. All except for the Burning Man, of course, who was after all dead and damned, and no longer subject to such lesser torments. They had passed through the Listening Gallery, evaded the Stalking Tatters, and fought their way through the Coil of Dreams. All to reach the sunken spire with its single room and its final terrible secret.

The only entry to the room was through a simple wooden trapdoor above them, held shut by a single steel bolt. Hawk was somewhat reluctant to approach it, given his experiences with the trapdoor that had brought them into the Inverted Cathedral, but in the end Fisher managed to bully him into opening it. Hawk pushed back the bolt with the head of his axe, just in case, and then used the axe to push the trapdoor up. He waited a moment to give anything nasty that might be waiting inside its chance to be cranky, and then he pulled himself up into the room beyond. Fisher quickly followed him, and the two of them stood close together, glaring suspiciously about them. For all their tired and aching limbs, they were almost disappointed that there were no obvious demons or guardians to face.

The room in the Cathedral spire was simple and unadorned, empty and featureless except for the single window in the far wall, covered with wooden shutters. Not much bigger than an average attic, with a low ceiling and

no furniture, its only interesting feature was that the entire
room had been constructed from solid gold. The floor,
walls, and ceiling gleamed with their own inner light, and
the beaten metal walls contained dark, distorted reflections
that looked balefully back at Hawk and Fisher as they
turned in a slow circle. Even when they'd been Prince and
Princess of their respective lands, they'd never seen so
much gold in one place, or put to such ostentatious use.
The walls were perfectly smooth, the golden metal showing
no signs of workmanship, and when Hawk cautiously approached his reflection and placed one cautious hand on
the metal, the gold seemed uncomfortably warm to the
touch.

The Seneschal called up plaintively to find out what the
delay was. Rather than explain, Hawk and Fisher each
reached down a hand and hauled him through the trapdoor.
He took one look at the golden room and was immediately
dumbstruck. Lament joined them soon after, muttered
something about vanity and folly, and then strode angrily
around the room, prodding the walls here and there with
a stiff finger, as though searching for signs of fool's gold
or some other evidence of trickery. There then followed a
somewhat awkward pause, as absolutely nobody was willing
to put a hand down through the trapdoor to pull up the
Burning Man. He finally floated up through the trapdoor
all on his own.

"You can fly?" asked Hawk. "I didn't know you could
fly."

"Lots of things you don't know about me," said the
Burning Man.

"Then why didn't you just fly all the way up?" Fisher
asked. "Why climb up with us?"

"To watch you struggle and suffer, of course."

"This room must have cost a fortune all on its own,"
said the Seneschal breathlessly.

The Burning Man shrugged, and the flames on his shoulders danced for a moment. "Nothing was too good for my
Cathedral. Alchemists say that all gold is formed in the
hearts of suns. The purest of all metals. What better way
to surmount my finest creation? Tons of gold went into the

making of this room. All of it donated by the goodly and the righteous. I'm sure thoughts of buying their way into heaven never entered their minds at all."

Hawk and Fisher moved over to study the closed shutters covering the only window. Both of the great wooden panels were covered with a single, heavily stylized painting of heaven. There were green fields under a warm sun, where men and beasts walked side by side, and winged angels with harps and halos sailed across a perfect blue sky like graceful swans on an endless lake. The style was naïve, almost primitive, but the scene had an undeniable charm and power. The temperature rose sharply behind Hawk and Fisher as the Burning Man came over to join them, and they moved quickly aside as he leaned forward to study the painting. He sniffed loudly and turned away.

"Very tasteful, I'm sure. Dated now, of course. And nothing like the real thing."

"How would you know, murderer?" the Walking Man asked him.

"Part of Hell's punishment is the knowledge of what you've lost," said the Burning Man. "Hell knows all the forms of cruelty. Your just and merciful God didn't miss a trick."

"Tell us about the Gateway," Hawk said quickly, to stave off yet another doctrinal squabble. "Where is it, exactly?"

"Right beyond those shutters," responded the Burning Man. "Open the shutters, go through the window—lo and behold! Reverie awaits."

"It can't be that simple," said Lament, striding over to frown at the portrait of heaven. "We must be deep in the earth by now. What's really beyond these shutters? Dirt that's never known the light of day? Or perhaps a glimpse of Hell itself."

"You're really far too literal-minded for a religious man," chided the Burning Man. "It doesn't matter anyway. You won't be able to open the shutters."

To no one's surprise, Hawk immediately took that as a challenge. He'd already noticed there were no locks or bolts or handles, so he took the next logical step and hit the shutters with his axe. He put a lot of effort into it, but the heavy steel blade rebounded from the wooden shutter without doing it the slightest harm, or even damaging the painting. Hawk dropped his axe to the floor and spent some time walking around in tight circles as he tried to rub some feeling back into his jarred fingers.

"Interesting," said Fisher. "Even the High Warlock's enchantment on your axe wasn't enough to make an impression."

"Interesting," Hawk muttered through gritted teeth. "Yes, that's the word I was just about to use."

Lament raised his long wooden staff and rapped imperiously on the shutters with the steel-tipped end. "Open! In the name of the Lord!"

Nothing happened. The Burning Man sniggered. "You didn't really think it was going to be that easy, did you? It wouldn't be much of a secret Gateway if just anyone could open it. No mortal hand can open those shutters. Reverie isn't meant for human eyes."

They all turned to look at him, and he laughed at them, flames leaping in his open mouth. Hawk picked up his axe again.

"You knew this all along," he said flatly. "That's why you were willing to lead us here. To enjoy our anger and despair as we failed."

"Of course," Burning Man stated simply. "The damned must find their pleasures where they can."

"There's got to be a way," said Fisher. "And you're going to tell us what it is."

"Or what?" challenged the Burning Man, sneering openly. "You can't hurt me and you can't kill me. I have already been punished far beyond anything you could achieve."

"Don't let him provoke you," warned Lament. "We need to concentrate on the matter at hand. God would not have brought us all this way for nothing."

"I think," the Seneschal said diffidently, "that this is where I justify my presence here." He slowly approached the closed wooden shutters, holding out before him the Hand of Glory. "I can find my way to *anywhere*. That has always been my gift, my magic. And the Hand can open any locked door. With my magic focused through the Hand, I think I can open these shutters. That's why I'm here. Stand back and give me some room to work in."

They all fell back, even the Burning Man, as the Seneschal held up the Hand of Glory before the shutters. And as the Hand drew near the painted wood, its fingertips burst into flames, but instead of the usual soft yellow candle-glow, the little fires this time were bright and blue-white, shining brighter and brighter until the glare was almost blinding. The Seneschal narrowed his eyes against the radiance, but didn't turn his head aside. An inch away from the shutters, the mummified fingers began to twitch, then slowly move as though the long dead Hand was awakening.

"What the hell is happening?" Fisher asked softly.

"Beats me," said the Seneschal hoarsely, not looking at her. "It shouldn't be doing anything. I haven't activated the Hand yet."

The Hand of Glory's fingers were flexing strongly now, almost yearning to reach the shutters, and it was all the Seneschal could do to hang on to the Hand. There was a strong feeling of presence in the room now, as though someone else had joined them. And then the Hand closed suddenly into a fist, snuffing out its flames, and knocked twice on the painted wood. The sound seemed to carry impossibly far, echoing on and on as though crossing unimaginable distances, and then the view of heaven split slowly apart as the shutters swung silently open, fanning back into the golden room to reveal an endless darkness beyond. A blackness so deep, none of them could look at it, not even the Burning Man; a dark beyond anything seen in the Darkwood or the long night. A complete absence of light and everything else. The dark at the end of the universe, when all the stars have gone out, never to be relit.

Everyone looked curiously at the Hand of Glory. It had uncurled now and looked like just another dead man's preserved hand. The Seneschal shook it gingerly a few times, but its role was apparently over. The feeling of an extra presence in the room was gone, too.

"Shutters that could not be opened by any mortal hand," said Lament.

"Just who's hand was that originally?" Hawk asked.

The Seneschal frowned thoughtfully. "According to legend it was cut from the body of the first Forest King. The man who gave the order for this Cathedral to be built. I found it in the Old Armory. I suppose he still has authority here."

"What made you bring that thing along?" asked Fisher.

The Seneschal's frown deepened. "The Hand told me to. And no, I don't feel like discussing that. Could we talk about something else now, please?"

"All right," agreed Hawk. "We now have our Gateway, unsettling as it is. Isobel and I are going in. Lament, I assume you're in, too?"

"Of course," Lament responded. "The situation hasn't changed. The world must still be saved from chaos."

"I'm not going," said the Burning Man. "I've gone as far as I can. I am bound to the site of my achievement and my crime."

"In which case the Seneschal will stay here with you till we return," Lament said immediately.

"I will?" asked the Seneschal. He looked uncertainly at the Burning Man, who smiled nastily back. "And just why would I want to do that?"

"You have to stay here with the Hand of Glory to keep the Gateway open," Lament said patiently. "Otherwise I wouldn't put it past the Burning Man to shut the Gateway behind us and strand us in Reverie forever. You can keep an eye on him and make sure he behaves himself."

"Alone?" asked the Seneschal, just a little plaintively.

"You can handle him," Hawk said briskly. "You're the High Warlock's grandson, remember? He gives you any trouble, kick his smoldering arse around the room a few times."

The Seneschal gave the Burning Man a long, considering look. "Yes. I think I could do that."

Fisher grinned at him. "Keep a light in the window for us. We'll be back before you know it."

"No one human has ever come back from Reverie," said the Burning Man spitefully. "You go to your deaths, or worse."

Hawk, Fisher, and Lament ignored him. They took a few deep breaths to brace themselves, and then turned as one to stare determinedly into the darkness beyond the window. And as they made themselves watch, a line of shimmering light suddenly appeared, spreading horizontally before them. The line quickly broadened, growing wider, brighter; and then opened all the way to form a huge Eye, filling all the window, looking in at them. The Eye shone very brightly, more luminous than any star, an overpowering glare that should have been blinding, but they were unable to look away. The Eye was vast and inhuman, alive and aware, watching them. It grew and grew, coming closer, and inside its great dark pupil they could see a galaxy of stars and planets. The Seneschal and the Burning Man looked away, covering their eyes with their hands, unable to bear the Eye's awful unblinking glare.

Soon all Hawk and Fisher and Lament could see was the amazing contents of the Eye. The room, their journey, and even their mission were all forgotten, lost in the fascinating vistas within the Eye. There were galaxies in the dark pupil now, slowly swirling, impossibly vast, impossibly detailed. As one, answering some unheard but undeniable call, Hawk, Fisher, and Lament stepped forward and entered the Gateway.

They were walking along an unsupported crystal bridge, eternally long, looking out over an endless abyss. Comets and shooting stars rained down through the endless night, above and below. There were suns and planets and constellations, all unfamiliar. A huge sun drifted by, borne along by some unguessable tide, close enough that they could almost have reached out and touched it, but its light didn't dazzle them, and they could barely feel its heat. They stopped walking for a moment to watch the sun pass, and as it drew level with them, they could sense something hibernating or gestating deep in the heart of the sun. Something almost unimaginably powerful, waiting to be born, or born again. It stirred in its deep sleep as it sensed their presence, and they were touched by an awful fear they couldn't put a name to, but the sun passed on, and whatever was within went back to sleep again.

Hawk walked along the sparkling crystal bridge with Fisher on one side and Lament on the other, and didn't know either of them. All of his exhaustion and muscle pains were gone. It was like walking through a dream, and he felt as though he could walk forever. Up ahead the three of them saw the Blue Moon shining in the dark, full and fat and potent, and in a moment they remembered who they were and why they had come to this place. Hawk and Fisher stood and looked out over the impossibly long drop, then grabbed each other by the hand. Lament murmured a prayer in an unsteady voice. And then they moved on again, heading toward the Blue Moon growing very slowly greater before them.

And as they walked, their appearances changed. Subtly at first, and then more radically, they became other versions of people they might have been, or might yet be. Their clothes changed first, colors and styles coming and going as they strode on. Hair and eye colors changed next, and then the way they walked and held themselves as their ages altered. Sometimes they were young and sometimes they were old, but the differences seemed strangely natural at the time.

Prince Rupert and Princess Julia walked together with the easy confidence of youth. Rupert had both his eyes, and Julia's hair was a bright frizz of golden yellow. Then they were Captains Hawk and Fisher, striding along in the black-cloaked uniforms of the Haven city Guard. Hawk's scarred face had only the one eye, and Fisher's blond hair hung in a single thick braid. And then they were older, in strange, unfamiliar clothes. Hawk was in his early sixties, and his thinning hair was nearly all gray, but he had both eyes again. Fisher's hair was as thick as always, but now it was a mane of pure white held back by a silver headband. With them walked their two adult children, Jack and Gillian Forester. Jack was a smiling, eager sort in a monk's robe. Gillian had a shaved head, a mean look, and a positively disturbing grin. She wore leather armor studded with silver runes. The four of them walked easily together, their eyes fixed on some distant goal, and woe to any fool who got in their way.

Time suddenly snapped back to the present, and Hawk and Fisher stopped abruptly, themselves again on the shimmering crystal bridge. Lament stopped with them, one hand rising slowly to his face, as though bothered by some unfinished thought. Hawk and Fisher looked at each other.

"What the hell was *that*?" Fisher asked finally.

"A possible future, maybe," said Hawk. "People we might become."

"And the children we might have," said Fisher. "They looked like good kids."

"Yes. They did. Though how we ended up with a monk for a son . . ."

"Probably the only way he could rebel against us. She looked like a one-woman army." Fisher looked carefully at Hawk. "You had both your eyes again. How is that possible? We tried every shapechange spell we could find but never found anything strong enough to overcome the amount of Wild Magic you'd been exposed to."

"Maybe it's from a life where I never lost my eye," said Hawk. "I've never understood those multiple time-line theories."

They both suddenly realized that Lament was being very quiet, and turned to look at him. He slowly lowered his hand from his face and straightened his shoulders through an effort of will.

"What did you see, Lament?" asked Fisher. "Did you see who and what you're going to become?"

"I'm not sure," said Lament. "If that was my future, it's not at all what I expected. I really don't think I want to talk about it."

"Did you see us?" Hawk asked.

"No. Just myself. As I was, am, and might someday be. You must remember, this is a place of chaos and Wild Magic. Nothing is certain here, and nothing can be trusted. Least of all any futures we might see in visions. There's no guarantee any of us will survive this."

"You know, you're a really cheerful sort for a man of

God," said Fisher. "Whatever happened to tidings of comfort and joy?"

Lament smiled slightly. "Why do you think I ended up as a monk in an isolated community?"

All three turned to look as a new Eye opened in the darkness beyond the crystal bridge. Within the Eye was another Eye, and another within that. The Eyes seemed to fall away forever, and all three people on the bridge had to turn and look away for fear they might fall in. When they looked back again, the Eyes were gone.

"Just how many Gateways and hidden Realms are there?" asked Hawk.

"God knows," said Fisher.

"Yes," agreed Lament. "He probably does."

"I'm going to slap you in a minute," warned Fisher.

"Let's get moving again," Hawk said firmly. "I can only handle so many mysteries at one time. See if you can find something for me to hit. I always feel so much more secure when I've got something to hit."

"It's true, he does," said Fisher.

"Head for the Blue Moon," directed Lament. "That's where all our answers lie, and perhaps our destinies, too."

They continued along the crystal bridge, and the universe wheeled around them. There were suns and moons of all shades and colors now, and comets that screamed like dying children as they rocketed past. Constellations formed unnerving shapes and huge unseen presences drifted past, scattering planets in their wake. But the bridge was firm and unyielding under their feet, and the Blue Moon shone before them like a beckoning finger. They were drawing near something now. They could feel it.

The bridge turned down suddenly, and plunged them into a realm of swirling, glowing mists. Hawk, Fisher, and Lament were in among the shifting mists and standing on what seemed like solid ground almost before they were aware of it. They looked quickly behind them, but all traces of the crystal bridge were gone. They had apparently arrived at their destination. Up above them, blazing down through the concealing mists, the Blue Moon shone like the open door of some unearthly furnace. The dreamlike feeling of uncertainty clung to the three of them as they inspected their surroundings.

The mists curled around them in streams and eddies, revealing tantalizing glimpses of the place they'd come to. It wasn't hot or cold, pleasant or unpleasant, or anything they could easily put a name to. Instead there was a constant unsettling feeling of anticipation, as though everything was in the process of becoming something. Places, shapes, and structures were constantly forming and disappearing, just on the edge of their vision, gone the moment any of them turned to look at the apparitions directly. Some would linger for a few moments, like fragments of dreams barely recalled on waking, while others came and went so swiftly, they left only disturbing impressions behind them.

Hawk thought he saw a great fairy-tale castle with impossibly high walls and slender turrets. He thought he saw vast tomblike structures hanging on grim gray walls like huge limpets. And sometimes he thought he saw familiar places from his past, only half completed. But none of the visions lasted for long, and none of them felt very real. It was as though the world they had come to was trying on various clothes to see what would most appeal to its new visitors. There were sounds all around, rising and falling and overlapping. From the crying of birds to the howls of animals to the chattering of men in unknown languages. These, too, sounded somehow artificial, as though the world was speaking in tongues, perhaps trying for some common ground they could communicate on, perhaps not.

"I don't know where we are," Hawk said finally. "But I don't think I like it. Nothing feels solid here. Nothing is certain."

"What else did you expect," asked the Magus, "in the land of Reverie?"

They all jumped a little as the sorcerer appeared suddenly before them. He looked like he always did; a short, almost self-effacing man wrapped in a great black cloak. His face and voice were still deceptively mild, but his pale gray eyes were unusually direct. He seemed entirely unperturbed by the shifting world around them.

"This is the world the Blue Moon orbits," said the Magus

calmly. "This is the place whose light the Blue Moon reflects. This is Reverie. I told you you'd come here eventually, Captains Hawk and Fisher. Remember?" He looked sternly at Lament. "But I wasn't expecting you, Walking Man. You should not have come here. You could ruin everything."

"We're here because we chose to come here," Hawk said. "Now what the hell is this place, exactly?"

"Not so much a place, more a concept," said the Magus. "This is Reverie, the world of the Transient Beings, home and source to all Wild Magic."

"Hold everything," said Fisher. "How did you get here, Magus? You weren't in the Inverted Cathedral with us. How did you get to the Gateway?"

"I belong here," stated the Magus. "I am a Transient Being." He looked briefly about him. "It's not much, but I call it home. I've been away for a while. Going back and forth in the world, and walking up and down in it. We can only come to your world when you summon us, knowingly or unknowingly, and once we return, we have to wait until we are summoned again. I chose to stay in reality, limiting as it is, because it fascinated me. *You* fascinated me— humanity, in all its many wonders and mysteries.

"And now I'm back here again. I've been plotting this meeting for such a long time, Captains. Not for you specifically, but for people like you. Heroes who understand duty and courage and honor. Together we have the chance to do something splendid and marvelous and very necessary. If the Wrath of God doesn't screw it up for all of us."

"If I'm such a threat to your plans," Lament said, "why don't you just strike me down?"

"Because it's too late now," the Magus said sourly. "You're already here. You must be very careful, Walking Man. Reverie is the place of belief, and a faith as strong and uncritical as yours could make you very dangerous. If you value the continued survival of humanity and reality itself, whatever you see and hear, or think you see and hear, keep your mouth shut and don't interfere."

"Isobel," said Hawk in a rather strained voice, "your hair is blond again. When did that happen?"

Fisher's hand went to her hair and pulled the end of the braid in front of her. All traces of the black dye were gone, and her hair was its familiar dark yellow again. She looked at Hawk, started to shrug, and then stopped and looked closely at Hawk's face.

"Hawk, take off your eyepatch."

"What?"

"Your eyepatch, love. Take it off. I have this strange feeling . . ."

Hawk slowly removed the black silk patch that covered the empty eye socket where his right eye had been before a demon clawed it out of his head. He let the black patch fall to the ground. He didn't need the wonder in Fisher's face to know that something marvelous had happened. His right eyelids, so long sealed together, opened slowly, and he looked at Fisher with two eyes for the first time in twelve years. They smiled at each other for a long moment, and then Hawk looked at the Magus.

"What's happening here, sorcerer? What are we changing?"

"Belief is everything here," said the Magus. "Reverie is the place of concepts and ideas, dreams and fantasies and everything in between. Thoughts have power here. Physical presences are passing things, unless vested in some specific viewpoint. Your self-image decides who and what you are here. So don't let your thoughts wander. If you forget yourself here, you might not come back."

Fisher looked closely at Lament. "You haven't changed at all."

"I know who and what I am," said Jericho Lament. "I made myself the Walking Man by my own free choice and desire."

But he didn't sound quite as sure as he might have, and everyone could hear it in his voice, even him.

"I anticipated everything but you," said the Magus. "A man who willingly made himself into something both more and less than a man."

Lament looked at him sharply. "What do you mean 'less'?"

"You gave up free will," said the Magus. "In return for

something I am unable to comprehend. But then, I'm not a man and never was."

"So you're a Transient Being," said Fisher. "Maybe you could explain just what the hell that is."

"We are many," said the Magus, "for we are legion. Forgive me, the old jokes are always the best. We are what you created to be here. Don't blame us if you don't like the shape and texture of your own dreams."

The ground shook suddenly beneath their feet, and something huge lurched out of the mists to stand behind the Magus, towering over him. Over nine feet tall, it was a great ill-formed skeleton, as much like a man as not, held together only by ancient and awful magics. Blood ran from his grinning jaws in a steady crimson stream, falling down to splash on his chestbone and ribs. His bones were browned and yellowed with age. Blood dripped thickly from his fingertips and oozed out from under his flat, bony feet. More ran down his long, curving leg-bones, and welled from his empty eyesockets like tears. He stank of carrion and the grave, and things that should have been safely and securely buried long ago.

Hawk and Fisher had their weapons in their hands, and were standing shoulder to shoulder, ready for any sign of attack. Lament studied the huge skeleton, leaning on his staff.

"What the bloody hell is that?" asked Hawk.

"That is Bloody Bones," said the Magus, not even glancing behind him. He seemed entirely unruffled, even amused, by the naked anger and threat in Hawk's voice. "He's a Transient Being just like me. Some kind of ancient funerary god or demon. It's often hard to tell such things apart. There were those who worshiped him centuries ago, but he never cared. It is his single nature to frighten and to terrify, and the blood you see is the blood of his countless victims. He's here to take you to the present spokesman of our ephemeral kind. I really would advise you to go with him. You have nothing strong enough to hurt him."

"Just how many Transient Beings are there?" asked Fisher, not lowering her sword.

"As many as there need to be," said the Magus. "And they're all very interested in you."

Even as the Magus spoke, Hawk, Fisher, and Lament became aware of other presences watching silently from the concealing mists. They were moving slowly, unhurriedly, just beyond the limits of human vision, circling the new arrivals to their realm; awful and unsettling things that watched and studied with unseen eyes. They were pressing closer now, and Hawk, Fisher, and Lament began to catch glimpses of ugly shapes and unquiet details, as though their own passing thoughts were giving shape and purpose to what lay in the mists.

"Keep your gaze fixed on me and Bloody Bones," the Magus said sharply. "You'll find things much less disturbing that way. Our shapes and natures are fixed and determined by long belief, but just by being here, you have undue influence. Believe me, you don't want to see some of the things your arrival has attracted. Just follow Bloody Bones and he'll take you to someone who'll answer all your questions. But don't blame us if you don't like the answers."

The huge skeleton turned abruptly and lurched off into the mists, the Magus close behind him. Rather than be left alone in a place of mists, surrounded by unseen enemies, Hawk and Fisher went after them, their weapons still in their hands. Lament brought up the rear, carefully not even glancing behind him, his lips moving soundlessly in one of the more martial psalms. The presences kept up with them as the small party moved through the churning mists, but they maintained their distance. Shapes slowly began to form out of the mists; a tree here and there, spiky shrubs, branches hanging down or thrusting up to form a canopy overhead. The shining sourceless light of the mists gradually died away to be replaced by the baleful, ghastly light of the Blue Moon. Hawk and Fisher realized in the same heart-stopping moment that they were back in the Darkwood again. It seemed entirely real—as dark and oppressive and soul-destroying as they remembered. All the trees around them were dead and rotting, and the horrid spiritual dread of the darkness beat upon their minds and their souls with all its old remembered strength. Hawk and Fisher stuck close together, breathing deeply despite the stench to try and calm themselves. Lament was singing his psalm aloud now, but it was a small sound in such a dark place.

Hawk knew where they were going, where they had to be going. And what terrible deathless thing was waiting to greet them again.

But even so, his heart slammed painfully in his chest when they finally came to the awful dark heart of the Darkwood, and there, sitting on his rotten throne, the Demon Prince. The malevolent, terrible creature that had come so close to destroying everything Hawk had ever cared for. The Demon Prince looked like a man. He had looked like other things before, and might again, but for now it amused him to look like his prey. His features were blurred, as though they'd melted and run. His long, delicate fingers ended in claws, and his burning crimson eyes held no human thoughts or emotions. Unnaturally tall, easily eight feet in height, he was slender to the point of emaciation. His pale flesh looked like something left too long in the dark, grown soft and rotten. He dressed in rags and tatters of darkest black and wore a battered wide-brimmed hat, pulled down low over his burning eyes. His wide slash of a mouth was full of pointed teeth, and when he spoke, his voice was quiet and sibilant, and grated on their nerves like fingernails down a blackboard.

"So good to see old friends again," said the Demon Prince. "I told you we'd meet again. You can't destroy me, little human. Banish me, and I just return here and wait for some new fool to summon me back into the world of men. I am of the Transient Beings, ideas made flesh, and we live on long after our every human enemy is dead and gone."

"Of course," said Lament, apparently unmoved. "Evil is eternal. I've always known that."

"Strictly speaking, we're neither good nor bad," said the Demon Prince, leaning back in the rotting tree stump that was his throne and crossing his long legs casually. "Those are human terms, human limitations. We are archetypes, reflections of what's on man's inner mind. We are the shadows humanity casts. We are the physical manifestations of abstract concepts, forces, fears, and preoccupations. Neuroses and psychoses, given rein to run free and potent in the mortal world. We are the rod you made for your own back. We sprang full-grown from humanity's brow, created in simpler times, when the Wild Magic was all there was."

"You always did like the sound of your own voice," said Hawk. "You're saying the Transient Beings are everything we ever dreamed of."

"Yes," the Demon Prince agreed. "Especially the bad ones."

"But the world and humanity have moved on," said the Magus, and there was something in his voice that made them all look at him. "Man has become more complex, replacing the chaotic Wild Magic with the more easily understood and controlled High Magic, and now more and more with the logical, more useful science. Humanity is entering, or creating, the time of the rational mind, and soon he will have no use for such as us anymore."

The Demon Prince stirred restlessly on his decaying throne. "It has been a long, long time since you have returned to Reverie, Magus. And as always, you bring bad news with you. You were created too closely in humanity's image. No wonder we despise you so much. You remind us of everything we hate."

"Why do you hate humanity?" asked Hawk. His mouth was dry and his voice was rough, but his gaze was perfectly steady. "If we created you, you should be grateful to us."

The Demon Prince laughed briefly, a harsh, unpleasant, hateful sound. "You know nothing, understand nothing, little man. We hate you because you're real. Because humanity is real you can grow and change and evolve, become more than you were. Transient Beings are bound by their nature to be only what they are, trapped and limited to the form your kind imagined. Eternally existing, eternally damned to never be more than what we were when humanity coughed us up.

"But now you have opened the Gateway, an unexpected back door into Reality. And every Transient Being in Reverie is free at last to have its revenge on you. We shall all go through into the world of mortal men, in all our awful glory, without having to be summoned. After so very, very long, our time has come round at last. We're coming in force, to overthrow the upstart reason, and crush the tyrant science. Logic and order, cause and effect, and all the other constraints on our freedom shall be swept aside, and the Wild Magic shall once again have dominion over every unfortunate living thing. Once the Blue Moon's orbit has intersected with your own moon once again, we will all cross over and remake your world in our own hating image. Then there shall be chaos, loose in the world like a wolf in the fold, for forever and a day. And oh, the terrible pleasures we shall take in what used to be your world."

"We'll fight you," said Fisher. "We'll never give up. We beat you last time."

"I was alone then," said the Demon Prince. "And I laid waste your whole Kingdom. There are more of us here than your mind can comprehend, and under a never-ending Blue Moon we shall be very powerful indeed. And in this new world of eternal chaos that we shall make, perhaps the limitations of the Transient Beings themselves shall be broken and overturned. We will all become real, and able to change and evolve at last. What creation doesn't want to turn on its creator, to become greater than was intended, to outgrow and overtake the creator?"

"And if you can't?" asked Lament. "If what you are is what you'll always be, what then?"

"Then we'll punish humanity forever," answered the Demon Prince. "And the hell we'll make for him on earth will be worse than any hell he can escape to by dying."

"You always did have a way with words," murmured the Magus. "But let's not forget I made all this possible. It was my creation of a Rift in space and time that raised the level of Wild Magic in the mortal world, and awoke the Gateway to life once more. The Rift was such a useful toy; I knew they'd never be able to resist it."

"You have our gratitude," the Demon Prince said coldly.

"We will find a way to stop you," Lament said doggedly. "God will not allow you to triumph."

"Wild Magic is the magic of creation," said the Demon

Prince. "Perhaps we'll remake God, or create a new God of our own. All things are possible under a Blue Moon."

"Exactly," agreed the Magus, and once again there was something in his voice that drew all eyes to him. "Everything that is happening now is happening because of me. I have planned for centuries to bring this about, manipulating the mortal world and certain useful people in it, to bring us all to this place, this moment. But not, alas, for the reasons you might suppose. The truth is, I intend to close the Gateway, separate reality from Reverie forever, and shut the mortal world off from every form of magic." He smiled vaguely about him, as though inviting comments, and then continued. "I have lived a very long time in the world of men, and seen reason slowly replace superstition. I have watched the world become a better place as the wild madness was controlled and put aside. It just got in the way of humanity's maturing.

"They'll be so much better off without magic, with all its temptations and perversions of hope and ambition. The Transient Beings have outlived their purpose. Humanity doesn't need them anymore. They're growing up and leaving their toys behind. And that's all we ever were, really. Dangerous toys that bit at the hands that made them. Forgive me, I drifted off the point, didn't I? The point is, I intend to re-Invert the Cathedral, send it soaring up into the sky again, and thus close off the last remaining Gateway, and make it useless and powerless for all time. It is the very last Gateway, you know. That's why the Darkwood always manifested in the Forest Kingdom."

The Magus nodded thoughtfully, and smiled at the ominously silent Demon Prince. "Long and long I walked in the world of men, living among them as one of them, and slowly I came to love humanity; for all their many undeniable faults, they have such potential. The very thing you condemn them for is the one thing that will eventually make them greater than we could ever be. With or without a Blue Moon. So I have betrayed my own kind and returned here to stay with you, locked away from humanity forever, because our time is over."

The Demon Prince surged to his feet and stalked forward

to tower threateningly over the diminutive form of the Magus. "Your time among humans has driven you insane! Have you forgotten we can only exist here in Reverie during the time of the full Blue Moon? That as it passes, we vanish away, become nothing and less than nothing, until we are summoned into the world of men? Once we pass through the Gateway and take their world away from them, we can exist forever and have power over all that is!"

"We're not worthy of it," said the Magus. "Give us the world and we'd just break it by playing too roughly." He turned to face Hawk, Fisher, and Lament, fixing them with a calm, implacable gaze. "Understand what I'm saying. All magic comes from Reverie. Closing the last Gateway will mean the end of all magic and magical creatures. Not immediately. It will take centuries for all the magic left in the world to be used up. But finally there will be no more wonders and no more nightmares. Science will replace magic in an entirely human world."

"No more dragons," said Fisher. "No more unicorns."

"No more vampires, or werewolves," added Hawk. "No more demons."

"Exactly," said the Magus.

"This last Gateway," Lament said slowly. "Did the Burning Man create it when he Inverted the Cathedral with his blood sacrifice?"

"No," said the Magus patiently. "There have always been gaps, weak spots, in reality, through which magic could enter. The Inverted Cathedral merely provided the last Gateway with a home, a focus. Just as I planned. I set things up so that Tomas Chadbourne would go to the Demon Prince for his compact, and set this all in motion. I arranged for the first Forest King to build his Castle around the Inverted Cathedral, thus isolating and containing the last Gateway while I waited for just the right combination of people, at just the right time, to close the Gateway forever."

"I have a really bad feeling I'm not going to like the answer to this," said Hawk. "But just how are we supposed to close this Gateway?"

The Magus looked at him sadly. "By dying here, Prince

Rupert, Princess Julia. You must die by your own hands, of your own free will. A willing sacrifice, to undo Chadbourne's blood sacrifice. Your deaths in this place will be a moment of undeniable reality; and I will use that moment to make the Gateway real, and destroy it."

"No," said Lament immediately. "There has to be another way. There has to be."

"I told you," the Magus said sharply. "Don't interfere! You could still ruin everything. There's something of the magical about you, Walking Man, and I don't trust it. Be still and silent, and stay out of this."

Lament looked at Hawk and Fisher. "I've always known who you were. You were my heroes. Let me die in your place. You're legends, you matter more than I ever have or will. There'll always be a Walking Man."

"It can't be you," the Magus said flatly. "I told you, you made yourself useless for this purpose when you made yourself more and less than a man. But then, a part of you has always wanted to die, hasn't it? Ever since the demons killed your fellow monks, you've felt guilty about surviving. Part of why you fight evil so relentlessly is because deep down you hope to find something powerful enough to kill you, and let you make amends at last. But you mustn't interfere now. For this to work, it has to be a wholly human sacrifice."

"Meaning us," said Hawk. "Somehow it always comes down to us. It's last man on the bridge again."

"Right," said Fisher. "Been there, done that."

They both sighed reluctantly and turned to look at each other, and it was as though they were the only two there.

"Why is it always us?" asked Fisher.

"Because we're the only ones who can be trusted to get the job done," said Hawk. "Whatever it takes. But I'm not giving up yet. We've only the Magus' word that our deaths are necessary, and he's already admitted to lying about practically everything else."

"But if there really is no other way . . ."

"Then we'll do what we have to. Just as we've always done. Personally, I'm more in favor of killing everything that moves in this appalling place, and then dancing a jig on the remains."

Fisher smiled briefly. "Yeah. That's always worked for me. But if the Magus is right, these things can't die."

"I know," said Hawk. "Ironic, really. We had to come all the way home, all the way back to where we began, to find our ending. Just like one of those bloody awful ballads I always hated so much."

"We're legends now," said Fisher. "I suppose we couldn't be allowed to die like ordinary people. We made a good team, didn't we?"

"The best. Just in case there isn't time later . . . I have always loved you, Julia."

"I have always loved you, Rupert."

"How very touching," said the Demon Prince, smiling his awful smile. "Did you really think we'd just stand here and let you ruin all our plans? I've got a much better idea. It seems we can't risk killing you, but we can certainly render you helpless and then take you with us when we go through the Gateway. And back in the mortal world, what games we'll play together. I shall enjoy hearing you scream through all eternity."

Hawk and Fisher looked around quickly. Bloody Bones was still watching them, grinning his crimson grin, and they could feel new presences closing in around them. Something was moving through the dead trees, just beyond the limits of the clearing's light. Huge shapes, lumbering on all sides, no longer bothering to conceal themselves. Hawk and Fisher hefted their weapons. They were surrounded now, and some of the new arrivals began to reveal glimpses of themselves. Lament cried out softly. There were worse things than demons. Concepts so hideous, so abstract, they should never have been permitted physical shapes. Madness, walking in bare flesh, nightmares from the darkest depths of the human mind.

The Magus glared at the creatures. "Stay back! I have learned much while I sojourned in the world of men, and I will not permit— "

The Demon Prince knocked him to the ground with a single blow and slammed a heavy foot down on his chest.

The black cloak squirmed helplessly, trapped under the Magus' weight.

"You've been gone too long, Magus," said the Demon Prince, and there was a thunderous growl of approval from the presences out in the dark. "This is *our* place, and we are as strong as we believe ourselves to be. We're going to take turns tearing you to pieces, Magus, over and over again. And when we all go through into reality, we'll take what's left of you with us, so you can watch all the terrible things we're going to do to your precious humanity and their world."

The awful presences around the clearing began to press forward, horrors and fancies beyond bearing. Hawk and Fisher raised their weapons. The Magus called out desperately for them to kill each other while there was still time. And Jericho Lament, the Walking Man, turned his gaze inward.

The box. Remember the box.

Lament reached into the pocket of his long coat and took out the small wooden casket he'd found in the Inverted Cathedral's Ossuary. Inside the box crafted by Christ's own hands still burned the original spark, the very beginnings of all creation. If he were to open that box, as perhaps only he could, and let the holy light out, he had no doubt it would sweep away all the threatening shadows of Reverie, and undo all the Transient Beings and their disturbing ephemeral realm. And he would die, of course, and Hawk and Fisher, but that had ceased to matter long ago. No, if he destroyed Reverie, the source of all magic, would he also be destroying the religion he had served and believed in for so long? Would a world of cold remorseless logic and science have any room in it for the miracles and majesty of God? Would he be responsible for destroying angels and devils, heaven and hell, and all the imponderable glories he had given his life to? To save humanity, could he murder God?

He took a slow deep breath and settled himself. God was more than magic, more than miracles. It all came down to one last terrible act of faith. His hand moved to the lid of the wooden casket.

"No!" the Magus cried out desperately, struggling under the Demon Prince's heavy tread. "That light would destroy Reverie and reality! The spark of creation would sweep *everything* away, wipe it all clean and start over!"

"Let him open his little box," said the Demon Prince. "This is my place, and I will set my darkness against any light."

Darkness closed in around them, sweeping forward like a black tide, heavy and threatening, enveloping the surrounding trees and the uneasy presences there, until there was only the clearing, and those in it, like principal players picked out by the ghastly spotlight of the Blue Moon. And Hawk suddenly smiled.

"Damn, I'm slow," he said wonderingly. "I'd forgotten. I've been here before. Lost in the darkness, facing the end of the world, and all the time the answer was right there with me."

"Yes!" said Fisher. "The Rainbow sword!"

Hawk dropped his axe and his hand went to the sword at his hip, the sword the Seneschal had brought to him in case he had to save the Land again. And the Demon Prince laughed in his face.

"That only worked in the real world. This is Reverie, where I belong. You can't banish me twice, little Prince."

"The Rainbow isn't the answer," Lament said slowly, following the surety of his feelings, of his belief. "Neither is the Source. But put them together, the Source to give the Rainbow power, the Rainbow to give the Source direction and purpose. You were wrong, Magus; I was meant to be here. We all were. Have faith, Rupert and Julia. In the end, in the dark, that's all there is."

The Demon Prince and Bloody Bones and all the Transient Beings howled with rage and horror as Hawk, who was once and always would be Prince Rupert, drew the Rainbow sword from its scabbard. He raised the ordinary-looking blade above his head, and Fisher's hand joined his on the long hilt, as together they called down the Rainbow; not for themselves, but for all humanity and all the fragile treasures of the real world. And as they did, Jericho Lament, the Walking Man, who had always been so much more than the Wrath of God in the world of men, opened the casket just a crack and whispered in a voice not entirely his own, *Let there be light!*

The Rainbow slammed down into the dark heart of the Darkwood, a thundering waterfall of shades and hues and colors, sharp and vivid and beautiful almost beyond bearing. And a brilliant light flared out from the small wooden box, to join and merge with the Rainbow, in a primal elemental force that could not be denied. Hawk and Fisher clung together, fighting to hold on to the sword as the Rainbow's holy light buffeted them like a raging storm that might sweep them away at any moment. The Demon Prince, Bloody Bones, the Magus, and all the other Transient Beings cried out in a single loud voice, and then they were gone, dissolved in the inexorable power of the falling Rainbow; mere shadows of reality swept away by a greater clarity. Reverie and the Blue Moon were no more.

And only Jericho Lament, God's chosen, had the strength of will to force the wooden box shut again, holding the Source within.

The Rainbow faded away, and with it went Hawk and Fisher and Lament. The long, dark night of the Blue Moon had come to an end at last, in a single glorious moment of light.

CHAPTER TEN

Redemptions

Through an open window in a golden room the Rainbow came home again. Shouldering aside the darkness, the Rainbow plunged horizontally across the room, hammering forward like a living battering ram of colors. It shot between the startled Seneschal and Burning Man, and they fell back from its thundering elemental presence. The Burning Man cried out and turned away, pressing his flaming hands over his screwed-shut eyes, unable to face the glory of the Rainbow. The Seneschal stood and stared, dazzled and delighted. He'd always wondered what the Rainbow looked like up close. The vivid hues burned in his eyes, suffusing his whole body and wiping away all hurts and pains. And then the Rainbow faded away, and there in the middle of the suddenly tawdry golden room stood Hawk and Fisher and Jericho Lament.

Hawk looked slowly around him as though surfacing from a dream whose hold had temporarily been greater than reality. "Damn," he said finally. "We're still alive. How about that."

"I thought we were finished for sure when the whole of Reverie gave up the ghost," said Fisher. "Lament, why aren't we dead?"

"The Rainbow brought us back because we belong here," explained Lament. "We were never a part of Reverie, so we escaped its doom."

"Is it really gone?" asked Hawk. "I mean, forever?"

"Who knows?" said Lament. "What matters is that we are cut off from it forever. No more magic . . . what will the world be like without it?"

"Quieter, probably," said Fisher. "Do you suppose the

Magus knew he was going to die with all the other Transient Beings? Was that part of his plan all along?"

"He knew his time was over," said Hawk. "What place could he have had in the world that's coming?"

"Excuse me," said the Seneschal. "I mean, welcome back and all that, but would it be too much trouble for just one of you to explain what the bloody hell you're talking about? Where have you been? What happened? What did you find? And how come Hawk's got both his eyes again?"

Hawk grinned. "Sorry, Seneschal, it's all been a bit overwhelming. What did we find? The stuff that dreams are made of. Including all the bad ones. And then we watched them all die. Including the Magus." He sighed. "What matters is that the threat to the Land is over. We're all safe again. And it will be up to generations to come to decide whether the price we paid was too high. So, did the Burning Man give you any trouble while we were gone?"

The Seneschal blinked a few times. "You've only been gone a few seconds. How long did it seem to you?"

Hawk and Fisher looked at each other. "Days," Fisher said finally. "Years. I don't know. It doesn't matter. The Blue Moon isn't a threat anymore and never will be again. We'll give you the full story later, Seneschal."

"In the meantime," said Lament, "what are we going to do with the Burning Man?"

They all looked thoughtfully at the dead man wrapped in his own flames, and he glared defiantly back at them. Something had changed in those who had gone through the Gateway and returned. He could feel it. They weren't afraid of him anymore.

"He's guilty of mass murder, blasphemy, and desecration, and God alone knows what else," said Lament. "But he's already been judged more harshly and more terribly than anything we might do to him. I don't want to hurt him anymore, even if I could. I've seen too much judgment, too much destruction. And yet the Cathedral can never be clean while he's still here."

"You'll never be rid of me!" the Burning Man said spitefully. "This is my greatest achievement and my greatest crime. The first Forest King bound me here, and only another Forest King could release me. And unfortunately for you, the King is dead. I'll always be here to foul the waters of your holy place and stain its lousy sanctity."

"Not necessarily," said Hawk, and there was a weary reluctance in his voice that made them all look at him, as though he was about to pick up some terribly heavy but necessary burden. "You all know who I am. Who I really am. I was, am, and always will be Prince Rupert of the Forest Kingdom. As Harald's younger brother, the Throne and crown are rightfully mine if I wish. I am King Rupert if I choose to be. So, for my first and only order as King, I release you, Tomas Chadbourne. Go back to the place appointed for you. Go now."

The Burning Man made a sound that could have been a laugh or a sob. "I should have known. They always find a way to cheat you. All right, send me back to the pit. But you can't take away what I did here. I did terrible, awful things, and would have done far worse, and I'm still proud of it! I was a monster and I loved it! Damn you all . . ."

And all the time he was fading away, screaming his spite and hatred and defiance, until finally there was nothing left of him in the room but a faint waft of brimstone and black scorch marks on the floor where he'd been standing. For a long time nobody said anything.

"I sent a lot of people to Hell," Lament said finally. "For what seemed good and just reasons at the time. But I never really thought about what that meant. How can anyone look upon such torment and not feel pity, even for such as he? But there are texts, very old texts, that say the damned are only held in Hell until they have realized the true horror of their sins. Once they truly understand, and repent, they are free to go."

"Do you believe that?" asked the Seneschal.

"I have to," said Lament. "I have to."

Fisher looked away rather than see the turmoil in his face. She cried out in amazement and ran over to the open window, and the others came to join her. The darkness beyond the shutters was gone, replaced by a breathtaking view of the Forest Land, from the highest point any of them had ever known. The Forest and the Land spread out for countless miles in all directions. There were great swathes of woodland, checkerboards of huge open fields, shining rivers and stone and timbered towns. The Forest Kingdom, in all its majesty. And all around the miraculously re-Inverted Cathedral, the Forest Castle spread out in a great sprawl of halls and rooms and courtyards, like waves of stone in a great gray sea.

"Where did all this come from?" Hawk said.

"The Cathedral has resumed its proper place in the sun," said Lament. "It soars up into the sky, as it was always meant to do."

"And the Castle's expanded to its original size, *around* the Cathedral!" said the Seneschal excitedly. "I can feel it! This is what the Castle was originally meant to look like before its interior collapsed into the mess we're all used to! A place where rooms stand still, and passageways go where they're meant to, and doors always open onto the same location." The Seneschal grinned happily. "For the first time in centuries, the Castle makes sense. This is going to make my job so much easier. No more shifting rooms, no more seasonal migrations. A place for everything and everything in its place. Permanently. I may cry."

"You can see all the way to the Forest boundaries," said Fisher in amazement. "This place is higher than Dragonslair Mountain."

"It's not all good news," said Hawk. He pointed, and everyone saw the dark patch in the depths of the Forest, like a black stain in the greenery, a shadow on the Land. "The Darkwood's still with us."

Fisher took his arm and hugged it to her. "The Demon Prince is gone forever. And with no Gateway to anchor it here, and no more Wild Magic to sustain it, the Darkwood will probably just fade away over the years. No more long nights of the soul, Rupert. For any of us."

They all looked out over the Forest and the Land, and with the Cathedral returned, the sky seemed bluer, the sun seemed brighter, and the air seemed fresher, as though an ancient burden had finally been lifted from the Forest Kingdom.

"All the sacrificed dead have been released from the Ca-

thedral," said Lament, almost dreamily. "I felt them go.
Free at last to go to their rest and their reward."

"All the blood is gone from the Castle interior," said the
Seneschal. "God, my powers are sharp right now. I could
see a pin drop. All the art and statues are whole again. I
feel like I could read the contents of the prayer books if I
wanted to. And I could point to every room in the
Castle . . ." He broke off suddenly and looked at Lament.
"The Ossuary. The Museum of Bones—it's still there. I
suppose because it was constructed by human hands rather
than magic."

"It must be dismantled," Lament told him. "Bone from
bone until they can all be identified and returned to their
proper graves and their proper rest. If only for the peace
of mind of the families involved."

"There are bound to be some old records, if I dig deep
enough," said the Seneschal. "I'll do everything I can."

Hawk looked at Lament. "You've still got the box. The
Source. What are you going to do with it?"

Lament considered for a moment. "Only the four of us
know the significance of the box. And since it cannot easily
be opened, I think I'll take it back to the Ossuary and leave
it there, hidden in plain sight among all the other relics.
Just a small wooden box with a dubious provenance. And
when the Ossuary is finally gone, let the box go to some
small country church and be forgotten. Disappeared from
history until it's needed again."

"You were meant to be there in Reverie," said Hawk.
"Only you could have opened the box . . . and closed it
again. That light . . ." He stopped and shuddered briefly.
"It was like looking God in the eye."

"Part of my job," said Lament. "Part of being the Walking Man. But I don't think I want to be the Wrath of God
anymore. I don't think I could ever be happy sentencing
even the most evil of men to Hell, not after what I've seen.
I'm only a man, after all, with a man's fallible judgment
and temper. But I'm not sure I can stop being the Walking
Man. The compact I made doesn't allow—"

"Compacts are drafted by men, for men," Fisher broke
in. "I think God knew you needed to be the Walking Man

after what happened at your monastery, so he let you hold the post for as long as you needed it. Now you don't anymore; maybe it's time for someone else to be the Walking Man. Someone who needs it more than you."

"But how can I be sure?" asked Lament.

"Ask your voice," said Hawk. "Nothing to stop you from hearing it now, is there?"

Lament listened, and knew immediately that the voice was gone. God had freed him to be just a man again, with all a man's weaknesses and limitations. His life no longer had a purpose and a destiny, and Jericho Lament thought he'd never been happier.

They all looked out over the glorious view, and it felt like the morning of the first day.

Hawk and Fisher went straight to their rooms, collapsed into bed, and slept around the clock. At ten o'clock the next morning, after repeated attempts to awaken them by knocking loudly, shouting even more loudly, kicking the door with steel-tipped boots, and then all three together, the Queen's messenger finally summoned one of the Seneschal's people, and had him unlock the door with his passkey. The Queen's messenger then stormed into the room, nose stuck firmly in the air, and Hawk and Fisher snapped out of their deep sleep in a moment.

Alert to the presence of a possible enemy, they tossed back the bed covers, snatched up their swords, and threw themselves at the startled messenger. In a moment they had him slammed back against the nearest wall, with two swordpoints at his throat. The messenger started to scream for help, and then swallowed it immediately as two swordpoints dug deep enough into his throat to draw blood. He whimpered feebly, and would have fainted if he dared. Not least because Hawk and Fisher never bothered with nightshirts, and were in fact both stark naked. The messenger stared determinedly at the ceiling, averting his eyes so fiercely, they almost rolled back to the whites, and shouted the word *Messenger!* so loudly, he hurt his throat.

"A likely story," said Fisher. "Probably a peeping tom. He looks like a peeping tom."

"Be fair," said Hawk. "That is a messenger's uniform he's wearing, now I look closely. And no one else would wear an outfit that garish unless absolutely forced to. You couldn't get me into it on a bet."

"It had better be a bloody important message," said Fisher. "Or I am going to makes sausages out of you, messenger. I was right in the middle of a really nice dream, and now I'll never know how it ends."

"Was I in it?" asked Hawk.

Fisher grinned. "Tell you later."

"Messenger, why are you doing that thing with your eyes?" asked Hawk. "It looks really painful."

"You're not wearing any clothes!" yelled the messenger. "So I'm averting my gaze. I can't look upon honored guests unclothed. It wouldn't be at all proper. And by the way, that's a really unfortunate place to have a mole."

"You looked!" accused Fisher.

"I've never liked nightshirts," said Hawk. "They creep up on you in the night. If it got cold in Haven, we just threw another blanket on the bed. Now, what do you want, messenger?"

"The Queen is holding a special Court," said the messenger. "Right now. She wants to see both of you there, as soon as possible. Though probably not quite as much of you as this. Could you please put me down? I think I'm going to have one of my funny turns."

Hawk and Fisher lowered their swords, and let him go. The messenger edged away from the wall, trying to locate the door while still averting his eyes.

"Never burst in on us again," said Hawk.

"Absolutely not," agreed the messenger. "Can I go now, please? I'd really like to change these trousers and put them in to soak before the stain sets."

"The door's right in front of you," said Fisher. "Tell Felicity we'll be there in a while."

"I'm sure she's counting the moments," said the messenger. He found the door and left the room, walking just a little stiff-leggedly.

Hawk and Fisher dropped their swords on the bed and got dressed, picking up their clothes from where they'd dropped them the night before. They didn't bother hurrying. It was only the Queen.

"It's probably all over the Castle by now," said Hawk.

"What, about my mole?"

"No, that we've saved the Land one more time. The Seneschal never could hold on to a good piece of gossip."

"So what does Felicity want to see us for?" asked Fisher, sitting on the edge of the bed to pull on her boots. "It's a bit late for a progress report."

"It'll either be a medal or a kick in the arse," said Hawk. "That's all Royalty ever hand out at sudden, unexpected meetings."

Fisher buckled on her swordbelt, and went over to look at herself in the mirror. Her hair was a mess and there were deep shadows under her eyes. She stuck out her tongue, grimaced, and reluctantly put it back again. She looked moodily at her blond hair.

"I wonder how people will react to seeing us," she said slowly. "I've suddenly gone fair, and you've got two eyes again."

"The Seneschal and Lament know who we are," said Hawk.

"I think the Seneschal always did. Do you think they'd talk?"

"Hell with them all," said Hawk. "We'll bluff it out."

When they finally entered the Court, breezing past the guards at the double doors like they weren't even there, Queen Felicity was sitting on the Throne with a drink in one hand and her long cigarette holder in the other. She didn't seem unduly upset at her guests' tardiness, which rather annoyed Fisher, and beckoned for them to approach the Throne. Hawk and Fisher ambled forward, taking their time and casually checking out who else had been invited to this special Court gathering. Sir Vivian and the warrior woman Cally were standing on one side of the Throne, surprisingly close together. In fact, Cally was being openly affectionate to Sir Vivian, who seemed embarrassed but quietly appreciative. As if that wasn't astonishing enough, Jericho Lament and Duke Alric were standing on the other side of the Throne. Lament had given up his traditional long trench coat for more usual Court attire, and was in actual danger of appearing fashionable. Fisher barely nodded at him, amazed that Felicity let their father, the Duke, stand in such a favored position, and actually astounded that the Duke was standing comfortably erect without any of his usual metal and leather supports. He was even smiling slightly. Fisher couldn't help wondering if perhaps the Rainbow had brought them back to the wrong world, and seriously considered pinching herself to see if she was awake.

The Questor, Allen Chance, and the witch Tiffany were standing together before the Throne, and Hawk and Fisher stopped to chat with them. Chance and Tiffany had that special glow that comes from recent bedroom gymnastics, though Fisher had to quietly point this out to Hawk before they got there. He never noticed important things like that. The two couples greeted each other happily, indulged in a few rather obvious double entendres, and did their best to ignore the dog Chappie, who was currently lying on his back at Chance's and Tiffany's feet, all four paws in the air, tongue lolling out and showing everything he'd got.

"A lot's happened while you were gone," said Chance.

"So I see," murmured Hawk, and Tiffany blushed.

"What's happened with the Duke?" asked Fisher. "Where's that cage he usually lurches around in? Where are his guards? And he's *smiling,* dammit. Who died?"

"He gave up the Candlemass Charm to save Felicity's life," said Chance.

"The Duke did?" Fisher had a hard job keeping her voice down.

"It was very brave of him," Tiffany said firmly. "Once the Charm was gone, I was able to cure him. He's almost been in a good mood since."

"You pinch me," Fisher said to Hawk. "Better yet, slap me round the head. I don't believe I'm hearing this."

"You'd better move on," said Chance. "The Queen's been waiting for you very patiently, but . . . well, she is the Queen."

"Hell with that," said Hawk. "Sir Robert? Is that you?"

He and Fisher moved over to join Sir Robert Hawke and Ennis Page, standing grinning together, just a little apart from everyone else. Hawk clasped them both by the hand, smiling so hard, his cheeks hurt.

"What the hell happened to you two? You look twenty years younger!"

"The Magus did it," said Sir Robert. "Not exactly out of the goodness of his heart, but . . . We both feel like ourselves again. Strong and sharp and ready to cause trouble in all directions. You know, Lament and the Seneschal have been telling your recent exploits all over the Castle, and singing your praises in quite embarrassing detail. You two are the heroes of the moment. Pretty much what I expected, really. I always knew you'd save us all."

Hawk gave him a sharp look, and turned to Ennis Page. "You're looking much improved from when I last saw you. Do you remember— "

"I remember everything," said Page. "You were kind and honorable to an old comrade, not that I would have expected anything less from you."

"Hold everything," said Fisher. "What are *they* doing here?"

Not too far away, in a little space all their own, stood the Shaman and his Creature. The Shaman stood hunched over, looking and smelling as foul as ever, glaring at everyone from behind his mask of woad and clay. As always he was fuming with barely suppressed anger, but surprisingly he wouldn't meet Hawk's or Fisher's eyes. The Creature stuck close to him, crouched on all fours, showing nasty yellow fangs as he snarled at everyone.

"The Queen said she wanted them here, so here they are," said Sir Robert distastefully. "I just know he's got fleas. And God knows what the Creature's got. If you want to know why we're all here, well, a lot's happened in your absence, and the word is the Queen has a lot she wants to say about it all."

"Anyone else expected?" asked Fisher.

"Just the one," said Sir Robert. "And the Seneschal's never been on time for anything in his life. I think he does it on purpose, just to annoy people."

"Yeah," said Fisher. "That sounds like him. Though he has mellowed. I haven't seen him spit at anyone since I got here."

The double doors flew open and the Seneschal bustled in. He nodded briskly to everyone, sneered at the Shaman, and hurried forward to bow before the Throne. He was carrying a long sword in an old scabbard, which rather baffled Fisher. Everyone knew the Seneschal wasn't allowed weapons. Not since the unfortunate incident with the insolent visiting dignitary and the blunt end of a pike. Fisher watched with interest as the Seneschal had a quiet word with the Queen, glanced back at Hawk and Fisher, and then moved over to stand with Lament and the Duke.

"All right," said Hawk. "That is the last straw. We leave you lot alone for ten minutes, and the whole world goes through changes. Has someone been putting something in your coffee? What the hell did happen in our absence that could bring so many disaffected people together in one place without trying to kill one another? Don't tell me sanity's broken out at last."

"Well, to start with, we put down a rebellion against the Queen," said Chance as he and Tiffany and a reluctant Chappie came over to join them. "The Duke started it, but was in turn betrayed, and risked his life to save the Queen, so everything's all sweetness and light in that department now. Supposedly. Anyway, the Duke and his armies are no longer a threat to the Kingdom."

Fisher sniffed dubiously. "I'll believe that when I see it. The Starlight Duke never gave a damn for anyone but himself and his own ambitions."

"No, really," said Tiffany, radiating sincerity as only she could. "I've offered to set up some conciliation meetings, where they could discuss abandonment issues and the like, and they almost said they'd think about it."

"Yeah," growled Chappie, scratching his ear fiercely as though determined to dig something interesting out of it. "There's so much harmony and good will in the air these days I may puke. It's not natural. Still, at least these two idiots finally got it together. I was beginning to think I'd have to draw pictures. They're inseparable now, of course, so I've had to adopt her as well as him. I always wanted to raise some puppies."

"We don't plan on having any children just yet," Tiffany protested, blushing again.

"You were trying hard enough last night," said the dog. "Though if you do want children, one of those things you were doing won't— "

"Shut up, Chappie," interrupted Chance. The dog sniggered and started licking his balls. Everyone looked away quickly. Chance fixed his gaze on Hawk. "Lament's been saying the returned Cathedral is no longer a threat to anyone. Is that right?"

"I would like to hear the answer to that one personally," Queen Felicity said loudly. "If you could spare the time, Captains Hawk and Fisher . . ."

Hawk and Fisher approached the Throne, and nodded briefly to everyone there. They didn't bow to Felicity, but no one said anything. "The Cathedral is back to normal," said Hawk. "Back to what it was always intended to be, a beacon of light in a dark world. That's the good news. The bad news is that magic is going out of the world. Permanently. It won't happen overnight, the Magus said it could take centuries. But it does mean the Rift is fundamentally unstable. So make the most of it while you've got it."

"You mean we could be cut off from the south again?" asked Felicity, taking a large gulp from her glass. "Sweet Jesus, that's all we need. There'd be riots. I think I'd join them. I couldn't live without my morning coffee anymore."

"As magic goes out of the world, the Deadlands will settle down, too," said Hawk. "If I were you, I'd start planning trade routes and new territory acquisitions."

The Queen thought about that, and then smiled suddenly. "If the Deadlands were to become habitable again, we could be on the verge of the biggest land rush in history. And if we could grab and control most of it, we wouldn't need the Rift anymore!"

"Don't get too excited," said Fisher. "The Magus said there was so much magic seeped into the warp and weft of the world that it would take ages to disappear completely."

"You're sure the Magus is gone?" asked the Queen.

"Quite sure," said Hawk.

"Good," said the Queen. "He always disturbed the hell out of me."

"Has anyone got around to telling Lightfoot Moonfleet that the Magus is dead?" asked Fisher. "They always seemed very close."

"We were," said the tiny winged faerie, appearing suddenly in their midst before the Throne. She grew quickly to human size and looked coldly about her. She was wearing a long black dress for mourning, and her face was scrubbed clean of all makeup. She looked somehow less human without it, more alien, otherworldly. Her delicate wings shone with a pale pearlescent light. "I always loved him," she said flatly. "Even though I knew he wasn't Real, and that one day he'd have to go where I couldn't follow.

"Now it's time for me to go. He was the only reason I stayed in the mortal world anyway. All my faerie kith and kin are long gone, walked sideways from the sun. I am the last faerie, and there's no place for me in a world without magic. I go to join the rest of my kind, in the place where shadows fall. Good-bye, everyone. It's been fun."

She blew Hawk a kiss and winked at Chance, and then shrank down to nothing and was gone.

"It's started," said Lament. "The world is changing."

"Everything's going to change," Hawk pointed out. "Nothing will ever be the same again."

"Sometimes that's a good thing," said Lament. "I'm going through changes myself. I am no longer the Walking Man; just a man now, as any other. No faster or stronger, and certainly not invulnerable anymore."

"Don't I know it," said the Queen. "He stubbed his toe earlier, and you'd have thought he was dying."

Lament looked at her fondly. "And to celebrate my newly restored humanity, I have chosen of my own free will to marry the woman I have loved for so many years. Felicity has agreed to be my wife. Which to my mind says more about my courage than my common sense, but I never could resist a challenge."

"Oh, I'll make you suffer for that later," said Felicity, smiling.

"Hold everything," said Fisher. "You mean you're going to be King of the Forest?"

She looked quickly at Hawk, who was staring thoughtfully at Lament, but for the moment he had nothing to say.

"I will be King to Felicity's Queen," Lament answered carefully, "but we're both really only Regents for Stephen, until he comes of age and takes the Throne for himself. And then the Forest and Hillsdown will join together, peacefully, uniting two long-sundered Lands into one, as they were originally. No more wars, no more border skirmishes, no more young men going off to die too soon." Lament smiled. "I spent far too much time dreaming of heaven. I'm going to spend what's left of my life trying to make some here on earth, for everyone."

"This all seems rather sudden," Fisher said.

"We've waited a long time for this," said Queen Felicity. "God knows, if we hadn't both been so damned stubborn we'd have done this long ago. Do you have any objections, Captain Hawk?"

"Not my place to make any," Hawk said mildly. "I think you'll make a good King, Jericho. You always did care more about other people than yourself. Just try to remember you're not the Wrath of God anymore."

"With magic leaving, the world will, I hope, become a quieter, saner place," said Lament. "A world that will no longer need a Walking Man."

And then everyone turned sharply as there was a loud growl to one side, but it was already too late to tell whether it had come from the Shaman or the Creature. The Shaman was glaring fiercely at Felicity and Lament, and hugging himself tightly, as though to keep from flying apart. His eyes were fierce and piercing behind the clay skull mask, but his lips were pressed tightly together. Disturbed by the Shaman's anger, the Creature stirred restlessly at his side, showing his fangs and flexing his claws. His slow cunning eyes moved restlessly back and forth, searching for an enemy he could attack. But the Shaman said nothing, so everyone turned back again.

"You've done very well, Captains Hawk and Fisher," said the Queen, finishing the last of her drink and tapping

ash from the end of her cigarette. "You've saved the Forest
Kingdom from another Blue Moon and changed the lives
of everyone you've met. A shame you couldn't find my late
husband's killer, but—"

"Oh, but we did," said Hawk, and it suddenly went very
quiet as everyone looked at him. "It really wasn't that difficult to work out once we'd got all the distractions out of
the way. There was only one person it could have been.
Only one person with the means, the motive, and the opportunity. Only one man who could do such a terrible
thing." He turned to look at the Shaman. "Isn't that
right . . . King John?"

He held out his left hand, and there in his palm was a
small polished ruby, like a drop of blood. The Crimson
Pursuant, glowing brightly in the presence of Forest Royalty. Everyone in the Court gasped a little as Hawk advanced on the Shaman, and the ruby glowed more and
more fiercely. Hawk stopped right before the Shaman and
closed his hand abruptly, cutting off the bloody glow.

"You look very different now," said Hawk. "And your
voice is very changed. But there were always clues. The
Creature is your old friend the Astrologer, transfigured by
the Demon Prince. He would never have accepted anyone
else as a friend. Then there was your dedication to the
people, added to a complete disregard for the new established authorities. Of course you weren't impressed by any
of the new faces at Court. You'd been a King here. And
of course, the Shaman comes and goes, and no one knows
how. Everyone said that, but they put it down to magic.

"As King John, you knew all the hidden entrances and
secret passageways in the Castle. Including some that only
the Royal Family knew, for reasons of security. It was easy
for you to get past Harald's guards and into his private
quarters. You knew all the ways in. After all, they'd been
your quarters when you were King. And finally the Magus'
protective wards couldn't keep you out because they'd been
set up to allow Forest Royalty to come and go as they
pleased. That should have been safe enough. Everyone
thought the Royal line now consisted only of Harald and
Felicity and Stephen. Rupert was long gone, and everyone

knew King John was dead. How did you become the Shaman, Your Majesty?"

There was a long pause as everyone watched breathlessly, and then the Shaman slowly unfolded his arms, straightened up, and stood like a whole new person. There was authority, even aggression, in his stance now, and when he spoke, his voice was still rough and hoarse, but nowhere near as bad as it had been before.

"I only wanted to be a hermit," he said slowly. "After all that had happened in the Demon War, I knew I wasn't fit to be King anymore, so I walked away from it all. Leaving the Throne for someone wiser than I. There were a lot of people living rough in the Forest in those days, finding food and shelter where they could. People broken by the horrors of the long night, physically or mentally, and often both. No one noticed one more hermit. And then I found the Creature that used to be my friend. I first learned magic trying to find a way to cure him, to turn him back into his old self. It wasn't difficult to learn magic in those days; there were a lot of magical hot spots in the darker parts of the woods, left behind by the Blue Moon's passing. Power, just waiting for someone to come along and pick it up. And I had lots of time to learn how to control and use it. But nothing I found or learned was enough to undo the Demon Prince's curse. My old friend remained a Creature. I like to think he knows who I am somewhere deep within him.

"But even after all I've learned, I would still have been happy to remain nothing more than a hermit. A man apart, free at last from duty and responsibilities. But over and over again the peasants came to me, seeking help and advice, because everyone knows hermits and magic-users are always wise men. They told me of the changes in the Court and in the Land, and how King Harald was throwing away everything we'd fought for through his own stupid intransigence. So I put on my mask of woad and clay, changed my voice and my stance, and came back to Forest Castle. And no one knew me. No one recognized the man who was once King. I was almost disappointed. I came back to try and make a difference, to save the Land one more time, as the Shaman." He smiled coldly at Hawk. "I always knew that if anyone was going to see through my disguise, it would be you. I always knew you'd be the greatest threat to my plans."

The Creature reacted to the rising anger in the Shaman's voice, roared once, and then surged forward, heading straight for Hawk. On some level the transformed Astrologer still knew his old enemy. The Shaman cried out for him to stop, but the Creature threw himself at Hawk's throat, his terrible claws reaching out before him. And Hawk spun expertly on one foot, his sword already in his hand, and he cut the Creature out of midair, the heavy blade smashing through the Creature's ribs and deep into his side. The Creature crashed to the floor, screaming and kicking, still trying to get to Hawk as blood gushed from his side and sprayed from his snarling mouth. Hawk jerked his sword free and stabbed the Creature through the heart, the blade sinking half its length into the heaving malformed body. The Shaman and the Creature cried out together, and then the Creature convulsed and died. The Shaman stumbled forward as Hawk pulled his sword free and looked coldly down at his kill.

"Payment for an old debt," he said, almost viciously. "For all the harm and evil you did, Sir Astrologer."

The Creature's shape shuddered and twisted, shrinking in on itself, bones creaking and joints snapping as he resumed his old human shape again. His curse had finally been broken in the only way it could be, by his death. The Shaman stood over him, and no one could see his face behind the woad and the clay.

"You never knew him in his young days," he said finally. "He was good and true then. He could have been a sorcerer, and a great man in his own right, but he gave it up to be my man because I needed him. Any of you would have been proud to know him then. He just lost his way, that's all. It can happen to the best of us." He shook his head slowly, weighed down by a great tiredness of the body and of the heart. "No tears. I ran out of tears a long time ago."

"Why did you kill Harald?" asked Hawk. "Why did you kill your own son?"

The Shaman looked at him. "You ask that, standing there with my old friend's blood dripping from your sword? I killed Harald for the same reason you did this. Because it was necessary." He looked across at Felicity, sitting stiffly on her Throne, numbed by shock and an answer she'd never expected. "He wasn't worthy, Felicity. He couldn't, or wouldn't, see the world was changing; and he wouldn't, or couldn't, change with it. He was determined to be an absolute monarch, even when it was clear the time for such things was over. He was prepared to see the whole country plunged into civil war and worse, just so he could be King. He had to be right, whatever the cost." The Shaman sighed wearily. "The last thing I ever expected from Harald. He always understood politics so much better than I ever did. But in the end the power seduced and corrupted him just as it did me. You start to believe you're the only one who can see the big picture, that you're the only one who understands what needs to be done. You're the King, so you must be right.

"I came back to the Castle as the Shaman, hoping to show him the right way by example. But he ignored me. Wouldn't even meet with me. So I went to see him in his rooms, my old rooms, and revealed to him who I was. I told him I hadn't come back to be King. I just wanted to help and advise him. I didn't want the Throne. Didn't want anyone else to know who I was. I had come back to save the Land. To save him.

"And he laughed at me. Laughed right in my face and told me I was a fool, and always had been. It was his turn now, and he knew what he was doing. I saw then that he could never change, never be what the Land needed, so I killed him, for the good of the Kingdom. It was my duty. I brought him into the world, so I had to send him out of it. One thrust with a hidden blade, right through the heart. He died so easily, but it was the hardest thing I've ever had to do. I've always known my duty. I've always done what had to be done. Just like you, Rupert. And Julia."

Hawk and Fisher looked at each other, and then looked quickly about them, and were almost shocked to discover that no one else seemed at all shocked or even surprised by the revelation. If anything they all seemed a little relieved they could finally stop pretending not to know.

"All right," said Hawk to no one in particular. "When did you know? Chance, did you tell them?"

"He didn't have to," said Queen Felicity. "Everyone here knew who you were the moment you walked in. It takes more than a few scars and a cheap dye job to hide faces as famous as yours. But we all decided that if you wanted to be here incognito, that was your right. So we all went along with it. Officially, Prince Rupert and Princess Julia were never here."

Hawk turned slowly back to face the Shaman. "I always hoped I'd meet you again someday, Father. I never really believed you were dead. But I never thought it would be like this. Why did you go away? Why did you let everyone, let me, think you were dead?"

"It was necessary," said the Shaman flatly. "How many times do I have to say it? I wasn't fit to be King. I left, so someone else could take the Throne. Someone more worthy. You, or Harald. I hoped it would be you, but you never did have the courage to be King. You never wanted it badly enough."

"I never wanted it at all," said Hawk. "I wanted a life of my own. So I went out and made one."

The Shaman looked at him and finally nodded, grudgingly approving. "You've grown up, Rupert."

"I had to. My father was dead." Fisher came to stand beside Hawk, and he smiled at her for a moment before turning back to the Shaman. "Harald spoke to me after his death. Told me to beware our father's legacy. It took me a while to work out what he meant, but once I realized you had to be the murderer, I understood. Might makes right; that was always your way and his. Using your power and position to enforce what you believed in, and to hell with everyone else. It lost you the Kingdom and it got Harald killed. I was starting to go that way myself in Haven, but I pulled myself back from the brink. There has to be law and justice for all, to protect the world from people like us. So, Father. What do we do now? I can't let you escape. Are you ready to face justice?"

"Justice?" asked the Shaman. "Who are you, any of you, to judge me? I am the King, and the King is the Land. I did what was necessary to save the Land. None of you have a right to judge or condemn my actions. I caused the problem by allowing Harald to take the Throne, and I put a stop to it in the only way possible. Now he's dead and the Land is safe, and I will go back into the Forest to be a hermit again. And let us all pray my duty never calls me back here."

"What for?" asked Hawk. "To kill again? Who would you kill this time if you didn't like the way things were going? Lament? Felicity? Stephen? You haven't changed at all, Father. You still believe might makes right."

"I may have given up my Throne, but I still have my responsibilities," the Shaman said fiercely. "I would have thought you of all people would understand what duty means. Now get out of my way, boy. I'm leaving."

"No," said Hawk. "I can't let you go, Father."

"What will you do, Rupert? Cut me down like you did the Astrologer? Can you kill your own father? I killed my son, and it nearly destroyed me. None of you understand what it cost me to do what I did. To do my bloody duty."

It began to rain, right there in the middle of Court. Great heavy drops of rain falling out of nowhere, faster and faster, quickly forming into a slim blue figure of living water. She looked around her, her wet mouth moving in a slow, gentle smile. Sir Vivian stepped forward, and knelt and bowed his head to her.

"Vivian?" asked Cally, one hand at her swordhilt.

"Sir Vivian?" asked Queen Felicity uncertainly. "Who is this . . . person?"

Sir Vivian looked up into the calm watery face, and she nodded. Sir Vivian rose to his feet and turned back to the Throne. "This is the Lady of the Lake, Your Majesty. An elemental formed around the ghost of a dead woman. She is the spirit of the Land, our ancient mother moving through the wet earth, the force that makes the green life grow, and nurtures us all."

The Shaman moved slowly forward, all the strength and arrogance gone from his face. The Lady turned toward him and he stopped abruptly, looking into her face, unable to approach any further. "Oh, dear God," King John said softly. "It *is* you. Eleanor . . ."

Shock and surprise moved through the whole Court as they looked numbly at the Lady of the Lake.

"*Queen* Eleanor?" asked Chance.

"Mother?" asked Hawk.

"Yes," said the Lady in a voice like a sparkling stream, smiling on them all like a benediction. "Or at least, I was. Eleanor died long ago, and what was left of an ancient Transient Being called the Lady of the Lake merged with her dying spirit so that she could continue. I am the last Transient Being in the world of men now, and with Reverie gone, I shall fade from the world as magic departs."

"Mother," said Hawk. He started toward her, but the Lady stopped him with a kind but implacable look.

"Your mother is dead, Rupert. I'm the Lady of the Lake now. The spirit of the Land. I remember you, but I have to be everyone's mother now." She turned her attention back to the Shaman, who actually shook under her gaze. "I am here to judge you, John. Who has the better right than the woman who was your wife, Queen to your King, mother to the man you murdered?"

The Shaman sank to his knees before her and tears ran down his face, cutting thick trails through the clay and the woad. "Oh, God, Eleanor; I killed our son! And I killed you, too, through my jealousy. And I think perhaps I've killed all that was good and honorable in me. I'm not the man you knew, Eleanor, the man you married. There's so much blood on my hands, and not all the water in the world can ever wash them clean again."

"That's for me to decide," said the Lady of the Lake. "Will you accept judgment from me, John?"

"I would tear the living heart from my breast and give it to you," said the Shaman. "Do what you must, Eleanor. I deserve it."

"You committed a terrible crime, John," said the Lady. "Not for you the peace of verdict and sentence, and the balm of punishment. Instead, I sentence you to sleep in the

Land, in my embrace, not to wake again till you are needed. To redeem yourself and the Land one last time."

"To make amends," said the Shaman. "That's all I ever wanted, really. I'm so tired, Eleanor."

"Then come to me, my love," said the Lady of the Lake. "And sleep the sleep of centuries."

The Shaman rose to his feet and looked slowly around him. He nodded to Felicity on the Throne, and Lament beside her. "Guard the Land, King and Queen. You have my blessing, for what it's worth." He turned to Hawk. "Good-bye, Rupert. It takes a wise man to know he's not a King, and a strong man to walk away from it. I have always been proud of you, son." He looked at Fisher. "Proud of you, too, Julia. You were like the daughter I never had. Watch his back, and try and keep him out of trouble." He turned to the Seneschal. "One last gift and command to you, my loyal servant. Go and see your grandmother, the Night Witch. She's currently the Mother Witch at the Academy of the Sisters of the Moon." He smiled as general consternation ran round the Court, touching everyone but Tiffany. "The Night Witch founded the Academy after the long night ended. I always knew, but I said nothing. She has the right to work out her own redemption. I thought you ought to know, Seneschal, before I left. Family is precious." And finally he turned to face the Lady of the Lake. "I'm ready, Eleanor."

She held out her arms to him, and water spilled from them like fountains. "The first Forest King was married to the Lady of the Lake. A true marriage of the Land and the King. Now the Cathedral is returned, the Castle is restored, and all things come full circle again."

King John walked forward into the embrace of the Lady of the Lake, and her liquid form closed around him, washing away his appearance as the Shaman as he faded away and disappeared within her. The Lady smiled around her one last time, perhaps especially at Sir Vivian, and then her watery shape exploded into a mist of tiny droplets that hung on the air and then was gone. The Shaman and the Lady of the Lake, King John and Queen Eleanor, not to be seen again for many, many years.

"It's time Isobel and I were leaving, too," said Hawk after a respectful pause. "We've done everything we came here to do. There's no need for anyone else to know who Harald's murderer really was. It would only complicate things. Blame it on the Magus. No one ever trusted him anyway."

"You *could* stay," Lament said suddenly. "The Throne is rightfully yours, by line of succession. Felicity and I would step down for King Rupert and Queen Julia."

"Well, yes," said Felicity. "Who are we, after all, to compete with legends?"

Fisher caught her eyes briefly. The Queen hadn't sounded all that enthusiastic. "No," she said kindly. "We could have been King and Queen long ago if we'd wanted."

"I always knew I wasn't the stuff Kings are made of," said Hawk. "And I'd always be worried about my father's legacy coming out in me. You'll make a much better job of it, King Jericho."

"Then stay anyway, as Captains Hawk and Fisher," said Lament.

"No," said Hawk. "I'd always be tempted to interfere. The Forest Kingdom needs a new start, with no reminders of its troubled past. The truth of our identities would soon spread, and I've never been comfortable being a legend."

"Right," said Fisher. "You have to watch your language all the time."

Duke Alric cleared his throat awkwardly and stepped forward. Fisher turned to look at him. "I was wrong," the Duke said flatly. "And there's not many people who've heard me say that. I'm sorry, Julia."

"For having your people beat us to a pulp, or for sending me off to die in the dragon's cave all those years ago?" asked Fisher, her voice cold as ice.

"I thought I needed to set an example," said the Duke. "You've done well, Julia. You could come back to Hillsdown with me."

"I don't think so," said Fisher. "We'd be at each other's throat in a week. We're too much alike to ever be close."

"Yes," agreed the Duke. "There is that. You always were your father's daughter."

Fisher looked at Felicity, sitting on her Throne. "So, Fliss . . ."

"So, Jules . . . Good to see you've gone blond again. Black never did suit you."

"Keep an eye on our father."

"Of course. It's a dirty job, but someone's got to do it."

They nodded, smiled, and looked away, glad that was over. They'd never had much to say to each other. Hawk made his good-byes to Sir Richard and Ennis Page.

"Give Jericho a hard time over Reform," said Hawk. "For the good of his soul."

"Of course," said Sir Robert. "You are sure he isn't the Wrath of God anymore? I'd hate to be hit by a sudden plague or boils. Or frogs."

"One last thing," said the Seneschal, stepping forward with a certain ceremony. "Not everything has changed for the better. The Darkwood is still with us, and still a danger to the Forest. Therefore, Captain Hawk, I must formally require you to leave the Rainbow sword with us."

Hawk slowly unbuckled his swordbelt and hefted the weight of the Rainbow sword in his hand. He knew the Seneschal was right, but it still felt like giving up an old friend, only newly recovered.

"And you left your axe in Reverie," said Fisher. "The High Warlock's last gift to you."

"Ah, hell," said Hawk, handing the Rainbow sword over to the Seneschal. "I've got both eyes again. I can always find another weapon."

"Precisely," said the Seneschal. "And so the Forest Kingdom grants you one last gift." He held out the sword and scabbard he'd brought into Court with him. "I found this in the Old Armory. It is the sword of the first Forest King. I'm sure he would want you to have it. So that wherever you go, part of the Land will always be with you."

Hawk smiled and buckled the old sword onto his waist. "Now I remember why I sneaked out of the Castle last time. I hate these drawn-out good-byes."

"So, Sir Seneschal, what will you do now the Castle's geography has returned to normal?" asked Fisher. "They'll be replacing you with maps and signs."

"And a good thing, too," said the Seneschal. "I got tired of chasing rooms round this dump long ago. I'm going to be heading a team investigating all the wonders and mysteries of the returned Cathedral. More than enough work there to see me out."

Hawk and Fisher stood together and looked around the Court one last time.

"Try and get it right this time," Hawk said finally. "I'd hate to have to come back and sort you out again."

"Right," said Fisher. "Being a legend's bloody hard work."

Sometime later, Hawk and Fisher rode away from Forest Castle on the horses they'd brought with them from Haven. They didn't look back. There were no crowds to cheer them on their way because no one knew they were going. Which was just what Hawk and Fisher wanted. It was mid-morning on a warm and pleasant day, with the sun shining bright in a clear blue sky. The air in the green woods was crisp and sharp.

"So," said Fisher. "Who do you want to be now? You've been Prince Rupert and Captain Hawk."

"I think I'll stick with Hawk. He's someone I chose to be. You still happy with Isobel Fisher?"

"I suppose so. But I'm definitely not going back to Haven."

"No," said Hawk. "We've burned our bridges there."

Fisher laughed. "Burned a hell of a lot more than that. They won't forget us in a hurry. In fact, I think it could truthfully be said that we did about as much good for Haven as that city could stand. Time for a new start. Again." She looked sideways at Hawk. "And there's always the children to consider . . ."

"Yes," said Hawk. "They seemed like good kids. There's no guarantee they're what we'd end up with, of course."

"Oh, of course. No guarantee of any kids at all."

"No. But we could have a lot of fun trying."

They grinned at each other and then rode on a way in companionable silence.

"Let's just go out into the world and see what's there,"

Hawk said finally. "Go adventuring again. Help people where we can. Kick the bad guys where it hurts. Because that's what we do best."

"Sounds good to me," said Fisher. "Who knows? Maybe we'll win another Throne along the way."

"God, I hope not," said Hawk. They both laughed and urged their horses on.

And so they rode out of Forest history once again, and back into legend, where they belonged.